Acclaim for David Perry's Thrillers

The Cyclops Conspiracy

". . . a pharmacist's death turns into an adventure of international proportions in this fast-paced thriller...Perry builds—and deftly sustains—a momentum that will have readers engrossed in this page-turner." —*ForeWord Clarion Reviews*

"I am an aficionado of a good conspiracy. . . I found one here in *The Cyclops Conspiracy*. David Perry has written a fast-moving, engrossing book. . . Action is fast and riveting. . ." —*Paul Lane, Net Galley*

". . . a top-notch thriller that you won't want to put down!"
—*David Compton, best-selling author of Executive Sanction*

"*The Cyclops Conspiracy*. . . ramps up the pace revealing a new twist and a new turn by the page. I will be adding him to my must read list."
—*Alan Williams, Book Reviewer*

". . . Perry . . . gives an extra zing to an already interesting story . . . there are so many lovely twists and turns . . . kept thinking of Robert Ludlum novels . . . I couldn't put it down at night until I starting seeing double. If you like political conspiracy thrillers, then check this one out!" —*Popcorn Reads*

"A prescription for excitement." —*Virginia Gazette*

Second Chance

"There are not many books that keep me up reading all night but this one I could not put down. It had my interest from the very first page. This is the best I have read so far this year. Looking forward to the next book from Mr. Perry. Shame I could not give it more stars than five."
—*Julie's Reviews, GoodReads*

". . . a wonderful read if you are not checking into a hospital anytime soon." —*Rosemary Smith, NetGalley*

". . . fast-paced and kept me awake all night long."
—*Theresa Nelson, NetGalley*

THE CYCLOPS
REVENGE

THE **CYCLOPS REVENGE**

DAVID PERRY

Published in the United States by Pettigrew Enterprises, LLC
Cataloging-in-Publication date is on file with the Library of Congress

Library of Congress Control Number: 2017946086

ISBN: 9780983637592 (hardcover)
ISBN: 9780998853208(softcover)
PRINTED IN THE UNITED STATES OF AMERICA
10 9 8 7 6 5 4 3 2 1
First Edition

For Walter and Betty. . .
A son couldn't have asked for a better pair to guide
me into adulthood. I chose my parents well…

For Uncle Billy. . .
To the ultimate ham-and-egger, you live on in our
hearts and the memories of your wonderful anecdotes
and tall tales. You taught us that no one gets to
heaven except through Chicopee Falls.

"…if you wrong us, shall we not revenge?"
The Merchant of Venice

WILLIAM SHAKESPEARE

"If we open a quarrel between the past and the present,
we shall find that we have lost the future."

WINSTON CHURCHILL

ACKNOWLEDGMENTS

This work would not have been possible without the selfless assistance of many individuals:

Deborah Gonzalez: thank you for your insight into the world of prisons and corrections;

Pastor Charles Bang: for allowing the use of his name, for his faithful stewardship of Gloria Dei Lutheran Church and School;

To the federal agents (who wish to remain unnamed): for their observations and input about protocols and procedures;

Doug Atkins: for his communications and signal tracking expertise;

Scott Perry: for always being available to explain the complexities and intricacies of technology in a way that this writer's simple mind can comprehend;

Ed Levy: for his editorial advice and counsel;

Donna Robinson: a wonderful sister who donates her time to the business of my writing;

To Anne: my devoted wife who offers her unending support and insightful critiques, delivered with directness yet cradled in love;

To Alex, Katlyn, Brandon, Sarah and Landon: a man could not ask to have better young people in his family. You are our future, the world is in great hands.

PROLOGUE

Friday, October 13th
One Week after the Christening
of the *Jacob R. Hope*

"You are still distressed, Miss Lily?"

The words were delivered as a question. But they hit her with the force of a statement speaking the bold truth.

Delilah Hussein lay on the beach lounge chair with a tall, exotic libation sitting on the glass table beside her, untouched. The warm tropical breeze was strong this late afternoon, whipping the silk sari. The wind on the secluded, well-secured, mountaintop villa was a constant.

Hussein looked up at Oliver with a distant gaze. Despite her distraction, she could see true concern etched on her manservant's face. They had been through a lot together. And he had stood by her without a hint of trepidation.

"Would you like a cool wet towel?" he asked.

Hussein did not speak. She simply looked up at him with unfocused eyes. The trauma of the events of a week ago was still too painful to bear.

Oliver extended the white towel toward her. Her eyes moved lower to see it clutched in his dark-skinned hand. The fingers were long, all except the pinky which was nothing more than a stump.

Hussein was responsible for its loss. She had snipped off both pinky fingers on separate occasions. She could never remember which one she'd amputated first, the left or the right. Each time he'd let her down, failed her in a mission. And on both occasions, Oliver paid for his incompetence with the loss of the smallest digit. The most recent failure was not more than a few weeks ago—though his mistake did not have any effect on the outcome of their calamitous failure.

"Thank you," she replied in a whisper barely audible over the wind. "You are a good man, Oliver. A true and valuable companion."

Oliver was a tall, muscular specimen. His silk shirt was unbuttoned at the neck, revealing the sculptured muscles of his chest. Adept in many forms of hand-to-hand combat, he was also deadly at medium distances with many small arms. He had killed countless times for her. And, Hussein knew, he could kill her quickly if he so desired.

Hussein sighed. "I can't believe we failed. The last three years had been planned to the smallest detail."

"It was a bold mission, Miss Lily. Very risky."

"And they're both gone now."

"Unfortunately, it does seem that is the case."

"Are you sure, Oliver?"

"Yes," Oliver replied. "Hammon sent the message twenty-four hours after the christening. Jasmine was killed. Your son was taken into custody. He does not know where he is being held or if he is even alive."

Hussein closed her eyes and tilted her head back, shaking it slowly. She pushed out a long breath. "*Mon Dieu*, I still can't believe it."

"It is not good for you to lie around like this. You must move about. It will make you feel better, get the blood flowing."

Hussein smiled. "Are you worried about me?"

The tall manservant smiled and nodded. "We must get you back into circulation, n'est-ce pas?"

"I suppose so."

Oliver kneeled beside her chair, looking deeply into her eyes.

"You have been despondent for a week now," he said. "We must move on. I will help you forget."

Beginning at her bare foot, he gently ran his hand along the inside of her leg. When he reached her knee and his hand began to disappear under the cloth of her garment, Hussein held up her hand.

Oliver's hand froze in place. She could see the confusion in his eyes. They were asking a question: *Have I gone too far?*

Hussein knew Oliver was only trying to help. He would not kill her. He would never raise a hand against her. He owed her too much. She held a marker Oliver could never repay. One she would always hold over him.

She had saved his life from her lover and dictator, Saddam.

His four fingers remained against her soft skin, the pads of each digit connecting with the inside of her thigh, just above the knee. They were four electrodes, pulsing current into her, bringing her flesh back to life. Hussein tilted her head back again and slowly sucked the Caribbean air into her lungs. She held that position for a long time, weighing the events and trying to kill the pain.

Was it too soon?

Hussein felt her nipples become erect and a warm flush swam over her body, back and forth like a violent, storm-laden tide.

"Oliver, help me forget."

Hussein reached for him, clutching the fabric of his shirt in her clenched fist, pulling him to her. His hand resumed its trek inside her sari, inching higher.

When it reached the confluence of her thighs, Oliver spread his fore- and middle fingers gently as a cue. Hussein responded and separated her legs, elevating her knees. The length of silk along her leg drifted toward her abdomen as the warm breeze caressed her exposed womanhood.

Slowly, with the deftness of a master craftsman, his fingers crept toward their goal. They dipped slightly, touching the skin just beneath the moist haven.

Hussein arched her back and sucked in a loud sharp breath. The electricity of his touch arced with mounting voltage. She reached up with her other hand, desperately clutching another fistful of cloth and pulling his lips to within an inch of hers.

Oliver moved his fingers higher, touching her moist mound with the gentleness of a moth landing on a leaf. Hussein's body spasmed. His lips made contact with hers as he pushed two fingers inside her.

℞

"Are you feeling better?"

"Oui, mon ami," Hussein replied. Her head rested on his bare chest as they lay naked in bed. "Much better."

Hussein ran her hand down his belly under the sheet. His skin, coated with a patina of perspiration, was taut and firm.

"Thank you, Oliver. I needed that."

"Pleasing you is my only mission."

With the blood coursing potently through her veins again, Hussein's mind began to race with more coherent thoughts for the first time in seven days.

As if sensing her impatience, Oliver asked, "You are thinking of something, Miss Lily?"

"Oui, I am."

"What do you need me to do?"

"Nothing yet," she answered. "I am still upset. I've lost a daughter and my son is gone. And even more, the failure was my fault."

"The pharmacist?"

"You realized my mistake was allowing the pharmacist to get involved?"

"Yes."

"And you said nothing?"

"It was not my place."

Hussein rose up and looked into his eyes. "You are right. It is not your place. And the pharmacist was the problem. It was my fault that I allowed him to come so close to our operation. I misjudged him."

"Again, what should I do?"

"Nothing. I will need your help in the coming months. Our compatriots in Washington are, no doubt, in a state of crisis. Have you been able to contact Hammon?"

"No, Miss Lily. The secure phone number is dead. I have tried each of the last three days."

"I feared as much. They are going deep underground. Word of the assassination attempts has spread quietly through the American government. . ."

"I have been monitoring the newspapers and news shows. There has been no mention of anything."

"Nonetheless, the FBI, Secret Service, and CIA are tracing all clues. And, I fear, they are torturing my beloved Sharif, trying to extract any shred of information from him."

"I fear you are correct," Oliver replied, running his fingers across her naked back.

"They will come after us."

"Yes, they will."

"I want you to contact Damascus. I will need to meet with them in the coming days. Arrange a meeting for a month from now. They are probably most concerned. I must smooth the waters and make them understand that this was only a temporary setback. We must continue with the mission. We must strike at the Americans again.

"Just as bin Laden did after the first attacks on the World Trade Center, we will strike them once more. They will beef up the security of all government officials. But we will hit them in a different way . . . in a way they will never expect."

Hussein pulled herself up to Oliver's lips and kissed him deeply as she reached for his groin. She massaged him and felt him growing firmer in her hand as her tongue probed his lips. Hussein ripped the bed sheets from his body and straddled him.

Without warning, she slapped him hard across the cheek, whipping his head to the side. She leaned in and hovered over him, her breasts caressing his chest. "Make love to me again once more. Then we have much to do."

"What?"

"I will fill you in when the time is right. The details must be worked out. But, trust me, the Great Satan will feel our wrath and we will not fail. I want you to track the movements and communications of Jason Rodgers, the pharmacist. I want to know everything he does and everywhere he goes. Every aspect of his life is to be scrutinized. When we strike again, I will avenge my daughter and my son. And Jason Rodgers will know the pain I have felt and will feel for the rest of my days. He will suffer as I am suffering. Do you understand?"

"Yes, Miss Lily."

"He doesn't know it yet. He is, no doubt, recovering right now. When the time is right, I want him to know that I am the one who has rained down vengeance upon him."

"Yes, *Madame*."

Delilah Hussein slapped Oliver once more, on the opposite cheek. With her hand still stinging from the blow, she reached down and grasped his swollen manhood.

"Make love to me, Oliver. I need to ease the pain but not forget the mission."

She lowered herself onto him as she whispered a verse from the Qur'an to herself. "Help me ease the pain."

PART ONE

CHAPTER 1

Friday, April 10
Two-and-a-half years later

Jason Rodgers was about to implement the mission to finally bury his ghosts.

The carefully laid plans had been in place for weeks. Tonight marked their beginning. The first step to making his life whole again. And in the days to follow, he would put his past behind him —and keep it there.

He leaned back, satisfied, pleased with himself. Everything he planned was going perfectly. Almost perfectly, anyway.

The meal had been fantastic, the service exemplary. Everything went off without a hitch. Except, that is, for Chrissie's demeanor.

"Are you okay?" he asked Christine Pettigrew. "You seem tired."

Chrissie sat across from him on the balcony level of the restaurant, looking uninspired and melancholy for most of the evening. Jason had noticed a change in her in the last few weeks and sensed her frustration mounting. She had been working very hard lately. She had achieved a level of success in her career that both Jason and Chrissie were extremely proud of. But tonight she seemed particularly bothered. Jason had a plan to change that, too.

She has no idea, he thought, sipping his coffee. *She will be pleased and surprised. That will change her mood! It will change everything.*

They completed an exquisite dinner capped off by a mountainous dessert of chocolate cake dripping in thick fudge. The Freemason Abbey in downtown Norfolk, Virginia, had been one of the premier dining establishments for decades. Nearly a century and half old, it began, as the name suggests, as a church, changed hands numerous times throughout its history, and was finally converted into a beacon of fine dining, sating the appetites of Hampton Roads inhabitants ever since. Jason had chosen it because they had never eaten there together. It was a special occasion, and the ambiance was perfect.

Chrissie looked over the half-eaten dessert they had shared, pressing her lips into a thin line. Jason had scarfed down most of it. Chrissie had only tried a small forkful, maybe two.

"Yeah, I am," she replied in a lifeless tone.

"Chrissie, something's been bothering you all night. I can tell. You should be excited. You finally got the partnership you've been shooting for. The firm is exploding with business. The Colonial ownership has transferred back to you. That process is finally over with. And we are filling more prescriptions than we did last year. This year is going to be a very lucrative one. And I'm talking about more than just dollars."

"What is that supposed to mean?"

Jason turned to look for their waitress. She was standing off to the side, waiting for his signal. He made eye contact with her and winked so Chrissie couldn't see it.

"I said," Chrissie asked again, "what's that supposed to mean?"

"You'll see."

The waitress appeared, pushing a narrow cart on which sat a large bottle of champagne and two flutes. She showed the bottle to Jason and began uncorking it.

"Jason, I've already had three glasses of wine. I don't need any more."

"Just a small taste," he replied. "Just take a sip."

The waitress poured a small sample into Jason's glass. He placed his nose over the glass and inhaled, pretending he knew something about champagne. He sipped it and nodded his approval. Then the server poured two glasses and placed before both of them.

"A toast," Jason said, lifting his glass. "I love you, Chrissie. To you and me, we are a great team."

The waitress had turned her back to them. Just as Jason finished making his toast, she turned around to face them. She placed a round white bread plate on the table between them.

On it rested a small velvet box.

℞

"You've been acting like an ass all day, Michael," Jenny told her son. "Do you want to talk about it?"

She was sitting on the edge of Michael's bed. Michael was lying on his back staring at the ceiling. His face was a palate of frustration and worry.

"My life sucks," he hissed.

"I know it seems that way," Jenny counseled. "But your father getting remarried isn't the end of the world."

Michael rolled on his side and propped himself up on an elbow. "You knew and you didn't tell me?"

"I'm your mother, Michael. Your father told me that he was going to tell you yesterday. It was the proper thing to do. You should feel good that he gave you a head's up that he was going to propose."

"Why didn't you tell me?"

"Because it wasn't my place."

"I don't like her."

"Chrissie? I've met her several times. She seems like a nice person. Why do you say you don't like her?"

"Because she's making him move. When they get married they're going to live at her house."

"I know your father. She's not making him do anything. If he's moving, it's because he thinks that's what's best for them."

"I didn't like it when you and Mark moved us out here to the Salt Ponds. What was wrong with the house in York County?"

"There was nothing wrong with it."

"Then why did we move?"

"It was just time," Jenny replied, looking away.

"Bullshit!"

"Watch your mouth!" Jenny slapped his leg as he lay there. "I don't want to hear language like that again."

"You and Mark put the house up for sale a week after whatever happened to dad. What happened that night?"

Jenny sighed.

"I know it was something bad. And don't tell me it was a car accident. Because I know you're lying."

Jenny looked out the window into the darkness shrouding their oceanfront home.

"Aren't you going to tell me?"

"I'm not having this conversation now," Jenny declared. "Your father loves you very much. You're still going to see him, Michael. He has a right to live his life. These are the types of issues we all deal with as adults."

Michael got up from the bed and walked to the window. It looked out on the waves of Chesapeake Bay crashing in the dim wash of light. He studied the line of rotting pilings disappearing into the water.

"I still don't like it!"

"You can visit Pity City, Michael. But you can't live there. You will have to get past this."

Michael's response was a frustrated grunt. Jenny continued speaking without acknowledging Michael.

"Your father told me that you really haven't given Christine a chance. You've been distant since the first day you've met her. Has she treated you badly?"

Michael stared into the darkness as his mind wafted back to that night. He'd heard her voice before he'd met her, and the words he'd heard spoken that night between his father and *that* woman had stung him to his core.

Chapter 2

"Ladies and gentlemen," Brad Lane, the FBI deputy director began. He was standing behind a podium emblazoned with the Bureau's seal—a red and white shield centered under a white streamer that read Fidelity, Bravery, Integrity. "We have been tasked with analyzing this information. This analysis and our recommendations will be presented to the National Security Council and the president a few hours from now at the White House. We haven't much time."

The briefing room occupied by the nine men and two women sat deep inside the forty-thousand-square-foot Strategic Information and Operations Center (SIOC) complex of FBI headquarters, overlooking a large, theater-like command center housing banks of computer and television screens fronted by workstations, each with three monitors, manned by analysts and agents who were typing and talking on phones. Equipped with legions of printers, fax machines, shredders, secure telephones, satellite phones, and high-frequency radios with state-of-the-art secure bandwidth, the SIOC could monitor and direct actions simultaneously for up to eight crises around the country and world. The normal contingent of three dozen staffers had swelled to the hundreds in response to the perceived crisis developing along the East Coast.

"What the latest, Brad?" the director of the National Security Council, Elizabeth Rankin, asked. "I understand we've determined she's alive, is that correct?"

Lane nodded the slow, emphatic nod of a man delivering necessary but unpleasant news.

"How the hell could this have escaped detection?" Rankin demanded, looking every bit a septuagenarian, with graying blonde hair and a wizened and wrinkled face. Lane had had many dealings with this witch. She played by her own set of rules. Get in her way and you ran the risk of being steamrolled. Her actual age, fifty-five, was masked by her puckered visage and the effects of a three-pack-a-day smoking habit. "This woman and her team nearly killed two chief executives in Newport News. What was missed? The president wants answers."

"I'll take that," CIA director of operations John Beck, intoned. He cleared his throat, loosened his tie, and sipped from the water glass before him. The poise of his well-coiffed dark hair was offset by the three days of razor stubble coating his face and the swollen, dark bags beneath his eyes.

Brad Lane knew the director of operations well. Beck would endure an incredible amount of scrutiny and stress in the coming weeks and months. The discovery that Delilah Hussein was alive would continue to bring a shit storm of pressure on his department. Beck's office, also known as Clandestine Operations, would bear the brunt of the blame for this oversight. But Lane also understood that, if word leaked, the media would find a way to blame every government agency.

"Madam Director," the CIA man began, "Hussein created a credible ploy to make us believe she was dead. The bodies on the yacht in the James River were exact matches to Hussein and her henchman, Oliver. Right down to the dental records. We had no DNA samples to compare. We believed the bodies belonged to them. The daughter, Jazan Hussein, aka Jasmine Kader, was dead, killed by the pharmacist with a sniper shot in the rain at the James River Bridge. We had and continue to have Sharif al-Faisal, aka Sam Fairing, the son, in custody. Everything was covered. There was no reason to look for her. The threat, we believed, had been neutralized."

The NSC director leaned forward. Her jowly face hung over the burnished conference table, the skin waggling with each syllable. To be on the receiving end of the piercing gaze of the penetrating gray eyes was almost painful.

"Obviously, it wasn't, was it? The bodies were not an exact match, sir. She's alive, and it escaped the notice of our FBI technicians and analysts." She waved her hand as if pushing away the past. "We are not done visiting this issue. There will be a reckoning about how the ball was dropped here. But I guess that point is moot now. How did we discover the news?"

"Madam Director," interrupted CIA deputy director Alvin Senski, Beck's direct supervisor, "let's leave the grandstanding for the Senate hearings, please. A lot of people missed the boat on this one, just like with 9/11. Let's talk about the issue at hand, dealing with finding her!"

"Then shed some light for me."

The deputy director continued. "SIGINT in the NSA intercepted an electronic communication two weeks ago. It appeared benign, at first. But as we continued to track it, more ominous information became clear. The communication was between two parties, one code-named The Watcher, and the other unnamed, an unsub. In a series of texts and emails, The Watcher used some key words that drew the attention of the NSA. They tracked the source and location of the electronic intel and discovered that The Watcher is in the United States."

"Where?"

"In southeastern Virginia. Newport News to be exact."

"What key words did they lock onto?" The question came from the far end of the table and the deputy director of the Secret Service, Vince Gagliano.

"Excuse me, Mr. Gagliano, what is the Secret Service doing at this meeting?" Rankin demanded.

"Well, Madam Director, the Secret Service is responsible for the safety and protection of the president. Any operation or threat which impacts him or his safety, is the Service's concern. And I believe that the assassination attempts in Newport News were facilitated by an unseen mole somewhere in our government. The secretary of the Treasury instructed my boss, the director of the Secret Service, to be a part of this meeting. I can assure you, the director will be present at the NSC meeting in a few hours. So, if you don't mind, I'd like to stop fucking around, and get some answers."

Madam Director shrunk at the rebuke. Her face flushed at having been dressed down by someone lower on the food chain. Rankin's lip curled into a frustrated snarl.

"Proceed," she instructed the deputy director of the CIA.

"The keywords were Simoon, Hammon, and Jason Rodgers. The Watcher was reprimanded for using these words in a subsequent communication by the unnamed individual on the other end. They occurred three times. It was enough to trigger our surveillance protocols. The NSA and FBI working together using satellite communications surveillance and cell-site simulators were able to determine that The Watcher is in the Newport News area. He has been tracking the pharmacist Jason Rodgers."

"Cell-site simulators?" Rankin inquired.

"You probably know them as stingrays. The IMSI-catcher, known by various trade names, mimics cell phone towers and routes nearby cell phone signals through the device, allowing us to track suspects and persons of interest."

"I am aware of the technology. Why is this Watcher following Jason Rodgers?"

"We have not as yet determined that."

"I don't see how this leads us to the fact that Hussein is alive," the NSC director added.

Brad Lane spoke up. "As soon as we heard the keyword between this Watcher and his associate, we reopened the case. The FBI began re-examining every piece of evidence and intelligence. We looked into the information about the bodies found aboard the yacht, *Vengeance*. One of our analysts discovered an anomaly."

"An anomaly?"

Lane motioned to the only other woman sitting at the table, a twenty-something cutie wearing large, round-rimmed, black eyeglasses. If she weren't an agent for the FBI, she could easily have been on the cover of *Vogue*. Her blonde hair had been pulled tight into a ponytail. She wore a button-down, stiffly starched white shirt revealing a pearl choker around the alabaster skin of her throat.

"Yes, ma'am," the analyst began. "It came to our attention after interviewing the witnesses in Newport News after the assassination attempts, especially the pharmacist Rodgers, that Delilah Hussein—and all her team—had the same tattoo inked on their inner forearms. It looks like this . . ."

The woman pressed a button on a remote in her hand. The flat television monitor at one end of the room flared to life, showing a photograph of a person's arm. The arm, delicate yet muscular, tapered to a portion of a hand revealing a thumb. The nail was long and painted. The swarthy skin held the bluish-gray pallor of death.

"That's a woman's arm. Obviously not Delilah Hussein's," Rankin observed.

"Correct, Ma'am. This arm belonged to the daughter, Jasmine Kader. Searches of the Iraqi records show that Hussein gave birth to a daughter. At the time of her death, Kader, whose real name is Jazan Hussein, was twenty-nine years old. Jason Rodgers confirmed that every member of her team possessed one of these tattoos. Agents from the CIA interviewed Hussein's son, Sharif al-Faisal, aka Sam Fairing, who's being held at a black site—"

"Where is he being held?" the director asked.

"Sorry, ma'am. I'm not privy to that information."

Rankin looked to the two CIA men in the room. "Where?"

"Sorry, ma'am," the deputy director of the CIA replied. "That's highly classified. Not even the president knows."

"But you do."

"No, Ma'am, I don't. Only my, boss, the director of the CIA and a handful of high-level White House staff know."

Rankin bristled at the second snub.

"To continue," the female analyst said, "the CIA agents confirmed during an interview that the son, al-Faisal, does in fact have a marking on his right inner forearm that matches this design. We then went back and looked at the photos of the bodies on the yacht—"

"Let me guess," the director interrupted once more. "The bodies do not have tattoos on them."

"Well, ma'am, one of the bodies was so badly burned there was no way to confirm. But on the female's body, the skin of the right arm must have been protected from the blast because it was mashed against the torso. The skin was relatively undamaged. And you are correct, ma'am, there was no tattoo."

Homeland Security's Director of National Protection Kyle Gill interjected. "With the knowledge that Hussein was probably still alive, we activated our emergency national security protocol, Operation Brick Wall. Every governmental agency with security jurisdiction is currently on alert and has been for the last few weeks. Additionally, we have instituted Operation Dust Storm, in keeping with the simoon terminology. A simoon is—"

"I'm well aware of what a simoon is, Brad," Rankin advised. "I've read all the briefs."

"Operation Dust Storm is looking for Delilah Hussein and any accomplices."

"And so far?"

"Communications to The Watcher occur approximately every six to eight hours in Newport News. We are trying to triangulate the origins of the texts to the unsub with little luck so far."

"We have the most sophisticated electronic surveillance technology in the history of man. We should have been able to locate the source by now."

The second FBI analyst, a middle-aged man wearing a bow tie and a scowl, chimed in. "Ma'am."

"Who are you?"

"I'm an analyst with the FBI on loan from the DIA with a specialty in SIGINT."

"Continue."

"The burst communications that The Watcher is receiving from and sending to come from a generalized location on the planet. The Caribbean. The source of the transmissions varies with each dispatch."

"So they are moving around?"

"It would appear so. But there's one problem."

"Which is?"

"The transmissions always occur over water, never on land. And they occur within a 1000-mile radius. The bursts occur, then the signal disappears. Kind of like when you turn off your cell phone."

"So they are on a boat or plane. But, they must have a base of operations. Can't you use some kind of algorithm to find a common spot somewhere within that radius where they could house a base of operations?"

"Very good, ma'am. We tried that. There are several intersecting points in the defined area. Bring up the next picture, please," the male analyst instructed his young female counterpart.

The massive television monitor flashed again. A flat map of the world appeared. On it, a red line had been overlaid on an area extending from the tip of Florida to the eastern Caribbean Islands, creating an irregular trapezoid. The picture zoomed in, filling the screen with the search area. Yellow lines appeared inside the trapezoid radiating three hundred and sixty degrees from various points. The lines intersected at multiple spots.

The male analyst continued. "These highlighted intersection points show the likely areas to search. Each one is over water and miles from any land mass. Surveillance satellites have captured hundreds of images over these sites. Nothing has been found."

"We're talking about the Caribbean, not the Middle East. It's not like it's a hotbed of terrorism. Are we searching over land with the satellites?" Rankin spat.

"Madam Director," Claude Feasal offered, "the Caribbean covers five hundred thousand square miles." Feasal, sitting closest to the podium, was director of the National Security Branch of the FBI.

"And satellites?"

"Allan, would you care to chime in?" Brad Lane addressed one of the men who had yet to speak, Allan Cummings of the National Reconnaissance Office.

"Yes, we have re-tasked all available intelligence satellites to surveil the area. We have seen nothing conspicuous of yet. We have analysts reviewing digital images round-the-clock. You have to remember, we just learned two weeks ago that Delilah Hussein might still be alive. It will take time. It took ten years to find bin Laden. There are hundreds of islands in the Caribbean."

"How do you know this person The Watcher is communicating with is Hussein or anyone associated with her?" Rankin demanded.

CIA DO John Beck sucked in a deep breath and offered his opinion. "We have an asset in Syria. Damascus, to be exact, who has been in contact with another asset we have turned. The asset has ties to ISIS and a faction that has been communicating with someone in the Caribbean. They have mentioned The Watcher and Hussein's name together. We believe the person communicating with The Watcher is with Hussein, or works for her, wherever she is. We believe it may be her manservant, Oliver."

"How certain are you of this information?" Rankin persisted.

"More certain than not."

"That's not very encouraging."

The DO fired a salvo at the NSC director. "Would you prefer we ignore it?"

Vince Gagliano drummed his fingers on the table in front of him. "What is it, Vince?" Lane demanded.

"We are missing an important issue. The communications to and from The Watcher mention Jason Rodgers. It's obvious that Rodgers is being watched and followed for some reason. Remember, Rodgers saved the lives of the president and his father. She may be plotting revenge or have a plan to kill him. Rodgers's life is in danger. We should alert him. He might be able to shed some light on Hussein and what is going on."

"Are you crazy?" Rankin shot back.

"Not the last time I checked. But my wife has a different opinion. She says these Italian genes don't work in my favor. She calls me a crazy guinea."

This brought smiles to the faces of everyone except Rankin.

"Vince," Brad Lane added, "Rodgers could lead us to Hussein. If she is reaching out to him for any reason and we alert him, it could spook her and ruin everything."

"We owe that man a lot. He saved a lot of lives, including two commanders-in-chief. A lot of people died that day. Good agents. He also saved the life of Clay Broadhurst, one of our own. Broadhurst has worked tirelessly in the last two years, despite his illness, to figure out what went wrong and how we can prevent it. We have revamped a lot of our procedures because of Clay's efforts. If Broadhurst were not around, a lot of that insight might never have materialized. Rodgers deserves to know he's in danger."

"Vince," NSC Director Rankin replied, "I will not make that recommendation to the president. We don't know what Rodgers will do. There's too much at stake."

CIA Deputy Director Senski offered one last piece of information.

"We're wasting time. We know Hussein is alive. But we have bigger fish to fry, ladies and gentlemen."

"What's that?" Brad Lane demanded.

"Not only is Hussein alive, but the CIA has just learned that she is planning an attack inside the United States. And it is imminent. I suggest we get to work on finding out what it is and how to stop it. Let me show you what we know."

CHAPTER 3

Chrissie's eyes widened at the sight of the small velvet box sitting on the plate between them. Its presence sent a barrage of mixed feelings coursing through her. The box represented the culmination of two years of excitement and anticipation which, in the last few months, had melted into an array of ominous despair and regret. Despite the torrent of conflicts assaulting her, Chrissie attempted to keep her face a mask hiding her true feelings.

Jason smiled. His grin relented, as determination seemed to fill his features.

The waitress stood over her two customers, transfixed with anticipation. She stepped back, the smile on her face widening. Jason slipped out of the booth. Two other waitresses stopped serving their tables and watched, along with everyone else in the small balcony dining room, their faces replete with expectation.

He dropped to a knee beside the table. Chrissie glanced around. She felt her face fill with color.

"Jason, what are you doing?"

He picked up the box. It squeaked open. He gazed down upon its contents. The glint from the jewel inside was briefly captured in his deep blue eyes.

He turned it toward her. She saw a massive, round-cut diamond solitaire, glittering in the soft candlelight.

Her countenance brightened. Her eyes sparkled.

"Oh my!"

Jason placed the box on the table and took her hand.

"Will you marry me?"

A rainbow of emotions danced over her delicate features. She felt them ebbing and flowing like surf pounding over the sand before a nor'easter. The other diners all gawked. Jason waited for Chrissie's response.

Tears flowed down her cheeks. Chrissie wiped away a tear as she lowered her eyes. She took Jason's hand in both of hers, blinking away more droplets as they overflowed and streamed down her cheeks.

"Oh, Jason," she whispered.

"Is that a yes?"

Jason eyes never left hers. She stroked the top of his hand with her fingers in rapid, nervous twitches. She felt her brow furrow. A melancholy curtain of dread seeped in. Chrissie's lower lip fell then began to quiver.

Since they'd nearly been killed two years ago, it had taken forever to reach this point in their lives. At this moment, time slowed, agonizingly so, like frozen syrup.

Jason glanced about, forcing a smile.

"Did she say yes?" one diner whispered.

"Yeah, what did she say?" another chimed.

Jason turned back to Chrissie. His eyebrows lifted, imploring her for an answer.

"Chrissie," he begged, "everyone's looking at us. They're waiting for an answer. *I'm* waiting for an answer!"

Her head remained motionless. Then as if set in heavy, wet concrete, she began to move it. She saw Jason's eyes following the tip of her nose. The tip of her perfect, sexy nose shifted a fraction from side to side. Back and forth, it gained momentum, swinging in larger, torturous arcs. Tears streamed along the margins of her delicate nose, dripping unabashed over her lips. She tasted their saltiness. Nevertheless, her mouth and tongue, barren and parched, found great difficulty in forming words. To utter each syllable was a Herculean task. In a choked whisper, Chrissie said, "No . . . no . . . no. I can't!"

Chrissie tried to slide from the booth. Jason did not move, blocking her way.

"Jason, move . . . please!"

He gazed into her watery, red, swollen eyes. The look of amazement and shock on his face cut her. She had just wounded him more deeply than if she had tried to cut out his heart. His gaze seesawed back and forth between her eyes. He said, "Chrissie . . . I don't understand. . ."

Chrissie reached out and pushed him back, shoving away his hands. She grabbed a cloth napkin, and rattling a cup and saucer, shouldered her way into the aisle and ran.

℞

Jason lowered his head. He remained crouched by the table as Chrissie, descending the stairs, dropped out of sight. He lifted his eyes and glanced around the room.

Faces now registered the embarrassment rippling through him. They looked away, returning to their meals, their heads rigid and bowed, as if restrained by an invisible force field from glancing his way. The waitresses vanished like wisps of fog. A tightening spasm of anxiety clutched his gut.

"Well, don't just sit there," someone whispered. "Go after her!"

Jason whipped his head in the direction of the words, trying to absorb them. Seconds evaporated as his mind clutched. Then he stood up, grabbed the ring, and ran.

℞

The Watcher moved his eyes to peer through the darkened cab of his black Cadillac CTS-V into the rearview mirror. The familiar blue van was still there, sitting three hundred yards back on a cross street, masquerading as a plumber's truck. The three small but noticeable antennae mounted on the roof did not escape his trained eye. He had been aware of their presence for the past several days. It was the Americans monitoring his whereabouts using his cell phone signal. They had been following him, monitoring his actions and communications, for at least the last week and a half.

The covert agent lurched upright from his slumped position behind the wheel of the Caddy. A loud crash from across Boush Street startled him to alertness. That alertness turned to alarm when he saw the Pettigrew woman emerge from the old church-turned-restaurant. The alarm melted into a knowing realization, as a curt smile creased his lips.

She darted down Freemason Street like she was running away from . . . something or someone. His eyes followed her until she disappeared from sight past a building.

Everything was happening as predicted!

Operation Hygeia was underway. There was no stopping it now. The Watcher was a part of it. And so was Jason Rodgers. The Watcher didn't have all the details about Rodgers' unwitting involvement in Hussein's plan. But he hoped to learn everything very soon.

Rodgers would rendezvous with two men in the next twenty-four hours. The Watcher had called both of them in the last hour to warn them and give them last-minute instruction. These men had been a part, albeit it a miniscule one, of the assassination attempts two years ago. Though neither liked the idea, they would face the pharmacist again very soon. Both men had no choice.

The Watcher killed the engine and exited the Caddy. Stepping off the curb and circling the creaking engine compartment, he was halfway across the street when the door of the restaurant burst open a second time.

It was the pharmacist.

The Watcher pretended to check his watch, an IDF Krav Maga, as Jason Rodgers whipped his head in all directions, searching for the woman. Trying to avoid being spotted, The Watcher turned right, away from the restaurant and Rodgers, toward the Southern Bank and Trust and West Brambleton.

He glanced back over his shoulder and glimpsed Rodgers darting down Freemason after the Pettigrew woman. The Watcher doubled back to the corner and poked his head around the corner of the building. He watched Rodgers march into the restaurant parking lot out of view. A crooked grin slanted up The Watcher's face as he stepped carefully down Freemason Street.

The Watcher had been following Rodgers, examining and reporting every aspect of the druggist's life for the last year. His email, phone calls, texts, and Facebook, Twitter, and Instagram activity—all were being monitored by his associates, as were those of his girlfriend, Christine Pettigrew, and his son, Michael. The Watcher's job was to keep eyes on Rodgers. Though he knew what was happening, he could not resist witnessing the carnage. Like watching a car wreck in slow motion.

For Rodgers, however, tonight would feel like a Swedish massage compared with what was to take place in the days to come. The Watcher was a cog in a very delicate machine. A machine manipulating governments, people, and events in the hopes of the right outcome. This covert machine was more delicate than a house of cards, ready to implode if the wind blew in the wrong direction.

For the past twelve months, The Watcher had communicated with his handler through electronic means, updating and apprising weekly. To ensure secrecy, the communications always used coded words and phrases.

At first, his orders had been clear. Monitor and advise. Report movements. Now, his role changed. He was ordered to place items for Rodgers to find. Those items were in the trunk of his Cadillac. They would direct the pharmacist, if all went well, along a predetermined route on a collision course, The Watcher guessed, with Delilah Hussein.

Two weeks ago, The Watcher sent a text in which he purposely used Rodgers and his handler's real name, Delilah Hussein, rather than their code names. It was a calculated gamble. It was the first and only time The Watcher had breached protocol. But it had been a necessary move.

The misstep would be chastised as a careless mistake. His handler had replied to his text with a stern warning not to repeat the error. A second would result in the end of his participation in Operation Hygeia.

The implications were clear. His life would end violently. But it was part of his job to take such risks. He'd realized it when he signed up.

His gambit had worked. The fact that the plumber's van was sitting a few hundred yards back and had been following him was evidence that his ployed had worked. He had alerted the Americans. Only time would tell if his risky move would payoff. If it did, he might just be able to save the lives of Christine Pettigrew and Michael Rodgers. And he would prevent Jason Rodgers's life from being totally ruined. More importantly, The Watcher might be able to prevent something much worse.

The pharmacist was involuntarily involved in a plot against his own country. If The Watcher was a piece in this chess match, it was as a medially-powered one, perhaps a bishop or a knight. Jason Rodgers's role was that of the lowly pawn. As in many chess matches, the role of the weakest piece could be the most vital. Once most of the pieces were removed from the board, it was how a player manipulated one or two pawns that determined success or failure.

The target of Operation Hygeia was still a mystery, as were the how and when. The Watcher only knew that it existed and was underway. As he gazed at Jason Rodgers's back striding toward the ashen-faced Christine Pettigrew, he pushed his fedora tighter onto his head, hoping this pawn could lead him to answers.

$$R_X$$

Jason caught up with Chrissie as she reached his Mustang.

"Chrissie, what the hell is going on?"

"I can't marry you!"

"What! Isn't this what you've wanted all along? Isn't it what we've talked about for two years?"

Her face, covered with angled streaks of mascara and tears smeared by swipes with her hand, seemed to have shrunk. The cheeks were hollow. Her skin was drained of color. Her autumn locks fell on either side of her narrow face like steel curtains. She studied the pavement, refusing to look up.

She shook her head again, with greater emphasis than in the restaurant. "I can't marry you right now, Jason."

"What? Why?"

"You're not the same man I knew. You're hiding something."

"What are you talking about?"

Chrissie lifted her eyes, meeting his.

"Take me home," she whispered.

"Tell me what's going on first."

"No. I don't want to do this here."

The finality in her voice caused a sharp stabbing pain in his chest. He sucked in a long breath and forced it out as he looked to the murky sky above.

"You don't want to do what here?"

"You didn't pay for dinner, Jason."

Jason scoffed. "That's my Chrissie. Always taking care of business . . . and avoiding the topic at hand."

Jason called the restaurant and asked for the waitress who had served them. He explained that he would not be returning. She took a credit card number and he included a sizable tip.

"I hope everything works out," the waitress said, her voice professional but concerned.

He ended the call and directed his next statement at Chrissie. "Now tell me why you can't marry me."

"Take me home!"

CHAPTER 4

"I can't be with a man who has secrets," Chrissie whispered later in the living room of her house in the Deep Creek section of Newport News, the house she now shared with Jason.

It was the home in which they had shared a bed and their lives for the last thirteen months. Jason still owned his home in Running Man up in York County. Though it was filled with horrific memories of Chrissie being attacked by the killers, he did not want to put it up for sale until they were engaged. At the moment, though, it looked like the place would stay off the market for the foreseeable future.

The knife of truth pierced him again. The pain he'd endured in the parking lot in Norfolk was the first blow. Jason realized now what was causing the trauma. It was more than her refusal to accept his proposal. It was a long, cold blade cutting him to his core. With each word Chrissie spoke, the knife seemed to twist in his chest.

Does she know the truth?

"I don't have secrets," he lied.

Chrissie sat on the edge of the sofa with her head cradled in her palms. She stared at the carpet. Jason paced. The lamp on the end table provided the only light in the entire house, a beacon illuminating his sins.

Even before her words confirmed it, Chrissie cocked her head and lifted her eyebrows in a way that told Jason she was not buying it. "Bullshit!" she whispered.

"I don't know what you're talking about," he persisted.

How much does she know?

"You're keeping things from me. We can't start off our marriage with secrets."

Jason shook his head, willing himself to convince her. He held her defiant gaze with all the reserves of strength he could summon. It was better that she didn't know everything. Jason felt the earth beneath his feet beginning to shift and crumble.

He *had* been keeping secrets from her. Now, his job was to limit the damage.

"You remember after all that crap that happened at the shipyard, how we were working through our injuries and our fears. Then it seemed like we had turned a corner. Do you remember?"

Jason nodded, admitting she was correct. "Yes, I remember."

"Things got better. We had a great ten months. Then things changed . . . again. You became sullen and withdrawn once more. You wouldn't talk to me. You were keeping things from me. I was supportive. I told you I wanted to get married, to have children. But you didn't hear me. Do you remember that huge fight we had right before Christmas last year?"

Jason bobbed his head once.

"Do you remember what I said?"

"Yes."

"What did I tell you?"

"To stop living in the past."

"I said, 'If you live in the past it will kill you.' That's what I said. 'Don't leave me again!' But you have. You have left me up here!" Chrissie pointed to her temple. "I can't live this way. I thought your memories of that day, the day of the christening at the shipyard, were haunting you. But it's not that, is it? It's something else."

Jason swallowed hard. He could not look at her.

"Tell me about Headlights."

Jason swallowed again, trying to temper the bob of his Adam's apple and contain the rising guilt.

"Headlights?"

"Don't play dumb."

"Chrissie . . ."

"Headlights . . . you know the strip joint on Warwick Boulevard up by Fort Eustis? Tell me about it."

Oh shit! She knows!

Jason shook his head. Chrissie bolted upright, stepping closer with a perfectly manicured, polished fingernail pointed at his nose. He looked away and sighed.

"Well?"

Jason turned his back on her and ran his hand through his hair.

Chrissie persisted. "Tell me why you drive up to Headlights and park on the street and sit there waiting."

Shit!

"How do you know about that?"

℞

Oleg Gundersen, the crusty captain of the Norwegian rust-bucket, *Thor*, chomped hard on the unlit, saliva-coated stump of a CAO Italia cigar that had gone out ten minutes ago. The appointed moment, the moment Gundersen had been highly anticipating and deeply dreading for the last week, was hours away. Less than four to be exact. His nervousness edged higher as the minutes ticked down.

He gulped hard. A healthy dose of cold, tobacco-laden saliva slipped down his throat. Gundersen scratched the five-day scrabble of beard.

This was the most dangerous part of the trip!

Gundersen had done his homework on the Tidewater area and the lower Chesapeake Bay prior to departing with his lethal cargo. He had navigated the ship through the Mediterranean Sea and the Strait of Gibraltar and across the Atlantic to this point without incident.

But now they were entering the Kraken's den. Except this creature did not reside in the cold Norwegian Sea, waiting to drag ships to the murky depths with its long, octopus-like tentacles, as in the folklore of his childhood. The creature lurking in or about these waters was not an undersea monster. The strength and tenacity of the American forces stationed in the area surrounded his ship. They were more lethal than any collection of military force in the world.

That fact pressed on him with a leaden discomfort.

Dritt!!

The Elizabeth River and Chesapeake Bay housed a formidable military presence. The Norfolk Naval Base, the largest in the world, yawned a few miles to the southwest with detachments of marines. Little Creek could helicopter a nasty contingent of Navy Seals to his location in minutes. The coast guard patrolled these waters from locations in Elizabeth City, North Carolina, and Yorktown, Virginia. With the current state of affairs in the world, they were always on alert and waiting for any sign of trouble.

Despite his growing anxiety, he knew that if he stayed calm, his payday was growing closer. He would be well compensated once the pair of deliveries were completed. The last thing he needed or wanted to do was poke the American beast into a reaction.

"Have you entered the coordinates?" he asked his first mate.

"Aye, captain."

"Set our course. All ahead two-thirds."

He had navigated the rusting vessel past the Chesapeake Bay Bridge-Tunnel into the southern tip of the bay. His official port of call was the Virginia International Terminal. Gundersen stepped out of the bridge onto the small deck and the rail, allowing the cool air to dry his sweating skin.

The *Thor's* bridge, located astern, provided him with a panoramic view of the darkened, cloud-filled skies and the hold. Hundreds of metal containers, filled with clothes, shoes, and other retail items from Europe, were stacked for maximum effect in the hold. All save one. The lone exception held a single panel truck. Gundersen would deliver that truck himself. He jangled the keys in his pocket. The placement of the containers in the hold had been carefully planned, leaving an open valley in the cargo area. Until an hour ago the valley was covered with a massive black tarp.

That cover had been peeled back a few minutes earlier, exposing what lay beneath.

The brisk stream of salty air buffeted his curly locks, exposed beneath his faded kommander's cap. He flicked what was left of the cigar toward the smooth, dark waters of the Chesapeake. The sight of the once hidden contents renewed his doubts about what he'd agreed to do.

Two black Zodiacs outfitted with massive outboard engines and five ten-gallon cans of reserve fuel rested side by side. Inside each water craft, a five-man team relaxed as they waited for h-hour. Many of the faces covered with camouflage paint were at rest, eyes closed, waiting. Their helmets, sporting night-vision goggles, lay on the mercenaries chests like empty skulls. A fully loaded pack provided each man with a coarse pillow.

Gundersen had been paid his down payment by a mysterious intermediary through a Swiss account. He'd asked many questions about the mission and received no answers. He needed the money. When the emissary said, "No problem we'll find someone else. And, by the way, you'll never find another decent cargo for your vessel," Gundersen relented.

"Don't worry, Oleg," the man said. "It's a simple delivery. Drop off the cargo and you are done. I will send you the coordinates."

The military nature of their gear sent a chill down his spine. Under the wash of the few flood lights mounted on the ship and before the camo paint had been applied, the captain noticed the swarthy complexion of the men in the boats. They looked to be of Middle Eastern descent. That fact made the bile in his gut, which swirled with acidic tobacco juice, bubble into a volcanic mixture.

An hour before, he'd approached the leader of the mission, trying to extract a morsel of information.

"I will turn this ship around if you do not tell me what is going to happen," he threatened.

The leader pulled him aside out of earshot of his soldiers.

"If you fail to deliver us to the designated drop point and deliver the truck at the terminals, you will not only not be paid, I will shoot you and your crew myself."

Gundersen had trudged back to the bridge, nervous and muttering. He now prayed that he would not see the results of their work on the evening news. Americans could be ruthless about terrorist attacks on their own soil.

The captain checked his watch. The first drop would happen soon. He willed the time to pass faster. He never should have agreed to this. He wanted to be done with all of it.

℞

"Vince, I want the entire Service placed on full alert," Giles Doyle, director of the Secret Service, commanded. I want one man from each of the field offices west of the Mississippi to send an agent to Washington. The president has ordered all agencies to prepare for an attack. All leaves are cancelled until further notice,"

"The NSC meeting?" Vince Gagliano replied.

Gagliano peered through the windows of the ninth-floor office of his boss out onto H Street and the Grant Hyatt Washington across the way. The sun had disappeared hours ago. Both men had logged sixteen hours in the last twenty-four. That was a common occurrence in the last eighteen months. Gagliano's mind raced through recent history.

Giles Doyle had taken over as director eighteen months ago. The former director, Vince Mahoney, was relieved of his duties by President Gary Hope in the aftermath of the investigation into the failed assassination attempts of Hope and his father, Jacob Hope, two years earlier in Newport News. Gagliano was promoted to deputy director after the death of Woody Austin, who had died after jumping from his Watergate East apartment balcony. Gagliano currently wore two hats—he was deputy director and he oversaw the Presidential Protection Division. No special agent had been appointed to replace Austin since his death. Director Doyle just didn't trust enough people.

The investigation into the assassination attempts pointed many accusatory fingers at the Service. Classified information had been leaked to the terrorists. The investigators suspected a mole, and Woody Austin made a convenient scapegoat, though no concrete evidence had been produced. Nonetheless heads had rolled.

"The threat is credible. Hussein is alive. The intercepts presented by the CIA at the NSC meeting a few hours ago confirm that something is in the works."

"But what?"

"We don't know. The CIA has intercepted email from Syria that make mention of a site on the East Coast as the target. They gave it a name . . . Hygeia. Hygeia is the target."

"What is a Hygeia?"

"Not a what. A who. Hygeia in Greek and Roman mythology is the daughter of the god of medicine, Asclepius, and his wife, Epione. Hygeia represents good health and hygiene. That's where the word comes from. She is associated with the prevention of sickness and continuation of good health."

"Thanks for the lesson, Giles. That doesn't tell us anything."

"No, it doesn't. But it does tell us we need to be ready. I want extra details on all the president's trips. I have asked the president to re-examine his travel plans and cut back where possible. We almost lost two on Mahoney's watch two years ago. I will not let it happen again. If anyone so much as farts too close to the president, I want them arrested!"

"Got it," Gagliano replied.

"And contact Broadhurst. Tell him we need him in the office. His insights into this woman might help."

"Sir, Clay just finished his last round of chemo. He may not be up to it." Special Agent Clay Broadhurst had been in charge of security in Newport News that day. His team, with the help of the pharmacist and his brother, had thwarted the plot. His work after his recovery and return to the halls of the Secret Service was instrumental in changing the Service's protocols. Broadhurst, despite the cancer diagnosis, worked tirelessly to upgrade the Service's security apparatus and to research how they had allowed a calamity to occur.

Doyle looked over his reading glasses, squinting at his subordinate. The smoke from an ever-present cigarette curling in front of his face.

"Good. If he's done with chemo, he should be feeling better. It wasn't a question, Vince."

"Yes sir."

Gagliano stood and walked to the heavy oak door. Halfway there, he stopped and pivoted.

"I think we should tell him," Vince Gagliano blurted.

"We should tell Clay what?"

"Not Clay, sir. The pharmacist, Rodgers. He needs to know what's going on."

Doyle began shaking his head before Gagliano finished his sentence. The cigarette dangled from his lips. The blue line of smoke wavered with each oscillation.

The Service's headquarters was government property and, therefore, a nonsmoking facility. It was a poorly kept secret that Doyle regularly broke that law. No one, however, dared to mention it to the former army ranger.

"Vince, I'm gonna say this one time, and one time only. If anyone—you, Broadhurst, or anyone connected to the Service — reaches out to Jason Rodgers to warn him, I will personally place their balls in a vice and crush them into raisins. I will not fire them. I will make sure that the rest of their career is spent cleaning out the sewers in Washington with their bare hands."

"It's not right, Giles. Clay is dying. He made great contributions to this case in the last two years because he was alive. The pharmacist saved his life. Clay is going to be pissed that we're keeping quiet. He wouldn't have been around if it wasn't for the pharmacist. Neither would the presidents . . ."

"I agree with you. Clay Broadhurst has worked his tail off in the last month to investigate leads and look into this issue. Despite his health, he's worked harder than most of the other agents. But the National Security Council recommended and the president concurred. No communicating with Rodgers. It's a direct order from my boss. It's not fucking negotiable. So, leave it alone, Vince!"

CHAPTER 5

Reprisal One moved over the mountain, humming a hundred feet above the ocean waves. Its four helicopter blades allowed it to hover as the pilot, at a computer station inside the residence, assessed the winds around Morne du Vitet. Delilah Hussein and Oliver watched from the stone patio at the rear of the residence. The landing struts unfolded from the body of the octagonal craft. A phalanx of eight men waited near the open, grassy area between the main building and the guard barracks.

The wind died. The pitch of the battery-powered engines whined higher. The specially designed drone rolled, turning into its final approach. Three minutes later, the craft was earthbound and the attendants secured it to four fifteen-foot high cement posts in the southern quadrant of the massive compound. A fifth attendant flipped a lever and a massive green tarp framed with large-diameter steel bars slid over the craft, hiding it from the prying lenses of satellites.

"Oliver, explain to me again how this drone prevents the Americans from learning our location?" Hussein asked. She didn't understand the technology or the strategy behind the flying machine's capabilities. Only that it worked. Nonetheless, Oliver's detailed answer put her mind at ease.

"Oui, Madame," her manservant began. "Reprisal is a communications drone equipped with a remotely switched 4G/satellite high bandwidth connection. All electronic communications, email, video files, pictures, and text messages are uploaded to the hard drive when Reprisal is on the pad via a direct secured connection. The hardware is kept off, unpowered, except when files are being transferred. While it is in flight, the software and hardware are again switched off so as not to send out signals that can be intercepted."

"Now I remember," Hussein said. "And how does it stay invisible?"

"Reprisal lifts off from the pad here in the compound. It flies directly south, since that is the shortest distance to water. It stays below five hundred feet, flying preprogrammed routes which change with every sortie."

One of the men climbed under the drone, sliding on his back on a wheeled dolly. Oliver and Hussein watched the technician complete this task. He reappeared with a small black case and ran toward Hussein and her male concubine. The remaining men stood at rigid attention, guarding the communications vehicle.

"We will have the information downloaded, Madame. The messages will be decoded within ten minutes," the minion said.

He disappeared inside the residence. When he was gone, Hussein addressed Oliver once more.

"Continue," she said.

"The aircraft flies the preprogrammed route, a different one every time. When it reaches the predetermined location—again these locations change with each trip—it ascends to transmitting altitude, about three thousand feet. The pilot, in the residence, turns on the software and hardware remotely and begins the transfer. All incoming and outgoing encrypted messages are received and sent. The hardware is then turned off. Reprisal descends below radar detection. Since it is always far out to sea, land-based radars do not see it until it climbs.

"Every route Reprisal takes is a different one. It is quite ingenious actually."

"Excellent. That makes me feel better. Make sure the drone's batteries are changed out and it is airborne as soon as possible," she commanded. "I want messages and updates every hour going forward. We are entering the most crucial phase of the operation."

"I understand, Madame. I will make it so."

"How does the drone know what route to take?"

Oliver was ready for the question. "Our pilot," he motioned toward the house, "has plotted and programed thirty-five different courses all around the Caribbean. The drone follows a different path on each and every sortie. It flies less than fifty feet above sea level and possesses infrared sensors and artificial intelligence allowing it to detect ships and other obstacles. If it encounters an object or group of objects it will divert, giving a wide berth. This reduces the possibility of detection by warships or drug interdiction patrols. It has also been outfitted with thermite charges. If forward movement ceases or altitude changes abruptly without computer involvement or if its sensors detect that Reprisal is being followed, it will self-destruct.

"The Americans no doubt have been and will be trying to intercept all communications. The messages are routed through the pods on the drone and transmitted at various locations over the ocean, depending on the sortie and the time they were sent."

"You're sure the Americans cannot extrapolate our position from these communications?" Hussein asked.

"Extremely unlikely. We will be gone before they figure it out. And each message is written in code." Oliver had not told Hussein that, a few weeks ago, The Watcher had slipped and used her name in a transmission. It was a one-time occurrence and had not been repeated.

Hussein nodded.

"Is the old wine cellar prepared?" she asked.

"It is. Everything is ready. Charlie and Pierre and two more of my best men are ready to monitor our guests. They will be most uncomfortable."

"Excellent," Hussein frowned. "Is Charlie under control?"

"The situation has been addressed with medication," Oliver assured her. "I personally monitor that he takes it each morning. There will not be a repeat of last time."

℞

"I followed you, Jason. Stop lying to me. What's her name? I've known for a month now."

"Who are you talking about?"

"Are you screwing one of those tarts that work up there? You are, aren't you?" Chrissie seethed. "Look at me! Tell me the truth!"

Jason refused to lift his eyes. She had been at him for the last few hours, unrelenting in her sporadic interrogations. Jason had refused to answer during their first confrontation. He had escaped and retreated to his bedroom. Ten minutes later, she pounded on the door until he opened up.

The second battle was louder and more virulent. Again, Jason managed to withdraw without revealing the truth. He had to retreat back into the living room to get away a second time. Chrissie left him, slamming her bedroom door only to reappear fifteen minutes later. They were now embroiled in their third skirmish in front of a muted television flashing scenes of *The Matrix*.

"How do you expect me to marry you if you can't be honest? What's her name?"

Jason shook his head. "Who?"

"The woman at the strip club. You make me sick. You know that!"

Jason struggled to cast a halting glance in her direction. "Chrissie, it's hard to explain."

She wrinkled her lips into a smirk. "No, it's not. You just tell the truth. How long has it been going on?"

He refused to speak, averting his eyes for the tenth time.

"I need a drink," she said.

Chrissie moved to the small portable bar in her living room. She poured herself a large shot of tequila. "What happened to the man I knew?" She lifted the glass to her lips and threw her head back. Jason watched her face contort as the harsh liquid slipped down her throat. "The Jason I knew a decade ago would never have done this. The Jason I met two years ago loved me. At least, that's what I thought."

Jason moved to her. Chrissie poured another two fingers of the liquid and was holding it. "Chrissie, I love you very much."

She shook her head. A pained snicker consumed her features. "Fuck you!"

Chrissie tipped the shot glass, hurling its contents at Jason. The tequila splashed into his eyes. He staggered backward. He felt her fist smash into his face. Tumbling toward the floor, he tripped over the coffee table. Jason landed on his back between the sofa and the table.

His hands went to his face and eyes. The stabbing of a million white hot needles obliterated his sight. On the periphery of his consciousness, he heard Chrissie stomp out of the room. A minute later, the slam of a door reverberated throughout the house.

$$\mathbf{R}_{X}$$

Thimble Shoals Light bobbed unseen in the darkness. Oleg Gundersen had ordered all running lights extinguished. He wanted as little illumination as possible on the activities of the next few minutes. The crescent moon found a crack in the clouds, sending what felt like a spotlight onto the ship and the silent waters.

Forsiktig! The American Kraken is out there!

When the lunar sickle ducked behind another bank of cumulus cover, Gundersen lifted his arm and moved his index finger in a circular motion. He watched as the forward derrick operator of the *Thor* pushed a lever and the crane swung into place over one of the Zodiacs. The only sounds were the gentle lapping of Chesapeake Bay against the hull, the thrumming of the crane's hydraulic motor, and the occasional creaking of the aging ship.

A harness had been placed under and around each water craft. As the large iron hook dangled a few feet over the first Zodiac, one of the paramilitary types, standing in the raft, brought the four ends of the harness together and hung them on the hook. He motioned for the crane operator to take up the slack.

The rest of the five-man team climbed aboard. Two short whistles preceded the whining of the motor. The craft was hoisted out of the hold, swung over the deck, and lowered to the black waters of Chesapeake Bay.

Thirty seconds later, the rubber boat was free and motoring into the darkness.

The tension in Gundersen's chest eased, if only for a moment. He removed his kommander's cap and ran his cracked hands through his mangy hair. Removing a cell phone from his pocket, he punched in a text addressed to the number he had been given. The first delivery was made a few hours ago. The second craft was now off his vessel.

Second delivery made! Moving to final destination!

℞

Hussein ambled into the converted bedroom two doors down the hall from her own massive master suite. Sitting at a desk in a high-backed leather chair before two massive, high-definition monitors was the drone's pilot, wearing a creased pair of khakis and a black cotton polo. Hussein's eyes followed the young man's left arm from his shoulder to his wrist. A large-faced Gucci watch adorned it. Her eyes continued past the small, squiggly tattoo on his forearm to the hand. The third finger sported a college ring from École Polytechnique.

"Bonsoir, Michel. As-tu l'information?" she asked. Good evening, Michel. *Do you have the information?*

"Oui, Madame. C'est ici." *It's here*, the young man replied, pointing to one of the monitors.

Hussein had recruited him a year ago. A true follower, the young man had demonstrated his value in computer programming and communications. The removable communications hard drive taken from the drone was being downloaded in another bedroom.

"*Excellent.* Download the data to my phone, *s'il vous plaît.*"

A moment later, Hussein's cell phone beeped, the familiar chirp letting her know she had a message. The messages from the drone had been uploaded.

"*Merci beaucoup*," she said. "*Le drone* will be ready for its next flight in about an hour."

"As you wish."

"And the social media accounts?"

"Monitored every day, *Madame*. There have been no inappropriate posts or tweets."

"*Excellent!*" Hussein smiled. Each one of her thirty men on the compound had been issued his own cell phone, provided by The Simoon. All phones were preprogrammed to block the use of social media and were collected and stored while her *soldats* were on the premises. Only she and Oliver were allowed to possess cell phones or any other electronic device inside the compound. The only other person associated with their cause who was allowed the use of an electronic device was The Watcher. And they communicated by encrypted text messaging and used the communications drone to play hide-and-seek with the signals.

Otherwise, her charges were all single men with no family ties who had been sequestered for this mission. Some had committed criminal acts in the past with no lapses to date and had demonstrated a strong allegiance to their cause. The troops were given as many nonelectronic distractions as possible to enjoy when not on duty: movies, magazines, board games, and television. But she also knew that people would always try to find a way circumvent the rules.

Her French computer expert monitored the social media platforms, making sure that no posts originated from any of the devices on her compound. Each man was allowed twenty-four hours off the compound each week. They were searched and body scanned with a wand upon their return to make sure no contraband of any kind made its way onto the grounds.

She had left Oliver to supervise the preparation of the next flight. She smiled at the ingenuity of the drone's utility. The American intelligence community had the best, most comprehensive networks available to intercept and decode communications. By accessing cell towers, servers, and databases legally and illegally, the CIA, the Defense Intelligence Agency, the FBI, the National Security Agency, Homeland Security's Office of Intelligence and Analysis and the National Reconnaissance Office, among others, could ferret out threats with amazing speed and accuracy.

Hussein had tried to bypass this technical ability during the assassination attempts twenty-four months ago. Electronic communications were forbidden. Communications took place through Cold War methods, dead-drops, and human transfers. The Americans had gotten away from these techniques, preferring to rely on drones and electronics to collect intelligence. The old ways had worked, for the most part, until Thomas Pettigrew had stumbled upon her plan.

Out of necessity, he had been disposed of. So had her reliance on outdated spy craft.

Jason Rodgers had inserted himself into the mix, trying to find out how and why Pettigrew died. Hussein shook her head, recalling her mistake. She had tried to involve the pharmacist in her pharmacy operation, an operation that was a cover for her ultimate pursuit—the assassination of two presidents. She had misjudged Rodgers. And he had brought down the plan and saved the two American criminals.

She had allowed him to get too close!

Hussein was not finished with Jason Rodgers. She owed him. This time Rodgers himself would deliver her weapon of destruction to America's doorstep. She owed him the agony he had caused her. And Delilah Hussein always paid her debts.

With financing from their allies in the Middle East and beyond, she had overseen the installation of modern, high-tech equipment that would allow her to complete this mission, the most important example of which now sat on the landing pad in the southern quadrant of the island compound.

The octagonal-shaped communications drone equipped with folding antennae and transponders had an operational range of eight hundred miles. It flew to within this distance in an arc from the east coast of Florida to a location north of Bermuda, returning to Hussein's compound after each sortie. Flight was powered by four fifteen-foot helicopter-like blades mounted on rotating stanchions that could tilt along a three-dimensional axis, allowing it to steer and fly in any direction. The engines and removable computer hard drives were powered by four rechargeable lithium batteries, each the size of a suitcase. The hard drive was removed from the craft after each sortie and its information—mainly, messages from The Watcher—downloaded. Communications with her compatriots in Syria were transmitted by secure satellite phone.

When Reprisal One reached a preprogrammed location, it dispatched any messages from its cache and received incoming messages by polling the various devices, secure phone, and computers that were programmed into its software.

When all the information was gathered, the computers were turned off and disconnected from their battery source. This prevented any signals from being intercepted by the Americans as the craft followed a different preprogrammed route each time. The $10 million aircraft had performed flawlessly.

The data from the latest flight had just been received on her phone. Hussein opened the first message. It was from the captain aboard the *Thor*:

First package delivered. En route to second.

The second was from The Watcher:

The first package is wrapped and ready. The second is also home now. Await my signal before moving in.

She was interrupted by a knock at the bedroom-cum-communications-room door. Oliver, her tall, athletic manservant and concubine, poked his head inside.

"Madame, your guest has arrived on the other island," he declared.

Hussein smiled. She had made several attempts to entice her American guest to visit her. Reluctantly, he had agreed. He possessed information she needed. Information that would make what remained of her family whole again. And she was going to extract it from him.

"Excellent. Have the boat made ready," she instructed. "Tell them that I will be there within two hours."

She wanted to look her former ally in the eye. She smiled once more. *It was all coming together!*

He had been flown to another island on which sat a second isolated but smaller compound. It was a risky move to bring this man so close to her operation. But a necessary one. Then she would fulfill a promise she had made to The Watcher.

Hussein turned her mind back to Jason Rodgers. She had vowed revenge. And she would have it. She—and her allies in Syria—had planned, financed, and implemented the current mission. They would strike again at the Americans. And in a fitting twist, Hussein would make the pharmacist experience the same kind of devastating agony he had caused her. The need to see the pharmacist's face fill with terror was unbearable. It was a need she would see satisfied.

CHAPTER 6

Jason pressed the cold wet towel to his face, concentrating the pressure on his eyes. Both were on fire. The cool dampness helped. He sat on the floor, his back against the vanity. He had tried to flush the tequila by splashing cold water into them. It was ineffective. After five minutes, he could still not open his eyes.

He summoned the strength to lift himself off the floor. Crawling to the tub and shower, Jason climbed in fully-clothed. The fire in his eyes intensified when he removed the wet towel.

Fumbling for the handles, he managed to turn on the cold water through the tub spigot. He lay on his back with his face under the cold blast of water, drenching his face, eyes, and upper body.

He managed to pull open each eye with a hand, allowing the water to flush his corneas. After a minute, he exited the tub.

Jason stood dripping on the tile when he heard footfalls at the door. He turned his face in the direction of the sound. "Is that you?"

After a long moment of silence, Chrissie replied with a whisper. "Yeah."

Jason wiped his hair and face with the towel. "Give me a minute."

"No, I don't have a minute," she retorted.

Jason felt her grab his wrist and lift his arm. "This is yours."

Chrissie turned Jason's palm upward. She placed the small velvet box in his and closed his fingers around it.

Jason pried his eyes open with extreme difficulty, trying to look at Chrissie. He caught a Dali-like image of her through the tears and water. With the pain too great, he squeezed them shut again.

"Jason, I want you out of the house by tomorrow afternoon. You can sleep in the guest room tonight."

Jason paused, summoning will. With his eyes still closed, he spoke in her general direction. "Don't worry, I'll be gone in thirty minutes."

He heard the bedroom door close. Jason slammed the wet towel to the tiled floor. He cursed out loud, hollering at himself and the world.

His anger and frustration mounted in seconds. He needed to get away from here, from Chrissie. He was pissed at her—and at himself. Right now, he was pissed at the world.

Now in the bathroom with his eyes closed and burning, his anger flared, erupting like a massive solar flare. His past still haunted him. It was time to exorcise that demon.

That deviant emotion needed to be satisfied.

He wanted it now. He needed to hurt something . . . no . . . not something . . . someone.

℞

The leader of Team Mohammed kept the GPS device under a small tarp to keep the screen's green glow out of sight of passing boats or aircraft. His satellite cell phone bleeped.

The leader read the message from his handler. He did not know his name or location. If they were captured, they could not divulge information they did not possess.

Your package is tucked in. Mission is a go!

"Where to now skipper?" his lieutenant asked. Though they had trained hard in the last weeks for this mission, his men still did not know the location of the target.

"We'll approach from the beach in two hours. We'll stay offshore until then. The houses are crammed close on the waterfront. The target is northwest of this location. It's a little more than four and a half miles from here. It's a neighborhood called the Salt Ponds." He pointed at the helmsman. "Make our course three-two-zero. You all know your jobs. Now stay low and out of sight."

℞

Jason rubbed his left flank above the belt line with one hand as he rested his hand on the Colt on the passenger seat with the other. Pain from the healed-over stab wound kicked up whenever he sat too long or felt stress. Tonight, the throbbing was caused by both, Jason thought.

His target was a regular at this strip joint, showing up every Friday night to ogle his favorite dancers and down a pitcher of suds. Headlights catered to the enlisted of Joint Base Langley-Eustis in northern Newport News, where the urban sprawl morphed into more rural environs.

Jason checked the Tissot. He squinted, rubbing his eyes to focus on the glowing hands. When they came into relief, he read the time: one thirty in the morning. Friday had turned into Saturday.

His eyes still burned. But at least he could keep them open.

After Chrissie had returned the ring, she stormed out. He couldn't see her but he thought he heard her crying. Her slow, laborious utterances were laden with sadness. It had taken thirty minutes to get his eyes functional again. He'd placed the ring in a drawer in the guest room. He'd tried to get Chrissie to come out of their bedroom, knocking for five full minutes. But she refused to answer or make a sound.

Finally, he gave up and hastily pulled on a pair of jeans and a shirt retrieved from a pile of dirty clothes in the laundry room. He had already removed the gun from the gun safe in Chrissie's night stand and put it in the glove box of the Mustang. His own weapons were locked away in his gun case in Yorktown.

He had no idea that Chrissie had been following him. He smirked in disgust.

You sure wouldn't make a very good spy, he thought. *How much does she know?*

It could not be too much, he reasoned. He had not done anything except sit in the Mustang and watch the place, tracking and monitoring his quarry's movements. Chrissie had surmised that he was waiting for a woman, an exotic dancer, because the place was a strip joint. Of course, there was no other woman. Chrissie was the one woman he loved with all his heart.

Jason had not corrected her when she'd tossed out her accusation of infidelity. He allowed her to think that was his secret. He hated lying, especially to her, but it was easier this way. In a kind of twisted stroke of good fortune, Chrissie had handed him the perfect alibi.

Jason *was* interested in someone inside Headlights. That someone was a man. A man he wanted to kill. A man who had tried to have him killed. In the past, Jason had killed out of necessity, in the heat of battle. Kill or be killed.

But would he take a life in cold blood?

Jason lifted the dog-eared composition notebook from the seat beside the Colt and leafed through the rumpled pages. His mark was nothing if not habitual. Jason had been observing him for almost three months. He showed up at Headlights faithfully every Friday night and closed the place down. Jason had ventured inside on two occasions to see what he did in there. Both times, he'd parked his ass at the elevated runway and craned his neck at the pasty and panty-clad dancers.

He shook his head.

They should be calling friends and announcing their engagement, then making passionate love and falling asleep in each other's arms. He should not be sitting here like some private eye in a cheap detective story.

Jason should have stayed at the house, pounding on the door or breaking it down, demonstrating to her that he would not let her walk away. He wanted to tell her the truth. But it would only make her worry. Jason didn't want Chrissie bearing the weight . . . or the worry of the past. She had been through enough. She would have to deal with the lie, for now. It pained him to think that she was dealing with the ravages of infidelity. Even if they never reconciled, one day, he promised himself, he would tell her the truth.

After the deadly events of the christening, it had taken months to get right again. But Jason's ghosts never really left. They just hung around, waiting for a break in his mental armor. The shipyard, The Colonial, the Regional Jail. They haunted him. They visited often from the dark recesses of his tortured mind. In the days immediately after the assassination attempts, Jason promised himself he would hunt down Tattoo Man and the guard who allowed him into his cell in the Regional Jail in Williamsburg. As the days passed and he and Chrissie started rebuilding their lives, the need to avenge the mortal deeds waned, practically disappearing as he healed and dealt with his demons. Jason and Chrissie settled into a comfortable existence, getting to know each other once more. They filled their lives with newer, more pleasant memories. It had taken months for him to control the post-traumatic symptoms. He—they—had turned a corner. All had progressed smoothly for a year.

Then he received the note.

He wanted to tear it up and burn the shreds. But something in him refused to allow him to. The words dragged him back into the past. The anonymous missive, scribbled in perfect cursive on thick, fancy stationery tucked under the windshield wiper one November morning a year ago, was a simple one:

Two men are still out there. One a former guard.
The other covered in art. Your life and the lives of
your family are still in danger!

Twenty-five simple words ushered in a torrent of flashbacks and unresolved issues. They were ominous and chockful of threat.

He tried to dismiss it. But the more he thought about it, the more he understood its meaning. And the more the desire to finish the job filled him.

Your life . . . and the lives of your family . . .

Someone was threatening Chrissie and Michael. Two sleepless nights and distracted days after receiving the note, Jason decided he needed answers. That's when he started his quest. He would find Tattoo Man and the guard.

Keeping Chrissie in the dark, at least until a few weeks ago, Jason toiled in the shadows, trying to hunt down the two men. Tattoo Man had disappeared. But the guard was still around. Jason had tracked him and watched his movements.

Jason believed in justice. He always had. He was obsessive about it. It's what caused him to pursue the reasons behind Thomas Pettigrew's death. It caused him to be sucked into an assassination plot. It almost cost him his life . . . and Chrissie's.

That need for the truth and justice drove him to right past wrongs. And it was this same need that had just cost him his relationship. It was his own damned fault.

He thought he had defeated that constant yearning, barreling past it. But the note sucked him into the vortex once again. It rekindled his latent anger and need for vengeance.

Jason shook his head, trying to clear the frustration like a wet dog shedding water. He needed a clear head, no distractions. He needed to be able to focus on his target. He rubbed his eyes once more, checking them in the rearview mirror. It was dark. He couldn't see, and he didn't dare turn on the dome light. His eyes felt red and swollen.

He should be plastered by now!

The man was a heavy drinker. Jason didn't know if he'd acquired the habit since being fired or if he'd always been a drunk. It didn't matter. Jason would confront him after he'd downed enough beer to slow him down, to cloud his mind.

He checked the Colt lying on the seat beside him once more, reassured by its cold heavy metal. He had taken it from Chrissie's small gun safe near their bed in the master bedroom two nights ago after she was asleep and placed it in the trunk of his Mustang. He wanted it available when the time was right.

The last thing he wanted was to be fumbling around for the gun and have Chrissie walk in on him. His own weapons were tucked away in his house in York County. He wanted Pettigrew's aging Colt to be the weapon used to avenge everything from two years ago.

Chrissie had told him approximately where she dropped the gun in the James River as she fled Lily Zanns's estate that evening two years ago. He had combed the shallow water on Saturday, three months after the christening, found the gun, and returned home with it. With Peter's help, he restored it to pristine condition. It had remained locked in the small gun safe at the side of the bed ever since. Now, Jason caressed its glistening steel.

Tonight, he would begin the healing process, get answers, and put it all behind him.

Jason drew several quick, deep breaths, willing away the anxiety. He checked his Tissot. *A few more minutes!* Then he would make his move.

Chapter 7

The black Cadillac CTS-V glided to a stop in the shadow of a large oak. Its tires crunched on the gravel of the road's shoulder. The Watcher had extinguished the headlights five minutes earlier as he followed Jason Rodgers, using the moonlight to guide the vehicle along the roadway. He did not fear driving too long without the headlights. The Watcher knew where Rodgers was going.

Lifting the powerful night-vision binoculars to his face and studying the Ford Mustang, he saw the green heat signature inside the vehicle. Rodgers was seated behind the wheel.

The agent lifted his smartphone and typed in a coded text message: *JR about to make contact with CH. It will happen tonight.*

The agent hit send and his message turned blue and moved higher on his screen. The message would not be received for at least an hour, maybe two.

He removed the fedora from his head and placed it on the seat beside him.

He studied the rearview mirror again. As expected, a van disguised as a service vehicle rolled into place a hundred yards back. The American FBI stood out like a gentile in a synagogue. They had been following for him for a week, watching him as he watched Jason Rodgers. The Americans knew something was up.

It was all part of the plan!

They didn't know who he was or what he was doing. This was the most dangerous of games. If he was not careful, The Watcher could get himself . . . and others . . . killed.

There would be time to worry about the FBI later. They would not interfere or make themselves known to the pharmacist.

The spy turned his attention back to Rodgers. He imagined his current state of mind. He'd been rejected by his woman. Based on their conversation picked up by the microphones in her home, it appeared to be over. She'd sent him packing. He was hurt and confused. She'd known about his secret mission, thinking it was a carnal desire.

Jason Rodgers had a score to settle. The last thing The Watcher needed was for him to end up behind bars for murder or manslaughter. His latest directive returned to him now.

Report his movements and be there to pick up the pieces.

Jason Rodgers would kill. In fact, that was part of the plan. It was The Watcher's job to make sure he did not get arrested . . . or killed himself.

Rodgers was about to confront a man who had been responsible for nearly ending his life. *That would be enough for me*, The Watcher told himself. *He'd be matzo!*

Though he didn't know it, the pharmacist had several jobs ahead of him. Dangerous, risky tasks. The Watcher would make sure he checked each one off his list. If he failed, his orders were to make sure Rodgers's targets were taken down . . . and that Rodgers made his appointed rounds.

The Watcher reached over to the passenger seat and lifted the black cloth covering the item in the seat. In the dim glint of moonlight sifting through the window, he studied the small black remote. He flipped a switch. The green light came on, indicating it was ready to go. The charges had been placed. Wondering when he would need to use it, he switched the device off and covered it once more with the black cloth.

He turned the knob on the dashboard ensuring the dome light would not come on when he opened the door. He slipped out and walked to the trunk. Unlocking it with the key fob, he peered inside. The items were there, ready to go. They were clues. Clues Rodgers would be asked to find, decipher, and act upon. He closed the trunk softly and re-entered the Cadillac.

The Watcher had many motives. He served many masters. Too many. Taking lives might be necessary and was not something he relished. This mission was vital and would provide answers. Answers that might save more lives later.

$$R_X$$

The helmsman of the second rubber skiff shuttling Team Isaiah pushed the tiller hard to port. The rubber boat rolled into its turn into the deepest part of the James River from the Carrollton shoreline, having passed under the James River Bridge three minutes ago. He angled the craft away from the bridge, a half mile north of the Crab Shack restaurant and the fishing pier. The black raft with its black-clad passengers ducking low, skipped along the small waves.

"Stay as far away from any boats as possible. We are 8.5 kilometers from our landing point," the team leader demanded in a voice loud enough to be heard over the soft hum of the outboard. It was barely audible, but its authoritative timbre made the fresh-faced rookie on the tiller nod emphatically. The camouflage paint on the leader's face made the whites of his eyes stand out. He looked at each member of his crew. "Believe it or not, this is the part of the mission with the greatest risk of detection. Hug the Isle of Wight coast until I give the order to cross the river."

The *Thor* had dropped them into the darkness at the mouth of the James River. The first team, Team Mohammed, had been dropped in the Bay, the team leader thought, and were probably waiting for the right moment to stage their assault.

The helmsman pushed the tiller to the side. The craft arced into another turn, making the southern bank visible in the dim moonlight. They motored north for thirty more minutes. With a wave of his hand, the leader motioned for a direction change. They crossed the river to the Newport News side in under fifteen minutes. Luckily, they had not seen any other water craft.

Farther up river, the leader made a slashing motion across his throat. The helmsman cut the engine. The craft inched over the dark water.

"Paddles," he ordered.

Halfway to the beach, the helmsman killed the engine. The raft coasted toward the shore three hundred yards away.

"Habib, Ahmed, bring her in!" the leader ordered.

Habib, the helmsman, and Ahmed turned the pair of clamps holding the large outboard to the wooden transom. With muffled grunts, they lifted the massive engine and lowered it onto the floor of the raft.

Each man lowered his short metal oar into the water and began stroking.

Twenty minutes later, the craft entered the narrow Deep Creek tributary, maneuvering around the slim point. Stroking every five seconds, their oars dipped soundlessly into the black water.

The boat scraped to a halt at the James River Marina. A rock-strewn jetty protected them from view to the south. A small beach littered with debris led to a gravel parking lot. To the north, they were exposed to waterfront homes and any curious onlookers with a decent pair of binoculars.

The five men slipped over the pontoons into the water, standing in the waist-deep water. Before he gave his next command, the leader swiveled his head, taking in every possible danger with the night-vision goggles he'd just donned. If they were detected, the mission would be aborted. He'd catch hell for it, but better than being captured or detained.

"It looks good."

The leader removed a large knife from the scabbard strapped to his calf, showing it to the other four men. They each removed their knives. Each man stabbed the black blades into the thick rubber. Air hissed from the multiple slits.

As the raft deflated, they pushed it toward deeper water. Twenty feet offshore, the heavy outboard motor dragged the limp rubber under. The brown hue of the James would hide it until a bather happened to stumble upon it. The river's murky brown cast could hide a small car for months.

The quintet swam until their boots hit the asphalt boat ramp.

"Stay low and move slowly," the leader commanded, as he tapped his best recruit on the shoulder. "We'll wait here. You have three minutes."

The leader watched the large, muscular man emerge from the water and make his way across the short stretch of gravel to the asphalt parking lot. He banked around a tree and angled into the shadows.

One of the men behind the leader whispered loud enough for the leader to hear.

"Why in Allah's name did we land here? It's too open. Too easy to be seen."

The leader turned and glared at the youngest member of his assault team. *The kid was good*, he thought, *but very naive.*

"Because," the leader said, "it's a marina and the only place where we can park a vehicle without arousing suspicion and have it be so close to the target."

The leader withdrew a Makarov PMM pistol. The barrel had been extended by a long cylindrical sound suppressor. He placed it between the young man's eyes. The rookie's eyes crossed as the barrel dimpled the skin of his forehead.

"Every aspect of this mission has been accounted for. If you question any part of it again . . ."

Sounds from the tree line interrupted him. He turned. Muffled words were exchanged. Someone in the parking lot on the other side of the marina was confronting his point man. Scrapes and grunts filled the night air.

Shit!

CHAPTER 8

The Watcher leaned his head back on the car's headrest as he wiggled his ass against the black leather, trying to get comfortable. His eyes never left the Mustang, waiting and watching for any movement from the pharmacist.

His mind drifted back to the day eighteen months ago when he'd managed to secure an audience with the murderous matriarch, Delilah Hussein.

He had arrived at the rendezvous point in al-Qiza, a small hamlet east of Damascus held by ISIS. The sun burned like a blast furnace. Sweat poured down his back. His parched throat hurt every time he swallowed. The slight breeze kicked up powdery clouds of sand. The white SUV stopped three feet in front of him. Three large bearded men alighted.

They had shoved him into the backseat; his wallet, watch, and contents of his pockets were confiscated. His hands were cuffed in front of him, a black hood placed over his head. The ride seemed to last for hours. What mattered was gaining access to Hussein's organization, The Simoon.

They stopped inside a walled compound. Once inside, the hood was removed and The Watcher guided down a long white hallway. He was deposited in a well-appointed living room.

A fine leather sofa sat along a large wall from which hung a massive woven tapestry. The couch was flanked by identical walnut side tables inlaid with mother of pearl and a matching coffee table.

The Watcher was forced into a comfortable arm chair angled beside the couch and tables. He sat, wrists cuffed, guarded by his host/captors for several long minutes.

A door opened and a smallish woman appeared wrapped in a green silk thobe with ornate embroidery at the neckline and a black woven belt wrapped several times around her thin waist. Her dark eyes gleamed from behind her hijab as she stepped forward.

One of men from the car nudged The Watcher.

"Stand."

He complied and looked at the woman.

The small amount of hair visible around her face and the fine wrinkles at the corner of her eyes hinted at her age. This woman was well beyond forty, maybe fifty.

"Are you Delilah Hussein?" The Watcher asked.

The woman nodded and motioned for a tray to be brought. A servant wearing a brown tunic offered The Watcher coffee. He waved it away.

"I'm told you wish to become part of my organization."

The Watcher nodded. A skeptical frown weighed down the edges of Hussein's lips.

"Tell me why."

"I have skills and resources that will benefit your cause."

"Such as."

Movement coming from the Mustang interrupted The Watcher's trance. Jason Rodgers had opened the car door. The dome light came on. The Watcher noticed the weapon clutched in his right hand.

$$\mathrm{R}_{\!\mathrm{x}}$$

Rodgers slipped into a chair at an empty table along the wall. He waved down a waitress and ordered a Miller Lite. He scanned the room. It didn't take long to find his target. Clyde Hutton, the former guard at the Williamsburg Regional Jail, was exactly where Jason expected him to be.

Hutton sat near the elevated runway jutting into the throng of male gawkers looking up at the exotic dancer. The drunken Hutton pulled a single from the wad in his hand and laid it on the stage in front of him beside the ten or eleven other bills residing there.

The dancer was a forty-something grandmotherly type who looked like she'd had various tucks and lifts, giving her face a plastic appearance. Her fake breasts were too large for her medium frame. It looked as if her surgeon had stuffed a pair of over-inflated soccer balls in her chest. Two tasseled pasties covered her nipples and a flap of wrinkled belly skin hung over her bikini bottom, neutralizing what little sex appeal she possessed.

Nonetheless, Hutton seemed to be taken with the show she provided, attested to by the ones he loosely tossed at her feet. Leaning forward on his elbows on the ledge just below the stage, he saw no one but her. A wry smile curved up the side of his face. A pitcher, holding dregs of beer and coated by patches of suds, rested beside him and his half-full glass.

Jason's side view of the man confirmed the good news. The glassy look in his eye and the miniscule oscillation of his torso brought a smile to Jason's lips. He was shit-faced. It would make what he was about to do easier.

Jason scanned the large room and sipped his brew. The place was crowded but not full. The largely male audience sat at tables or along the runway quietly taking in the dancer and the scantily-clad waitresses, their oversized breasts bulging from tight tops and hips hugged by skimpy bottoms. They had perfected the bend-at-the-waist-to-give-the-patron-a-good-look-at-your-cleavage bow. By the high-and-tight haircuts, Jason knew many of them were military types out on the town from nearby Joint Base Langley-Eustis.

Hutton was flanked by two other men who did not appear to be with him, benefiting and partaking of the view provided by the former guard's money.

The man to his left caught the eye of a passing off-duty dancer and leaned back to say something to her. They chatted briefly. The woman nodded and smiled.

The man stood up and followed the dancer through the tables and smoke to a curtained backroom. Keeping it out of sight, Jason removed the Colt from the waistband of his back and slid it around to the front. Seizing his chance, he stood up and walked toward Clyde Hutton.

$$\text{R}\kern-0.3em\raise-0.5ex\hbox{x}$$

"Where's the body?" Isaiah's team leader whispered to his scout.

His soldier had returned holding a bloodied knife. The scout pointed toward the marina building. "Behind the building under the bushes."

"Who was it?"

"A drifter. He was huddled at the corner of the building."

"Anyone else?"

The man shook his head.

"Get the vehicle!"

The scout wiped the blade on the leg of his trousers. "Yes, sir!" He moved off toward their ride.

The leader turned to the rest of the team huddled in four feet of water just off the small beach. He waved them forward, pointing toward the dark SUV parked twenty yards beyond.

The leader jogged to the marina building and circled it. He found the body stuffed between the building and a row of thick bushes fronting the water. He pushed through the branches and shined a small flashlight up and down the corpse. The throat was expertly cut, sliced from ear to ear. A thick coating of blood covered the dirty, hole-filled shirt.

The soldier scanned the ground but found no trail of blood to the body.

Well done!

His soldier had dragged the man to this spot before killing him, then obliterated the drag marks.

Hopefully, this would be the only glitch in their mission.

He heard the engine of the SUV come to life. The leader emerged from behind the building and climbed into the passenger side.

Before closing the door, he said out loud to the other four men of his team, "Let's go."

CHAPTER 9

A thick line of heavy sweat dribbled down Jason's back as he approached the open seat. Perspiration popped onto his forehead. The adrenaline rush quelled the burning in his eyes. He lowered himself into the chair beside Clyde Hutton.

He did not look at the former corrections officer, pretending to study the dancer. His eyes stayed riveted on the woman, but his mind was occupied with the man to his right.

Jason sensed Hutton had turned to look at him just before issuing a curt statement.

"I think that seat's taken, buddy." The odor of the beer-soaked breath reached Jason in an instant.

Oh yeah! Definitely plastered.

Jason smiled at the dancer and removed a single from his shirt pocket. He placed it on the deck.

"That's okay. I won't be here long. By the looks of it, he won't be back for a few minutes."

Jason felt Hutton's gaze linger a moment. When Hutton turned back to the dancer, Jason spoke.

"You come here often, Clyde?"

Hutton turned back to him, wavering from side to side. His eyes widened, then shrank to a squint.

"Rodgers! Jason-fucking-Rodgers!"

Jason hesitated, caught off guard by Hutton's quick recognition of him.

"You know who I am?"

Hutton nodded through his beer-soaked stupor. "Been expecting you."

It was Jason's turn to register surprise. *Have I been that careless?* he thought. *Had he given himself away to Hutton as well?*

"You've been expecting me?" Jason demanded.

"Yup. Let's not do this here."

Jason removed the gun from his waist with his right hand and shifted it to the left in a slow, fluid motion under the overhanging ledge holding the drinks. He put his arm around Hutton's shoulder and pulled him close, jabbing the barrel into the man's ribs. A gasp of air escaped Hutton's lungs.

"Let's go outside," Jason whispered. "This better not be a trick!"

Hutton tried to pull his body away. But Jason squeezed him tight, pushing the gun deep between two ribs. Hutton winced and relented.

"I'll fucking waste you right here, asshole!" Jason whispered.

Jason glanced behind them. No one seemed to notice what was happening. The dancer had moved a few feet away and was plying her wares for another drunken gawker.

"Now," Jason continued, "you're going to stand up and walk out. I'm going to be right behind you. This gun is going to be pointed at your back. If you try anything stupid, I'll put a thirty-eight through your spine. Smile, Clyde!"

Hutton glanced Jason's way. Jason had his eyes on the dancer. He didn't feel the reaction he wanted.

"I said, 'smile!'" He removed the gun an inch and rammed it into a rib. Hutton grunted and forced a weak, nervous smile.

"This night is on me," Jason said. "Don't move!"

Jason removed the hand draped on Hutton's shoulder and reached into his pants pocket. He removed a crumpled fifty dollar bill and placed it under Hutton's glass.

"Stand up and walk!"

℞

Chrissie could not sleep. The digital numerals of the clock on the night-stand read 2:18 a.m. She had tossed and turned under the covers since climbing into bed, thinking about Jason pounding on the door to her room, their room. She had no intention of sleeping. That wouldn't happen tonight. Getting under the covers was the only thing she could think to do. Her mind raced.

She had lost him for a second time!

She lost him fifteen years ago to set of circumstances that were beyond both of their control. Jason—and by extension Chrissie—had been manipulated by unseen, dark forces.

Now, maybe, she had lost him to someone else. She wasn't sure it was a dancer, or if it was a woman at all. She had tossed that accusation at Jason to trick him into telling her the truth. She had confronted him with her concerns tonight, of all nights. For a month, she had refused to bring it up, afraid to allow the monster out of its cage, though it weighed on her mind. As long as she remained silent, there was still a chance she was wrong. But Jason offering her the ring had brought everything to a head. She had to deal with it.

He had given her no clue that he was going to propose. It was a complete surprise. Under different circumstances, she would have accepted instantly. She had hinted at it for months. But Chrissie stopped hinting six months ago. Jason didn't even notice.

Her concerns about his trips swelled slowly. At first, she thought he was going through a phase, brooding and withdrawn. But later it became apparent it was more than that.

That's when the doubts crept in.

She loved Jason. Parts of her always would. She wanted to be his wife. No. She had wanted to be his wife. Now, she wasn't sure. Her child-bearing clock was ticking down to zero. She had wanted to be married and have a family. And she had wanted Jason to be the father.

But now her mind was clouded with uncertainty. The brave man who'd come back into her life, the man who'd risked his life to save hers, and the lives of two presidents, had changed.

In the months following the assassination attempts, they'd both recuperated physically. Getting over the trauma of the assassination attempts at the shipyard had taken time. She thought they'd reached the point where they'd both put it behind them. And she'd thought that once they'd done that, it would be smooth sailing on the ocean of life. She'd never considered the possibility that he would be interested in another woman. Or something else, whatever or whoever it was.

This time she had been the one to make the break. Not Jason.

Maybe their destinies were never meant to merge. Maybe they were paddling against the current of fate!

Chrissie got out of the bed and walked to the bathroom. She splashed water on her face, patted it dry with a towel, and looked into a pair of swollen, red eyes. Padding back to the bed, she cast a glance out the window. The moon, bright in a now cloudless sky, cast a silvery glow on the shed and the deck of the house. Chrissie froze in her bare-footed tracks.

She moved to the glass.

Had a shadow moved out there . . . under one of the trees?

Chrissie backed out of a direct line of sight but continued watching.

There was something out there . . . in the shadows. She could feel it. All her fears, past and present, resurfaced.

Remembering, she visualized the generic dark sedan across the street two years ago. The click of the lock on the front door. The two armed men slipping into her house. Stealing Mrs. Liggieri's car to escape.

Checking the window again, she studied the scene.

Nothing! Stop it! she told herself. *Get a grip!*

Chapter 10

Thirteen miles away, four members of Team Mohammed emerged from the pounding surf of Chesapeake Bay north of Buckroe Beach. With each step, another few inches of their bodies and equipment became exposed. As they inched from the waves, the waterproof night-vision goggles gave way to black uniforms and short, powerful automatic weapons. They moved in unison, each step synchronized, sweeping back and forth, scanning and assessing.

Once clear of the water, they moved to the grassy dune fronting the beach house. They lay on their stomachs, side by side. One man pulled out a map covered in plastic.

"Is this the place?" one soldier asked.

"It's the last set of pilings before the entrance to the Salt Ponds Marina." The man with the map pointed to the rotting row of pilings disappearing into the water. "The house is the one with the two ocean kayaks lying on the boardwalk leading to the beach. I recognize it from the photographs. This is it." The man pointed with a vertical slash of his hand.

The house, a large two-story, with roll-down hurricane shutters above the windows on each level, sported a gray and white deck sprawled across its entire width. Three high-top tables with closed umbrellas, each surrounded by captain's chairs, sat evenly spaced on the back porch.

The team leader checked his watch. "You all remember the floor plan?"

Each man responded with a nod.

"Good. You and you . . . check the street. Make sure we will not have visitors. I'll wait here with Salaam. And for Allah's sake, stay out of sight."

The two men belly-crawled along the sand to the north. In ten yards, they turned left across the dune, churning sand, before elevating to all fours and slipping into the narrow space created by the neighboring house.

Fifteen agonizing minutes later, they returned on their stomachs.

"All clear."

"Excellent. We'll wait ten minutes to make sure they're all tucked in. Then we move!"

$$\text{R}_{\text{X}}$$

The waves pounded the sand. Each swell was an angry beast reflecting Michael's mood. He couldn't see them but he could hear them. He could always hear them. Michael stood at the window peering into the darkness. They were loud and thunderous, penetrating the walls. It had taken him a month to get a decent night's sleep since moving here with his mother and stepdad. Only recently had he become accustomed to the briny smell and the noise associated with coastal living. But tonight the waves were winning.

Michael hadn't liked being uprooted from their home in York County. Something had happened to his father. His mother and Michael had driven to the house of his Aunt Fran, his mother's sister, in Richmond. His mother was a wreck for the few days they were there. Michael overheard some of the whispered conversations. "Danger" and "precautions" had been bandied about. Eventually, the panic passed and they returned home. Michael learned his father had been injured. Something had happened that put him in the hospital with serious injuries.

It was a car accident, his mother explained. But one day on the way to the hospital, they drove past his father's house in Running Man.

Michael spied his father's bright red Mustang sitting in the driveway. Undamaged.

There had been no car accident.

A week later, a For Sale sign was planted in Michael's front yard.

The memory still clung to him like a hangover.

Michael moved away from the window and plopped onto the bed with an audible sigh. He'd never told his mother about the night he'd visited his father in his hospital room. He simply lied and said his father was asleep.

That night returned to him now.

They had driven to Tidewater Regional Medical Center. As they walked to the elevator, Michael asked his mother if he could visit alone. She initially refused. But he begged for two full minutes. Finally, he demanded.

She relented, and told him she would accompany him on the elevator. His mother waited in the visiting area as Michael trudged to his father's room.

"I'll be waiting right here," she said, a look of anxiety painted on her face.

Michael was very close to his father and loved him very much. He knew that he could convince his father to tell him the truth.

On previous nights, cops and a man in a suit wearing an earpiece were stationed outside his father's room. On that night, they were not present. Relieved he had one less confrontation to deal with, Michael turned the corner to enter the private room. He was stopped by the sound of an unfamiliar voice coming from behind the privacy curtain. A woman's voice. A voice he'd never heard before. It didn't belong to that bitch, Sheila Boquist. It possessed a higher timbre. And it was filled with concern.

"Now lay back and get some rest, Jason. The doctor said no moving around," the woman said.

"I'm sick and tired of being in bed," his father retorted. *"I want to be out of here, Chrissie!"*

"I know . . . I know," she replied. *"But you were seriously injured, Jason. You lost a kidney. You've just been moved out of intensive care."*

"Alright. Alright. But I feel fine," he replied *"How are you feeling?"*

"Better. The headache is starting to go away. But I need to take it slow. Concussions are a bitch. I get dizzy if I move too fast. Thank you for saving my life. If you hadn't been right behind that guy, I would be dead."

"I let him get the better of me in the hallway. He never should have gotten away. I'm sorry I left you there alone afterward. I didn't have any other choice."

"I understand. That doesn't matter now. What's important is that you were there for me . . ."

"Yeah, but I brought a shit storm to your door."

"If you hadn't gotten involved . . ." The conversation continued. But Michael became distracted at that moment. The words were spoken, but didn't register in his mind. He quickly regained focus. *" . . . you cared about Daddy's legacy. You believed in him when I had stopped. You put your life on the line for his memory."*

"I'm going to be there for you from now on," his father replied. *"I never should have left. I wasted all those years. Chrissie, you are the only woman I ever really loved."*

Michael remembered the feeling in his chest as his father uttered those words. His father and the mystery woman were silhouettes behind the sterile curtain.

Wasted years?

What was he talking about? Had his father been saying he regretted marrying his mother? Had he not wanted a child?

That evening, Michael's world entered a new, uncomfortable place. His father's words clashed with the knowledge of the man he'd loved since his first memories of him. His dad had always been very attentive. And Michael had grown close to him. In his mind, he was the perfect father. He coached his baseball teams, made sure Michael was doing his homework and getting good grades. And even though Michael did not like it, when necessary, he chastised him for not doing his chores at his mom's house or creating mischief.

Anger had welled that night. It swelled in him again now as he recalled the words and memories. The goings-on and the secrecy surrounding his father during that week confused and frustrated him. Those emotions attacked again. His first impulse was to charge in and confront them. He wanted answers. Those feelings short-circuited his self-control. And the impulse had taken over . . . only for a moment.

Michael took two quick steps toward the curtain, prepared to interrupt the private conversation. For some reason, the physical action triggered and, briefly, erased his anger. He was eavesdropping. His father had always told him it was not polite.

He stopped short.

His torn and dirt-stained tennis shoes scuffed on the tile. A loud rubbery screech shot through the space and the room.

The conversation on the other side of the privacy curtain stopped. Michael saw the shadows of both heads turn in his direction.

He swallowed hard . . . and ran.

Michael never told anyone about what he'd overheard. He wanted to pretend it never happened. Tears erupted from his eyes now, running down his cheeks and onto his pillow. He lay on the bed in the darkness of his bedroom. His father had probably already asked Miss Christine to marry him. And she had probably already said yes. That realization felt like a hot sword gouging his belly.

Michael had had a chance to confront his father about his feelings the day before, when he told Michael about the proposal. But Michael sat silently, withdrawn and petulant. They had a quick dinner before Michael asked to go home.

Michael promised himself that he would unload his thoughts on his father the next time he saw him. There was still a chance that he could turn things around. His father owed him answers. Michael deserved an explanation. And he vowed he would get one.

Angry with himself, he reached through the neck of his t-shirt and withdrew the medal hanging on the silver chin around his neck. His fingertips caressed the dime-sized circle, feeling the embossed image on the sterling silver.

St. George, the patron saint of England, and courage.

Michael recited from memory the inscription on the back.

Always do the right thing . . . no matter how hard it seems.

Michael's crying intensified. He'd not shown much courage around his father, a giant in Michael's world. A godlike figure. Tomorrow, he would summon his courage and get the truth. Once and for all.

He wiped the tears with the sleeve of his t-shirt, turned out the light, and tried to sleep.

Chapter 11

"Je me vengerai!" Delilah Hussein demanded. *I will have my revenge!*

Her enormous guest shifted his bulky frame in the freshly painted Adirondack chair situated on the covered patio. The warm breeze dissipated the blue smoke wafting from his lips. Through a slit in the silk mask that covered his face, a curved pipe rested between his lips.

"Why the mask, Hammon?"

"Precaution. I'm sure your cameras are recording this meeting."

"Thank you for meeting me in person," she said. "It was hard to convince you to come."

"Your communication intrigued me," Hammon replied. "You mentioned that there is something in it for me? A way out?"

Hussein nodded. "If we can come to an agreement."

"There is much going on in Washington. It's much too soon," he replied. The small droplet of sweat running down his temple belied his anxiety. It stopped, absorbed by the top edge of the large scarf covering his nose and mouth.

"I need something from you," she said.

"I met you face to face as a courtesy," the three-hundred-pound man said. "It has only been two years since the attacks. My government is still on high alert. They are actively searching for you and my moles. My men have gone underground and will stay that way until I decide it is safe."

"Searching for me?" Hussein asked, picking up on the spy's comment.

It was amazing he could function at all, she thought. How a man possessing Hammon's girth could perform the subtle manipulations of a spy escaped her. But, she concluded, this man sat behind a desk, covertly directing others. Such duties required an adept, sharp mind but little physical dexterity or energy.

Hammon nodded with one emphatic head bob. "They have knowledge that you did not die on the yacht in Newport News. They have begun a massive manhunt. It is only a matter of time before they come across the recordings made by Jason Rodgers and the dead private investigator, Waterhouse."

Hussein felt her pulse quicken. "How did they come by this knowledge?"

"I do not know that. My access to that intelligence is limited."

"The Americans may find the recordings, but they are inconsequential now. The government will never let them become public. It will be too embarrassing."

"Perhaps," Hammon replied, clicking his pipe stem against his teeth.

"What else do you know?"

"They also know that you have a plan underway. You should withdraw to fight another day. You risk capture and failure."

She shook her head. "We have an agenda and a timeline. The attacks on the presidents were part of a larger, coordinated effort to bring America to its knees. It will happen. We have worked too long and too hard to turn back now."

"Our participation," Hammon continued, "only extended to the assassination attempt. We were unaware of a larger plot. That is of no concern to us. We are simply being prudent, Lily," he continued, using Hussein's alias. "You have a beautiful estate here on this island. It was a stroke of genius to build a compound on a resort island. It's the last place they will look."

"This is not my estate, you idiot. Do you think I would bring you to my headquarters? This is a secondary property. My headquarters are far from here."

Hussein watched the eyes of the spy grow wide for an instant. Then they reacquired their steely glare.

"This surprises you? We have many resources."

Hammon shrugged, trying to feign indifference. But Hussein could see his frustration. The man had thought he still had her trust and could waltz into her headquarters. He had struck a deal with his government to save his own ass. Of that Hussein was certain. It's the only reason he would agree to such a meeting.

"Has our failure to kill the father and the son caused you to become meek and timid, Hammon?"

Hussein smiled. Her impression of him had changed in the first thirty seconds of their meeting. He was no longer the all-powerful, never-to-be-questioned font of wealth from which she had once drawn support. He was transformed in her mind to a morbidly obese means to an end. Delilah Hussein did not know this man's real name. She did not care. It did not matter. She knew him as Hammon, the leader of a secret faction embedded deep within the American Central Intelligence Agency. He was a spy. She no longer needed his money. She needed something else.

"Hammon, what happened to the $24 million that was supposed to be transferred into the accounts after the assassinations?"

Hussein saw the skin around the fat man's eyes crinkle as he smiled beneath the scarf. "That money was dissolved back into secret accounts automatically after the assassinations failed. You are not asking me to pay you for a failed operation, are you?"

Hussein returned the smile and shook her head. "Non, mon ami. I would never do that. But I do want something else. A favor, actually."

Hussein had already aligned The Simoon with the growing, wealthy terrorist organization known as the Islamic State in Iraq and Syria or ISIS, an organization spawned by the power vacuum in those two countries. Hussein had secured additional funds from The Watcher, the disgruntled, former colleague of Hammon and his terrorist organization, al-Nusra.

The round man shifted again in the wooden Adirondack chair. Its planks creaked in protest. Hussein sighed and leaned back, looking like a beached whale covered in a large floral print shirt. He placed the Sherlock Holmes-style pipe through the slit in the mask, revealing plump lips. He relit the blackened tobacco in its bowl.

Winter in America was winding down. Soon the tourists would vacate until the Northern Hemisphere autumn reappeared. Hussein liked it when the island became less populated. She had more freedom to move around. During the tourist season, she was a recluse.

"A favor?" Hammon replied with air of indignation.

Hussein could almost read his thoughts. *This bitch has the audacity to ask for favors!*

"I do not believe you are owed any favors, *Madame*! You have forgotten, Miss Lily, without my organization's help, your operation would never have gotten off the ground. Do not blame us for the failings and incompetence of your operatives. If you are to proceed with further endeavors, you will do it without our assistance or funding."

"Your Steven Cooper--or whatever his name is--was a key cog in that failure," Hussein retorted. "He folded like a cheap lawn chair."

"There were plenty of mistakes and failures to go around."

"I see," she continued, "that you will not be swayed by my words." Hammon nodded. "That is correct. I have no money or favors for you."

"I feared as much," Hussein stated flatly. "You can't blame a girl for trying, can you?"

"It never hurts to ask." The crinkle around the man's eye above the scarf told her he was smiling.

"So this meeting is not a complete waste, Hammon, you will give me something else. Something that is actually of much greater value than money. It is in fact the real reason I wanted to meet you."

"And what is that?" His voice filled with concern.

"A piece of information."

Hammon's forehead wrinkled. "I don't understand."

"*Non*, this information I wanted you to deliver personally."

"I have no information for you."

"Mais oui, you do."

Hammon turned his palms toward the black night sky.

"I want to know where my son is being held."

Hammon glared for a long moment. "I do not have such information."

Hussein's lips flattened into a thin line. She removed a handgun from beneath her silk gown and leveled it at her guest.

"I know you do."

"I cannot give you something I do not have."
"Then we will have to use other means to extract it."

℞

Chrissie felt as if she'd been teleported back in time. Her body shook. All the demons she'd fought and managed to suppress for more than a year lurched at her. Simply because she'd thought she seen a shadow move in the back yard.

I thought all that was in the past?

She truly understood how war-ravaged veterans felt. She watched the shadows for two more minutes. Nothing.

She refused to let the ghosts in.

The thought of removing her father's Colt from its lock box in the bottom draw of the night stand flashed through her mind. She had slept with it under her pillow, loaded, for nearly six months after the presidential ordeal.

No! she told herself. *I'm not going to be held captive by those memories. I have enough to deal with.*

Chrissie climbed back into bed. Her thoughts shifted back to Jason. Her eyes found the familiar crack in the plaster of the ceiling and focused on it, her mind reliving the emotions and hurdles of the past two years.

Even if there were no other woman, should she marry Jason? Hell, should she stay with him?

In the last months, two critical issues had bubbled to the surface.

One was Michael, and the way he acted toward her. She couldn't put her finger on it, but she sensed Michael's inability to accept her had something to do with the assassination attempts or something that had happened because of it.

The second was the way Jason himself acted.

In the beginning, after things had calmed down, they grew into a routine, keeping The Colonial running and getting to know each other again. In the days and weeks that followed, she saw the warm, sensitive man she'd fallen in love with all those years ago. He worked hard and was very attentive toward her. She knew that he, too, was in love.

As days turned into weeks and then months, their thoughts turned to building a life together. Confident that they would make it work this time, they discussed combining their households and their finances, where they would live, and even children. Chrissie told him that she wanted to get to know his son, Michael.

"He will always be the priority in your life," she had told him one night. He comes first. And I want to build a new family around the three of us."

Jason seemed motivated and enthusiastic about all of it. And they started to take steps to make it all happen. Jason introduced Chrissie to Michael at dinner one night at his house in York County.

Jason thought it would be best to have the meeting take place in surroundings the boy was familiar with. Dinner was simple: hamburgers on the grill, corn on the cob, macaroni salad, and watermelon wedges.

Jason and Chrissie did most of the talking. Jason tried to draw Michael out, prompting him with questions and observations. Michael seemed shy and withdrawn, responding with one-word answers.

Chrissie chalked it up to Michael's understandable discomfort with Jason's new girlfriend. But the distance between her and Michael never seemed to close. He was standoffish and avoided her whenever possible. It frustrated Jason. Chrissie told Jason to leave it alone. But Chrissie's presence in Jason's life seemed to be driving a wedge between Jason and his son.

Then there was the subtle evidence she'd found that Jason was doing things behind her back. He'd say he was going out for a while and disappear for four and five hour stretches. The phone would ring and Jason would go into another room and close the door to take it.

After four weeks of ignoring it and trying to convince herself that it was nothing, she'd finally asked, "What's going on?"

"Nothing you need to worry about," was his reply.

She pressed him on it. "*Just mind your own business, please,*" Jason demanded. Chrissie backed down and did not bring it up again. The matter, however, festered.

After enough gut-wrenching, she'd decided to follow him. He'd stopped at the strip joint. He sat outside in the Mustang waiting for almost fifteen minutes. Chrissie could not bear to see Jason with another woman. She left before her heart could be broken.

<h1 style="text-align:center">CHAPTER 12</h1>

Sweat poured from Hammon's forehead. It was early in the morning. He had not slept for almost twenty-four hours.

"You . . . you think that threatening to kill me is the answer? If I'm dead I can't give you any information. And I took precautions."

"Such as?"

"I have a thick file and electronic data about the assassination attempts locked away in a safe deposit box on the East Coast. It details everything about your operation. If I do not return to America in the next twenty-four hours, I have left instructions for that box to be opened and delivered to the Secret Service and the FBI."

"That's ancient history. It will not give them my location. They already have my son and Cooper in custody. I'm sure your CIA has extracted information from them using very persuasive and horrific techniques. You cannot provide them with much more than they already have."

"Perhaps. But I can give them you."

Hussein let the direction of the gun's barrel slip a few millimeters toward the patio bricks. "No, you were brought here by a very circuitous route. Five different planes and two boats. You were strip searched. Your electronic devices were confiscated long ago. I told you this is not my base of operations. There is no way . . ."

Hammon was desperate now, clutching at anything to gain an advantage. He was trying to stay alive. If he had information she needed, she would not kill him. The CIA, his own service, was getting close. They would discover enough evidence to implicate him in high treason.

He had resisted Hussein's queries to meet face to face. But that was when America did not know she was alive. Once they'd discovered she was not dead, Hammon saw a way to mitigate his precarious situation. If he could bring them to Hussein, he might just be able to negotiate himself a lesser punishment. Hammon was acting on his own. If he could go to the intelligence community with information about where Hussein was, along with her operation, he could negotiate a deal—perhaps the chance to not die in prison.

But she had thrown him a curveball. She led him to another location, away from her base of operations. Hammon had hoped that she would still trust him enough to allow him a glimpse into her web. But he knew when he arrived he had been duped. There was nothing in this small resort villa that revealed any communications equipment, weapons, or a human apparatus of any kind.

She had played him. Now, it was his turn to play his hand, as weak as it was. He was about to play the bluff of his life.

He could see the frustration etched on the woman's face as he smiled under the scarf. "You are too trusting, Delilah. I'll show you," he said. "Do you have a knife?"

Hussein shot him a quizzical look.

"You can keep the gun on me. I need a knife. A sharp knife."

$$\text{R}_{\text{X}}$$

"I'm going to ask you questions. Just move your head to answer. Do you understand?"

Hutton nodded. Jason was grasping Thomas Pettigrew's Colt firmly in his right hand, the distal half of the barrel buried in the former guard's mouth. The effects of the alcohol had evaporated, replaced by abject fear played out in Hutton's wide, terror-filled eyes. By the angle of the weapon and the pressure Jason exerted, Clyde Hutton must have thought it would be shoved down his throat.

Jason escorted the smaller man to the Mustang, forced him on his back onto the front seat by way of the passenger door. He led Hutton out just prior to closing time. Jason, perched atop the man, waited until the crowd filed out of Headlights. The parking lot had emptied minutes ago. With his left hand planted on Hutton's chest, supporting his body and pinning him to the front of the Mustang's bench seat, Jason began his interrogation.

He had taken a slew of photos of this scumbag from a distance. Jason now studied him up close for the first time. His ferret-like face, thin with a long nose, was reddened by drink. The weak chin disappeared into his neckline. The sad, gray eyes pleaded from under a shroud of pockmarked skin.

"Good," Jason said smiling. "If you try anything, your brains will be splattered all over my car. And if I think you're lying, same result. Got it?"

Hutton blinked slowly, and nodded again.

"How long were you a guard there?"

Hutton tried to speak, but the gun barrel stopped him. Jason removed it from his mouth but kept it trained on Hutton's nose.

"CO," Hutton answered.

"What?"

"We are corrections officers, not guards."

Jason lifted the hand from Hutton's chest and rammed his fist into the nose with a sickening crack.

"Don't play games with me, Clyde! I'm not in a good frame of mind."

A rivulet of blood dripped from both nostrils.

"Let's try this again. Two years ago, you allowed someone to enter my cell at the Regional Jail in Williamsburg. He was sent there to kill me. The man with all the tattoos. Is that correct?"

Hutton nodded.

"How much?" Jason pushed the barrel between his lips. It clicked against teeth.

"How . . . mush . . . wha?" Hutton replied, his words muffled.

Jason removed the gun once more from Hutton's mouth, raised it, and smashed it into Hutton's cheek. The skin ruptured. A crimson trail snaked past Hutton's ear, dripping onto the vinyl.

"How much were you paid?"

"If I could go back and do it over, I'd never have agreed. I lost my job and was lucky I didn't go to prison. They never knew that I was paid off. I told them I made a mistake putting him in there with you. And they bought it. I lost my house and my wife left me. I got nothing left."

"I know, Clyde, you weasel. I've been watching you for a long time. I almost went to prison, too, for murder. I've killed a few men. I don't have a problem with adding you to the list. How much were you paid?"

"Five thousand."

"That's it! That's all my life was worth? What's his name?"

Hutton shifted his gaze from Jason to the weapon pointed at his nose.

"I'm not going to ask again."

Jason pressed the Colt into the weasel's neck. Hutton took several deep breaths. He pressed his eyelids together. Beads of sweat popped out on his skin. Jason smelled urine.

"If you don't tell me, you're a dead man. If you tell me, you live a little longer."

Hutton swallowed hard. Jason pulled the hammer back on the Colt.

"Okay, okay," Hutton said, pleading. "I'll tell you. Just relax with the gun, will ya?"

"Who is he?"

"I don't know, man. You fucked him up pretty good in the cell. I never saw him again."

Jason pressed the weapon deeper into the neck. "You're lying."

Hutton closed his eyes one more time. His body shook. Weak, pitiful sobs escaped his lips as his body quaked. "Just do it, get it over with. I'm a dead man anyway! Even if you don't kill me, I'm still a dead man!"

"You weak-ass pussy." Jason pulled the weapon back and aimed it between Hutton's eyes. "So be it, Clyde."

Jason sucked in a breath, held it a beat, and pulled the trigger.

Chapter 13

Oliver returned from the villa and handed Hammon a kitchen knife with a four-inch blade. The tall manservant stepped back and trained a handgun on the overweight spy. Hammon removed a box of wooden matches from his shirt pocket, striking it against the arm of the chair. A long, thin flame flared. Hammon held the knife to the flame, moving the blade back and forth along its length.

"Can't be too careful," he explained. "I understand MRSA is a bitch."

He blew out the match and lifted the tent-like floral print shirt exposing his fat-filled girth. Pressing a fold between his fingers, he dug the blade into his belly. Blood seeped along the incision. Hussein watched Hammon's face. His expression never changed. No sign of pain moved over his countenance.

With two bloody fingers, he removed a small capsule from beneath the skin. He picked up one of the cloth napkins from the small table between them and pressed it into the wound. Using the other hand, he showed the small implant to Hussein.

"This device has tracked my travels since I left Washington. The data has been transmitted to a secure computer in my home office. If I do not enter a pass code into the program within twenty-four hours, that data along with your file will also be sent to the authorities."

Hussein nodded with a tight smile. "Impressive. You're a regular James Bond!"

"I know how much you despise technology. But I thought you'd like it."

"I do," Hussein answered, taking the small implant. "You are quite ingenious." She paused and continued. "Why would you reveal the device to us?"

"I want you to know that my movements are being tracked. If you kill me, the information I possess, including my last known whereabouts, will be delivered to the highest levels of government. They will be able to find you."

"You haven't been listening, Hammon," Hussein spat. "We are nowhere near my compound. They will not find me."

He tried to remain stone-faced under the mask. His eyes leveled an unflinching stare at Delilah Hussein. He had been a fool to think she would allow him to lead the Feds to her.

"You can't be sure," he replied.

Hussein grinned, dropping the tiny, bloodied tracker to the patio. She crunched it under the heel of her sandal. Hussein raised the gun again, aiming for the fat man's torso. She winked and fired.

$$\text{R}_{\text{X}}$$

The leader of Team Muhammed pressed his back into the wall beside the back door and nodded to his young team member. The recruit removed an electronic lock pick from his satchel. He dispatched the storm door with ease. The storm door creaked but its sound was swallowed up by the waves crashing on the beach. The back door followed a moment later. The team leader turned the knob and pushed the door in.

With one man watching the beach and another in the shrubbery out front, the two mercenaries crossed through the living area to the stairs. Intel had told them there was no security system. After a moment's hesitation, they climbed the stairs, stopping on the second floor outside the master bedroom.

As they had practiced countless times in the last three weeks, they burst in. The husband shot up.

"What the hell . . ."

They covered the distance with two long strides. The architect husband was in the process of whipping off the bed sheets when the butt of the machine pistol rammed into the bridge of his nose. The crunch of the breaking cartilage snapped in the darkness. The man crumpled back onto the bed and did not move.

The young soldier grabbed the woman by the hair, cutting off her shriek with a gloved hand. He jerked her off the bed and onto the carpet, dragging her a few feet. The woman opened her mouth to scream. The gunman rammed a balled up cloth into it, covering it with his hand. He wrestled her to the floor before sitting on her chest, pinning her arms. With his hands free, he pulled a length of duct tape from a roll on his belt and pressed it across her mouth.

He produced a syringe from a sheath on his thigh. The woman saw this and squirmed, bucking him. He uncapped the needle awkwardly and rammed it into her neck. In less than three seconds, she was unconscious.

Though not moving, the husband was sedated in the same manner. The two intruders waited thirty seconds to make sure the couple was down. They exited the master bedroom and headed down the hall.

The door shot open before they could kick it in. The boy's eyes widened at the sight of the black-clad men.

"Michael, it's me," the leader said.

The boy's face twisted with confusion at the sound of his name.

"Who are—"

The young Muslim soldier grabbed him by the neck and turned him as he drove him down, pressing Michael's face into the carpet, pinning him with a knee to the back. Michael Rodgers tried to rise up.

"Hel—" he began to scream. The leader covered his mouth with a gloved hand and pushed a cloth into it. Another needle was inserted into his neck.

"Get some clothes," the leader commanded. He removed a business card from his shirt pocket and placed it on the nightstand.

℞

Chrissie kicked her legs twice under the sheets, trying to free herself. They felt as if they were stitched with lead, crushing her beneath an iron curtain of anxiety.

Her potent, latent angst would not allow her to rest tonight. Her mind went back to the second time she'd followed Jason. Her trepidation and curiosity had kept her awake that night also.

A sharp, single creak penetrated her bedroom door from the hallway.

Her heart skipped.

Screw the ghosts, she thought. *I'm getting the gun!*

Chrissie rolled over and pulled open the bottom drawer of the night stand.

℞

The bullet had missed Hutton's skull by millimeters, rupturing the interior of the driver's side door. Jason averted his aim at the last instant, trying to scare the drunkard into an answer. The report beside his ear caused his muscles to seize and had probably ruptured an ear drum. Hutton tried to reach up to cover his ears. Jason's legs pinned them down.

"The name?"

Hutton turned away thinking he was going to take a bullet in the face. Jason grabbed the stringy, unwashed hair and forced Hutton's face back toward him. Hutton went into panic mode.

Somehow, he managed to free his right arm. It arced in wildly. Before Jason could react, a fist slammed into his temple, blurring his vision. His head slammed into the rearview mirror. Jason's eyes began to water and burn, the remnants of the tequila. A barrage of wild punches hammered about Jason's head. Unable to see clearly, Jason brought his arms up to block. Hutton's hand clutched the gun, wrenching it away from his face. It toppled, thumping onto the floorboard.

The former guard managed to raise a knee, placing it against Jason's sternum. Hutton's right hand continued to pelt Jason. Jason scrambled to block the blows. His own fist was forced back into his face multiple times. Clyde Hutton was a desperate—and therefore—a dangerous man.

Jason attempted two wild punches that missed. Hutton raised up, forcing Jason farther backward. Hutton's arms pistoned back and forth, connecting up and down Jason's face and neck. Jason was completely defensive.

The pressure on Jason's chest released a moment after the driver's side door opened, illuminating the cab. Hutton scampered through the opening.

Jason grabbed his boot. Hutton kicked. The heel connected with his chin, snapping Jason's head. Hutton's foot slipped from Jason's hand as Jason slumped into the passenger-side foot well.

Dazed, Jason collected himself as he leaned against the passenger-side door. Shaking away the dizziness, he raised himself up and looked through the windshield. He shook his head, trying to clear the disorientation and pain, but with no success. With the acid sting still burning his eyes and his nose on fire, he tasted blood flowing over his lips.

He managed to reach into his pocket and remove his keys. His eyes followed Hutton through a curtain of water as he climbed into his pick-up truck. Two seconds after the headlights came to life, the truck lurched forward onto Warwick Boulevard, spitting pebbles and dirt.

Jason wiped his eyes and fired the engine. By the time he was on the road, Hutton's pick-up was two hundred yards away.

Jason slammed the steering wheel. *Idiot!*

He floored the accelerator, willing power from the Mustangs eight cylinders. They engaged and the engine pitched higher. Forced deeper into the seat, he wiped his eyes once more.

All the months of planning and watching, Jason had managed to keep his surveillance of the former jail guard secret. Then tonight, he'd fucked it up.

If Hutton got away, he would disappear!! And Jason would never know the real name of the man who'd attacked him in the jail. Tattoo Man.

The Mustang hurtled north on Warwick Boulevard gaining on the twin taillights of Hutton's pick-up truck.

℞

Four members of Team Isaiah had moved in from the tree line beside the decaying shed in the back. The fifth man sat in the black SUV down the street, waiting for them to reappear.

They entered the house and moved to their designated positions. One man at the front door, one at the back. The team leader and his second moved up the stairs single file, taking each step as if it might explode.

Now, they were frozen at the top of the stairs. The floorboards beneath the carpet in the decades-old house had creaked seconds ago. The two men had waited for any sign that the woman had been alerted. *Nothing!*

After a series of quick hand signals, the pair inched down the hall.

Chapter 14

"Tout va bien?" Oliver demanded. *Everything okay?*

Charlie nodded a single, defiant nod. Oliver bristled at the reaction. It was becoming more and more frequent. After Madame had shot the overweight spy, Oliver did not wait around. He left to check on his most talented *soldat,* who had been acting and talking like a prima donna. The boat trip back to the main compound took two hours.

Hussein's second-in-command reached and grabbed the long-haired *soldat* with both hands, pulling his face to within inches of his. "I have protected you from Madame. But I will not be able to protect you much longer. Toe the line or you will be dealt with. I said, 'Is everything ready?'"

Charlie again provided a single nod again, this time adding a single word. *"Oui."*

Oliver had reached his breaking point. He recalled the days back in Newport News as he searched Thomas Pettigrew's and his daughter's homes looking for the box of files. He remembered thinking that the assassinations would be his last mission. That he would retire when the job was done.

Then they had failed. He should have known Miss Delilah would not allow them to stop until they had avenged her daughter and her son. *So much for living the good life,* he thought. *Now he had to babysit this idiot!*

"Très bien. I will be over to check the accommodations shortly. I am here for your evening dose."

Oliver scanned the space. Standing inside the single-story barracks at the southern end of the compound, three other guards looked on with rapt curiosity.

"Allez!" Oliver demanded.

They dispersed, disappearing out the door.

Charlie moved his head in the direction of his bunk area. On a short shelf above the neatly made cot sat three prescription bottles. Oliver released his grip on the senior guard and picked up the amber vials. He palmed a pill from each and grabbed a bottle of water from a small refrigerator in the kitchen area.

Oliver picked up the prescriptions personally every month at the local *pharmacie*, delivering them to the barracks. He made sure that Charlie swallowed every dose. It was the only way he could guarantee Charlie could continue his service to the cause.

"Now!"

Oliver handed the pills to Charlie. Charlie placed all three on his tongue and closed his mouth. Oliver unscrewed the cap from the bottle and handed it over. Charlie gulped down a swig.

"Show me!" Oliver demanded. "I must return to Miss Delilah on the other island."

Charlie stuck out his tongue.

"They will arrive in six hours. Make sure you and Pierre are prepared. Si vous vous vissez . . ." Oliver switched to English for emphasis. *If you screw up. . .*

Charlie responded with another single nod. Oliver felt his jaw muscles tighten. He cocked his head and lifted his arm, prepared to launch a backhand across Charlie's face, but stopped.

"*Batard!*" he whispered, walking away.

Charlie waited until Oliver exited the barracks into the Caribbean morning. When the door closed, Charlie walked into the bathroom, reached into his mouth and from under his tongue and removed each of the wet, sticky tablets. Palming them, he moved to the five naked toilets. He dropped the pills into one and flushed.

He had stopped taking the pills a week ago. He'd practiced the maneuver for weeks: rolling his tongue and lodging the tablets beneath it. He was feeling like a man again, his energy and strength returning.

But so were the urges. The pills dulled his senses, making him lethargic and clouding his mind. The irrepressible urges had almost gotten him killed and incarcerated. Charlie held no illusions about his illness. As a serial rapist and sex addict, he needed to feel the power and the raw energy he experienced when he ravaged a woman beneath him.

Miss Hussein, the Boss Woman, had saved him from a long sentence in an Algerian prison for raping and mutilating a young local. Oliver took up his cause, insisting the team needed him. His skills could not be replaced, Oliver had pleaded. To save one of her trusted *soldats*, Hussein intervened by bribing a corrupt judge. But she insisted that he be treated. That was six months ago.

Charlie hated the pills. He didn't like what they did to him. They made him feel weak and sluggish, always tired. Worse, yet, he couldn't get it up. His member hung between his thighs like a limp sausage.

Pas plus! *No more!*

At the moment, he didn't give a shit about Hussein. It was good to feel like a man again.

℞

They hurtled toward the Lee Hall Depot. Jason in the Mustang trailed Hutton's Ford pick-up by a car length. Hutton jerked the truck to the right, negotiating the two-ton vehicle north onto Yorktown Road. They had several close calls, barreling through junctions with intersecting roads in the populated sections of schools and businesses along Warwick.

Jason was cautious and lost ground three times at the lights. Fifty yards behind now, he closed the distance again. Yorktown Road cut through a rural area with dense forests punctuated by large, flat fields. On this stretch, Jason closed to within a few yards. Hutton's adrenaline must have waned and his drunkenness had taken over again. The truck weaved and swerved along the roadway, hurtling through the night toward Jefferson Avenue.

Jason pulled alongside, the Mustang's grill even with Hutton's door. Hutton pushed the barrel of a rifle out the window, laying it across his left arm.

Taking an unsteady bead and glancing back and forth between the Mustang and the roadway, Hutton pulled the wheel left, crumpling the Mustang's quarter panel. Jason braked, swerving left, catching the shoulder of the two-lane road. A blast erupted from the barrel. The passenger side of the windscreen crackled into multiple spider webs. Chunks of glass sprayed his face.

Jason slammed the brakes. His car nosed down. The engine of the pick-up pitched higher. The vehicle lurched forward and sped up, creating separation. Fifteen seconds later, Hutton hung a left, west onto Jefferson Avenue. Jason floored the pedal, fishtailing back onto the road.

He roared into the intersection. A horn blared. Tires screeched. Jason narrowly missed a compact car as a horn wailed then died away.

A burning sensation crept up Jason's shoulder to his neck and down his right arm. A rosette of crimson circled the holes in his sleeve. A trail of blood oozed from the wounds. Glass from the windshield had sprayed his arm and shoulder.

Nausea welled in his throat. His right hand shook. Jason drove for another mile, never letting his eyes leave the pair of taillights ahead. The Mustang drifted toward the right shoulder as Hutton's taillights became fainter through the web of cracks in the glass.

Then in the distance, the taillights disappeared. The disappearance coincided with a cyclone of smoke and dust and the sound of twisting metal. The sight of intermittent flashes of red taillights pulsed as the truck cartwheeled along the roadway. Jason yanked the steering wheel hard to the left, overcorrecting. The Mustang responded, its tires grabbing asphalt. Jason recorrected in the opposite direction.

Through the passenger-side window, he saw a large fireball mushrooming up from the overturned vehicle. An instant snapshot singed into his memory a spilt second before he felt his own car leave the roadway.

Jason's stomach plummeted. The car became airborne. Tree trunks and branches along this northern stretch of Jefferson Avenue hurtled at him.

The front end crumpled. Metal screamed. The car stopped, but Jason's body kept moving, stopped instantly by the deploying airbag. Something penetrated the already weakened windshield, tearing at the flesh of his face.

The last sensations Jason experienced were the whiplash of his head and neck followed by the warm gush of blood over his eyes.

Chapter 15

The goddamned idiot had panicked!

The Watcher couldn't help but cuss out Clyde Hutton as he careened his Ford along the densely traveled Warwick Boulevard with the pharmacist. The spy's Caddy hadn't been able to keep up with Rodgers and Hutton. Not because of a deficit in horsepower, but simply bad timing. The Watcher had hit several red lights at intersections in which he'd been stopped as the third or fourth car in line.

With his hand on the gearshift lever and his palm bouncing up and down on the knob, The Watcher counted the seconds before the light turned. He couldn't see them anymore. They had taken a right onto Yorktown Road, disappearing around a bend at the old train depot.

Moments before, The Watcher had let a sardonic grin slip over his lips as he watched the two men inside the darkened cab of the Mustang. Jason had pressed himself onto the smaller man. The Watcher's mind had recalled watching Christine Pettigrew a month or so ago sitting in almost the same location from which The Watcher now scrutinized the pharmacist and his prey.

With his reverie interrupted, The Watcher was jolted back to the present when a light strobed inside the car and the loud report cracked.

Had Rodgers killed Clyde Hutton?

Had Hutton delivered the item?

The answer came a moment later when Hutton extricated himself from the car and fled, initiating the high-speed car chase.

When the light changed, he caught a break. All the traffic ahead of him stayed north on Warwick allowing him to floor the accelerator, gunning the eight cylinder four-hundred-horsepower power plant of the Cadillac.

The Watcher shook his head as he trained his eyes on the road.

The Watcher had explained to the nervous Hutton last night that Rodgers would not kill unless he was provoked. It was not in his nature to kill without cause. The agent had given Hutton a simple assignment. An assignment passed on from Hussein. *Give Rodgers the name and the damned device!*

One simple directive. One a child could have carried out. Even grown men become idiots under pressure.

The double agent's heart sank. He brought the Caddy to a screeching halt at the intersection with Jefferson Avenue. In the distance to the north, he spied a fireball along the right side of the road. Without waiting, he spun rubber through the red light at the deserted roadway.

As he approached, he breathed again. The wreckage belonged to the pick-up truck. He pulled onto the shoulder a quarter mile from the accident scene. He scanned the roadway for any sign of the Mustang but didn't see it.

Donning the goggles, he checked again. He spotted a soft red glow in the trees to his left. The red luminescence from the still hot engine. The car was impaled by a thick branch, penetrating the windshield, holding it aloft like a pig on a spit. Inside, the skull-shaped green circle of Rodger's head on the driver's side lay motionless near the large branch. Rodgers's body was still warm.

One question assaulted him: was he still alive?

℞

Jason opened his eyes. He was rewarded with a warm, sticky darkness. He pushed himself back into the seat and away from the steering wheel. A plastic fabric covered it. Jason tugged at it but it did not give.

Walking his hands along the plastic, he could feel it anchored into the center hub of the steering wheel. The deflated air bag.

He blinked, trying to accommodate to the darkness. He turned his head to look toward where the flames would be engulfing Hutton's truck. His head hit something rough and sturdy.

He ran his hands along it. It was a tree limb. A gruesome death had been inches away. He could see no yellow flames in the distance. He saw nothing at all.

Bringing his hands to his face, his fingers came away coated and sticky with blood. Tracing it to its origin, his fingers caressed the skin of his forehead. The depression was wide. Touching it sent electric daggers coursing through his skull.

Jason tensed, clenching his fists and his teeth, fighting off the agony.

When it passed, he wiped the sticky curtain from his eyes. Faint slivers of dancing yellow and crimson seeped in.

Jason ducked under the thick tree limb holding the car aloft and looked west. Yellow flames licked up from the angled undercarriage of the pick-up resting on its roof.

The unmoving silhouette of Clyde Hutton hung, still strapped in on the driver's side, backlit by the yellow flames. Jason checked to make sure his Colt was tucked in his belt. He crawled out of the shattered passenger-side window and fell six feet to a grass-covered ditch.

At this early morning hour, this stretch of roadway was deserted except for the two mangled vehicles. No sirens wailed and no flashing lights pulsed . . . not yet. He had no idea how long he'd been unconscious. He scampered up the slope to the roadway and ran on weak, wobbly legs to the burning truck.

Dropping to his knees, he poked his head inside the cab. The heat from the flames above them stung his face. Hutton hung motionless by the seatbelt, his right arm bent in a way unintended by nature. That's when he saw the copious amounts of blood.

Jason's head and scalp screamed in pain as he ducked inside the cab, where the combination of his own pain and Hutton's blood dripping onto the upturned roof made his stomach turn. He repressed the urge to vomit as his own blood seeped down his face from the deep scalp laceration. He felt a wave of dizziness as bile filled his throat.

He jabbed a bloody finger onto Hutton's neck. The pulse throbbed intermittently. This man was still alive but bleeding to death.

There's not much time!

Jason reached up and tried to unbuckle the seatbelt holding the man aloft inside the overturned pick-up. It would not give. He tried three times to yank it free with the same result.

A loud whoosh swept over the vehicle. The heat in the cab intensified. The yellow glow brightened around the vehicle. Jason tugged once more at the seatbelt. Again, it would not budge.

Jason removed the Colt from under his shirt and took aim. Two blasts strobed inside the cab. Hutton's torso flinched. The belt gave way. Hutton dropped into Jason's arms.

He dragged Hutton onto the brush and checked for a pulse once more.

Still alive!

Jason slapped Hutton twice across the face, once with a forehand then a backhand.

"Wake up, Hutton!"

He grabbed skin just under the jaw and twisted it with as much force as he could summon. Hutton twitched and blinked.

"Hutton, what were you going to tell me?"

Hutton's eyes registered relief at being saved. Then he must have realized who had saved him.

Grabbing hair, Jason shook the weasel's head.

"Tell me! Who was the man in the jail?"

Hutton sighed, blinking away the pain.

"It's not over! They're back . . . The Simoon . . . They're looking for . . . "

Hearing the name of the organization again, spoken aloud, stunned him. Jason recoiled. He hadn't realized it until this moment. He'd not said the name in nearly two years. "How do you know that name?"

"The guy who visited me told me."

"Who?! What did he look like?"

Hutton shook his head. "It was a guy in a hat . . . you know, like Dick Tracy's hat . . . he wore all black."

Hutton tried to move his right arm, but dropped it like a discarded tree branch. His eyes widened a moment before he screamed.

"My arm! What the fuck did you do to my arm?"

Jason grabbed Hutton's shirt, drenched with sweat and blood. That's when he noticed the fragment of bone protruding from the tissue. Blood spurted in pulses from the wound.

"Oh shit," Jason said.

He removed the laces from both tennis shoes and placed one below the shoulder of the mangled arm, creating a tourniquet. The pain in Jason's shoulder surged. Nausea followed and Jason puked on the asphalt. He recovered, wiped his mouth with his good arm, and tied the fabric. He moved his weakened arm to hold the lace as he pulled hard with his right hand. The pressure was so tight the visible skin dimpled.

He swallowed hard and tore away the sleeve of Hutton's shirt. Still, blood seeped from the hole around the three-inch section of gray-white bone. Using the second shoe lace, he applied a second tourniquet near the elbow, tying it as tight as he could. The flow stopped. Jason sucked in rapid, quick breaths fighting his own urge to collapse. Blood continued to ooze from the laceration on his head.

"Hutton, stay with me!"

The weasel floated in an out of consciousness. Jason slapped him hard, twice. His eyes fluttered.

"What are they looking for?"

Hutton mouthed one word. No sound escaped from his lips. Hutton tried again. Jason leaned in.

"Say it again!"

"You . . ."

"Me?"

Jason saw the tourniquet give way, unraveling at the elbow. Blood pulsed from the wound again. The slick crimson did not allow him to gain purchase. He tried several times. The flow could not be staunched.

"They . . . are . . . looking . . . for you . . ."

Jason pushed away from Hutton and shook his head. He ran a hand through his bloody hair. "I don't fucking believe this!"

A large oval of black blood widened on the asphalt under Hutton.

Jason grabbed the weasel by the shirt with both hands, ignoring the slicing shards of pain in his body. "Clyde, listen to me. I don't care about what happened in the jail. It's over. You're dying. They medics won't get here in time. I can't stop the bleeding."

Part of Jason knew he should be doing more to save this man's life. Another part of him wanted this scumbag's life to end. He deserved nothing less. But, he needed him to stay alive long enough to get as much information as he could from him. Jason's adrenaline kicked in, chilling his own pain and fueling him.

"Clyde, make things right. Tell me Tattoo Man's name!"

Hutton's eyelids fluttered. The eyes began to roll into his skull.

"Clyde, the name." Jason slapped Hutton across the face three times with all his might. Hutton opened his eyes. They were glassy and unfocused.

"Luther . . . William . . . Luther . . ."

"Where is he?"

Hutton shook his head. He swallowed and grabbed Jason's shirt with his good hand, pulling him down.

"I'm sorry . . ."

Jason leaned in again, trying to hear Hutton's weak words.

"In the pocket of my pants . . . take it. I was supposed to give it to you."

"Give me what?"

"I've known you were watching me. He said to wait until you made contact. They're watching, both of us."

"Clyde, what the fuck are you talking about? Who told you?"

"The man in the black hat. They're watching."

"Who are watching?"

"The same people who hired me to put Luther in your cell. The Simoon!"

"What?"

A sharp, slice of agony cut through Jason's chest. *Were these the rantings of a dying man or did Clyde Hutton know more?* Jason wanted to keep him alive and ask him more questions. But there was no time. Hutton was bleeding to death.

Jason glanced around. He saw nothing but the glow of the burning truck. He patted down Hutton. There was something in the right-hand pocket. He pulled it out and looked back to Hutton. Jason placed the item in his pocket.

"If you knew I was coming for you, why did you run?"

"I got scared. I'm a dead man. I deserve to die."

With those words, Clyde Hutton closed his eyes for the last time.

$$\text{R}_{\text{X}}$$

What to do?

The Watcher had waited, trying to determine his next move. Eventually, the pharmacist had crawled through the passenger window of the mangled Ford. He had staggered and stumbled toward the inverted truck. Flames licked up from the exposed undercarriage.

He checked the rearview for the FBI. Nothing.

Lost them in traffic.

Through the night-vision goggles, he watched as the pharmacist struggled to free Clyde Hutton. After several tense minutes, Rodgers dragged the limp body from the cab and onto the shoulder of the road. Rodgers himself appeared to be injured.

Was Rodgers talking to him? Or was he trying to revive him?

The Watcher had no idea why the pharmacist wasn't simply given a message through a dead drop or another means. Hussein wanted the message and the smartphone delivered by Hutton. There was some kind of symbolism in all of it.

The agent saw Hutton's head and lips moving. He was talking and responding. There was nothing else to do . . . for now.

Delilah Hussein was toying with the man like a cat with a captive mouse.

The cops would be on the scene soon. If Hutton had evidence linking him to The Simoon in the vehicle, it had to be destroyed. The Watcher was under orders to make sure nothing could be traced back to Hussein. Later, after the man was dead, he would search Hutton's double-wide in Williamsburg.

He lifted the small black box from the seat beside him, turned the red knob to the on position. The green light illuminated. He checked to make sure Jason Rodgers was not going back to the vehicle, then he pressed the round black button.

A second later, the charges rigged in the overturned truck exploded.

Chapter 16

Fifteen hundred miles to the southeast, Delilah Hussein knelt in her massive master suite. She would miss her appointed time for the first *salaat* of the day. Normally, she prayed the *Fajr* at six in the morning. It was just after four now. There would be no time later. This would be a very busy day, so she performed it now, two hours early.

She had only managed a few hours of sleep in the last twenty four, mostly through short twenty or thirty minute naps. With her energy level high, Delilah Hussein cleansed herself and covered her hair. She stood on her prayer rug with her hands at her ears, palms forward. Her thumbs tucked behind her earlobes.

"Allahu Akbar!"

She then placed her right hand over her left on her chest and looked at the rug before her. She offered the traditional opening supplication followed by the *Fatiha*, the first surah of the Qur'an.

She lowered hands and bent at the waist. *"Allahu Akbar!"* she whispered, as she lowered her torso. When her back was parallel to the floor and her eyes saw her feet, she continued.

"Subhanna rabbiyal 'Azeem!"

Hussein repeated this three times.

The door to her bedroom opened. Hussein sensed the man waiting until she was done.

"What do you want?" she demanded without looking in his direction.

"Hammon, he is bleeding . . . a lot. There may not be much time."

Hussein sighed. She could not afford to let this man die. She had shot him on the island in the shoulder, missing any vital internal structures. With his implanted tracking device destroyed and his body scanned for any other devices, her minions had dragged Hammon back to the boat for the two-hour trip to the main island. They deposited him by the pool under the covered pergola while she prepared to pray. It was time to extract what she needed.

"Je serai la!" *I'll be right there!*

℞

"He abducted someone from inside the club, sir."

"What?"

"Our agent on the ground said he came out of the strip club with a gun. He forced someone into his Mustang. Minutes later, Rodgers left the car and is now chasing him. Very high speeds."

"Where are they going?"

"We don't know, sir. The agent lost them at an intersection. We are blind again."

Brad Lane, the deputy director of the Bureau who had been personally asked by Director McNamara to supervise this operation, spat a string of expletives.

"And the pharmacist and the pick-up truck are being followed by a third vehicle. A black Caddy. Is it The Watcher?"

"We believe so, sir."

℞

Hussein watched Hammon clutch at his left shoulder from the comfort of the padded Adirondack chair. The round had penetrated below the clavicle. His plump fingers tried in vain to stem the flow of blood.

"You are bleeding profusely, Hammon. I guess a man of your size has a few extra liters."

Hammon's arms were crossed over his torso. One clutched the bullet wound while the other pressed the bloody napkin into the self-created knife wound in his belly.

"You stupid bitch," Hammon moaned.

Hussein leapt from her seat and was on him with a dexterity that surprised even her. She maneuvered the barrel of the gun between the fingers of Hammon's hand over the belly wound and pressed. The fat spy shrieked.

"You are bleeding all over my patio and furniture, you fat slob. So much blood, it scared my man. He thought you were dying."

Hammon breathed heavily, trying to quiet the pain.

"I have brought you back to my island, Hammon, as you wished. But the tracking device is on the other island, destroyed."

"I'm not giving you a penny. I can't!"

"I know that, you idiot! You are delirious. We already talked about this. I never intended to take any more money from you. I need information from you."

"What kind of information?"

"One piece. That's all I need. I know you have it. If you give it to me, I will kill you quickly, painlessly. If not, Oliver will carve you, while still alive, into bite-size morsels to be used as chum," Hussein seethed.

℞

Jason awoke in a large, square ambulance rig parked at an angle across Jefferson. He lay on a stretcher as a paramedic palpated him for more wounds. A second rig was visible through the open doors. Jason stared into its open bay. In it lay a stretcher with a blanket-draped body.

The night was punctuated by a kaleidoscopic array of blue and red lights reflecting off the foliage and tree trunks. Two fire trucks, three police cars, and a HAZMAT vehicle also blocked Jefferson Avenue in both directions. Two fire hoses were aimed at the smoldering truck, dousing it as a string of black smoke wafted skyward.

The first responder wore a tight-fitting, dark blue t-shirt with the Newport News Fire Department's logo over his left breast. In his peripheral vision, he could see the man's lips moving. He was speaking to Jason. But the words were muted by the humming in his ears.

"What?" Jason shouted, barely able to hear his own voice.

The paramedic began to roll Jason over. The metal lump under him made Jason push him away. The Colt was still in his waistband. He did not own it and had no license for it.

Jason shoved the first responder. The firefighter looked at him with confusion.

"I'm fine," Jason shouted.

The EMT held up his hands as if asking, "What the hell?"

"I'm fine."

"You need stitches on the gash on your forehead and those glass wounds in your shoulder."

Jason shook his head. "I'm fine."

"That's not a good idea. We can't let you drive, sir. That gash on your forehead is deep and the wound in your arm needs medical attention. You may have a concussion."

Jason glanced at his arm and shoulder. It had been expertly bandaged and wrapped. His hand went to his forehead. Another thick wad of gauze had been placed over his head.

A Newport News uniformed cop climbed onto the back bumper of the rig. The paramedic and the cop exchanged words. Jason could not hear what they were saying.

The cop moved beside the stretcher, switching places with the firefighter. He asked him several questions including his name and address.

" . . . what happened?"

Jason shouted several partial truths. "The truck was swerving all over the road. I came up behind him . . . looked like he was drunk. He finally flipped it. I lost control too."

"Have you had anything to drink tonight?"

Jason shook his head.

"Do you have identification?"

Jason fished out his wallet and handed it to the cop, who read the driver's license.

"Do you know the gentleman in the pick-up truck, Mr. Rodgers?"

"No."

"The EMT tells me you do not want to go to the hospital. Is that correct?"

"Yes."

At that moment, a man appeared outside the rear of the ambulance. He wore a black suit and a fedora and flashed a leather wallet and a badge. Jason, again, had trouble hearing. He caught snatches of the conversation between the uniform and the suit.

"I'll take care of this," the suit said to the cop.

The man climbed in as the uniform exited.

"Is there someone you want to call?" the man asked, placing a pretend phone to his ear.

Jason nodded. He pulled his phone from his pocket. "My girlfriend."

He placed his free hand over his ear and listened to Chrissie's land line ring. It sounded as if it were in the far end of a long tunnel. As it rang, he couldn't help but notice that the hat on the man's head looked like a black version of the one worn by Dick Tracy.

It rang ten times. He tried her cell with the same result.

He left messages on both phones for her to call him. He bent his arm to look at his Tissot. The dome was shattered but the second hand was still moving.

Four-twenty-three in the morning.

Where the hell could she be at this hour!

℞

Delilah Hussein forced a reluctant smile. The man was stubborn. This was taking much longer than anticipated.

Back in her seat, she put the green, tapered bottle of Perrier to her mouth, took a sip, then patted her lips with a starched white cloth napkin.

Hammon lay half on his side, bleeding from the two wounds, groaning.

"One piece of information. That's all I require. I know you're in a lot of pain. One word will put an end to all of it. Comprenez-vous?" *Do you understand?*

Hammon's floral print shirt, soaked in blood, clung to his skin as his chest heaved. He did not respond.

Hussein nodded toward Oliver, her manservant, standing behind Hammon's Adirondack chair.

Oliver, having returned back to second island, grabbed a fistful of the thinning hair. "Answer the lady! Do you understand?"

The spy managed a feeble nod.

"Good," Hussein said.

"What . . . do . . . you . . . want?"

"Remember, if you lie to me, you know what will happen . . ."

"What do . . . you want?"

"Où se trouve mon fils?" *Where's my son?*

Chapter 17

Lisa Rodgers had heard the ring before and knew who it was. She hated that shrill ring—an imitation of a wild cat screeching in a fit of agitated distress. Her husband had a twisted sense of humor.

What kind of trouble is he in now?

Peter could sleep through a hurricane, tornado, and nuclear blast if they hit all at once. He did not flinch when the damned thing began to vibrate, flash, and scream from the nightstand on his side of their massive king-sized bed.

She rolled toward her husband when the third screech of the feral cat pierced the darkness of their Smithfield home. She bent her arm and dug her elbow deep into his rib cage.

The former marine arched his back. "What the hell?" he spat.

"Peter, answer the damned phone."

She heard him fumbling with the device and the noise stopped.

"Jase, what's up?"

She lay on her back, staring into the blackness as she listened to Peter's half of the conversation.

"When did this happen?" he asked.

More listening.

"Okay, give me forty-five minutes," Peter said as he ended the call.

He swung his legs off the bed as he spoke to Lisa. "I have to go, Jason needs my help."

"What else is new?"

℞

"Your son," Hammon gasped, "is being held in a place that cannot be penetrated. He cannot escape . . ."

"I did not ask for your opinion, Hammon. I just want the location."

"If I tell you, you will allow me to leave."

"No. You are going to die. It's just a matter of how long it will take and in what manner. The longer you refuse, the longer Oliver is going to inflict unspeakable pain on you. If you do tell me now, we will kill you quickly and as painlessly as possible."

Hammon closed his eyes and mouthed a silent prayer. Panic invaded his pained expression.

Hussein nodded again. Oliver moved in once more. He tied Hammon's wide arms to the wooden rails of the chair. Then he tied the neck with a length of rope to back of the chair.

"Last chance," Hussein declared as if speaking to a disobedient child.

Oliver slammed the butt of his handgun into Hammon's face. Blood and teeth sprayed. Hammon cried out.

"Où est-il?" *Where is he?*

Hammon shook his head, blood dripping from his chin.

"Okay," Hussein said with a tone of resignation.

Oliver removed a long, thick, bladed knife from a scabbard under his pant leg. He forced Hammon's head to one side, holding it firmly with one hand. Climbing atop him, Oliver forced his knee onto Hammon's chest for additional stability. The blade descended between Hammon's right ear and his scalp, resting there. He drew the blade back.

With each stroke, the blade carved back and forth, separating the ear from the spy's head. Hammon cried out with the intensity and volume of ten men. Blood-tinged spittle plumed forth, hitting Oliver in the face and chest.

Oliver dropped the severed ear, now a ribbon of flesh, to the patio. It hit with a dull, wet splat.

Blood flowed from the wound, down Hammon's neck, in a wide triangular path. Hammon hyperventilated, trying to block out the agony. Tears seeped from his closed eyes. Low, moaning sounds emanated from his throat.

"I . . . can't . . . tell . . . you," he whispered. "I don't . . . know . . . where he is."

Hussein shook her head and frowned.

"You just told me that he's being held in a facility from which escape is impossible. That tells me you must know where it is. You're being inconsistent. Your skills as a spy have eroded, Hammon. Either that or the pain is unbearable. I'm guessing it's the pain."

"No . . . more . . . please . . ."

"Give me the information I want."

"How will you know I'm not lying?"

"We have narrowed down the possibilities to a few places. If you give us an off-the-wall answer, we'll know you're being untruthful."

Hussein sat stone still. She'd just lied to Hammon. They had no idea where her son was being held. This was her only hope. She's was bluffing. Though he didn't know it, Hammon held all the cards.

"So, shall we continue," she asked. "Or do you have an answer for us?"

℞

The sinking feeling in Jason's stomach plunged deeper when he saw the house.

Chrissie's place, their place, was dark. Not a single light glowed. Something was wrong.

"You need to have those wounds looked at," Peter said for the third time, nodding toward the blood-soaked bandage plastered to his head.

"Later," Jason retorted. "This doesn't look right, Pete. There are no lights on."

"It is early morning, Jason. She's probably asleep."

"She always leaves at least one light on upstairs and downstairs ever since the attacks on the presidents."

"Maybe she's out. Didn't you say you guys had a fight?"

"At this hour? Look, her car's in the driveway. There's something wrong. I've called her five times. She hasn't answered. I'm worried about her." Jason moved to exit Peter's Hummer.

"I'm going in with you."

$$\text{R}_{\!\text{x}}$$

Hammon's chin rested on his heaving chest. His head bobbed with each respiration. The warm blood from the wound where his right ear once resided flowed over his back and down his chest, seeping into the folds of his neck.

I need to find a way to die!

He had been working his tongue against the back tooth of his lower right jaw for the last few minutes. It served two purposes. One practical, one necessary. The undulations of his tongue against the tooth helped him focus on something other than the agony circling his head and body. The second reason was more vital to his and his team's mission. He needed to get at the small capsule beneath the false molar.

The right side of his head and face felt as if a blowtorch were searing the skin and muscle. The gunshot wound in his shoulder had a strong, acidic pulse. The incision in his gut stung with pain, occasionally out-screaming the intense agony of the other wounds just to remind him it, too, was still there.

The angry signals ping-ponged back and forth. Vomit welled in his throat. If he wasn't seated, he would have fallen over. His whimpering and tears were impotent, involuntary reactions to the interminable horror.

He knew the location. But Hammon couldn't reveal it. Revealing the site had to be avoided at all costs. His colleagues at the CIA were getting close. They were hot on his trail, the trail to discovering what Hammon had done in aiding The Simoon and Hussein's people in the failed assassination attempts. Hammon held no illusions. These people, like him, were good at what they did. They would eventually have proof that he was the mastermind of the leaked information about the christening in Newport News.

Hammon's only chance was to locate Delilah Hussein's base of operations, her compound, so they could apprehend her. Once she was in custody, he could cut a deal to save his life . . . or at the very least . . . keep from spending the rest of his life in a federal prison. But that option had evaporated. Hussein had brought him back to her compound. Hammon knew that meant he would not leave the island alive.

Hussein, no doubt, wanted her son back. If she knew his whereabouts, she would try to free him. The Simoon had assets living secretly inside the United States. Hammon's cause was lost. He was going to die. He needed to die on his own terms . . . before he revealed the location. There would be no reversal of fortune. Consumed by the sense of duty and a need to have the agony end, he redoubled his efforts to loosen the molar. Hammon needed to keep Hussein from getting her son back.

He sighed heavily and felt his eyes beginning to roll into his skull. He shook his head, willing the vomit and shakiness back.

Unconsciousness would be a welcome albeit temporary relief. It would not be the end. Hussein would not kill him; she would not allow him to find the sanctuary of death until he had given up the location

I need to die now!

The false molar had been hollowed out, stuffed with a cyanide capsule and cemented back into place. With free hands and a small pair of grips, Hammon could have freed the tooth in a matter of seconds. But with only his tongue, it was a gargantuan task. The tip of his tongue was worn with irritation and shook with fatigue.

"Shall we continue, Hammon?"

Hussein's words sounded as if they were coming through a poorly tuned radio. He felt the manservant move in, then the sharp grip of his thinning hair.

Hammon tensed with the anticipation of another bout of horrible agony.

CHAPTER 18

Jason tried to insert his key into the deadbolt lock of the front door. The key simply pushed the door open. It slid inward with no resistance. The hair on his neck stood up.

"Shit," he whispered.

Jason heard Peter's holster unsnap, followed by his brother racking the slide of his nine millimeter Remington 1911 R1. Jason removed the Colt from inside the waistband of his back.

He pushed the door wide with one finger and stepped in, leveling the gun. Flipping on the light switch, Jason swung the weapon in a horizontal arc.

The brothers secured the first floor in two minutes. Peter then exited through the back door, moving to Chrissie's Chrysler 300 in the driveway. Jason remained inside, continuing to scan the first floor. Peter returned, shaking his head, indicating that everything outside appeared normal. The pair climbed the stairs single file. Each room along the hallway was searched and cleared. Three minutes later, they arrived at Chrissie's closed bedroom door.

Jason turned the knob, pushing the door open. It crashed into the closet door. Jason jumped back as Peter pointed his weapon into the darkened room, scanning. Peter nodded and entered followed by Jason. Both had their weapons leveled, fingers on triggers.

Jason noticed the bed, sending a cold shiver through him.

"She never leaves it unmade."

Peter stepped past Jason and checked the bathroom. "Empty." Then Peter flipped on the light.

Jason sank onto the bed, put the gun on the disheveled covers and lowered his head into his hands. "What the hell is going on?"

"You said you two had a fight. Maybe she is staying with a friend."

Jason's gaze noticed a spot on the scuffed hardwood floor, just off the throw rug. Lowering himself, Jason reached out and touched the small circle. A droplet of crimson clung to his forefinger.

"I don't think so."

℞

The spy gasped, intensifying his already unbearable torment. Oliver had approached Hammon and nearly ripped the hair from the rotund man's head. Hussein grunted one word, "Attendez!" *Wait!*

She had studied Hammon for several minutes as Oliver held the man's head upright by his hair follicles. Hussein shrugged and said, "I guess he's not ready to talk. Go!"

Oliver tilted the bottle over the gaping, blood-soaked head wound. As the liquid dripped from the plastic container, an acrid, acidic stench filled the air. Muriatic acid sizzled, bubbling and smoking over the crimson flesh.

Three seconds later, Hammon's body tensed as if current flowed through it. His eyes, already closed, squeezed tighter. His lips parted in a silent scream. The enormous man's muscles quivered as the seizure gained momentum.

"Arrêtez!" Hussein shouted at Oliver. *Stop!*

Several more seconds elapsed. Hammon's body went limp.

"Merde," she spat. "I hope you haven't killed him."

℞

The ship had been docked for an hour at Pier Five under the massive derrick offloading the metal containers. The whine of motors told Gundersen that the transfers had begun.

Both five-man military teams had been delivered to their drop-off points, one in Chesapeake Bay the other at the mouth of the James

River. A ten-ton weight had been removed from the captain's shoulders. However, a small, uncomfortable pressure still niggled within his chest.

At least the commandos are gone, he thought.

One more delivery lay before him. One he would handle personally. This would be easy compared with the previous two—no guns, no night-vision goggles.

Deep in the stacks of containers still on board the *Thor*, Gundersen angled his body as he maneuvered among the containers looking for the correct number. He found it.

Above him, the monster derrick's gears whizzed as the large harness was brought into place over the remaining hundreds of metal boxes. It would be an hour before this container was moved to the yard of the terminal.

Gundersen had checked on this piece of cargo three times every day since they'd left the Ghanian port of Tema on the West African coast, fretting over it like a mother hen hatching a chick. The journey to Norfolk had taken twelve interminable days.

The captain removed his key, the only key for this box, and inserted it into the large padlock. He swung open the doors, stepped inside, and reclosed them, sealing him inside. Producing a small flashlight from his pocket, Gundersen looked at the medium-sized truck squeezed into the interior of the metal container. This shipping container had been specially modified to hold this vehicle and support its needs.

The gentle whirring sound coming from the front of the container and the very cold temperature of the ambient air put his mind at ease. Gundersen shivered. It would be a shame to have the cargo spoil after getting halfway around the world. He had been warned that if the cargo did not remain frozen inside the truck, he would be held accountable. The Norwegian held no illusions about what that meant.

Satisfied that he would not be disturbed, he wedged himself along the right-hand wall. He checked the cab of the white truck. All appeared in order. To save time, the sailor crawled beneath the chassis, scooting to the opposite side.

The electric panel mounted to the interior wall of the shipping box glowed with a series of red and green indicator lights over a panel of eight two hundred and twenty volt outlets. This container had been wired into the ship's electrical system which in turn fed current to the vehicle. Just above the electrical panel, a flat, rectangular black box, the backup generator, provided a twelve-hour backup in case of a power failure. When it was lifted by the derrick, the electrical connections would be severed and the back-up supply would take over. Gundersen had plenty of time to transfer the power to the truck's power plant.

Gundersen studied the wall unit. From two of the outlets, a pair of thick yellow power cables snaked from the console and draped to the floor. A foot past the truck's cab, they ascended to the refrigeration unit mounted on the front-facing wall of the truck's hold. The cables disappeared under and into the refrigeration unit, feeding the massive machine.

Gundersen stepped onto the running board of the passenger door and shined the light on the temperature gauge mounted on the ceiling of the cab.

Minus 2 degrees Celsius. Perfekt!

He placed his hand on the sidewall of the truck's cargo area. A patina of frost coated the outside. He removed his hand, leaving a hand print on the frosted metal. He smiled a thin, weary grin.

All was good.

He would soon be rid of this worrisome container. The sound of motors whirring and grinding above him told him the derrick was in motion again, removing another container. Soon this box would be removed from his ship.

Gundersen smiled, locked up the container and counted the minutes until he would make the delivery . . . and the moment he could relax.

℞

"J'ai besoin du nom, Hammon." *I need the name . . .*

Still alive, but barely conscious, the fat man slumped on his right side in the Adirondack chair. The pattern on his floral print shirt had become obscured by the large amount of blood soaked into its silk. Two of the wounds, the knife wound on his torso and the gunshot wound in his shoulder, were congealed with blood.

Hammon's head bobbed intermittently as he bounced in and out of consciousness. Hussein could not determine if it was a haphazard movement caused by extreme pain or if he was shaking his head in disagreement or simply nodding a capitulation.

His eyelids fluttered. The blackened, sizzling hole in the left side of his head continued to ooze rivulets of blood where the ear once resided, revealing a canal leading to the brain. The acid cooked the blood and eroded a trail of skin down to his neck. The excess caustic fluid dripped onto his shirt, burning holes in the collar.

"You must be in incredible agony, mon ami," she continued.

Hussein nodded to Oliver again. The manservant lifted the weapon sitting beside the severed ear, sitting in its own small pool of thick, sanguineous fluid. He pulled back the slide on the nine-millimeter in his pinky-less hands and brought it to Hammon's face, dimpling a small intact area on his temple.

"Just give me the location where he is and we will put an end to your misery."

Hammon's lips moved, mouthing incoherencies.

"I can't understand you. Speak up!"

Hussein did not look at her tortured captive. She studied her manicured fingers, frowning at a blemish. "Cut the other one off!"

Oliver yanked Hammon's head to the left, exposing the remaining ear. Hammon groaned. His eyelids fluttered, exposing glassy, unfocused eyes.

The manservant lowered the sharp blade, touching it to the valley of skin.

As soon the blade made contact, Hammon screeched two unintelligible words.

"I'm sorry," Hussein asked. "I did not get that."

"Onion," Hammon pleaded, drawing out each tortured syllable. "He's . . . at . . . Red Onion . . . with Cooper . . . Steven C . . ."

Hussein stood up, retrieving the nine-millimeter from the glass table. She raised the weapon and fired a round between Hammon's eyes. "Merci beaucoup, mon cheri!"

The matriarch of terror pointed to the corpse, then toward the ocean.

"Jettez ce morceau de merde dans le mer." *Throw this piece of shit in the ocean.*

"*Oui, Madame.*"

"Do we have anyone with access to the Red Onion?"

"We will have to pull some strings," Oliver replied, "but I believe we have an asset ready to go."

Hussein grinned. "Didn't I tell you they would keep him at a black site."

"*Oui Madame*, you did," Oliver replied. "What about Cooper?"

Hussein rubbed her chin with a thumb and forefinger. "Yes, indeed. It is fortunate that Hammon also divulged that Cooper is being held with my son. It is a fortunate turn. We can kill two proverbial birds, *n'est-ce pas?*"

Oliver nodded.

"Get al-Raqqah on the line. They will need to coordinate with our friends at the GRU," Hussein commanded, pointing at the satellite phone.

"The GRU?" Oliver asked with a tone of incredulity. "Do you think the Russians will want to be a part of this?"

Hussein had been performing a delicate balancing act over the past two years, juggling the desires of ISIS and their quest to bring harm to America with the agenda of the Russians, who tried to appear disgusted by the terrorist group but who secretly also desired to wreak havoc on the States.

She was on the secure satellite phone every day with her handlers in al-Raqqah, Syria, the de facto capital. Hussein also made frequent overtures to her contact at the main intelligence agency of the general staff of the Armed Forces of the Russian Federation, the GRU. Hussein was confident that day-to-day reports to her Russian counterpart were making their way to the Russian president.

"The Russians have hacked Americans emails, no ? With the right amount of money and the chance to help bring down the American economy, they will jump at the chance. We need to move quickly. They have the resources, we have the people on site. I want a plan in place in twelve hours."

℞

Twin navy-blue Lincoln Navigators skidded to a halt on the tarmac at Hampton Roads Executive Airport on West Military Highway in Chesapeake. A Gulfstream G-IV SP sat quietly outside a hangar in the dim predawn glow. The airport's posted hours were from seven to five. It would be another two hours before the airport would begin serving southeastern Virginia businessmen.

A five-man group emerged from each vehicle, now dressed in casual business attire. Two toted briefcases. Two clusters of three men from each Navigator moved with military precision to the rear of the SUVs. As soon as the lift gates had fully elevated, each trio pulled a wooden coffin-sized crate cratered with fist-sized breathing holes from the vehicle's bed.

As this occurred, the briefcase-toting men approached the jet. A sleepy-eyed airport official appeared from the main hangar holding a steaming Styrofoam cup of coffee, meeting them at the nose of the aircraft.

Each man lifted his respective briefcase and opened it, allowing the airport man a glimpse inside. With a satisfied nod, the cases were closed again. The airport official poured his coffee out onto the asphalt and dropped the cup. He took the cases, one in each hand, and disappeared into the hangar.

The two coffin crates were loaded onto the Gulfstream jet by the rear staircase. The Navigators zipped to a distant parking area and the drivers jogged back to the aircraft.

Inside the cabin, the senior team leader, commander of Team Mohammed, stuck his head in the cockpit. The former briefcase-carriers were now buckled into the seats checking dials and flipping switches.

A moment later, the twin engines whirred to life.

"Did you file the flight plan?" the leader asked.

"Yes," the pilot responded in perfect English. "We'll land in Georgia to refuel. The second leg was filed as going to Miami. After we take off from Augusta Regional, we'll turn off the transponder as if we've gone down. Of course, we'll be well over the Atlantic before anyone realizes we're not on course. We'll send out a distress call when we are a few miles offshore. Then we'll adjust our course to the final destination."

"Excellent." The leader turned and motioned for his compatriot, the junior team leader of Team Isaiah, to follow him through the cabin. They arrived as the lids were being removed from the coffin-like crates.

The Pettigrew woman—bound, gagged, and unconscious—was lifted from her crate, laid out on a small sofa, and strapped down. The boy's limp body was moved onto a second couch across the aisle.

Two men took seats in swiveling captain's chairs, watching over their prisoners.

"The next shift will relieve you in three hours," the senior leader commanded. "The rest of you relax and get some rest."

Five minutes later, the Gulfstream lifted off the four-thousand-foot runway into the receding darkness. The plane banked on a southerly heading and disappeared over the trees.

PART TWO

CHAPTER 19

Saturday, April 11

"What are you doing here on a Saturday morning?"

Angelo Sheppard swallowed hard as the moisture in his mouth evaporated. Quinton Boyd, vice president of Injectable Production, stood in the doorway to his cramped, paper-filled office, backlit by the harsh fluorescent light. Sheppard, director of Biological Manufacturing at Dawson Pharmaceuticals, could not remember a time when Boyd, an Englishman who Sheppard had heard had been knighted, ever came to the production floor. Especially this early in the morning . . . and never on a Saturday.

Boyd's eyes bore into Sheppard. "It's time, Angelo. It's bloody well time!"

"I see." Sheppard's gut tightened. Though he had been preparing for this moment for months, Sheppard had been petrified for the last two weeks. This was not what he'd signed up for! There was something wrong with the whole thing. He just didn't know what it was. But now he was in too deep. The events that would transpire in the next few hours could not be reversed. Up until this very moment, everything had been just a plan, a dream. Now, it was about to become a reality.

Whatever *that* was!

That made his anticipatory anxiety all the more intense. Meticulous preparation made failure all the more unacceptable.

"I want you to show me the area," Boyd said.

Sheppard stood and came around his desk. "Follow me."

They walked through a glass corridor bisecting the sterile production area, a gaping space filled with massive stainless steel vats dripping with tubing, with gauges attached to computer terminals like aluminum patients on life support. Boyd and Sheppard passed the egg-preparation facility. This is where, when the plant was in full production mode, fully gowned and masked workers wheeled towers of trays of manufacture-grade eggs to and from the topping machines to the candling and extraction rooms.

Once through, Sheppard led his boss past shelves of supplies and empty but ready-to-be-filled syringes, filing through two more pristinely organized sterile rooms. Sheppard opened one final door and allowed Boyd to enter first. When the vice president was inside, Sheppard checked to make sure no one had followed them or was in the hallway. All was clear.

He closed the door and locked it.

Sheppard looked at his boss and fellow conspirator with a sheepish, nervous grin. "I call it the Vault, sir."

Boyd scanned the room as a low-pitched drone filled the space.

Inside, a massive aluminum drum lay sideways. The size of two refrigerators, the gigantic cylinder rested on four steel support legs. A large-bore flexible-plastic pipe protruded from one of the two convex ends. Curving like an elephant's trunk, the black tube disappeared into the nearest wall, where it met the floor. A flat, dark LED panel with an attached keyboard sat perched on a small shelf attached to the machine. A thick power cord snaked from this portable computer to an electrical outlet. A frosted patina coated the colossal stainless steel vat. A chill hovered over the room, seeping into Sheppard's bones.

"It's loud," Boyd commented. "Are you sure no one can hear this?"

"The refrigeration unit is state-of-the-art," Sheppard replied, pointing out the condenser to the right. "We cannot decrease the noise. But the walls and the ceiling surrounding us have been filled with industrial-grade insulation. And these sound-proofing pyramids deaden the noise. You didn't hear anything before we opened the door, right?"

"No…jolly good," Boyd replied.

Sheppard moved his arm in an arc around the small room. All four walls, as well as the ceiling and the door they had just entered through were covered with triangular, sound-absorbing foam prisms. The tall, slim, gray pyramids pointed ominously toward the interior of the room, covering every inch like points of a giant torture chamber.

"Is it ready to receive the shipment?" Boyd asked.

Sheppard placed his palm on the skin of the drum and motioned for Boyd to do the same. It was cold. Very cold. Sheppard and Boyd removed their hands, leaving evaporating handprints on the metal.

"It will maintain a negative two degrees Celsius, or 28.4 degrees Fahrenheit. It's has a twelve-hour backup supply in case of power failure."

"Where will the drums be placed?"

Sheppard moved to the end of the device. He reached under the platform on which the massive cylinder sat and found a lever. When he pulled it, the dull whirring of an electric motor competed with the hum of the condenser. The container inched upward away from the supports. The belly of the sleek silver container rose, exposing a rectangular, grave-sized hole, trimmed in stainless steel. The cool refrigerated air mixed with the room-temperature atmosphere, creating a cloud that hugged the tile. From the underside of the vat, ten large-diameter tubes capped with stainless steel nozzles hung, unattached, reaching into the subterranean space.

"These tubes," Sheppard explained, "will be attached to the sealed drums. They will remain frozen. When we begin the production run and the diluent is to be added, I will activate the diverter. The contents of the drums will be fed into the product."

"And will the seals remain intact throughout the entire process?" Boyd asked. "We can't afford a leak. That cannot happen."

"Got it," Sheppard said. "No one has access to this room except me. I will place the drums and insert the tubes personally. Of course, I will be wearing complete head-to-toe double-suited protection, as instructed. When I'm finished, the clothing will be removed and burned."

"I want you to take all precautions."

"Why are all these precautions necessary?" Sheppard asked.

"Do you have a problem with that, Angelo?"

"Uh…no."

"Good. Because your life depends on it. What about the FDA inspectors?"

"I'm not comfortable with this, Mr. Boyd!"

Boyd leveled one of his patented stares at Sheppard. "We've been through this, Angelo!"

Sheppard averted his eyes to the frosted metal of the large horizontal container. He swallowed and continued. "Yes, sir . . . I programmed the software to keep select trays pure," Sheppard answered. We will only allow the experimental fluid in the drums into the lots slated for use by Dawson's business partner on the specified day. That will begin the experiment. We will produce those lots after the inspectors have certified the other products. As you know, the FDA inspectors are few and far between, with too much to do. It will not be hard to make this happen."

"And only you and I know about this? The contractors who installed this asked no questions?"

"They were told it was a holding tank for a new line of product. We buried the work order with the renovation of Building Four. No worries."

"When will the drums arrive?" Sheppard asked.

"They are on the way. And should arrive within twelve hours. I have a team of three men who will deal with the driver of the truck."

"I thought only you and I and a few of the board members knew?"

"Angelo, keep your mouth shut and do the job, mate! When they escort him away, you will take the drums to . . . the Vault . . . as you call it. Understood?"

℞

Oleg Gundersen placed the red flame of his jet lighter to a fresh cigar and puffed. Plumes of blue smoke whisked off, carried by the stiff breeze. The early morning sun burned off the cool air as he watched from the hard asphalt of Pier Five.

Nesten ferdig! he thought. *Almost done!*

He studied the markings on the last cargo container as the massive crane transferred it from the ship to the transfer vehicle. This container was not destined for the bed of a tractor-trailer. Gundersen climbed into the passenger seat of the transfer rig beside the driver. He nodded. The driver acknowledged the signal and caused the transfer rig to move. Appearing to be weeks out of puberty, the skin of the longshoreman's face was dotted with acne. Five minutes later, he braked in a secluded area of the yard. With adjustments from two levers, he lowered the metal box from the rig to the asphalt as a breath of dust escaped from under it.

Gundersen reached into his pocket, removed five one-hundred-dollar bills, and offered them to the young man, who placed them in the front pocket of his stained denim shirt.

Gundersen swiveled his head in a one-hundred-eighty-degree arc. The main bustle in the yard was a hundred yards away. The few dock workers were busy, pre-occupied with their tasks. Truck drivers waited in the coffee shop for their loads to be placed on the beds of the eighteen-wheelers.

Convinced the timing was right, Gundersen exited the rig and slapped the door twice. The rig moved off and disappeared through the multicolored stacks of containers. When it was out of sight, he strode to the doors of the cargo container.

He unsecured the padlock and swung open the steel doors. Gundersen entered the container and was assaulted by the hum of electricity. He sidled between the corrugated metal of the container and the truck, squeezing into the cab.

Several moments later, the engine roared to life.

He exited the cab, circled the truck, and inched his way along the opposite side of the container. After removing the electrical cables from the battery supply at the front of the container, Gundersen manipulated two switches. The refrigeration unit on the truck was now being fed by the Freightliner's M2 106 ISB Diesel engine.

He carefully backed out the Freightliner box truck. Gears screeched as he tried to find drive. He forced the gearshift into place and the refrigerated truck moved off. The ship's captain weaved his way through the yard and out the terminal's entrance. Showing his paperwork to the attendant at the small shack, he offered a friendly wave. Turning into a BP gas station off of Terminal Boulevard outside the gate, Gundersen recognized his contact by the bright red jacket swallowing him. The small, elderly man stood in a remote corner of the lot.

He braked ten feet from the hunched old man. Gundersen read the letters on the front of the jacket, "Red Sox." He did not understand the words or what they meant. Gundersen rolled down the window and stuck his head out.

The grizzled conspirator pointed to a spot. Gundersen gunned the engine and parked. He climbed out and tossed the keys at the man, who simply let them rattle to the asphalt.

Gundersen made a backhanded wave and began to walk away.

"Hey," the man hollered in a scratchy voice.

Gundersen stopped after four tentative steps and turned. The man had removed a gun from his jacket and had it pointed at the sea captain. "Pick those up," he ordered.

Gundersen smiled stiffly, ready to be done with all of this. He strode to the keys, picked them up, and walked to the old man.

"Drop them in there," the grizzled geezer barked, pointing to a sewer grate.

Gundersen, confused, said, "but how will someone drive it?"

"Another set is on the way!" the wrinkled human replied. He wagged the gun back and forth. "Now!"

Gundersen shook his head. "Whatever you say, *gubbe*."

He dropped them in and turned to the man. "We good now?"

The man forced a smile, revealing stained, rotting teeth. He nodded.

"By the way," Gundersen asked, "what's in the truck?"

The man smiled, wincing as he straightened up. "I'm betting it's a whole lot of trouble."

Chapter 20

The bedroom was dark except for a sliver of early morning light cutting through the opening created by the two drapes. A phalanx of prescription bottles of varying heights and diameters stood on the nightstand, creating a miniature plastic skyline. A half-full bottle of water and a box of tissues flanked the pills. His head resting on two overstuffed pillows, Clay Broadhurst lay on his side, willing strength into his sore bones and shrunken sinews.

Save POTUS! Save POTUS!

As with nearly all previous nights, last night had been no different. Those words infiltrated his dreams, interrupting what little sleep he managed.

Save POTUS!

He had uttered those words as he lay dying in the stairwell of the north tower in the condominium complex in Newport News on that October day two years earlier. Despite everything he had gone through, being severely wounded and left for dead, the surgeries, the pain, and the investigations, those words survived. He had almost lost two presidents on his watch.

The Secret Service agents who were on duty in Dealey Plaza had suffered for decades with the knowledge that they lost their president in '63. Broadhurst almost understood their grief. It visited him every night.

The cadre of medicine vials and the daily routine of swallowing the assortment of horse pills were, if not keeping him alive, keeping him as comfortable as possible. He studied the sliver of sunshine slicing between the curtains of the master suite. The small bit of luminescence interrupting the darkness summarized his life at this moment.

He was dying. Darkness was slowly engulfing him. The only beacon in his life was his family—his two daughters, Grace and Kelly, and his wife, Claudia. The burden of his cancer tugged at them, draining the sparkle from their smiles. Fear etched their faces like gouges in granite. They were as exhausted as he was.

Broadhurst was not afraid to die. He had stepped to the threshold of death's door once already, only to be pulled back. Every second, every minute since that day was a God-given bonus.

Since being shot in the stairwell of the condo towers overlooking the James River, its bridge, and the Penrose Gatling Shipyard, Broadhurst had endured countless physical and emotional hurdles. The quick action by the pharmacist as he lay on the landing at the top of the stairs had saved his life. He remembered the cool air hitting his bare foot after Rodger's pulled off his sock. The last thing he saw was the pharmacist's face as he rammed the balled up sock into the chest wound. The pain was so intense he'd blacked out. He woke up in the intensive care unit of Tidewater Regional Medical Center a day later. Two weeks after that, he was transferred to Walter Reed in Washington.

In the months after being released, the Service bestowed upon him the Director's Award for Valor in a secret ceremony attended by the president and a few high-level guests. Not even his family knew about the honor.

They couldn't, of course. Seeing Broadhurst, the father and husband, presented with such a medal, would invite questions. Questions Broadhurst could not answer. As far as his family knew, he was shot by a crazed counterfeiter and drug lord on a botched raid. Of course, the lie was necessary to prevent further questions.

Broadhurst had also received a Congressional Commendation, equally secret, for his actions and wounds that day. Any satisfaction he derived from the honors were exceeded only by the knowledge that he'd done his job and his charges, the presidents, had not died.

But the special agent-in-charge also knew the outcome could have been very different if it were not for the actions of Jason Rodgers. Broadhurst had only managed the situation. Rodgers's deeds and courage were the real reason for his success, and the reason he was able to lay eyes upon his family once more. Rodgers bought him precious seconds until the paramedics had arrived.

Since the near catastrophe, he filled his days recuperating and analyzing how the Service had allowed two assassins within the triple ring of protection, how they had failed, and what should be done to prevent another occurrence. Placed on restricted duty and confined to a wheelchair, Broadhurst manned a desk, working fifty hours a week—fighting through the surgeries, rehabilitation, and pain and interviewing everyone who had a role that day. To say the last two years were difficult would be like saying the Grand Canyon was a hole in the ground. But finishing his analysis had been his goal.

He'd finished his report three months ago and was looking for four weeks of relaxation, to enjoy his wife and daughters . . . before he became a memory.

One week after handing in his report to Director Doyle and a day before heading out for a well-earned and much-anticipated vacation with the three women in his life, the cataclysmic news hit.

An MRI had been performed on his left lung to monitor the progress of his recovery. It was the same lung that had been shredded by a phony agent's bullet. The test revealed spots on the lung. Broadhurst had stopped smoking three years ago. The lesions were cancerous.

To this day, he guessed that his gunshot wounds and recovery allowed his lung cancer to take root. The doctors would not confirm or deny this theory. But Broadhurst knew in his heart that his weakened state had allowed the disease to blossom.

The chemotherapy sapped his energy and strength. His body shriveled from 190 pounds to a paltry 150. His clothes hung on his frame. He could almost fit his closed fist between his neck and the collar of his dress shirts. The end was near. The cancer had spread to the intestines and liver.

It was a death sentence. Broadhurst held no illusions. The number of days left for him were dwindling. He'd made the decision to forgo further treatments. He wouldn't put his body or his family through the torture any more. He would go out on his own terms.

Broadhurst swung the heavy covers off his skeletal frame. He dropped his legs over the side of the bed and opened the nightstand drawer. Removing the large, leather-bound diary, he flipped it open to the page marked by two sealed envelopes.

One was addressed to his beautiful Claudia, Grace, and Kelly. In it, he'd poured out his heart and soul to them in two carefully scrawled pages. The second was addressed to Jason Rodgers, the Newport News pharmacist. Broadhurst thanked the man he barely knew for saving his life and giving him a few more years. In his first letter, he'd asked Claudia to make sure it was delivered.

He ran his fingers along the sealed flap.

Thank you, Jason Rodgers!

Now is the time! The girls will be at a friend's wedding shower for hours.

He laid the envelopes on the nightstand beside the pill vials. Slowly, and with enormous difficulty, the Secret Service agent rose, picked up his cell phone and slid it into his pajama pants pocket. Struggling to walk to the closet, he removed his service weapon from the holster hanging on the hook.

It took another full minute to make his way to the bathroom. He stepped into the shower and closed the curtain. Broadhurst pressed himself against the tiled wall and lowered himself into the tub. He pulled back the slide and chambered a round.

Flipping off the safety, he pointed the barrel at his chest, slightly off center between two ribs. The bullet would rip through his chest cavity, slicing through his heart. A chest wound would allow for an open casket.

Broadhurst removed his phone and found the number. His brother had agreed to call the authorities and would let them in to tend to his remains before the girls came home and found him. All he had to do was call him seconds before he fired the shot. He pulled up his brother's number from his favorites list and poised his thumb over the green circle. Tears clouded his vision. His breath came fast and shallow.

The phone began to vibrate in his hand a moment before it chirped.

Broadhurst wiped his eyes and read the caller ID. It was Deputy Director Vince Gagliano.

What the hell does he want?

A sense of duty honed from years of discipline and loyalty would not allow him to decline the call. He pressed the green circle on the screen.

"Broadhurst," he croaked, his voice thin and weak. His hand shook as he held the phone.

"Clay, it's Vince Gagliano. We need your help!"

Exasperated and distracted, Broadhurst said, "With what? I've given you everything I can give."

"Delilah Hussein is alive."

℞

The Gulfstream bumped onto runway ten of Gustav III Airport to the squeal of tires under the mid-morning sun and taxied to the terminal area. Instead of stopping, the pilot circled back as if he were going to take off once more, and crossed back over the runway to a service area. The plane came to rest inside an open hangar, away from prying eyes and overhead satellites.

A white Model 350 TraumaHawk ambulance appeared from behind the hangar and pulled alongside the jet's tail. A phalanx of six men exited the tail door of the aircraft, descended the stairs at a slow jog, automatic weapons at the ready. With their backs to the aircraft, they formed a semicircle around the medical truck, ready to stifle any prying presence.

Seconds later, Michael and then Chrissie, unconscious, were carried down the steps, bound and gagged in their crates, by the remaining four team members. A minute later, they were loaded aboard the van-like emergency vehicle.

The four men climbed into the rear compartment and swung the doors closed. The six men lining the perimeter jumped into two waiting Land Rovers mounted with flashing portable light bars.

The Rovers took up front and rear positions as the three-vehicle convoy sped off the airport grounds. Thirty minutes later, they were heading east along Route D209, curving southeast along Saint Jean's Bay and out of the city of the same name.

℞

"Where is she, Pete?" Jason demanded, thinking out loud, not expecting a response.

The brothers sat in the living room in a state of fidgety animation. Jason on the sofa, Peter on the edge of the cushion of the stuffed recliner. Angled trapezoids of light filtered through the curtains. After Jason had discovered the drop of blood on the bedroom floor, they returned downstairs. Jason tried to call Chrissie's cell phone again, only to discover that when he did, her phone chimed in the kitchen. It was on the counter, plugged into the wall, charging, hidden between the refrigerator and the Keurig machine. He then called two of her friends in turn. Neither of them had spoken to her last night. At that point, Jason called the police.

The Newport News Police Department sent a lone uniform in a cruiser to take Jason's statement and photograph the now-smudged droplet of blood. He'd asked the obligatory questions about a quarrel and if she'd decided to stay with friends. Finally, he declared he would file a report and a detective would call in the morning.

"I don't know how long it will take the police to respond," he had said. "But this will start the process rolling."

With nothing else to do, the brothers hunkered down and tried to find a way to relax. Peter lay on the sofa and Jason, not wanting to disturb any possible more evidence, slept in the spare room.

As he lay there staring around the darkened room, Jason battled the pain of his shoulder, his arm wound, and the deep gash on his head. As he popped some leftover tramadol, Clyde Hutton's words returned to him.

They're back . . . The Simoon! And they're looking for you!

It couldn't be. Hussein and Oliver were dead. The son, Sharif al-Faisal, aka Sam Fairing, had been taken into custody.

No, he told himself. *It couldn't be.*

"I don't know. How did the dinner go?" Peter asked, jolting Jason back to the present.

"Not good, she said no when I asked her to marry me."

Both of the former marine's eyebrows lifted. "Really? I thought you guys were making plans. You said it was a slam dunk."

"I thought it was." Jason rubbed sleep from his eyes.

"What happened? She must have given you a reason."

"She thinks I'm having an affair."

"What? An affair?" Peter paused, then asked, "Are you?"

"Don't be an idiot. Of course not."

"Then why does she think that?'

"Because she followed me to Headlights."

Jason had kept Peter apprised of his progress of the surveillance of Clyde Hutton. His nervous habit kicked in. The marine rubbed his eyebrow, the one cleaved by a scar from his days in the corps.

"Didn't I tell you to leave that shit alone?"

"Pete, don't lecture me."

"You know, Jason, your tenacity can be a real asset. But sometimes, you need to let things go. How much does she know?"

"She thinks because I was parked outside the club, I was waiting for a dancer. She thinks I'm boning one of them."

"Does she suspect anything else?"

"I don't know. I don't think so. She knows I've been sneaking around."

"Okay, well maybe she's just pissed and left for a while."

"I don't think so. Again, her car, remember?"

"Somebody could have picked her up." Peter's eyes got wide with realization. He peered at his brother. "Wait a minute. You proposed to Chrissie last night during dinner. Then you ran off to accost Clyde Hutton."

Jason nodded. "Yes . . . I mean no! I left the house after we fought, so I decided to take it out on Hutton."

"You are an idiot, you know that?" Peter delivered the statement with the excruciating honesty that only a sibling could get away with.

Jason shrugged. "Look," he began, "I know it probably wasn't smart—"

"Probably?"

"These guys, Hutton and Tattoo Man—Hutton told me his name's William Luther—tried to kill me. I came this close to being murdered in jail. I can't let it go. I've got the scars to prove it. These bastards got away with it. I can't find any record of either of them being charged or convicted of anything. We know Hutton was around. Luther could be, too. Would you feel safe?"

"All because some knucklehead left you a note!"

Jason had told Peter about the anonymous note that was left for him on the windshield of his car a year ago. The note that had catapulted him back into all the amorphous, gut-wrenching anguish.

"Pete, shut the hell up!"

Peter held up his hands. "Okay, okay. We'll have this conversation later."

"What do we do now?"

"We'll wait for the detective to call you. But first we need to get you stitched up. I'm going to the truck to get my medical kit."

Jason stopped Peter as he started for the door. "Then there's this," he said, pulling out the item he had taken from Clyde Hutton's pocket.

℞

The pair of Land Rovers climbed the rutted mountain road, their undercarriages scraping against the sandy earth every hundred yards for the last few miles. The serious-looking guard at the compound's gate was dressed in a crisp pair of jeans and a lightweight white shirt. He held up a hand as he palmed the black machine gun slung across his chest.

The driver uttered a few words. The guard nodded, pointed into the compound, and retreated to the guard house. The automatic gates peeled open.

The vehicles arrived in front of the main house three minutes later. Standing at the head of the circular drive, Delilah Hussein and Oliver watched the convoy circle and come to a halt. A cloud of dust engulfed the Rovers. The driver of the first vehicle, the leader of Team Mohammed, exited and circled to Hussein.

"Take them to the wine cellar," Hussein ordered. "But first, I want to speak to your men."

The leader turned and motioned for the men to approach. Car doors swung open. The ten-man group formed a semicircle around the matriarch of The Simoon. Oliver grunted a one-word command in French. The men all revealed their forearms and the squiggly tattoo etched into the skin.

Hussein made eye contact with each man, holding their gaze for a second or two, before moving to the next.

She cleared her throat. "Well done. You each have acquitted yourselves extremely well. We are one step closer to our goal. Soon we will plant the seed of terror and death on American soil. This seed will bear fruit in the coming months. This time we will not fail.

"Please remain diligent in your work. Charles and Pierre will show you where we will keep our guests." She motioned to the two *soldats* standing a few feet away. "After you unload them, get some rest —you have earned it."

Hussein held the gazes of the leader of Team Mohammed and then the leader of Team Isaiah. "I want to see both of you in my office in thirty minutes.

"Allahu Ahkbar!"

Hussein pointed to the Land Rovers. "Show me."

Hussein marched to the rear of the first Rover, leading her lieutenants. The coffin-looking container was offloaded, placed roughly on the gravel and its lid opened. Hussein gazed down on the unconscious Michael Rodgers, his hands cuffed over his abdomen.

Hussein's lips retracted into a satisfied smile. She reached in and caressed his cheek. "He looks like the father."

When the second container was opened, she scowled at the solemn, sleeping face of Christine Pettigrew.

"*Prostituée*," she spat.

Hussein motioned for them to be taken away. She turned to Charlie and Pierre. "Get them out of my sight! Make them as uncomfortable as possible."

"It is time to send the messages. Is the drone ready to depart?"

"Yes, Madame. The message has been saved to the hard drive. It will be sent once it reaches the designated waypoint and should be delivered in the next two hours."

After the drone, Reprisal One, had returned from its latest sortie, the messages from The Watcher were downloaded. Clyde Hutton was dead and Jason Rodgers was now in possession of the cell phone the dead man had given him.

Hussein turned to Oliver. "Have you heard back from al-Raqqah and our friend in Moscow yet?"

"I have. A plan is in place. It's crude, but it could work. We have an asset en route to the Red Onion."

℞

Jason flipped open the cell phone he'd taken from the dead guard's pocket. On the back of the device, a large number one was written in white grease paint.

"Where did you get that?" Peter asked.

"From Hutton, before he died."

He wanted to tell Peter, the person he trusted more than anyone, that the dying man had made a pointed reference indicating Hussein's people were back. But had Hutton meant what he said? Jason decided to wait. He didn't need his brother riding his ass anymore right now.

Jason shrugged and scanned at the home screen on the phone. A single red circle dotted one of the square folder's upper-right corners, indicating a communication of some sort had taken place. Jason touched the box and a message window appeared with instructions.

It read: *Find the password to see the message!*

The phone was not password-protected. Jason had been able to access the desktop by pressing his finger on the lower circular indentation. But the voicemail was blocked.

"It's asking me for a password," he declared.

Peter snatched the phone and played with it for several moments with no better results. "Where's the goddamned password?" Peter spat.

"Are you sure you got everything from this Hutton guy?"

Jason shrugged. "He told me to look in his pocket. I did!"

"So, what do we do now?" Peter asked.

Jason took the phone back. "We wait and see if it turns up somehow."

℞

"Have you called her family?" the female detective asked.

The woman had introduced herself as a lieutenant in the Newport News Police Department, Missing Persons Division. She had flashed a badge and stated her name, but it hadn't registered with Jason.

A fresh-faced youngster, her cheeks glowed with the blush of inexperience, framed by smooth dirty blonde locks pulled back into a tight ponytail. *They sent us a rookie,* Jason thought.

Jason paced the living room, Chrissie's living room. He had resided here with her for the last year.

"Did you understand the question, sir?" she demanded.

The sting of fatigue burned his eyes. Acid churned in his belly. His distraction delayed the processing of the officer's question

Finally, he managed a response. "She doesn't have any family. Her mother and father are dead. She had an uncle, but he died too. There's no one else I can call."

"What about friends?"

Jason had called a couple of Chrissie's girlfriends in the wee hours of the morning, waking them and, no doubt, filling them with some degree of concern. Neither had spoken to her in the last twenty four hours.

"I've tried them."

Chrissie also had a co-worker she was close to. In a husky, sleep-filled voice, the woman said she'd not seen her since she left work the previous day.

"Is everything okay? Is she coming in today?" the woman had asked. Alarm coated her voice.

"I don't think so," Jason had replied. "Don't worry anyone yet. Just tell her boss that she's in bed sick and that I called in for her."

"I phoned everyone I can think of," Jason explained to the cop.

"When was the last time you saw her?"

Jason stopped, noticing her hair. Strands of the brown-blonde coif bobbed and weaved as she moved her head. Her hazel eyes bore into Jason as she waited for a response. Her lithe body was partially hidden under a lightweight sports coat. A lanyard hung from her neck, holding the previously produced identification and badge.

"Last night."

"Did you two have an argument?"

"Why does that matter?"

"Did you?"

"You could say that."

"Maybe she's just blowing off steam."

Jason frowned. The cop turned her attention to the bandage on Jason's head. "What happened to you?"

Peter had employed his battlefield medical skills and the sizable medical kit in the backseat of his Hummer. Having a brother who was an ex-marine had its advantages. The bandages looked like Jason had visited a doctor's office or an emergency room. With syringes, needles, gauze, and 4-0 chromic sutures, Peter patched Jason back together, saving a trip to the emergency room, a possible hospital stay, and unwanted questions.

"I was in a car accident."

"Did your girlfriend hit you?"

"I don't think I like your question."

"I have to ask," the officer replied. "You asked me to come out. Begged, in fact. So just answer the questions so we can get through this."

"No, she didn't hit me."

"Was anyone angry with her? Have a beef with her?"

"No," Jason answered.

"Does she have any medical conditions that might create a situation in which she might become incapacitated? Diabetes? Drugs or alcohol?

"No!"

"There is no sign of forced entry. Or any other indications of foul play."

"What about the blood on the floor?"

"That's a very small droplet. She could have cut herself. It could be nothing."

Jason shook his head, communicating a sizable amount of disgust.

"I will file a report and list her as a missing person on the Virginia State Police website. Do you have a photograph of Miss Pettigrew?"

"I have one on my phone."

"Text it to me at this number." The woman handed Jason her business card. "We will also send out a BOLO . . . that's Be On the Lookout . . . to all police in Hampton Roads. But, I have to be frank, here, Mr. Rodgers. This does not sound like an urgent case . . . not yet anyway."

"That's it?"

"That's all we can do for now. Keep trying to contact her. Call me if you have not heard from her in forty-eight hours, if you learn any other salient facts, or she contacts you."

"Thank you, officer," Peter said cutting off Jason's reply, escorting her to the door.

When he returned, Jason studied his brother. "I don't have a good feeling, Pete."

"It'll be alright. Stay patient."

Jason texted the photo to the cop and then decided to level with his brother. "Hutton told me something last night before he died."

"Yeah?"

"He said they were back. They knew I was going to make contact with him. He said they were watching both of us."

"Who?"

"You know . . . Delilah Hussein and . . . The Simoon," Jason blurted.

"Hussein's dead! She died on the yacht. Did he specifically mention Hussein's name?!" Peter stroked his eyebrow.

"I'm just telling you what he said. He said he was visited by a man in a black hat, a Dick Tracy hat . . . a fedora. The cop who came to me in the back of the ambulance was wearing a black fedora."

"Did Hutton say the name Hussein? Or The Simoon?"

"No, he said , 'The Simoon . . . they're back and watching.'"

"It doesn't mean shit, Jason. He was panicked and dying."

A ringtone blared. Jason and Peter eyed the cell phone in his hand, Hutton's cell phone, expecting it to be ringing. It lay silent.

Jason felt the vibration on his hip. He grabbed his own cell phone and read the caller id. It was Jenny. Michael's mother. He answered.

"Jason?"

He had never heard the kind of panic her voice now held as she uttered his name.

"Jen, what's wrong?"

"He's gone, Jason! Michael's gone!"

CHAPTER 21

Jason and Peter barreled into the waterfront house Jenny shared with her architect husband, Mark. Out of breath, the brothers were stopped by a uniformed Hampton cop. Jason had had trouble punching in the pass code to the kiosk of Mark and Jenny's gated community, the Salt Ponds, because his hands shook uncontrollably. They'd parked Peter's Hummer and run the mile to the house on First Street.

"I'm the boy's father. Let me through!"

Jenny ran to the railing overlooking the foyer. "Jason!"

The cop let them pass. Jason vaulted the stairs three at a time. Peter followed a step behind.

Jenny wrapped her arms around him, hugging him in a death squeeze. Jason held her a moment, then placed his hands on her shoulders and pushed her far enough away to see her eyes. "What happened?"

Jenny began to cry, her voice tremulous. "They took him." "Relax," Jason whispered.

It took two minutes of gasped, watery whispers for Jenny to explain.

"They were . . . dressed in black uniforms . . . with helmets and those binocular-looking things over their eyes . . ."

"Night-vision goggles," Peter observed.

Jenny nodded. "They had guns . . . machine guns. They drugged me and Mark." Jenny motioned with her head toward her husband, who was speaking to one of the Hampton detectives on the scene. Jason spied Mark standing a few feet away. A bloodied bandage slanted across the bridge of his nose. His face was smeared with dried blood.

Peter tapped Jason on the shoulder. "These guys were pros. This was planned," he explained.

Jason nodded. "I know."

"Then they stuck a needle in my neck and I went down," Jenny continued. When we woke up, Michael was gone."

Jenny cocked her head toward the back porch. "Follow me." Outside, she handed something to Jason. "They left this on his nightstand." Jenny whispered the next statement. "The detectives don't know about it. I don't think they'll take this seriously. You will. If you think you should give this to them, I leave that to you. This has something to do . . . with . . . you know . . ."

The blank backside of the rectangular business card faced him. Jason flipped it over.

"Holy shit," he gasped, handing it to Peter. His eyes went wide.

"We need to go," Peter said.

Jason turned to Jenny and said, "I will get him back!"

℞

"You've studied this woman and her organization for the last two years. We need you to spearhead the effort to find her. We are calling it Operation Dust Storm. I want you . . . I need you in the SIOC. Will you help?"

The words were spoken by Brad Lane, the deputy director of the FBI, to Broadhurst. The Secret Service agent felt swallowed by the wheelchair he sat in at the conference table, along with Lane, Gagliano, and six other people inside the SIOC of the Hoover FBI Building. All eyes were trained on the dying agent seated to the right of Brad Lane and flanked by Vince Gagliano, his boss at the Secret Service.

Broadhurst ran his sweaty palms over the thighs of his trousers. The gray cotton suit was the smallest in his closet. But it still felt like he was wearing a tent. His mind drifted back to a few hours ago. He was ready to end his life, seconds away from completing the job. Now, he was back in the saddle and feeling alive again.

Seconds make all the difference, he thought. He had been given a second chance by the pharmacist. Now he was being presented with another opportunity to make things right. *Hussein was alive!*

Broadhurst leaned over to Lane and whispered, "You're putting me on the spot. My health is not good."

Lane whispered back. "You're right. That was my intent. Your country needs you, Clay. Your health has not been good for a long time. Yet, you managed to revamp all the Service's procedures and still research all there is to know about this woman. I want to hear a 'yes' from you."

Lane leaned back and sat stone still, smiling and staring at Broadhurst. A heavy quietude descended over the room.

"How the hell did you find out she was alive?" Broadhurst asked, breaking the hush.

In a few minutes, Lane explained what the group had discussed yesterday, then followed with, "We believe she has an operation planned. It might be underway now and its target is within our borders. It's called Hygeia. We need you. There is no time for delay." Broadhurst nodded.

"Just down the hall is the command center," continued Lane. "You will have access to whatever you need." He pointed to a young woman seated to his left. "This is Agent Maria Gonzalez. She will stay at your side for the next twelve hours. Beside her is Agent Bradley Day. He will take the opposite twelve-hour shift. They will get you whatever you need. Beside him we have Clint Hill with the CIA. He is assistant to mission chief for the Western Hemisphere. We have over a hundred agents from the Bureau, the CIA, the National Intelligence Agency and Homeland Security. They are awaiting instructions. Clay, you have complete operational control."

Broadhurst turned his eyes to each person seated around the room. Each pair of eyes either looked at the papers in front of them or smiled the uncomfortable moue of one at a loss for words.

The last stop for his gaze was Brad Lane. He nodded. "Okay."

"Excellent. Done! Agent Broadhurst has operational control. If he says it, it's an order." Lane turned back to Broadhurst. "I will need to brief a select group of directors in the SIOC conference room in a few hours."

"No problem. I need all the intelligence reports from the last two weeks," Broadhurst croaked.

"Done." Lane leaned toward Broadhurst. "There's one other thing . . ."

"Which is?"

"Jason Rodgers is involved . . . Hussein has targeted him . . . and his family"

"Where is Rodgers now?"

"Our men followed him to a rendezvous with an unknown man. Rodgers took the man at gunpoint. A car chase ensued and the unknown vic died. Rodgers was treated and released at the scene. We are tracing his cell phone now. We will know shortly."

$$\text{R}_\text{X}$$

One hundred and twenty-seven miles to the south in Newport News, Jason and Peter sat at the kitchen table. Two identical business cards lay on the bare table before them. After Jenny had given Jason the card left by Michael's hostage takers, they returned to Chrissie's and scoured the master bedroom. They found the second card placed inside a book Chrissie had been reading. Both cards were identical.

On one side of the card were printed a name and six words:

Lily Zanns
Owner, The Colonial Pharmacy

Jason had seen a card like this two years ago when he was hired by Lily Zanns, aka Delilah Hussein. The cards were pristine, as if they had just been printed, excerpt for a small dark line near the bottom of each. An apparent line of excess ink near the bottom.

"This is a sick joke," Peter said.

"They were kidnapped by professionals," Jason added. "What do I do now? It's Hussein's people. It has to be!"

Peter shook his head like he was trying to believe a fairy tale. "I don't know. I just don't know."

"Again, what do I do now?"

"We."

"What?"

"What do *we* do now?"

"Thanks, Pete."

"Since we found an identical card upstairs, we can assume the same person or persons took Chrissie as well," Peter observed.

"I agree. But what's the next step? Should we call the detective and tell her we have more information?'"

Peter had picked up one of the business cards as they talked, examining it. "What the hell is this?" he asked.

He pointed to the small thin line across the bottom of the front of the card.

"I don't know," Jason replied. "It's a line of ink."

"No, it's more," Peter answered. "We are not going to do anything else until we read this microprinting. Do you have a magnifying glass?"

℞

Torturous, evil slits adorned the small, rectangular room.

They were microscopic glimpses to an expansive, unreachable world beyond his cell. A world in which he would probably never set foot again. The inmate prayed to Allah that an escape was in place or being planned. It was one of those unanswerable prayers one uttered more for comfort than expectation. He knew his compatriots would not leave him in the custody of the infidels without at least making an attempt to free him. His mother would figure something out.

But the prisoner held no illusions. The chances of success for any escape attempt would be slim.

No larger than a small bathroom, the inmate couldn't even spread his arms out to full wing span. Three ten foot cinder-gray steel walls, painted a dull gray, surrounded him. In the fourth wall, the south wall, a solid steel door allowed the only entry and exit. This was his private, miniature hell.

The metal door was flanked by two vertical rectangular openings. Encased in the thick steel, filled with equally thick Plexiglas into which a thick wire mesh had been imbedded, the tall, narrow openings allowed him a view onto the small, exclusive prison unit housing him and four other captives.

The inmate sat on his metal cot, on the thin mattress, with his back against the cold concrete. His eyes studied the thin slit in the north wall, opposite the door. A single rectangular slash had been shaped into the concrete, allowing in the fading outside light, tantalizing its inhabitant with the sky beyond. As with the sidelights beside the door, the thick, rigid Plexiglas in the horizontal slit, no more than six inches high and a foot wide, was laden with wire. Notched at the nine-foot level, the Plexiglas and the miniscule dimensions of the frame precluded any normal-sized human from slipping through even if they could shatter the thick glass. As many times as he tried, he could not pull himself with his hands to reach the window and get a glimpse of the surrounding acreage.

It's unusual, he told himself, for a window to be allowed in a cell for someone considered so dangerous. There was only one reason the designers of the prison would have allowed it. They wanted the prisoners to see what they were being deprived of each and every minute of the day. In was the cruelest of punishments.

Solitary confinement meant twenty-three hours a day in the cell. Only one hour in his own private exercise yard each day was allowed. And then only if the COs allowed it. The privilege could be revoked . . . and often was . . . for any variety of reasons. Bad weather, poor behavior, or a corrections officer with an attitude.

The prisoner had been housed in this facility for two and a half years. He'd attempted and failed to carry out his crime of high treason. Well, it would have been treason if he were a citizen of America. To him, it was an act of bravery and consequence that would have shaken the foundations of world politics. Despite their failure, it was a crime serious enough for him to be held without American due process, held without ever having seen an attorney, and without the possibility of being set free by normal legal channels. And no one would ever know about his transgressions or his imprisonment.

And those two facts irritated the hell out of him.

The man, sitting on his metal cot with his knees elevated, closed the book he was reading and contemplated his surroundings. In the thirty months since he'd begun his incarceration, the prisoner had become a voracious reader. Television, radio, and newspapers, all portals to the outside, were not allowed. His only mental stimulation was his own imagination and the well-worn pages of the prison library.

He read every work available to him, more than once.

Six months ago, he'd found the one work defining his plight, capturing its full travesty. It was the mythological fantasy of the mightiest smithy in Greek mythology, the tale of Brontes, a Cyclops, the forger of weapons for the gods.

As he turned the pages those many months ago, the prisoner realized that, though allegorical, it was his story. Since the words had registered with him, his purpose had been reinvigorated, redefined. He decided that day, six months earlier, that his quest must continue. He had to free himself from this Underground, the same way Brontes had done. He would forge the weapons that would be used in the ongoing war and—as Brontes had done—he would become a vital cog in the battle against the infidels.

The man adjusted the eye patch covering his devastated right eye. He had lost it in a struggle with a weaker human being, a lesser man, a man not anywhere close to him in talent. A mere pharmacist, a pill pusher who'd stuck his nose where it didn't belong. A man who had thwarted their plan and bested him, causing him to spend his days in this eternal Underground.

It was on that day six months ago that the prisoner decided his mission was not over. He would need help, mind you, and the will to stay positive. He had to be ready if and when any plan to free him materialized. The matriarch of The Simoon, his matriarch, would send a message. He prayed each day that she would get word to him.

If and when his freedom was won, he would seek revenge in two ways. First, he would join his mother again and be at her side. And he would strike down the pharmacist, Jason Rodgers. Second, they would strike at the belly of the infidels again . . . and again, until they capitulated. This would be a blow more devastating and destructive than the attempts to kill the two pig presidents. He hadn't been given details. He didn't need them . . . yet. Sharif al-Faisal knew his mother would not rest until the United States was brought to its knees.

Al-Faisal lay back down on the metal cot and whispered a verse from his favorite surah. He tented the open book on his chest, placed both hands under his head, and looked up at the concrete ceiling. A sense of electric anticipation engulfed him, along with the serenity that accompanies dutiful preparation. The rest he would leave in Allah's hands.

When the time came, he would be ready.

He had been known by two names in his life. He was Sharif al-Faisal Hussein, son to a murdered dictator, slated to become an Arab leader of world renown, charged with ridding the Middle East of American imperialism. That plan failed when the assassinations were thwarted.

The Americans knew him as the straight-laced assassin-pharmacist Sam Fairing, a talented sniper and warrior skilled in martial arts and all manner of weapons.

Both of those personas were gone, vanished like vapor.

That fateful day in his cell, after reading about Brontes, the prisoner had forgone both names. He told his guards months ago that he was to be known only by his one true identity, one that fit his purpose and his physical state.

The one-eyed prisoner had only one name now:

Cyclops.

And he would have his revenge!

Chapter 22

"The president personally thanked Rodgers for saving his life, Giles. How the hell can we let this happen? He is not a pawn."

Broadhurst was more animated than he'd been in months. His body had summoned a reserve of energy he did not know he possessed, probably his last. He could feel his face flush as he directed his irritation at his boss in the SIOC Command Center.

"Clay, relax. I've conveyed your concerns to the president. I have his assurance that we will follow Rodgers and this Watcher fellow. And just for the record, Clay, everyone is a pawn if we need them to be. We will watch and wait to see if we can get a handle on what Hussein's operation is. If he's in danger, we'll go in and get him."

"Why don't I believe you?"

"Watch yourself, Special Agent! You still work for me . . . and the president."

"You asked me to supervise this operation, Giles. I want assurances. Rodgers put his life on the line for his country. He's a civilian. Grow a pair!"

Giles Doyle circled his desk. He towered over his best agent, now riddled with cancer.

"You listen to me you son of a bitch. I will not be talked to that way. You have been given an assignment. I expect you to carry it out."

"Yes . . . sir," Broadhurst mimicked. "But I'm telling you now that if it comes down to it. I will do whatever I can to assist that man. Is that clear?"

"You smug bastard. If you weren't so sick, Clay, I'd cold cock you right now," Doyle smirked.

"If I weren't so sick, Director, believe me I'd do the same!"

Giles Doyle, the director of the Secret Service and a former army ranger, smiled. "I believe you are scheduled to brief the brass about what you know about Hussein, what happened in Newport News, and The Simoon. Get to work, Special Agent."

℞

"Can you read it?" Peter asked.

They stood side by side at the workbench inside the garage of Peter's Smithfield home. Jason hunched over a microscope with his brother at his shoulder, demanding answers.

"Give me a minute," Jason barked.

They had spent an hour at Chrissie's trying to decipher the small mark on the back of one of the cards. Jason did not know which card it was, the one from Michael's or Chrissie's room. It didn't really matter. They appeared identical.

Jason found a magnifying glass in a desk drawer and tried to read the miniscule writing. When that proved futile, Peter remembered that one of his daughters owned a microscope that had been relegated to the dusty recesses of the garage. They drove from Newport News and had huddled over the workbench for the last twenty minutes.

"How the hell do you know it means anything?"

"I don't. But the marking doesn't look random. It was placed on the card. You see how straight and perfect it is along the bottom edge. See?"

Jason held both cards up for his brother to examine.

"It's not a pencil or pen mark. It's microprinting like you see on currency. But really tiny."

Jason placed the card under the microscope. "How the hell did you think of using the microscope?" Jason asked.

"Megan was caught up with science for many years. We bought her every kind of science kit we could find. I bought her this microscope three years ago. She would look at everything under it."

Jason stood up. "This magnification is too low. Are there any other lenses?"

Peter went back to the box and returned with an assortment of lenses laid out in foam cutouts. Jason tried two stronger magnifications with no luck.

"Got a flashlight? The light under the stage is burned out."

Peter rummaged around in his stack of clutter on the workbench and returned again with a mag lite.

"Shine it from underneath. I'm going to try this last magnification."

Jason slid the lens into place as Peter pointed the flashlight up under the small card clipped to the stage

"Okay, that's better," Jason said.

"What's it say?"

"Gimme a minute. Hold the light steady. I can barely make it out."

Jason twisted the focusing ring on the stem of the device in a long arc. He then twisted in the opposite direction as he played a visual version of warmer-colder.

"Well?" Peter persisted.

"Almost there."

Jason turned the ring back and forth in miniscule arcs, narrowing the focus.

"Holy shit!" Jason whispered. Jason removed the card and checked the second card. The micro printed message was the same.

"What does it say?"

"Let me see!" Peter pushed himself between Jason and the microscope. After a few seconds of adjustments, he exclaimed, "Son of a bitch!"

He read the words aloud:

Do not contact the police or the Feds or your son and girlfriend will die. . . . the password is . . . Vngnce . . .

℞

"Summarize for everyone, Special Agent," Giles Doyle, the director of the Secret Service began. "Explain what problems occurred two years ago in Newport News. Everyone here has been cleared to be read in on the details."

Doyle turned to the handful of high-level attendees. "Special Agent Broadhurst has been working for the last two years to analyze, correct, and anticipate future issues when it comes to presidential protection and prevention of future incidents."

Clay Broadhurst sat in the conference room overlooking the amphitheater that was the SIOC. The room was replete with large, wall-mounted screens and smaller desktop versions scattered throughout the space, along with secure phones, fax machines, and other high-tech devices. Agents sat at every terminal, monitoring their specific assignments. The floor-to-ceiling glass wall provided these top level government officials with a first-hand view of the FBI's capability to monitor ongoing crises. Broadhurst sat front and center, at the head of the gleaming conference room table, staring down his audience. He had managed to swallow his anger and frustration over his earlier meeting with Doyle regarding Jason Rodgers.

"Thank you, Director," he replied. "I will address two topics today. First I want to look at the deficiencies of the security apparatus at the shipyard in Newport News. And second, now, that we know Hussein did not die on the yacht, I will give you a profile of this madwoman and what we think her next moves will be."

Broadhurst cleared his throat and wiped his lips with a white handkerchief. He scanned the ten faces sitting around the table. "Before you is a three-page report outlining the failings that resulted in the near-deaths of two presidents, maybe more . . ."

"We've read the report, Clay," the director of the National Security Agency interrupted. "Just give us a quick summary. We all know how hard you've worked on this since the event."

"Yes sir. In short, we had a major infiltration in the Secret Service, the CIA, and possibly other agencies inside the federal government. Delilah Hussein's organization was—and may still be—far-flung, with assets all over the world, inside the federal government, and on the ground in Newport News. Her team had apparently planned this operation for several years, all along financed by a phony front organization called Cooper Venture Capital.

"Hussein purchased a local, independent pharmacy under the alias Lily Zanns as a base for her headquarters, and used Cooper Venture to funnel money through the pharmacy, pay her operatives, and finance the operation. Two of the major players were her son, Sam Fairing, a pharmacist, aka Sharif al-Faisal, and her daughter, Jasmine Kader, a physician. Both children were highly trained assassins. Kader is dead and Fairing was apprehended in the condo tower north of the shipyard with the help of the pharmacist named Rodgers. In fact, Jason Rodgers and his brother, Peter, are the only reason that we avoided a tragedy like Dealey Plaza.

"I interviewed Fairing three months after he was captured. He explained much of the operation to me . . . after some intense interrogation, of course. He was set up in Windsor Towers in a fourth-floor condo with a perfect view and sniping position for a shot on the christening. The daughter, Kader, aka Jazan Hussein, was perched atop the James River Bridge north tower under a tarp. Both shots were to have been taken from a mile away and to be placed through the protective white canvass we had deployed to block an attempt at such a shot.

"How were they able to even attempt such shots if the white canvass was obscuring the view?" George McNamara, the director of the FBI demanded.

"That, sir, was the million-dollar question," Broadhurst replied. "During the interview, Faisal informed me that information was being retrieved from a dead drop near the James River whenever key data was available. That data included the seating arrangements of the dignitaries on the pier that day, including the exact locations of both presidents. Two moles hired by Woody Austin, the former and late director of the Presidential Protection Division, had access to that highly classified information. Austin left a note explaining that he had been blackmailed into hiring the moles. This note was left before he jumped to his death from the Watergate East Apartments. That information allowed the snipers to know the precise locations of the intended targets. That was the most crucial breach.

"Those two moles have been apprehended. The mastermind of the infiltration of the governmental operation, a man codenamed Hammon, is still at large," Broadhurst said, stopping. He turned his attention to the director of the CIA's Clandestine Operations, John Beck.

"Special Agent Broadhurst is correct," Beck said. "We have a suspect under surveillance and are close to finalizing his arrest."

"How were they going to make the shots?" a voice interrupted. "You still haven't explained that."

Broadhurst nodded. "Yes, sorry. Hussein and her two snipers purchased a device they called Cyclops. We are still trying to track down the maker of the device. It was a dual laser system hardwired to a laptop that calculated wind direction, distances, rain, air temperature and humidity, and the curvature of the earth. These parameters were updated every two seconds and fed to the lasers mounted on motorized stands that would realign two target reticles, one for each sniper, onto the white screen we had deployed. The sights were invisible to our team of agents because they were visible only by using infrared scopes mounted on their Barrett fifty caliber sniper rifles. They were to have used these constantly updated reticles to know where to place their shots through the white canvass.

"The snipers, Fairing and Kader, perfected and practiced their skills at a covert site in northern North Carolina called the Camp. Oliver, Delilah Hussein's manservant, flew them down using the float plane. The same float plane, as we now know, that eventually carried Hussein and Oliver to a rendezvous somewhere on the ocean east of North Carolina."

"What about the changes to protocol for protection of the president going forward?" Giles Doyle, the director of the Secret Service asked.

"The Service has revamped all of its presidential protection procedures ," Broadhurst continued, "including expanding the ring of protection to a mile and a half out for all presidential events. The Towers that day were fully examined and searched. All windows were scanned by agents looking for open windows. No possible breaches were found. Fairing, the sniper in the north Windsor Tower had cut two three-inch holes into the window glass that morning and was to fire through one hole while the Cyclops painted the dual infrared targets on the white screen. The rifle was disassembled and stored in another condo in the south tower until it was needed.

"It is my conclusion, despite the near failure in Newport News, that our on-the-ground security precautions were adequate. The failure came from up the chain and the infiltration of the Service and the CIA. Nonetheless, we have enhanced security and the changes have already been implemented."

Broadhurst slumped in his wheelchair. Giles Doyle noticed this. "Thank you, Agent Broadhurst. You have worked tirelessly for two years. Your work here is essential to the current operation. Everyone can read the report. If there are questions, I will answer them later." Doyle addressed his colleagues sitting around the conference room: "Clay is still recovering. He needs a break. We will adjourn for thirty minutes. When we return, he will explain that Hussein is most likely going to attempt another strike on the United States and why this is so."

$$\text{R}_\text{X}$$

The password, *Vngnce*, a Twitterized version of Vengeance, unlocked the message on the cell phone Hutton had given to Jason. The message, short and to the point, sent a torrent of fear and panic through him.

I have Michael and Christine . . . Unless you do exactly as instructed they will die . . . First, find a second cell phone at these coordinates and follow the instructions . . . Do not go to the authorities.

Jason rubbed his forehead. His hand shook as it stroked the skin.

"Are you shitting me?" he whispered. "Hutton was right! They're back!"

"We don't know that, Jason. This could be from anyone."

$$\text{R}_\text{X}$$

"In short," Broadhurst explained to the reassembled group in the SIOC conference room, "Delilah Hussein has all the classic symptoms of a megalomaniac with a streak of narcissism. This diagnosis was determined using the limited information gathered from sources in Iraq during Saddam Hussein's rule and witnesses to his affair with Delilah Hussein.

"The FBI and CIA profilers have concluded that the megalomaniacal and narcissistic tendencies are derived from a traumatic event that took place in Delilah's childhood."

"How did you come by this information about her childhood," asked the director of Homeland Security.

The CIA man Beck fielded the question. "We had operatives in place in Iraq who were able to piece together some data from eyewitnesses, bodyguards, and servants who had witnessed Delilah spending time with Saddam over the years. They overheard her telling the dictator her woeful story. Sorry, Clay, please continue."

"Thank you, sir. When Delilah Hussein was ten years old, she lived with her parents, Henri and Imane, near Babil. They were murdered. Delilah found them upon her return from school. Evidently, she fled the house, thinking she would be next.

"She ended up as a servant and concubine for another family. The parents treated her cruelly. The husband beat and raped her sometimes for hours on end. This treatment lasted for at least a year. She managed to escape by killing the mother and father.

"Delilah wandered the desert for hours and was found by a cleric, a man named Ahmed, who took her in, clothed her, and treated her kindly. Ahmed was a confidant of Saddam Hussein. Eventually, Delilah was introduced to Saddam. And he took her as a concubine, siring two children through her. Sharif al-Faisal, aka Sam Fairing, and Jazan Hussein, aka Jasmine Kader.

"The kindness of the cleric apparently did not rub off on Delilah Hussein. Instead, her megalomania and narcissism had inculcated her as a result of the rapes and beatings, along with witnessing the excesses and brutality of Saddam. She freed herself from the brutal conditions, but they had instilled in her a sense of omnipotence, fearlessness, and grandiosity. Seeing Saddam's grip on his nation and the riches he'd acquired imprinted the narcissistic tendencies on her psyche. She developed a sense of invincibility. The narcissism drives her need for revenge. When Saddam was toppled and executed, Delilah used her influence and resources to form a secret group called The Simoon.

"Evidently, she has had an ultra-secret plan to take down America since Saddam was toppled and has been plotting to attack America with the same intensity and vengeance seen with bin Laden.

"There has been chatter in electronic transmissions from our sources in the Middle East hinting at another attack, Syria to be exact. But we have not been able to pin down the target of the attack or her location since finding out she is still alive."

"And you think she will not stop until she gets her revenge?" the director of the Defense Intelligence Agency asked.

"That's correct, sir. In fact, we are now watching the pharmacist, as we feel that her need to avenge herself and her family for the pharmacist's heroic actions will also be a key to this operation."

$$\text{R}_{\text{X}}$$

"Do you recognize it?" Peter inquired.

"Absolutely. This is where it all started for me almost three years ago. Come on."

The afternoon sun had dipped behind a large bank of dark clouds, dropping the temperature. The wind kicked up and buffeted the Hummer. They exited the vehicle and both men walked up the slope toward the gravesite. Jason knew exactly where he was going, leading the way to a terraced garden of grave sites at Peninsula Memorial Park

When Jason stopped short, Peter glanced down at the marker. "Is this her father?"

Jason nodded, silently reading the inscription on the ornate headstone:

Thomas Pettigrew

Loving Father and Husband

The date of death read September 14, almost three years ago.

Jason found himself being pulled into the past, recalling the large contingent of graveside mourners on the Tuesday following Pettigrew's death, and laying eyes on Chrissie for the first time in more than a decade. His heart had raced in his chest then and was doing so now . . . but for very different reasons.

Peter broke through Jason's trance. "If this is her doing, that bitch has a flair for the dramatic."

"I don't see any cell phone anywhere. Check the flowers, will you?"

Peter knelt by the headstone and pawed around the pot of fresh flowers. Jason couldn't shake the feeling that he was being watched. He glanced around the grounds. To the north, situated among a copse of trees, was a fifteen foot white marble statue of Jesus kneeling and praying with arms raised and outstretched. The quiet scene and the sunlight-and-shadow dappled sculpture felt too calm, too serene. To his right lay rolling acres of cemetery dotted with granite and marble memorials. Despite the placid surroundings, Jason could feel a torrent of evil simmering like the calm before a storm. A green canopy had been erected over an open grave 150 yards to the south, surrounded by mourners seated and standing. A preacher, Bible splayed and dripping over his hands, read passages.

Jason studied the scene and shuddered. Being here once again sent tremors of malevolent sensations through him.

Chapter 23

"I've found something," Jason declared. He dropped to his knees and probed with his fingers.

The brothers had circled Thomas Pettigrew's grave and headstone for several minutes, scanning the ground. Jason had noticed a disturbed, rectangular patch of green grass adjacent to the headstone.

He lifted the perfectly cut rectangle of grass, reaching into the six-inch-deep hole, he removed an odd-shaped box.

"What the hell?" Peter declared.

Jason's stomach flipped. He cradled it in both hands, as if it might explode. The pain in his bandaged arm flared. A strong, steady pulse erupted in the wounds on his arm and scalp.

The box, constructed of fresh-cut pine, was about the size and weight of two novels stacked together. A menthol pinewood scent penetrated Jason's nostrils. Moreover, the shape caught the brother's attention instantly. Jason shuddered.

Shaped like a miniature toe-pincher coffin—like those seen in old Westerns—wide at the torso and narrowing as it tapered toward the feet. Two words, two names, had been burned into the lid. A first name and a surname: *Christine Pettigrew*

"Jesus H. Christ," Peter whispered.

Placing it on the soft, grass, Jason pried open the lid with a fingernail and peered into the morbid container. Something had been wrapped in thick, sealed plastic. Praying it was not a body part, he peeled away the waterproof tape and pulled apart the packaging.

Relieved, he let out a sigh, removed another sleek, black smartphone, and held it up. The numeral two was scribbled in white paint on its back

"Another message?" Peter asked.

"Let's find out."

℞

The Watcher blended into the small crowd to the northeast of Thomas Pettigrew's grave. The dearly departed's graveside service provided a view of the Rodgers brothers scouring the earth around Thomas Pettigrew's plot.

His black Cadillac's dark paint job blended into the line of cars parked along the curving roadways meandering through the vast cemetery. As the preacher droned on, The Watcher paid little attention to the ceremonial words. He'd had an unobstructed view of Peter Rodgers's Hummer as it pulled to a stop three hundred yards away. The timing and placement of the graveside service had been fortuitous.

The Watcher had returned from Williamsburg and driven straight to the cemetery . Two hours earlier, he had completed his search of Clyde Hutton's mobile home, looking for anything tying him, Hussein, or The Simoon to the deceased man.

While there, he'd kept one eye on his phone, monitoring Jason Rodgers's whereabouts. Using the classified tracking software installed on his phone and accurate to within three feet anywhere on the planet, the program allowed him to monitor a subject's whereabouts using only a cell phone number.

The brothers spent several hours at the ex-marine's house, then returned to Newport News as The Watcher drove south from Williamsburg. They returned to Christine Pettigrew's home as The Watcher reached Newport News. From a hundred yards away, he'd observed the brothers driving through the arched wrought iron of the memorial park. He had taken an alternate route through the burial acreage, arriving graveside two minutes before the Hummer pulled up. The Watcher knew they had found and deciphered the microprinting on the business card and would go to the cemetery.

Things were ramping up!

He had placed two items. The first had been deposited twelve hours ago. Rodgers was digging it up now. The second item was waiting for them in York County. The Watcher had no idea why Hussein needed or wanted to manipulate Jason Rodgers's movements. Despite being in the dark about her motives, or because of that fact, the hairs on the back of The Watcher's neck stood erect.

Symbolism! Delilah Hussein loved it!

The Watcher smirked. He knew the pharmacist's history . . . and some of his future. As it had two years earlier, Jason Rodgers's current journey would alter his life forever.

$$\text{R}_{\text{X}}$$

One hundred and twenty miles west in southwestern Virginia, an off-duty corrections officer named Dalton Griffin dressed in pressed navy jeans, brown leather work boots, and a checkered flannel shirt followed the short woman in a black corrections uniform down the ascetic hallway. In his right hand, the man carried a thin manila folder, and in the left a leather carry-on bag.

"You Baker's replacement?" the woman asked.

A step behind her, the man studied her. *Nice ass*, he thought, smiling.

Her hair, pulled back into a tight ponytail, stretched the skin of her face, which was covered with only a hint of foundation. *Not bad!* The athletic mien and well-proportioned figure could not be hidden by the arsenal of gear strapped to her body. The derrière was the tell. Off duty, this CO was a one hundred percent, estrogen-filled, high-heeled clacking woman.

The shirt of her uniform covered a flak jacket, suppressing a pair of ample breasts. Pinned to her shoulder, near the collar, a radio microphone rested above a name badge that he had yet to read. A large utility belt dripped with the necessities of the job: a holstered pistol, ammunition, pepper spray, handcuffs, and a baton, all wrapped around a slim, toned waist. As she strode with the confidence of a prize fighter, the gear clicked, rattled, and rubbed, echoing off the painted concrete walls.

Having a corrections officer would be a first. He'd banged women from all walks of life. Flight attendants, nurses, grocery clerks, and loan officers.

"That would be me." Griffin replied. "Drove down as soon as I got the word."

"Where was your last tour?"

"Wallens Ridge. Four rookies just took the oath and came on board. So that freed me up to come here."

"I'm taking you to the deputy warden's office."

"What's your name?" he asked.

The woman shot him a look over her shoulder.

"My name is Don't Get Any Ideas. So you can take your eyes off my backside."

"I wasn't . . ."

"Bullshit. Besides it's not my best feature. And I'm too much woman for you to handle, Mac!"

The new CO smiled. "I don't think so!"

They walked in silence along the gray metal and concrete corridors. In the distance, the metallic boom of a door closing reverberated throughout the prison.

"Why am I here?" he asked, deflecting the sexual tension.

"They didn't tell you?"

"Nope," he lied. "Just following orders."

"Josh was a great guy, family man, and one hell of a CO. I still can't believe he's gone."

"What happened?"

"Apparently, he killed his wife and two small children with bullets to the head. Then he ate the barrel and splattered his brains all over the wall."

The woman pointed to the office door. "This is it here." The stenciled letters on the glass of the door read: *Deputy Warden Jeremiah Travis*

She knocked twice, opened the door, and stuck her head in. "Josh's replacement is here, sir."

A gruff, mumbled response rumbled from within. She held the door open for him. The woman whispered something as he edged past:

"You have some big shoes to fill."

The door snapped shut. Griffin looked down on a burly, barrel-chested man in a uniform identical to the woman's. This one, however, was decorated with a higher rank.

A pair of dainty Ben Franklin spectacles rested on a red, bulbous nose as the man read from a report. Griffin stood awkwardly for ten seconds before the deputy warden looked up.

"You Griffin?"

"Yes sir, Dalton Griffin, reporting for duty."

"This ain't the army, son. I'm Deputy Warden Travis. That's 'Deputy Warden' to you." He pointed to an uncomfortable looking metal chair that did not invite loitering. "Sit."

He motioned for Griffin to hand him the paperwork. Travis read through the chronology of Griffin's career.

"Been a CO in three maximum security prisons, six years' experience."

"Yes, sir."

"I'll be straight with you, son. You were not my first choice for this assignment. In fact, you weren't even on my radar. I'm looking at your history. We don't let anyone on that unit unless they have at least ten years at a super max facility. You've only been at Wallens Ridge for four.

"Some muckety-muck up the chain pulled some strings and said we were to place you, right away. They said you were the best. You've got some friends in high places. You better live up to it. Come with me. I'll take you to the unit."

The chief led Griffin farther along the same drab corridor.

"Not sure I wanted this assignment either, Chief. And I like to think I am the best," Griffin explained.

"Cocky son of a bitch, ain't you? You're gonna need every ounce of it. We're assigning you to a special unit. We call it the Underground. Earned the nickname recently. It was Unit D. It houses five of the most dangerous men in the state of Virginia . . . if not the country."

"The Underground?"

"One of the inmates came up with it. Yeah, he was Baker's charge before he offed his family and then himself. Now he's yours. He lost an eye in a fight before he got here. Don't know the particulars. He's been reading about the mythical Greek one-eyed monsters. They lived in a place called the Underground. So he's been calling this place by the same name. It's fitting and it stuck. It houses only five men, all of them vicious and lethal. One guard for each inmate.

"You'll be replacing Josh Baker and taking over his duties and his prisoner."

"His prisoner?" Griffin feigned surprise.

"Baker was responsible for one man. Assignments are switched out every four weeks . . . so no one gets too familiar."

They passed through three heavily guarded checkpoints and multiple sliding iron gates.

"What's his name?"

They were buzzed through a fourth gate into a circular unit with a hexagonal station centered among six cells. Each cell was numbered one through six.

"We don't use names here, son. Only numbers. His is number three. That's his cell, right there. But he likes to call himself Cyclops."

Deputy Warden Travis introduced Griffin to the four COs sitting behind computer terminals displaying closed-circuit screens of each cell. Griffin focused on screen number three and the dark-skinned, skinny inmate resting on his cot, reading some kind of book. Griffin could make out the word mythology across the faded cover.

"He don't look like much," Griffin said out loud.

"That kind of thinking will get you killed." The four men eyed Baker suspiciously. Travis heaved a plump forefinger at one of the men.

"Max, here, will give you the lowdown on procedures. You'll report for duty tomorrow at 6 a.m., sharp. Welcome to the Red Onion, son."

℞

"Bonjour, mon ami," the voice of Delilah Hussein chirped. Her words were laced with a vicious, self-satisfied smugness. "I know what you're thinking. I'm supposed to be dead. I can assure you I am very much alive. I can't wait to see your face, Jason. We have unfinished business."

Jason and Peter sat in Peter's Hummer on the paved roadway cut into the Peninsula Memorial Park's grounds. Jason held the phone between the two of them as they listened to the gruff, accented voice coming through the speaker. Weakness and fear fueled a slow, tremble that overtook his body.

"By now, you know that your son, Michael, and Christine have been taken. I am confirming what you must already suspect. I have them both in my possession. Do not bother looking for them . . . they are no longer on American soil. Open the text-message function on the phone and you can look at them."

Jason paused the recording and tapped the text-message icon. A single message appeared with photo attachments. Christine lying on her back, asleep, or unconscious, or dead, on a sofa of some kind on the right side of a cramped space. The curved walls in each photo looked like the interior of an airplane cabin. The second was of Michael, also unawake, on a sofa of a similar design. But it appeared to be on the left side.

Jason placed the phone on the console between them, bowed his head, and rubbed his temples. "I can't believe this is happening . . . again."

Peter picked up the phone and continued the voice message.

"Fear not, Jason. They are still alive. They were drugged during their abductions so as not to put up a fight and risk getting injured or shot. I will send you additional photos of your loved ones as we progress through your new mission.

Yes, you now have a mission to complete. A simple three-part job. You must find something for me. Then you will find someone. And finally you will make a delivery.

It is a mission that you must complete if you wish to see them again.

Now listen carefully . . . bring a laptop. You have one more package to retrieve . . ."

Hussein's gravelly voice, accented in a thick Mediterranean French, hung in the cab of the Hummer. Her utterances reverberated off the glass and leather interior, filling the space with an ominous timbre. The intensity and volume of Jason's fear swelled like a storm surge before an approaching hurricane.

Jason lowered his head, his chin falling to his heaving chest, his rapid breaths punctuated by short, groaning sobs.

R_X

Delilah Hussein stood between two eight-foot-high cases stuffed with dusty wine bottles, laid horizontally, watching her two captives. She'd wanted to observe their isolation and terror in anonymity. It was not time for them to know anything about her and why they were here. Their ignorance would add to their mental discomfort. She wanted them to hurt in every possible way.

Hussein was certain the boy had no idea why he had been kidnapped. The woman might have an idea, but Hussein doubted it. As far as Christine Pettigrew was concerned, Hussein was dead.

The subterranean wine cellar dug from the sand and clay of her island, mountaintop villa measured fifty by fifty with a dusty concrete floor. A small phalanx of racks had been removed to make room for her captives. The space held a variety of tools, rakes, hoes, and pitchforks, overflow storage from the utility shed. The folded clothes taken from their rooms had been laid neatly on one of the racks holding hundreds of dusty bottles of wine.

Hussein scrunched her nose at the musty, dank, and foul odor that suffused the air and walls. Her wine collection and now her hostages resided in the anteroom of the two-room cellar. A small, arched, doorless passageway led from the anteroom to a larger, less-utilized space filled with rotting, discarded wine barrels. The villa had once been home to a small winery. Hussein had the vines torn out after acquiring the property, installed a barracks, and had a landing pad poured for her drone.

Turning her attention back to her guests, she studied their uncomfortable accommodations. They were chained in distress positions against opposite walls, facing each other. For the moment, neither of them knew the other was there.

Blindfolded, their mouths were stuffed with dirty cloths secured in place by gags wrapped tightly around their heads. Their noses and a small patch around them were the only visible skin.

Hussein sipped from a glass of Bordeaux in a clear plastic cup as she contemplated the boy. Michael Rodgers's hands were cuffed behind him. The cuffs were chained to the east wall of the cellar. In a kneeling position, he leaned his full weight against the chained handcuffs, with each ankle chained from a different point on the wall. The ankle chains were sufficiently short that he could not sit back on his rump, but had to rest his weight on his knees and lean forward, pulling his arms backward and up.

Extrêmement inconfortable, Hussein thought.

The discomfort would grow with each hour, expanding through their bones and tissues. Muscles would cramp and tire. In a few hours, he would be begging and crying to be released. Hussein had ordered the use of this position many times. Seasoned soldiers and agents had been unable to withstand this position for longer than twenty four hours.

Before his eyes and mouth had been covered, Hussein had caught a long look at the boy's face as he was carried unconscious into the makeshift cell. The firm set of his jaw and lips resembled those his father. The eyes and the facial bones around them did not hold Jason Rodgers's genetic makeup. They were softer, more handsome than the pharmacist's. No doubt a quality derived from the mother. But nonetheless, he bore a strong resemblance to his father.

The sight of Michael Rodgers's face, so similar to that of his father, sent waves of hatred coursing through her stoic veins. It was an unexpected reaction.

Hussein smiled as she took another sip of wine. The photos and a video had been shot a few hours ago. The stills had already been sent to the cell phone Jason Rodgers would find in its hiding place.

Operation Hygeia was well underway. And Jason Rodgers was at its very core.

By now, Rodgers knew that she was behind the disappearance of the two people he loved most in the world. But she also knew that when he saw the pictures of them as her captives, his worst fears would be confirmed.

That's when the real fun would begin.

℞

"Here we go again," Jason sighed, tapping his pockets frantically. "Where's the cell phone number one. The one she sent us?"

"Calm down!" Peter tapped his shirt pocket. "I have it right here."

Jason climbed back in the Hummer with a small cardboard box after exiting the Grafton Post Office. He sliced through the thick tape using his car keys. Opening the flaps and rifling through the crumpled paper, he removed another symbolic container, a coffin identical to the first. This one had Michael's name branded into the lid.

Gently, Jason shook the box and something rattled inside. He pulled open the lid and peered inside. With two fingers, he removed a sleek black flash drive wrapped in clear plastic. The outside of the plastic bag was covered with a red liquid.

"What's that?" His brother asked.

Jason examined the pads of his fore- and middle finger. They were streaked with red.

"Is it paint?"

Jason sniffed his fingers then rubbed them together. A crawling dread swept over him. "I think it's blood."

He examined the box and found a red smear on the underside of the lid. Jason shook his head and exhaled.

"She's going to kill them, Pete. No matter what I do, she's going to kill them."

"You don't know that. She's screwing with you. Stay focused."

"Grab the computer."

CHAPTER 24

Consciousness seeped in, crowding out oblivion like the dawning sun nudging aside the night. As the darkness of her mind receded, Chrissie's last memories replayed with the flurry of an out-of-control slide show: the bedroom door crashing open, knocking her backward; the masked face; the monster-like goggles; and the sharp sting in her neck.

Pressure surged from the center of her skull expanding outward with each passing second, creating the sensation that her head would blow apart. Chrissie tried to open her eyes, but couldn't. Her eyelashes rubbed against something rough. The blindfold felt as if it would push her eyes backward into her brain.

She tried to suck in lungsful of air. Each inhalation was met with stiff resistance. A vile odor permeated her nose and mouth. Chrissie moved her tongue back and forth. A disgusting cloth had been rammed into her mouth, filling it, restricting the movement of her tongue and choking her.

She gagged and pushed forward with her tongue. The pressure against her throat eased. She managed to suck in some cool, moldy air through her nostrils. At the moment, her nose was her only connection to the world.

A searing pain scorched her arms and legs. The muscles burned. Her arms felt like they were being pulled apart from her shoulders. Behind her, outstretched, taut, her wrists were held aloft and she could not lower them. Every time she tried, the pain intensified, becoming molten. Something held them aloft. If she tried to force them lower, her arms screamed in protest.

The large muscles in her legs had begun to cramp and spasm. Tears tried to drip from her eyes only to be swallowed up by the repugnant cloth around her eyes. Chrissie's stomach wanted to expel its contents. If she did, she might choke to death because of the gag. She willed herself to focus on other things, blocking out the pain and the nausea.

Where the hell was she?

Who had taken her? And why?

Where was Jason? Had he been taken too?

Chrissie tried to cry. But her whimpers were absorbed by the filthy cloth in her mouth, her tears sopped up by the irritating fabric over her eyes.

She couldn't even weep.

Amid the rustle of her clothing and the brush of the blindfold and gag depriving her senses, another sound intervened, inconsistent with and independent of her movements. It emanated from somewhere close by. The soft, gentle whoosh, a scraping noise caused by two rough surfaces rubbing against each other. Faint but unmistakable, it was there.

The cold floor felt like concrete coated with dirt or sawdust. The sound coming to her was the same sound she made when she moved her legs along the floor. Chrissie froze and listened.

There it was again!

A panicked anxiety shook her. Another living creature was alive and moving in the space near her.

Was it a mouse . . . or a rat . . . or something worse?

Whatever it was, she realized she was not alone.

℞

The flash drive held a single video file. Delilah Hussein's, formerly Lily Zanns's, puckered puss dominated the computer screen. The recording had been paused. A large right-pointing triangle poised mid-screen waiting for a command.

They sat in Peter's idling Hummer in the parking lot of the Grafton Post Office. Before clicking the play icon, Jason studied the frozen image.

Despite the fact that he'd last seen her less than three years ago, Delilah Hussein looked fifteen years older. Her black eyes exuded a hard sadness. The skin around them was markedly wrinkled. Her lips were pursed in a condescending pout.

Acid in his gut roiled. The pulse in his temple and wounds raced. Jason sucked in a tremulous breath, pushing back hatred, frustration, and a horror-filled dread.

The scene behind Hussein, frozen on the screen, appeared tropical. Slanting palm trees jutted from thick ground cover. A serene azure body of water stretched calmly to the horizon, the antithesis of Jason's life at this moment.

Jason hovered the mouse over the triangle then clicked.

"So, Monsieur Jason, you have found the flash drive inside the second coffin. Michael and Miss Christine are only a few meters from me at this very moment. They are alive. Confused and afraid, naturally. But still among the living. Let me show you . . ."

The image on the screen shifted from the placid outdoor backdrop to a dark, murky room. Jason squinted, moving his face closer to the screen. Seconds elapsed, the videographer adjusted the aperture of the lens and the picture exploded in light. Another adjustment and the level of light corrected itself once more.

The same two silhouettes knelt before opposite walls, in a basement of some kind lined with racks holding wine bottles laid horizontally. Farm implements leaned in clusters against the four walls. The prisoners were blindfolded, perched forward uncomfortably before opposite walls. Their arms secured behind them as taut chains angled from their arms to the brick.

If any doubt existed, Jason had none now. He recognized the familiar outlines of Michael and Chrissie. The image zoomed in to Michael, filling the screen on the left, and then panned right.

Jason did not need to see their faces—Michael's mop of hair and his strong angled chin, and the curve of Chrissie's delicate, tear-stained cheeks. Their faces were swathed by gags and blindfolds. Miniscule patches of skin along the jawline and around the nose were visible.

Next, the image moved to the dirt-covered floor between them. A pristine newspaper lay there. The camera zoomed in on the masthead, focusing on the date. Yesterday's edition of the *Washington Post*.

His eyes welled with moisture. Jason blinked them away, finishing with a wipe of his sleeve. Delilah Hussein reappeared and spoke:

"Here are your three objectives. You must secure a vehicle. Go to the address inscribed on the underside of the lid of the second coffin, Michael's coffin, and retrieve a set of keys to a vehicle from the man there. You will be given the location of the vehicle later, if you survive. With these keys and the vehicle, you will make a very important delivery for me. It is out of state and will take no more than ten hours.

"Remember, the lives of Michael and Miss Christine depend on your success. It will be a difficult task, but one that you are capable of completing. I have complete confidence in you.

"Once you have obtained the keys from the male resident of the home . . . you are to use the cell phone from Chrissie's miniature grave . . . the one marked number two . . . and call the only number in the address book. You must report back to me by one am your time tomorrow. Monsieur Jason, after you retrieve the keys and before you make the delivery, you will need to do one more thing . . . You must kill the man who gives you the keys . . . Bonne chance!"

$$R_X$$

"We have to take this to Palmer," Peter demanded. "He's the only man who knows what happened. He can help us!"

Jason shook his head. His first inclination was to get the police involved. But he'd reconsidered. "I don't know. You heard her. 'No police or Feds.'"

"She has Michael and Chrissie. We don't know where they are. We can't do this alone. Let the police crash the house and shake this guy down!"

The video had finished a minute ago. The brothers sat in silence contemplating Delilah Hussein's instructions, absorbing the shock of the ultimatum, the enormity of their dilemma swelling.

"Stop and think a minute, Peter, will you?" Jason shot back. "We don't even know if this guy knows where they are. If we get the cops involved, Hussein will know. I can't risk it. If we take this to Palmer, the whole Newport News Police Department is going to descend on that house. Then they'll bring in the Feds. And she will kill Chrissie and Michael. I know it. We can't. We have to find another way."

"Jason," Peter replied. "This thing is way too big for you and me. Hussein could be holding them anywhere. If she's telling the truth and they are no longer on American soil, we have no way of finding out where they are, let alone mounting a rescue. Look, I love them, too. But we need help."

"I agree we are going to need help. But not yet."

"So what are you . . . we going to do?"

"We're going to follow her instructions to the letter . . . until I can think of a way of getting help without Hussein knowing it. Think about this: Hussein is trying to manipulate me. She took Michael and Chrissie because she wants me to deliver—whatever it is. She's taken them to control me, to make sure I do what she wants. I'm going to do just that."

"She wants you to kill someone! Are you planning on doing that too?"

"I'm going to try everything I can to avoid it. Let's go back to my place. I'm going to need some things . . . and I'm going to need a better weapon than the Colt. And I need to make a stop."

℞

"I'm not letting you go alone. You need someone watching your six," Peter declared.

They had driven back to Jason's place in York County and were standing at the kitchen counter. Peter had cracked a Miller Lite. Jason sipped from a bottle of water. Peter had placed the first cell phone on the counter between them along with the password scribbled on a piece of paper.

The determination in Peter's words possessed an iron finality. When this marine got something in his head, he would not let it go. Nonetheless, Jason put up a token effort to resist.

"Pete, you can't be involved. If I have to kill again, you can't be involved. What about Lisa and the girls?"

Peter held Jason's gaze. "Michael's family. So is Chrissie. I'm going. That's final."

Jason nodded. "Okay. Let's get out on the deck. You can have a cigarette. We'll need a plan."

On the deck, Peter shook a Marlboro from its box, lipped it out, and touched the lighter's flame to its tip. He sucked in two long draws and exhaled them into the cool, spring air. Jason sipped from the water bottle. The brothers stared into the wooded lot. They had done this countless times in the past under less trying circumstances.

"I have a question," Peter began, "with you here and Chrissie… unavailable, who's minding The Colonial?"

"I've got two great pharmacists. Billy Parks is in charge. I checked with him about fifteen minutes ago. Told him Chrissie and I were going on a long weekend. That we'd be back next week." Jason hesitated, his voice wavering. "If we get them back."

"Don't worry, we're gonna do everything. And I mean, everything." Peter placed a firm hand on his brother's shoulder as he pulled two quick drags from the cigarette into his lungs and flicked the butt away.

"Alright bro," Peter began, "where do you have to go to find this man you're supposed to kill. The video said it was on the lid of the second coffin. What's the address?"

Jason hefted a thumb over his shoulder. "It's in the house. We'll look at it in a minute. Where's your gun?"

"Under the seat of the Hummer."

"Ammo?"

"Three fifty round boxes, also under the seat. That should be plenty."

"That depends on where this takes us next."

"How about your weapon?"

"The Smith and Wesson nine mil is upstairs. I'll get it in a minute. I have two boxes of rounds. I've got about five hundred in cash in my dresser. I'll bring it . . . in case. Is your phone fully charged?"

Peter checked his bars. "I'm about half."

"You?"

"I'm good. I have a charger inside. You can fill 'er up on the way."

"So how should we play this?" Peter asked, withdrawing a second cigarette, lighting it, and sucking it down to half.

"Hopefully, he'll be alone. I'll approach the door by myself. You'll hang back in the car, waiting and watching. You'll be there in case anything goes wrong. And that's final. I go in alone."

"What about killing him?"

"I'm working on that."

"What about making him disappear?"

"What do you mean?"

"We could kidnap him and keep him incommunicado until we have Michael and Chrissie back, then release him."

"Who's going to babysit him? We don't have time to get more people involved. Plus we have a deadline . . . one in the morning."

"Good point."

"We're going to have to play it by ear," Jason declared.

"When do you want to leave?"

Jason rubbed his chin. "In a few minutes," he replied. "Is Lisa pissed?"

Peter smiled and nodded. "I think she worries more about me being with you than she did about my being in Iraq."

Jason nodded. "Can't say I blame her."

"You okay?" Peter asked. "You've been wearing out those jeans for the last hour."

Jason lowered his eyes and saw his hands running up and down his thigh. He stopped and looked at his brother.

"I should have left all this stuff alone, Pete. If I hadn't been chasing Clyde Hutton, I would have been there when they took her. I could have stopped it."

"Maybe, but you wouldn't have been able to keep them from taking Michael. We'd still be here trying to get him back. This was a well thought out op. She's planned this a long time. Don't worry, we'll get them back. No matter what it takes."

"Thanks. Give me a minute. I'll get the gun and the money. I'll come and get you. Have another smoke."

"Copy that," Peter said as he fished out his third butt.

℞

Jason descended the stairs after leaving his bedroom. He had retrieved his Smith and Wesson and two boxes of rounds, the cash, and two empty clips from the small safe in his closet

The two-story Running Man residence still held a household's worth of furnishings. The utilities were still on. He hadn't spent much time here since he'd moved in with Chrissie six months ago. He drove the twenty minutes from Newport News and checked on things twice a week. Once in a while, he'd spend the night.

A melancholy gratitude filled him. *Good thing I haven't sold it*, he thought. *I might be moving back here.*

Jason hesitated in the kitchen, peering through the window at his brother leaning on the deck the railing with his back to Jason. Intermittent puffs of smoke wafted skyward. He'd always chided Peter about his two-pack-a-day habit. And Peter always waved it away.

Tomorrow, he'd say. *I'll quit tomorrow.*

His brother always smoked outside, even at home. Lisa would have it no other way. Today, he was glad for his brother's addiction.

The keys to the Hummer lay on the counter beside the cell phone. Jason scooped them up.

He pivoted, exiting the kitchen through the foyer and opened the front door a fraction. The hinges squealed. He pulled it open wide enough to slip out and closed it silently behind him.

You'd run through hell in a gasoline suit for me, brother, Jason told himself. *I can't let you do it this time.*

Jason knew the moment Hussein's video instructed him to kill a man that he had to keep Peter out of it. He'd sacrificed too much. Lisa, Peter's wife, already hated that Jason had exposed her husband to so many dangers. She'd never say it out loud. But he saw it in her eyes. Jason was sure she lobbied Peter about staying away from Jason. Jason also knew Peter defended him . . . every time.

On the way back to the house, Jason had devised a getaway plan. The idea to have a smoke on the deck and invite Peter to stay there for a minute had worked.

Jason pressed the button on the key fob, unlocking the doors. He hopped in and slipped the key in the ignition. The engine hummed to life. He jerked the gearshift into reverse and backed out.

As he curled into the street, the front door opened. Peter appeared in the doorway, confusion etched on his face. He bolted toward his Hummer.

Jason rammed it into drive, slamming the accelerator to the floor-board. The rear wheels spun on the pavement, causing it to fishtail. Smoke enveloped the Hummer. Peter intercepted Jason as he gained speed. The former marine slammed the passenger-door window.

"Jason, what the fuck!"

Jason stayed hard on the gas, swung the wheel right, and hurtled onto Running Man Trail. He watched an irate, arm-waving Peter grow smaller in the rearview mirror.

Chapter 25

Pastor Charles Bang walked through the soothing environs of the earth-toned tile and chocolate timbers of the Gloria Dei Lutheran narthex making his final rounds, checking on the vast Hampton complex, before heading home for dinner. He had taken the position as senior pastor a few years ago, moving his family down from Buffalo. He did not miss the harsh winters of northern New York State and enjoyed the warm, welcoming weather and attitudes of the Virginia locals.

He'd been uncertain about the move at first. The former pastor had passed away after a long, distinguished tenure building the church, school, and daycare from the days when the congregation met in a bowling alley. Nonetheless, they had welcomed him with open arms. He fit in here. It felt like home. His flock's numbers were growing, and he looked forward to a lengthy tour at this holy duty station.

Through the inner glass doors leading into the sanctuary, he spied someone kneeling at one of the front pews. Not wanting to disturb the praying man, he opened the door and used his outstretched hand to keep it from bumping against the stop. Bang progressed up the center aisle at a leisurely pace, enjoying the view.

The sanctuary was nearly dark. The lights were off. The only illumination in the vaulted space seeped through the tall pentagonal-shaped windows cut into the nave walls and the more massive portals on either end of the transept. A fifteen-foot wood and brass crucifix hung suspended above the raised altar in a wash of supernal radiance. Bang loved the acoustics of the vast, stone sanctuary trussed with heavy, dark timbers. The massive pipe organ behind the altar brimmed the space with glorious Lutheran hymns each Sunday. The acoustically charged space carried his sermons to all corners of this place of worship with ease.

But in this early evening, the sounds reverberating through the vaulted ceilings were ones of despair and hopelessness. Bang had heard them before. And it signaled tragedy.

Ten feet away, Bang knew something was dreadfully wrong. The man's head was bowed. His shoulders bobbed in a frenetic fashion. Anguished sobs escaped his quaking body. The sobs ceased when Bang placed a firm, gentle hand on the man's shoulder.

"Can I help my son?"

The man turned and elevated his swollen red eyes to the cleric. The tear-streaked face was a familiar one to Bang.

"Jason? What's wrong?"

Jason wiped his eyes with the back of his hand. "I need a prayer answered."

"You're in the right place."

Jason searched Bang's eyes. Bang regarded him in silence, his eyes imploring him to share his burden. As he watched and waited, the clergyman searched his memory for specifics about Jason Rodgers. Jason and his girlfriend, Christine Pettigrew, had come to Gloria Dei eight months ago. As he recalled, they were looking for a new start and had mentioned marriage at some point. Neither one of them had been members of a church, but wanted to change that. A friend had recommended Gloria Dei. They attended services regularly, but their busy schedules did not allow them much time to participate in church activities. Rodgers had a son named Mark or Mitchell, and Christine was childless.

Bang took up a position in the pew forward of the pharmacist and angled himself to face the distraught man. Reaching out, he placed a gentle hand on Rodgers's arm and implored, "Tell me what's wrong."

Jason sighed. "I can't give many details. I'm in a very difficult situation, Pastor."

"Tell me what you can."

"I've lost two people I love very much."

"I'm sorry, Jason. How did they die?"

Jason shook his head. "They're not dead. They're missing."

"What happened?"

"I asked Chrissie to marry me yesterday. But I've messed it up, Pastor. My past has messed it all up. Michael is gone also. It's my fault. I may never see them again."

"I don't understand. Has a crime been committed?"

"Yes."

"Have you gone to the police?"

"No. I'm doing everything I can. I was praying for them. I need you to pray for them. Can you do that for me . . . and for them?"

"Most definitely, my son." Bang placed his hand on Jason's bowed head and whispered a short, emphatic prayer.

"Dear gracious God, we pray for the lives of three of our own, Jason, Christine, and Michael. We ask that you watch over them and bring peace back into their lives. We ask that you help Jason find the skill and determination to bring his loved ones back into his life. In Jesus' precious name we pray. Amen."

"Thank you, Pastor. I have to go now. I have to be somewhere. Before I go, I have one last question for you."

"Of course."

"I've been placed in an impossible situation. I have to do something that will cause someone's family great pain and suffering. I don't know if I can do it. But if I don't, I could lose the two people I love the most."

"How can that be so?"

"Pray for Chrissie and Michael, Pastor. I'm asking you for forgiveness . . . in advance. I have to do something ungodly. I promised myself I would never do such a thing again. My hand has been forced."

"Again? Jason, you're not making any sense."

"Is it ever justified to kill someone in order to save a loved one's life?"

Charles Bang stared at Jason in complete shock. He'd been asked many difficult questions and been put in many difficult situations over the years. This question, however, was a first. He felt the blood drain from his face.

"Jason, I guess that depends."

"Pastor, please pray for us."

Before he could utter another syllable, Rodgers slipped out of the pew and marched toward the rear of the sanctuary. Bang watched, stunned, as Jason plowed his hands into the double glass doors, causing them to burst open.

He tried to call after the retreating pharmacist. But his normally sanguine voice had been sucked away by fear and confusion. All he mustered was a half-hearted, "Jason . . ."

Bang hurried after the pharmacist, scurrying out of the dark sanctuary through the narthex and foyer to the entrance. He arrived in time to see Jason Rodgers backing out of a parking spot in haste and squealing tires into the intersection with Fox Hill Road.

℞

Jason pulled the Hummer to a stop at the curb on 65th Street, a hundred yards from the address that had been etched on the lid of the second miniature coffin. He was all too familiar with the street and building. He'd been here before. Two years earlier, he'd watched Douglas Winstead's head explode in the living room of the dilapidated structure.

His anxiety had waxed as he drove to Newport News from the church in Hampton. Bile had risen to toxic levels in his gut, threatening to explode out of his mouth in an eruption of acidic vomit. Peter had blown up his cell phone with threatening text messages and voicemails, adding to Jason's unease. He'd ignored all of them. He had not shared with Peter the address inscribed into the lid of the second miniature coffin.

Jason had not grabbed the first cell phone marked number one in grease. Peter had left it on the counter along with the password that gave access to the text message. Now he rubbed his pants pocket, feeling the hard case of the second phone, the one from the miniature coffin with Chrissie's name burned into it, beneath the denim of his jeans. He removed it and placed it on the Hummer's passenger seat.

I'm going to need that later to call Hussein, he thought.

Throwing his head back, he sucked in several breaths, choked back his stomach contents, and tried to steady his nerves. Over the past two years, the seminal events had faded, hanging in the gallery of his mind like the work of a semi-known artist relegated to near obscurity. With the events of the last twenty-four hours, those once obscure memories had been moved into the main viewing gallery, ever present and shone upon by the brightest of lights. His past deeds, his actions, were being revisited. Jason did not want to live in that hell again. But as Dante Alighieri mused in his *Divine Comedy*, one must pass through hell to get to heaven.

He started to remove the weapon from his belt. A car passed by. A large black Cadillac. Jason hesitated, letting it slip past. The brake lights flared. It stopped at the intersection with Warwick Boulevard, hesitated a moment, and turned left heading north on the one-way thoroughfare.

When it had moved off, he removed the Smith and Wesson M&P 9 mm from under his shirt and checked the fifteen round clip. *Full.* Briefly, Jason's mind flashed on his old gun, the Smith and Wesson 645 that Jasmine Kader had stolen from his house and planted in Sheila Boquist's bedroom in an attempt to frame him for murder. The police had never given the 645 back to him, not that he cared.

Jason shook the memory from his mind and analyzed the new gun.

The composite grips felt evil in his hand. He racked the slide, chambered a round, and replaced the weapon in his belt, in front this time, and lifted his shirt over it.

Would he kill an innocent man to save Michael and Chrissie? Could he?

As he opened the car door, the muscles in Jason's arm quivered. Hoping he would not have to pull the trigger, he walked like a zombie to the same rickety front porch he'd mounted with Walter Waterhouse a couple of years ago. Jason scanned the structure. Nothing had been done to improve its appearance. The paint was in a greater state of neglect. Absent shingles still dotted the old roof. Weeds had long ago crowded out any semblance of ordered greenery. The two-story neoclassical structure was proletarian in stature, having descended through the lowest socioeconomic strata.

None of that mattered. For Jason, this was a death house.

Jason had never had a reason to return to this neighborhood. And he would have avoided it at all costs if Michael and Chrissie's lives weren't depending on it. The images of Douglas Winstead's head disintegrating flashed in his mind's eye in a strobe-like, rapid-fire display.

The sound of the muted report, the crack of the glass, the smell of fear and sweat, and the tactile sensation of blood and bone hitting him in the face seemed real again, as if they had happened only moments ago. He wanted to turn and run, to drown the images and thoughts in a bottle of Knob Creek. It was a fleeting thought, however, whisked away by the image of Michael and Chrissie bound and blindfolded in a dark cell somewhere and frightened beyond all comprehension.

He climbed the steps and approached the front door. The floor boards creaked in the same manner and with the same devastating intensity. Jason smirked at the cloudy, convoluted irony of it all.

He had killed to save two important men. He had killed men . . . and a woman who had deserved to die. They had murdered a man he admired and respected. Thomas Pettigrew. Jason had dispensed a lethal justice with relative ease. At the time, he hadn't thought about the emotional and mental aspects killing would leave in its wake. The people he'd killed were depraved, vicious individuals who had tried to kill two presidents. And they had violated his way of life.

He had killed to save two men he did not know, and done it with relative ease.

Today, he was being asked to kill again. This time an innocent man, a man he did not know. A man with whom he had no quarrel. And Jason had to do it to save two more people. Two people who, in the scheme of world politics, were inconsequential.

But they were the two most important people in his life. Jason trembled at the thought of losing them. It would be just like Delilah Hussein to put him in such a quandary. The evil in that woman knew no bounds.

Jason placed his hand in his jean pocket, hooking the thumb outside, close to where the gun resided under his shirt. He mashed the doorbell and blew out a breath, vibrating his lips.

Seconds evaporated.

The curtain on the door moved. The painted, peeling portal swung open.

Jason studied the eyes of the man standing there. His eyes bore into the shrunken face of incarnate evil.

At that moment, Jason knew he had been wrong. He did know this man. He did have a quarrel with him.

"Come in," the man said. "I've been expecting you."

But would he . . . could he kill him?

CHAPTER 26

The Watcher had donned dark sunglasses. The position of his head gave the appearance that he was looking straight ahead. But behind the black shades, his eyes darted back and forth, scanning every inch of the scene before him.

He had followed Jason Rodgers from the church in Hampton. The dark-suited agent stayed hundreds of yards behind. He was not afraid of losing him. The Watcher knew the pharmacist's destination . . . and he was tracking him using an app on his phone. The detour to the church caught him by surprise. The pharmacist had stopped off for a bit of spiritual counseling.

At 65th Street, he spied Peter Rodger's Hummer, drove past, and circled back, taking Warwick Boulevard north, doubling back along Huntington Avenue, then turning back onto 65th Street.

He'd taken his time. When he returned, Rodgers was out of the car and nowhere to be seen. The Watcher concluded that he'd gone inside and met the man in the house.

The Watcher activated another app on his phone. An image appeared on the screen. The image showed two men, Jason Rodgers and the occupant of the house, standing in the foyer, talking. The old house had been fitted with several tiny cameras, allowing The Watcher a view of what was happening.

Every possible precaution had been taken to ensure The Watcher could monitor Rodgers actions. But now he was inside with a former killer. If things went south, The Watcher would rush in. But he also knew the amount of time it would take to arrive inside was a lifetime compared to how quickly one man could kill another. The house had been searched this morning. They'd found no weapons, even the utensils had been removed from the kitchen. The body language of both men was tense and rigid.

The Watcher lit a cigarette, keeping it below the level of the dashboard. Every twenty seconds, he would lift it and give a long pull, causing the tip to glow a deep orange.

Waiting . . . and watching was a bitch.

With nothing else to do but wait, The Watcher let his mind drift back to the day he'd first met Delilah Hussein.

He'd sat on the soft sofa in the modest house in al-Qiza, Syria. One of the guards nudged him, forcing him to stand. Hussein asked why he wanted to work for her organization.

"I have many skills to offer you and your organization," he replied.

"I was intrigued by your request for a meeting. I do not normally grant such requests."

"But you agreed to it," The Watcher said.

"Yes."

"Because I mentioned the name."

"Yes, the word. How did you come by this word?"

"Hammon. It is a very interesting word, isn't it?" The Watcher teased. "It is a variation on the spelling of Amun, the Egyptian god, meaning 'hidden one.' The lore is that he created himself, then his surroundings. But you and I know it means something else, doesn't it?"

"Enlighten me," Hussein replied evenly. The Watcher detected a hint of alarm in her voice.

"Hammon is your secret contact. The Hidden One within the American intelligence community. He provided your funding for the failed operation in Newport News. He wanted to overthrow the administration. He is your mole."

Hussein shrugged and tried deflect the comment. "What makes you think I need any more people in my outfit?"

The Watcher knew he had struck a nerve. "You need someone like me. You do not have people with my talents."

"What talents?"

"I can get inside the United States. You have an operation planned there. But you need someone on American soil who can move around without arousing suspicion. Someone who looks like a Westerner and not like a terrorist. I can follow Jason Rodgers. I am an American citizen. I will not arouse suspicion."

Hussein's eyes widened for an instant. The surprise was unmistakable. It dissolved quickly. "I don't know what you are talking about."

"I know about the assassination attempts on the presidents one year ago. They failed. You lost your daughter, killed by the pharmacist. Your son was taken. You want revenge on America . . . and Rodgers. I can help you get it."

Hussein stared at him for a long minute. Her eyes bore into him.

"I admit to nothing. But just to humor you, tell me how you know this."

"You need money. That's why you are in Syria. You are arranging financing through our friends in Moscow. I can get you more. And I can help you get your revenge."

With this last statement, The Watcher motioned to one of the guards who was holding the items confiscated from his person. "The slip of paper, please, that was in my pocket."

The guard handed him a folded piece of white paper. He placed it on the coffee table. Hussein signaled to another man to hand it to her. "What is this?"

"A numbered account in Zurich. It is yours. If you hire me. With more than $50 million in it, it will help you finance your operation. And I will help you complete your mission. That's just the first installment. A second will be dispersed on my authorization once your cargo has been delivered to the United States."

The Watcher had watched Hussein freeze, the astonishment in her eyes highlighted by fear. *He had her*, he remembered thinking.

His handlers knew that Hussein was arranging for something to be delivered to America. They did not know what it was. But just the fact that he knew of the delivery made him credible.

"Why are you trying to help us?"

Finally, an admission, he thought.

"I was once a colleague of Hammon's. He betrayed me. I, too, want revenge. This is how I will get it. My compatriots also want to strike a blow at the infidels. But we also want something from you as well."

"What is that?"

"We want you to kill Hammon. He is a threat. His resolve is weak. He is trying to sabotage your mission."

"Who are your compatriots?" Hussein demanded.

"Jabhat Fatah al-Sham."

Hussein nodded her approval. Jabhat Fatah al-Sham had changed their name from Jabhat al-Nusra many months ago, severing all ties with al-Qaeda. They no longer took direction from any entity. Hussein had heard and read that they were weary of maintaining an allegiance with al-Qaeda, afraid that an association with the weakened entity would prevent them from recruiting jihadists into the fold. Suspicion of al-Qaeda's international focus also contributed to their decision, she remembered.

"You have proof of this?" she asked.

The Watcher nodded. He handed her another slip of paper. "This is the private cell number for Mostafa Mahamed, one of JFS's leaders. He will verify my allegiance."

Hussein's lips curved into a sardonic smile. "You will need to show us that you are worthy," Hussein had replied. "Then we might do business."

And so it began, he thought.

Over the ensuing few months, The Watcher had demonstrated his trustworthiness to Delilah Hussein and her team. Ten months ago, he had carried out various missions, including killing two enemies of The Simoon.

Now, the man in the dark suit smiled as he jettisoned a plume of blue smoke through his nostrils. His eyes studied the quiet, sunlit, Newport News street before him, refocusing and relegating his memory to the past.

The pharmacist's success was crucial to The Watcher's mission and his handlers. The Watcher's respect and admiration for the pharmacist had grown over these past months. Jason Rodgers was a man of principle and justice.

The Watcher inhaled through his nose and let the smoke out slowly through pursed lips.

Time to move! I can't be too far away if things go south!

After checking his watch, The Watcher exited the Caddy, crossed the street, and ducked into the space between houses. In the back-yard, he climbed the steps and made his way to the back door. He peered through the dirty glass, looking and listening. It was then that the image of Jason Rodgers and the other man disappeared. The phone went dark.

℞

They were inside now, standing in the tiny foyer.

Jason stared into the shrunken demonic face of Tattoo Man.

He had no recollection of pulling it from his belt. It had been an instinctive, automatic action. The Smith and Wesson was leveled at the man who'd tried to kill him in the cell in the Williamsburg Regional Jail.

"You've come to pick up the keys."

It was a statement holding no malice or anxiety, no hidden mean-ing. He was simply acknowledging a business transaction.

Tattoo Man retreated, motioning for Jason to move deeper into the dwelling. "You can put that away. I have no desire to harm you. My job is to simply make sure you get these."

Reaching into his trouser pocket, he produced a keychain from which three keys dangled. One appeared to be to a car key with a large black bow adorned with push buttons for unlocking and locking the doors. The other two keys were silver with flat bows.

Tattoo Man's massive bulk had shrunk since their encounter in Williamsburg. He wore a wife-beater t-shirt and faded jeans over a pair of black running shoes. His head was still clean shaven displaying the incensed drawing of a dragon with drops of blood suspended between the eyes.

"If it's all the same to you, I prefer to keep my friend here as part of the conversation," Jason said, waggling the Smith and Wesson.

"Whatever."

Keeping a safe distance, Jason inched farther into the house. Tattoo Man retreated into the same living area where Winstead had drawn his last breath. Jason waggled the gun again.

"Stop!" Jason demanded.

Jason glanced around, looking for signs of danger. The tiny foyer split the front of the house into an open living area and dining room. The layout had not changed. The living room was small with distressed, dark, hardwood floors and dotted with three throw rugs on which sat a nondescript sofa and a well-worn recliner. The third rug, tattered and frayed, was spread across the small stretch of hardwood leading from the foyer to the living room.

The dining room also appeared the same. He couldn't be sure. Jason had a hard time remembering. The last time he was here he was so focused on its occupant, Douglas Winstead, he had not given the décor much notice. The distressed hardwood from the living room ran under a small, rickety dining room table. Hanging from the ceiling was a heavy, lead crystal chandelier, with dangling arrow-like pieces of glass. The piece was impressive but out of place in this shithole. Jason did not remember it.

"You alone?" Jason asked.

"Yeah, are you?"

Jason smiled. "It's just me. What happened to you? We have unfinished business. Show me the rest of the house," he demanded.

At gunpoint, Tattoo Man led Jason through the small, two-story structure. Ten minutes later, satisfied they were in fact the only people in the house, they returned downstairs.

"I told you. I don't want any trouble. I'm outta the racket," Tattoo Man declared at the foot of the stairs.

"I don't remember the chandelier being here," Jason observed.

Tattoo Man looked at the glass monstrosity. "What the fuck kinda question is that? You from Home and Garden Magazine? I've been here a couple of weeks. It was here when I got here. If you want to buy the place, talk to somebody else."

"Shut up," Jason said

Tattoo Man showed Jason his hands. "I just want to get this over with. I don't want no trouble."

His words sounded stilted. His jaw moved in an unnatural fashion when he spoke.

"You've lost weight. Stopped working out and using the juice?"

Tattoo Man spread his arms, showing Jason his shrunken physique. "This is all your doing."

"Excuse me?"

"You shattered my jaw, asshole. Remember? After you kicked my ass in jail, I was taken to Williamsburg Community. The left side of my face had been shattered. The doc said there were too many pieces to put back together." He ran his fingers along his jaw. "Had to have three surgeries. I got a titanium rod in there now. I set off metal detectors. I lost forty pounds, never got it back. Haven't eaten right since. Still trying to pay off the doctor bills. That's why I agreed to give you these keys. They're paying me. Not that I had much of a choice."

Jason smirked. "You're still getting paid to deal with me, huh? First, you tried to off me. Now, you're delivering keys. Don't expect sympathy."

"I guess I'd be feeling the same way if I was you."

"Let's get down to business," Jason commanded.

"Let's go in the living room."

Tattoo Man led Jason into the small sitting area. The furniture had changed. It was still inexpensive second-hand stuff but arranged much the same as before. Jason's eye went to the window of the side wall.

Of course, the glass had been replaced. But Jason's mind couldn't repress images of flying glass, bone, and blood. He paused and collected himself.

"What's wrong with you?" Tattoo Man asked. "You look like you seen a ghost"

Jason motioned for the assassin to move to the sofa as Jason moved to the threadbare recliner in the corner.

"A man was killed in this very room." Jason said. The recliner was in about the same spot he and Walter Waterhouse had found the false panel in the floor. "Yeah, I am seeing ghosts."

"Do you mind?" Tattoo Man said, stopping Jason's descent and pointing at the chair. "I'm more comfortable there. It's better for my back."

Jason wrinkled his lips and thought for a moment. "Fine." Jason backed away and let him have the seat.

Jason sat across from him on the far-right end of the sofa, not in line of sight of the window.

The cushions were shot. He sank farther than anticipated. He held the gun in his right hand, rested the stock on his knee, and trained it on his host.

"I got to take a piss." Tattoo Man started to rise.

"Stop right there! Sit down! You can urinate when I leave."

Tattoo Man sat back down. His eyes riveted on the handgun.

"So, William Luther," Jason said. "Let's talk."

"You know my name?" Luther replied with surprise. He shook his head. "What do you want to talk about?"

"Where you been? I tried to track you down. But I could never find you. Having your name would have helped. Why are you not in prison, William Luther?"

"You just said my name. So how *did* you get it?"

Jason was unable to locate Luther's name in the years since the tattooed Luther had attacked him. Every discreet inquiry had been met by a dead end. He'd spent most of his efforts tracking Clyde Hutton, the man responsible for hiring Luther, and planning the guard's demise. He wanted to extract Luther's name from Hutton. Luther had been a secondary issue . . . until now.

"It was given to me by a friend of yours. Clyde Hutton."

"The guard at the jail?"

Jason nodded. "He gave it to me last night, about ten seconds before he died." Jason raised the weapon and pointed it center mass at Luther's chest.

"I was in jail. Spent a year at Greensville," Luther croaked.

"I never read about it in the papers."

"I had a good lawyer. I pled it out. Part of the deal was that the agreement was sealed. I didn't want no one coming after me."

"Only a year?"

"It would have been longer, but like I said, I had a good lawyer. Cut a deal with the Commonwealth's attorney. They wanted a name. I gave it to them."

"Who's name?"

"Clyde Hutton." Luther licked his dry lips and swallowed hard. "You kill him?"

Jason smiled but did not reply.

"You gonna kill me?" Luther said in a near whisper.

"You certainly deserve it."

"Life's a bitch. Then you marry one," Luther quipped, regaining some composure.

"Do you even know why you were hired to kill me?"

"No, and I don't give a shit. The money was good. That's all I know."

"How many folks have you killed for money?"

"More than one, less than five. Can't say I recall. Don't matter much anymore. I'm outta the business. Don't have the body or the nerves for it."

Jason could not let the issue of the money out of his head. The fact that these guys could kill someone for any sum of money rankled him. "How much was I worth?"

Luther smirked and shrugged. "Why not? Ten large . . . and I never got pinched 'til I failed to off you!" The former killer smiled with a warped sense of pride.

"I'm worth a lot more than that. I ought to shoot you just for being an idiot."

"Well do it if you're gonna do it."

"Who hired you?"

"Hutton did."

"Who was he working for?"

"Don't know."

Luther's right hand slipped between his thigh and the arm of the chair.

"Hands on your knees. Now!"

Luther lifted his hand and showed his palms. "Easy man. It's cool. I don't want no trouble, I told you." He lowered a hand onto each knee.

"Who are you working for now?"

"Don't know."

Jason aimed the weapon at the drop of tattooed blood between Luther's eyes. "Bullshit!"

Shifting the gun from his right to left hand, Jason reached into the zippered breast pocket of his North Face jacket and removed a long cylinder. He screwed it onto the barrel of the weapon. Luther's eyes widened.

"I don't know his name. It's a dude. Tall, maybe six-two. Wore a dark suit and a hat. Drove a black Caddy. I met him two weeks ago. He showed up with the keys and the cash. Said that you would be by within the next couple of weeks to get them. I just had to make sure you got them. Matter of fact, he called me yesterday to tell me you'd be by today."

Jason hesitated. Hutton, and now Luther, had mentioned the man in the dark suit with the black hat. The man in the ambulance flashing a badge wore a black fedora.

"You still with me, Chief?" Luther demanded, seeing Jason's eyes become unfocused.

"How . . . how much money?"

"I don't remember."

Jason lowered the weapon and fired.

℞

From the bushes, The Watcher tapped the cursed phone against his leg, trying to get the image from inside the house back on his screen. The two men had approached the back door, nearly catching him by surprise. He spied William Luther making his way into the kitchen. The Watcher scampered behind some overgrown bushes for cover as the back door opened.

Luther had come outside and descended two steps, allowing Jason Rodgers a look. Apparently satisfied, they retreated inside once again. The Watcher remained out of sight for several minutes, fiddling with the malfunctioning phone.

Unable to retrieve the closed-circuit feeds, he had moved again to the back door. He thought he heard a muffled report, a thump, followed by a sharp, surprised exclamation.

℞

"For chrissake," Luther exclaimed, "I told you, chill out."

A round had ripped through the lower front of the recliner between Luther's legs. Luther slithered higher into the chair, using his arms to elevate his body. A small plume of stuffing erupted from the hole and still floated about from the shot, which had occurred thirty seconds before.

"How much?" Jason demanded

Luther swallowed. "Five large."

"The price went down?"

As if sensing Jason's displeasure at the paltry number, Luther tried to justify it. "I didn't have much choice. It was not negotiable. The guy pulled a gun and said if I didn't do it he'd kill me. Besides, it's just keys."

"Not a nice feeling, is it?"

Luther shook his head in agreement.

"Why are you living here? If I were you, I would have hightailed it out of here. I wouldn't want to run into the guy I tried to kill. Too risky."

"After I got out of the Big House, I was living up in Toano. Keeping to myself, staying out of trouble. Working in a tattoo parlor. But this guy in the Caddy found me somehow, someway. Said I needed to come down here and live until you came to pick up the keys . . . or me and my family would die. I'm getting the hell outta Dodge as soon as you walk out that door. You'll never see me again."

"I should kill you right here, right now," Jason said.

"Like I said. Do it if you're gonna." Jason watched Luther's Adam's apple bobbing. Sweat erupted on his forehead.

Jason raised the weapon once more and, aiming for Luther's chest, cocked the club-shaped hammer.

CHAPTER 27

"Any changes with our guests?" Delilah Hussein demanded. She and Oliver were now back on their compound on St. Barts.

Charlie, the senior man on the dayshift guard detail, shook his head.

"Non, Madame. They are chained as instructed in the wine cellar.

Two two-man teams will keep twelve-hour shifts. Pierre and I will take the day shift and two of my most trusted men will take the nightshift."

A wild-eyed, monster of a man, Charlie's stringy, dirty blonde hair hung below his shoulders and his face was perpetually covered with a growth of beard. His thick arms stretched the sleeves of his sweat-stained black t-shirt. The skin beneath his eyes hung in baggy bulges, as did the skin under his chin. He looked like a vagrant. But she knew his skills as a soldier of fortune had served her well over the years. Hussein estimated him to be about one 190 centimeters, or six three in American inches.

"Most excellent, Charlie. Keep a close eye on them. If things go as planned, we will only need them for twelve to fifteen hours. Then we can dispose of them."

"Oui, Miss Delilah," Charlie countered. "Pierre has already dug les tombes."

"Graves? I did not order you to dig graves."

"I thought it would save time. They are in the southern, deserted quadrant."

Hussein glared at the Frenchman, moving her head side to side in a displeased manner. She turned to Oliver for a reaction. He provided none.

"I do not pay you to think, *Monsieur*," she continued. "I pay you to follow orders. If no orders are given, you do nothing. Comprends-tu?" *Do you understand?*

Charlie lowered his head. "Oui, Madame."

"Have Pierre fill in les tombes. We will dispose of les corps at sea. Then we will burn the buildings. As soon as this mission is over, we will be leaving for our next destination."

She waved Charlie away. He bowed his head ever so slightly, then departed. Hussein turned to Oliver.

"Did you take the photographs of the boy and the woman?"

"Oui."

"Are they properly secured?" Hussein asked, not sure she believed the scoundrel Charlie.

"I checked on them *personnellement*, Madam Delilah. They will not be going anywhere. And they are in extreme discomfort. They will be fed and allowed to use the bathroom shortly."

"Très bon!"

Hussein checked the computer screen, studying a small blip on it. She looked up at Oliver.

"Did you talk to Charlie about what is expected?"

"I did. There will not be a repeat of the last time."

"Do you believe him? It seems he has a hard time following orders . . . or at the very least, doing things not ordered."

"Charlie is a well-trained operative. He understands any slip-ups will not be tolerated. He has trained most of the men on the compound. He is very good at what he does."

"He may be well-trained but he has a weakness. If he repeats his actions, he will not have to worry about making any more mistakes again . . . ever. I want you to personally check on our guests and the guards as needed."

"Understood. I am making sure he is taking his medication."

Hussein motioned for Oliver to sit beside her. She pointed at the computer screen. "What is going on with the pharmacist?"

℞

"You better explain this minute . . . and it better be good."

Peter opened his mouth to respond to his wife's stern directive, not knowing what he was going to say. She fired another question at him before any sound escaped his lips.

"Where are you?"

"I'm at Jason's."

After watching Jason drive away in his Hummer, Peter had returned to the house, trying to figure where Jason was going. Jason had never told him the address where he was to meet the character he was supposed to kill. The cell phone marked number one on the counter offered no help. The address was burned into the lid of the coffin . . . and the coffins were in his Hummer. Jason had taken the second cell phone, the one with the order to kill on it.

Peter had not been able to find transportation. He knew no one in Jason's neighborhood. A stranger asking to borrow a car would only result in a call to the cops. So, Peter did the only thing he knew to do. He called his most trusted employee at the gun shop and asked him to pick him up. As he waited for his ride, he'd called his wife to let her know he would not be home right away. In fact, he didn't know when he'd be home again.

"What are you two doing?" Lisa Rodgers demanded.

"It's complicated."

"It always is with that brother of yours. You said this type of thing would not happen again. You promised me!"

"He needs my help.

"That's it. That's all I get. We've been married for fifteen years and all you can say is 'He needs my help'? The last time he called you like this, you ended up shot and in the hospital. Is he being stalked again? Is he going to be arrested again for murder? And will you be sideways damage in the process?"

He could be, Peter thought.

Lisa Rodgers was an intelligent and attractive woman. Peter sensed her frustration. No, he felt her frustration. It was short-circuiting her brain.

"It's called *collateral* damage, honey."

Peter forced a chuckle. *If she knew the whole story,* he thought, *her head would explode.*

The former marine rubbed the scar bisecting his eyebrow as his wife bellowed. It was not an unwarranted rant. Peter had been in harm's way two years ago when he and Jason nearly died. Peter was shot in his own home.

In a moment of weakness in the hospital room in Suffolk, an hour before two assassins had killed a police officer and tried to kill Jason, Peter, and John Palmer, Peter had confided to his wife the major details of the adventure. It had been a mistake then, and he regretted it even more now. Lisa had hounded her husband ever since, wanting to know everywhere he went, what he was doing . . . and if it involved Jason in anyway.

When Jason called yesterday, asking for help after crashing his Mustang, Lisa harangued him for fifteen minutes. Peter had simply walked out, refusing to answer her questions.

She must be going out of her skull.

"I can hear the tone in your voice. Are you laughing at me?"

"No, Lisa. I just need you to understand. I need to help him. He's my brother, honey."

"Don't you honey me! Is this like it was last time? Does it involve the presidents again?"

Peter had no trouble picturing the look on her face. He decided to come clean, a little bit.

"Lisa, it's Michael. He's been kidnapped. We're trying to get him back."

"Oh, my God!" Lisa sobbed and wailed all at the same time. "It is happening again, isn't it?"

"I'll call you as soon as I can. You can't say anything to anyone. Do you hear me! I have to go. I need to make some calls. I love you."

Peter ended the call before she could say anything more. He needed to make another call. Consumed by anger that he'd been duped by his brother, Peter bristled. Though he fumed about Jason's duplicity, he understood why he'd ditched him. He wanted to keep Peter away from trouble, to protect him. But, it was not in his nature to sit idle.

I need to get to him!

$$\text{R}_{\text{X}}$$

Chrissie's words echoed in Jason's ears.

If you live in the past, Jason, it will end up killing you!

She had uttered those words in the months after he left the hospital and was still dealing with revenge issues. Chrissie thought Jason had gotten past them. At least she thought he had. He'd done a good job of hiding them from her.

Jason's could feel the muscles in his face twitching. He'd cocked the Hammer on the Smith and Wesson. He'd fired one shot into the chair. Luther seemed unfazed. The urge to pull the trigger battled with his conscience. In the months after the assassinations, Jason hinted to Chrissie that he wanted to seek out the men who had been responsible for his near death in jail. She begged him to reconsider. *"Don't leave me again, Jason. I want you back!"*

Jason promised her he would forget about the past. But eventually, he broke that promise.

Jason lowered the gun.

"I guess you paid your price in more ways than one. So just give me the keys and I'll be on my way," Jason explained.

"I put them back in my pocket. So I gotta stand up."

"Do it . . . slowly."

Luther rose and pushed his hand into his trouser pocket, extracting the three keys. He held them up, rattling them like a trophy.

"Put them on the floor and move into the corner behind your chair."

Luther squatted and placed the keys on the hardwood floor. He backed up and stood behind the recliner.

"Don't move."

Jason dropped off the couch onto his knees. He scooted toward the keys, keeping his gaze and the gun on Luther. Jason reached out and patted the floor, keeping his eyes on Luther. Unable to find them, his eyes left Luther in order to locate the keychain.

As his fingers wrapped around them, a darting movement caught his attention. Thinking Luther was on the attack, Jason recoiled, expecting a blow. He lifted his gaze and looked toward the movement.

Luther had leaned over the back of the recliner and was reaching into a hidden pocket in the arm. Jason's weight shifted backward. He pulled the trigger out of reflex. Another round burped from the suppressed barrel.

℞

Her actions, words, and emotions toward Jason in the last twenty-four hours were miniscule and inconsequential now. Yesterday, her relationship with Jason was falling apart. But now, that disintegrating romance was the impetus she used to try to keep from becoming consumed by fear. Thinking about her troubled relationship with Jason was keeping her mind off where she was and who was holding her.

Fear and the questions assaulted her. The two issues played ping-pong in her mind, creating a confusing maelstrom.

Was he following someone? How could I have misjudged him so badly?

But her mind would not cooperate. Like a flash of lightning, panic shot through her. Panic fueled by fear. And different questions ravaged her.

Why was she here? Where was Jason? Was he looking for her? Did he even know she had been taken?

She was on her knees on a hard, rough floor, leaning forward, her hands shackled behind her, elevated away from her back. The chains leading to the wall were taut and rigid, pulling at her wrists. She was unable to sit back on her haunches. When she tried, all her weight was placed on the shackles around her wrists, cutting into the skin. Her arms felt as if they'd break. Someone wanted her in great discomfort. And they had succeeded. Her muscles screamed. Her head pounded. The spot where they had inserted the needle in her neck still burned. Whatever chemical they injected into her had worn off and left a heavy hangover in its wake.

Chrissie heard the scraping along the floor again. She was growing accustomed to the presence of the vermin in the cell with her. At the moment, the rats were the least of her worries. More questions pummeled her as she set aside her physical pain as best she could.

Did Jason know she was missing? Had he even come home last night? Would she ever see him again? Was he worried about her?

Chrissie hoped he was looking for her. Then another thought struck her, sending another more potent wave of panic shooting through her.

Had Jason been taken too?

CHAPTER 28

The round missed, burying itself in the wall behind Luther's head.

Luther had ducked, causing his hand to withdraw from the pocket in the chair. He recovered, reaching in again. Jason, ready to fire once more, paused when Chrissie's words echoed in his ears.

Don't leave me again . . .

Now, Luther bent over the chair and reached into it again. He lifted something out of the pocket. Regaining his focus, Jason launched himself at Luther and the top of the tattooed head with the exposed, coiled dragon.

Luther swung his head around as Jason connected. His free hand grabbed at Jason's gun, clutching his wrist. His other mitt emerged from the pocket of the chair with a massive handgun.

Jason, in turn, clutched at Luther's wrist, stopping him from leveling the weapon. Their faces inches apart, the two men grunted and struggled in a waltz-like death dance. Luther pushed, Jason pushed back. Jason responded with a surge of strength, forcing Luther into the wall.

They wavered back and forth, sweat dripping from their faces, grasping each other by the wrist, their hands clutching weapons, their arms flailing in arcs, trying to bring weapons to bear, their strained efforts halted by the other man's hands and arms.

Jason pressed his chest into Luther's. The tattooed man, though smaller, still possessed enormous strength and countered Jason's surges.

Jason's strength and determination eventually won out, pressing Luther into the wall, forcing Luther's gun down. Luther's barrel was now pointed at the floor while Jason's Smith and Wesson twisted closer to the assassin's face.

Luther turned away. Ignoring the searing pain in his wounded arm, Jason pushed the advantage, his weapon a few degrees from its target.

If you live in the past, it will kill you.

Chrissie's words shouted in his ears, giving him another pause. His initiative faltered. Luther seized the opportunity. His head whipped forward, the temple connecting with Jason's cheek. White shards of light filled Jason's field of vision. A loud crack filled the space around Jason's head as it whipped to the side. His grip on Luther's arm slackened. He fell away, his body separating from Luther's.

An instant later, Luther's knee pressed on his chest. Then Luther planted a boot on Jason's sternum. Jason was catapulted through space. The whoosh of air past his head and the roller-coaster-like sensation of falling consumed his senses. The gun was out of his hand now, flying behind him. Landing on a throw rug, he slid across the hardwood floor, coming to a stop against the opposite wall.

With his left eye closed and stinging from the head butt, Jason could see only through his right. He saw the lower half of Luther's body approach, striding toward him with the hand cannon clutched at his thigh. The weapon moved up and out of sight as Luther stepped onto the crumpled rug.

Jason grabbed the cloth throw, rolling over and away from the barrel that was no doubt aimed at his head. He yanked the rug with all his might.

Luther's weight gave way. Luther's weapon discharged, the report pounding his ears.

℞

People experience varying levels of fear during the course of a lifetime. The severity and intensity of that angst depend on the causative stimuli, ranging from the simple anxiety of being reprimanded by one's boss, to the heart-skipping helplessness of your car careening out of control, to the life-stopping news that a loved one has died. Over the course of decades, most people will experience the whole gamut.

Thirteen-year-old Michael Rodgers had experienced all of them in the last twenty four hours. Awoken in the dead of night, his alarmed curiosity had morphed into electric anxiety as whispering voices called to him from outside his bedroom. Gut-wrenching panic ensued as a needle was plunged into his neck. He trembled before everything went black.

He woke kneeling, with his arms chained behind him, his body stiff and aching. Since regaining consciousness, he'd remained as still and as quiet as possible. He only moved when the agony in his muscles became unbearable. The discomfort reared in spurts, forcing him to wriggle in place.

When he wasn't trying to get comfortable, he listened. At that moment, Michael realized there was really no such thing as complete silence. It was amazing how noisy a quiet room could be. Wind blew outside, buffeting the walls. The creaking of wood cut the quiet. Tiny creatures scurried around the room.

Michael shook. Not from cold. At first, terror consumed him. Eventually, he depleted his ability to sustain fear. He decided to make the best of this problem. His father had always told him courage was doing what was necessary despite your fear. What was necessary right now was to determine where he was and who had kidnapped him.

The sound of a large keychain rattled from beyond a wall somewhere in the distance. Muffled voices spoke in a foreign tongue, followed by the metallic clack of a key inserted into the lock. A door crashed open behind and above him.

Thick booted footsteps descended a short set of stairs. Something metal was set down beside him. The presence of other humans floated nearby. Their soft breaths and whispers brushed about. The whoosh of clothing preceded a push of air.

Someone had stooped to his level. Then the whispered, accented voice filled with a manly scent.

"Do not make a sound or I will cut your throat."

A sharp, long piece of cold metal touched his neck. He stiffened, realizing it was a very large knife.

A forceful hand removed the cloth from around his head. He reflexively spit out the ball of material crammed into his mouth. The blindfold remained in place.

"Open your mouth!"

Michael hesitated but complied, opening his lips a fraction. A warm, soft piece of bread was rammed into his mouth. He chewed slowly, enjoying the ability to move his jaw freely. A second piece was shoved in before he'd finished the first. A plastic bottle was placed to his lips. Cold water spilled past his tongue, mixing with the masticated bread. Michael gagged, but choked down most of the water.

He managed to speak. "I have to go to the bathroom."

More words were spoken in a language he didn't understand. He thought it might be French. Seconds later, the chains securing him relaxed and he was lifted to his feet. Strong arms hoisted him up the stairs. Michael heard a second male voice speaking to someone else in the room.

Though he did not understand the words, he understood their meaning. They were commands, the same commands that had just been given to him. There was someone else being held with him. A muted response followed, then a high-pitched, muffled shriek.

When he was outside, the soft, warm breeze hit the exposed skin of his face. Michael felt as if he were being cleansed, even though he was dragged a distance over rough earth. In the distance, Michael heard something he recognized. Something familiar to him: pounding surf. Just like home.

Hands manipulated his jeans. They were tugged to his ankles.

"Go!" the voice commanded.

Michael peed where he stood. When he was done, the hands began to lift his jeans.

"I have to take a dump, too!"

"Qu'est-ce que c'est? What is this word dump?"

"I have to take a crap! You know . . . poop."

"Merde," the voice swore. "Vous êtes un cul!" *You're an ass!*

It wasn't a lie. His bowels had been touchy since he'd been taken. But he wanted to enjoy some of this half-freedom as long as possible.

He was moved again. His back was leaned against a tree with his legs angled a few feet from the trunk. Pressing his back against the rough bark, Michael relieved himself.

When Michael was finished, his guard put his pants back on and he was escorted to the cell. Michael heard a key inserted into the lock on the heavy door. It swung open and crashed against a wall. They walked down the stairs. His captor recoiled as Michael's foot touched the sandy floor.

"Charlie . . . Charlie, que se passe??" the guard called out to his partner. *What's happening?*

Quickly, Michael was pushed back into his spot and chained to the wall.

The cloth was stuffed back into his mouth and the gag tightened around his head. He listened as his guard tended to his partner. Hushed, clipped words were exchanged in French.

Scuffling followed, then harsh unintelligible words. Some sort of threat had been leveled at the other person being held with him. Fear welled in Michael. Not for himself but for the woman with him.

You can't tell much from a muffled shriek. But there could be no doubt that that person was a woman. Only a woman would make a sound like that. It could only be one person, he told himself. He would have bet his entire collection of baseball cards on the fact.

They had taken him. They had probably taken her also.

Michael knew what he needed to do next. He needed to communicate with her. He needed to let his mother know he was here . . . with her. Then they would figure out what to do.

When the guards left, Michael worked his tongue slowly, determinedly, against the cottony, acrid cloth balled in his mouth.

He needed to talk to his mother.

℞

She'd heard it plenty of times. And there was no time to waste.

Mildred Williams had grown up around firearms her whole life. Her father had been an avid hunter. He owned an assortment of rifles and handguns. She learned to shoot at a young age.

When she moved out on her own many years ago, she witnessed a shooting in the East End. She'd lived in the projects then. Drug deals were weekly fare. Gunfire a monthly occurrence.

That was then. She lived on 65th Street now. Crime rates were lower here. But the gunshot reminded of her days in the ghetto.

When someone got shot, living or dying meant getting them to the hospital quickly.

One shot meant more would follow.

She lifted the eighties-style handset off the wall and dialed.

"911. What's your emergency?"

"There's been a shooting on my street."

$$\text{R}_{\text{X}}$$

After the shot missed, Luther landed on his back, thumping to the floor. Jason whipped his body, arcing his legs at the fallen man, kicking at Luther.

His shin connected with the gun and hand. His kick followed through, striking Luther's face. Now, Luther's weapon went airborne, rattling along the floor into the dining area near the small dining room table.

Luther scrambled after it. Jason kicked Luther again, this time in the flank, slowing the desperate man. Luther, on all fours now, paddled toward his weapon. Jason reached out and grabbed Luther's jersey by the collar, pulling him back. Both men scrambled toward the gun. In concert with the sound of tearing fabric, Luther dragged Jason into the dining area.

The gun lay at the foot of one of the legs of the rickety table.

Luther flailed an elbow twice at Jason's head. The first missed. The second connected with his chest. Jason grunted, refusing to release his grip. The pharmacist countered with two futile punches, hitting Luther in the shoulder. He yanked the jersey hard, stopping Luther's progress for a moment. Fabric shredded in Jason's hands, leaving him holding half a shirt. Luther began to dart away. Jason leapt, wrapping both arms around Luther's neck.

With Luther's progress halted, Jason rammed Luther's head into the floor and vaulted over his back, stretching for the gun. He could see it clearly now. Walking to Luther's .357 Magnum with two fingers, he coaxed it into his hands. Jason rolled onto his back and started to level the weapon between his knees toward where Luther should be.

As he was bringing it to bear, Luther's large hand pushed it aside and the criminal lurched over Jason. Jason raised a knee and used

Luther's momentum to launch him over. Luther collided with the table and a chair, knocking them askew. The shaky table skidded sideways. Two of its chairs toppled.

Somehow, Luther recovered, and in a quick wrestling reversal, Jason found himself staring up at William Luther. The shrunken, tattoo-laden man was atop Jason, pinning his arms and torso to the hardwood. The gun was still in Jason's right hand but pinned by Luther's left knee.

Jason's free left hand flailed at Luther's head. Luther tried to grab it. In doing so, his weight shifted, allowing Jason to free his right hand and the gun. Jason swung the weapon at Luther's head, connecting with Tattoo Man's cheek and face. Blood erupted on his skin.

Luther grabbed Jason's gun hand once more, twisting the weapon free. It toppled from both their grips and landed a few feet from Jason's shoulder. With the gun removed, both Luther's hands dove for Jason's throat, the fingers closing around it.

The wild, menacing glare in Luther's eyes coincided with the pressure growing in Jason's eyes and head. The murderer's strong hands closed off his windpipe. He tried to gulp in air. But none found its way to his lungs.

Jason's hands went to the vice-like mitts, trying to pry them away. For an instant, a trivial amount of oxygen slipped into his lungs as Jason was able to relieve the pressure momentarily. Just as quickly, it closed again.

Jason attempted to elevate his chin and pull the hands away. But Luther only closed the fleshy noose tighter. He tried bucking him off. He dug his fingernails into Luther's skin as Jason flailed at the head and face with one hand. His vision turned red.

Time was running out.

The faint wail of sirens reverberated through his fading consciousness.

Chapter 29

Chrissie had been placed back on her knees with her hands behind her, elevated to the point of pain. Her breaths came hard and fast. She tried to catch her breath and block the episode from her mind. But her mind refused to cooperate, replaying the thwarted assault.

Minutes ago, she'd heard footfalls on the steps. The heavy door slammed closed with a wooden thunk spiced by the clank of metal. She tensed, cocking her head, listening.

Someone else in the room with her had been forced to eat and then ushered out. They had spoken in a whisper. *I have to go to the bathroom!*

She wasn't alone! Was it Jason?

She couldn't tell. The words were soft, barely audible. She had only a second to contemplate these questions. The guard's presence, the filthy, manly musk, filled the air around her.

"Who's there?" she asked.

"Je m'appelle Charlie," the gruff voice replied. *My name is Charlie.* The low-pitched words were slow and inviting, filled with lustful insinuation.

"Do you need to use *ze* bathroom?"

"Yes."

The chains holding her slackened. A rough pair of hands lifted her to her feet. The man stood in front of her, very close. His chest touched the tip of her breasts. Chrissie breathed his alcohol- and tobacco-saturated breath. A cold shudder passed through her. She stopped breathing to avoid sucking the unpleasant stench into her lungs.

Finally, she exhaled. "If you don't let me pee, it's going to get very messy in here."

The man stopped. Chrissie sensed her captor ogling her.

The guard walked her deeper inside the building. Her foot hit something. She stumbled. The guard lifted her roughly to her feet. They turned a corner. Chrissie's arm hit a doorway. They had entered another room. A vinegary odor hung in the air. Inside, Charlie stopped her with a hand on her chest.

"Turn around," he commanded.

Chrissie obeyed, fearing what would happen next. The guard's hand reached for her jeans, unsnapping them. Ripping them to her ankles, exposing a thin pair of panties, the guard slid them past her thighs, making sure his rough hands caressed her skin.

Chrissie heard him lift something and place it on the floor with a wooden thud. A deeper acidic, vinegary stench mixed with the ripe, disgusting fetor of excrement, filling her nostrils. Chrissie wanted to vomit.

Charlie then placed a hand under each of her armpits and hoisted her into the air with amazing ease. He pushed her backward. Chrissie's naked butt landed on something hard, round, and hollow.

"An old rusted wine barrel. Do your business. And be quick about it!"

She thought about asking for some privacy but knew it would be futile. Chrissie peed in the barrel. When she was done, Charlie pulled up her panties and jeans, fondling her as much as possible.

He dragged her back to her holding station, one of Charlie's arms reaching behind her. The hand squeezed a fistful of her hair, yanking her head backward, elevating her chin. Chrissie yelped.

His other hand touched her near her waist under her shirt, moving higher. The skin of the fingers and palm, rough and calloused, scraped her sweaty skin. As the hand inched higher, nearing her breasts, Chrissie's ire swelled.

Charlie moved his face into the crook of her neck. The stubble on his cheek cut her below the ear. Chrissie held her breath again.

"Mon petit," he whispered, "vous êtes très troublant. Ton beau est un homme fortune!" *You are very, very sexy, my sweet. Your boyfriend is a lucky man!*

The hand inched higher, cupping her breast through the bra. As he began to push his fingers inside the fabric and touch her nipple, Chrissie boiled over. She jerked her knee, hard and fast, into his groin. The guard's lungs expelled air into her face. He released his grip and collapsed in a heap at her feet. He lay there groaning. Still blindfolded, Chrissie envisioned him curled into a ball with his hands cupped over his manhood.

"Garce," he whispered. *Bitch.*

Chrissie prepared herself for what was to follow.

"Bring it on, Frenchie," she said, kicking at him. Her foot connected with soft flesh, landing hard in his gut. "If you want have your way with me, you're going to earn it."

His hand reached out and grabbed her ankle. That was when the heavy door crashed open. The attack had been interrupted.

℞

His eyelids began to close. Images began to swim through a half curtain. Darkness closed in. Deprived of oxygen, Jason's mind flashed a runaway, out-of-sequence slide show of the mistakes in his life . . .

Chrissie's tear-stained face on the park bench when he left her . . .

The sight of Jenny walking away, two suitcases in hand the day they'd decided to get divorced . . .

Thomas Pettigrew's face as he told him Jason had made a fatal drug error . . .

Chrissie being tackled by the intruder in his house . . .

Chrissie lying unconscious on his living room floor . . .

The body of one of the attacker's lying in a crimson halo on the living room floor . . .

The gun lying near him . . .

Delilah Hussein's face talking to him about a great opportunity . . .

Jason's mind froze on the image of a gun lying on the floor of his house after Chrissie was attacked.

The gun!

Jason tugged at the hands constricting his throat, albeit with less force. He managed to turn his drooping eyes to the weapon on the dark wood a few feet to his right. The .357 Magnum!

Grab it!

Doing so meant releasing his grip on Luther's hands. It meant letting go of the source of his impending death. He would have to go against every human survival instinct.

A few seconds more and it would be too late, he would lose consciousness, then die . . .

It was his last . . . and only option.

Jason released his grip, whipping his hand out. Luther, thinking Jason was trying to hit him, turned his head allowing Jason to miss. Luther's weight shifted. A gust of delicious air inflated Jason's lungs.

Realizing it wasn't a blow, Luther closed his fingers around Jason's larynx once more.

Jason's fingers slapped the hard black metal of the gun. He tapped his hand against the floorboards, trying to grasp it. The weapon spun but landed in his palm.

As his oxygen reserves became depleted again, the pressure in his head and neck once more became almost unbearable. Holding it by the barrel, Jason walked his hand down the gun's shaft, finally clutching the stock. His index finger found the trigger housing.

Then the trigger . . .

Luther's eyes darted left, seeing Jason bringing the gun to bear. He removed one hand from Jason's neck. Jason gasped in another torrent of oxygen. Luther lunged for the weapon but only managed to clutch Jason's forearm.

Jason wrapped his free arm around Luther's neck, pulling him away from the weapon. Luther managed to keep Jason's arm straight, not allowing him to bring the weapon around. Jason could only flex his wrist with the gun in it as he wrapped his opposite arm around Luther's neck, wrenching it tight.

They struggled again. Luther lay atop him, stretching for the hand and Jason's weapon. Jason wrenched him back onto his chest. Luther possessed the advantage. As he wrestled with Luther, Jason's eyes took in the ceiling.

And he saw a way to put an end to this battle.

℞

What the hell is taking so long?

Peter slammed a heavy fist on Jason's counter.

He had called one of his employees, Tim, from the gun shop over an hour ago. Desperate and despite being a stranger, he'd tried the neighbors. The elderly woman across the street did not answer his repeated bell ringing. The houses down the street had no cars in the driveways. Everyone was at work. If anyone was at home, they weren't answering the door.

He cursed for what seemed like the hundredth time.

I should have known Jason would try something. You were duped, marine!

Peter studied his phone, willing it to ring.

After several calls, Peter managed to get a message through to Detective John Palmer of the Newport News Police Department. But he had yet to return his call. Palmer had been involved in the mess two years ago.

Peter had leveled with the cop in his message. Jason was in trouble with the people who'd planned the assassination attempts. If he were Palmer, he would stay miles away from anything to do with this. Peter hoped Palmer was not that smart.

A horn tooted. Peter ran to the driveway and climbed into Tim Baker's used Ford Escort.

"What the hell took you so long?"

"Traffic on the JRB. Where to?"

"Police headquarters in Newport News," Peter demanded. For some strange reason, the former marine felt like he was forgetting something. He closed the door, leaving the first cell phone resting on the torn piece of paper on which Jason had scrawled the password.

℞

Jason squeezed the trigger. A round thumped into the ceiling. A shower of powdery bits sprinkled the two men. The hole was a foot to the right of the chandelier mount. Once more, Jason tugged Luther back on top of him, wrapping his legs around the tattooed criminal, trying to hold him still. Luther clutched at the skin of Jason's arm, reaching for the Magnum.

Jason readjusted his aim and fired again. The round moved closer to the fixture and again rained dust and chucks of plaster. The third round sparked the taut chain holding the multitude of glass blades. A link gave way, splitting it. The oval piece of metal began to pull apart. The entire chandelier cocked to the right. The heavy blades of glass swayed to and fro, clinking in a portentous symphony of sound.

A millisecond later, the entire consortium of crystal cut loose.

Luther's head was turned, his attention trained on the gun with no regard for where the rounds ended up. Jason watched as the chandelier descended, growing enormous in his field of vision.

At the last possible moment, he released his grip on William Luther. He slid out from under the man and rolled away a fraction of a second before the massive object crashed onto Luther's head and torso.

$$R_x$$

"Lui envoyer un autre message," Hussein demanded. *Send him another message.*

"This is dangerous, Madame," Oliver pleaded. "Reprisal is transmitting from its position over the ocean. The transmission could be visible if anyone is watching."

"Send him an uncoded message. It will be faster! Now!"

Oliver typed in the uncoded message:

Report on Rodgers needed! Reply immediately!

Hussein fidgeted, desperate for an update on what was going on with Rodgers. He was supposed to be meeting and killing the tattooed killer. The drone, in flight, at transmitting altitude, burst Hussein's urgent pleas for information. The aerial communications UAV would also be able to receive and forward transmissions to Hussein's compound. But they were receiving no traffic. Over the last ten minutes, Hussein had ordered several electronic missives to be sent.

Oliver picked up the secure cell phone and punched in a text to The Watcher.

"That was the fourth text I've sent him," Oliver replied. "He's not responding."

"Batard!" she spat. "I need to know what is going on."

"The drone is airborne and circling. It will take a moment for the message to be relayed. We are running out of time," Oliver replied. "The drone's batteries need to be replaced. There is barely enough energy to get them back to the compound. I can send another message, but if the drone circles too long. It may not make it back."

Hussein swore. "Bring it back. But I want it sent back out immediately."

$$\text{R}_{\text{X}}$$

The twenty-something communications technician sitting at his monitor inside the National Security Agency's remote monitoring station on the North Carolina barrier islands at Topsail Beach peered at his computer screen. The software running on his terminal monitored all electronic communications sent via the airwaves or bounced off satellites. In the last two weeks, the computer had been programmed to search for a list of thirty keywords related to The Simoon, Jason Rodgers, Hygeia, Delilah Hussein, or The Watcher.

The wavy line on the screen jumped in a crazy dance, bleeping an audio alert in the young technician's headphones. He clicked on the icon denoting the communications. The word Rodgers flashed in red.

Immediately, he began a trace on the source of the transmission.

$$\text{R}_{\text{X}}$$

"Show me your hands!"

A sinking feeling clutched Jason. The gold shield hooked to the cop's belt and the weapon aimed at him told Jason his quest to find Michael and Chrissie was over. Prostrate on the floor, Jason lifted his eyes and raised his hands off the floor, showing his palms. He would soon be processed by the criminal justice system . . . again.

The officer approached, sweeping his weapon between the two men.

"Is there anyone else in the house?"

"No," Jason replied.

The cop wagged the gun. "Slide over there against the wall under the window. Stay on your belly and keep your hands flat on the floor! Do it now!"

Jason pushed himself across the floor as the officer approached. The cop knelt beside the motionless William Luther.

"Holy Shit!" the cop whispered, swallowing hard. "He's done."

The detective stepped to Luther's handgun, lying nearby, and kicked it away. He produced a small radio and called for backup and an ambulance.

He winced at the motionless body. A pool of crimson expanded across the floor.

Jason managed a glimpse.

The chandelier possessed at least fifty bladed pieces of glass that dangled from six brass S-arms spoking out from a center column. From each S-arm, a multitude of weighted, crystal prisms hung, varying in length from an inch to at least eight or nine inches. The whole ensemble must have weighed fifty pounds.

It had landed on Luther's face. Jason could make out at least three prisms that had pierced Luther's head and face. A fourth had penetrated his jugular. Blood no longer spurted from the neck wound. The man who had attempted to kill him in the Williamsburg Regional Jail was gone.

Jason shifted his focus from the body. His eyes scanned the floor between the dining room and the living area. The keychain rested on the floor, nestled beside the crumpled throw rug.

"Do you mind if I get my keys?" he asked.

"Shut up," the cop demanded.

"I really need those keys."

"I said be quiet."

The cop was at Jason's side now. He twisted his right arm behind his back. He repeated the process with the left. The grinding of handcuffs locking over his wrists punctuated the movement.

"Here we go again," Jason sighed.

His eyes stayed glued on the keychain and the three keys clipped to it.

"So you've done this before," the detective snapped.

PART THREE

CHAPTER 30

The Watcher felt the blood drain from his face. He watched Jason Rodgers being led from the house, his hands cuffed behind his back. A young detective escorted him to an unmarked car and deposited him in the back seat.

His phone vibrated for the fifth time. Hussein had been demanding a status update. *Not yet!* He needed to focus. He did not need to cloud his mind with ranting texts and updates. He needed to act!

He had returned to the Cadillac when he heard the sirens. The gunfire must have triggered a phone call by a neighbor. He reached into his suit for the fake shield he'd used last night to rescue Rodgers after the car accident on Jefferson Avenue in the northern stretches of Newport News. The Watcher placed his hand on the lever and was about to open the car door when he hesitated.

Not a good idea, he told himself.

The thought that he could strong arm his way into the crime scene, flash the badge, and take Rodgers with him appeared at first to be an expedient method to free the pharmacist. But last night he dealt with one cop and a paramedic before others could arrive. And last night Rodgers was not in custody. The Watcher's mind recalculated.

Now, the pharmacist had been arrested. The place swarmed with cops and detectives. If he tried to bully his way to Rodgers now, the chance that he might run into someone like John Palmer was high. The Watcher hadn't seen Palmer arrive. For all he knew, Palmer might already be in the house. If not, he would arrive shortly. The Watcher would be exposed and even detained himself. And that he could not afford.

He would have to find another way.

His mind kicked into a gear rarely used. Quick improvisation was a must in his business. Plans *always* went to shit. There was no time for panic . . . or hesitation. Every second counted now. How he acted and the decisions he made in the next few minutes would decide the fate of at least five people. Maybe more.

Jason Rodgers was in custody. Presumably, the man in the house had been shot . . . and could well be dead. That meant Jason Rodgers was going to be held, interrogated, and charged with a crime up to and possibly including murder.

The Watcher recalled his one overriding directive: *Make sure Jason Rodgers carries out the madwoman's instructions.*

The keys! He needed to retrieve the keys

Reaching into his suit coat pocket, he palmed the gold detective's badge. The keys were everything. The whole operation would be bupkis if he didn't retrieve those keys.

He pushed out a long breath. There was only one way to get the keys: he *had* to enter the house. He wouldn't bully anyone. He would simply slip in the back and look like he belonged. Pulling out the badge, he exited the car, circled the block, and cut through two yards until he reached the back steps of the house.

Get the keys! Then get Rodgers!

He turned the knob, found it unlocked, and stepped inside.

℞

Two miles to the north and thirty minutes later, Peter's right knee jack-hammered up and down. The former marine studied his cell phone. He opened the crumpled pack of Marlboros. *Only one left*, he thought. He wanted one badly right now. A smoke would have to wait.

"Are you going in or not?" Tim asked.

They had been sitting in the parking lot of police headquarters for ten minutes as Peter contemplated going inside. He knew if he did there was no putting the genie back in the bottle.

The only thing on his mind was how he'd shown up at the fourth floor of the north Windsor Tower in Newport News as Jason was about to be shot by the Arab pharmacist. If he hadn't, Jason would have been killed.

Those thoughts and images filled Peter with angst. He'd always had Jason's back. It was not in his nature to be a bystander, especially where his brother was concerned.

Trust him! Peter told himself.

No this was a matter of life and death!

Fuck it, he told himself. Peter pulled the last cigarette from the pack, lit it, and filled the cab with smoke. He checked his watch. Just after ten in the evening. As he pushed out a blue cloud, a caravan of five police cruisers arrived at headquarters, lights ablaze. They sped through the parking lot and circled to the rear of the building. A prisoner was escorted by a phalanx of blue uniforms in the darkness. The group and the prisoner passed under a street lamp illuminating the prisoner. Peter's heart jumped when he recognized his brother's face.

His phone chimed out the Marine Corps Hymn. Peter dove at the device, picked it up. The caller ID said "Private."

"Peter Rodgers!"

"You are the brother of the pharmacist!"

It was not a question.

"Who's this?"

"A friend of your brother," the voice said.

"I need a name!"

"You don't get one. Your brother needs you! You will meet him at one this morning. You need to retrieve your vehicle. Don't be late! And don't go to the police!"

"That's going to be a problem. The cops just brought my brother in in cuffs."

"I know."

"Who are you?"

"Not important. Follow your instructions if you want to save your brother."

"He was driving my truck. Where is it?"

"It's on 65th Street. Go there now and retrieve it. Just be at the location on time."

The voice recited an address. The line went dead. Peter's anxiety ratcheted up several levels. He checked his watch. He had less than two hours.

The former marine could barely choke out his next directive.

"Change of plans, Tim. I need you to take me to get my Hummer."

$$R_X$$

An hour and a half later, Jason's hands were cuffed to a two-foot-long chain slipped through a hasp bolted into the steel interrogation table. His eyes were riveted on the red light on the camera mounted on the tripod in the corner over Palmer's right shoulder. A cord snaked from the camera to a small hole in the wall.

Rodgers had been interrogated by John Palmer, the homicide cop, for the last ninety minutes. At first, Palmer was shocked at the extent of his injuries: the head wound, the shrapnel wounds in the arm and shoulder, and a swollen left eye from his fight with William Luther. Palmer asked if he needed a doctor. Jason declined. And so the questions continued.

A generic clock on the wall indicated it was one minute past eleven-thirty at night. Fatigue clung to him like a dense shroud. This was no time to be tired. Closing his eyes and sucking in quick breaths through his nose, he leaned closer to John Palmer and whispered.

"I need you to do something for me."

Palmer's eyes shifted to the two-way mirror on the wall. Palmer had been interrogating Jason for the past hour about the dead man in the house on 65th Street. Jason had avoided answering questions to this point, to Palmer's obvious growing consternation.

"Jason, you're wasting my time. You want me to do something for you. Give me something and I'll consider your favor."

"I'm about to ask for my lawyer. But not yet. When I do, you'll get nothing. I know my rights, your partner read them to me. I don't have to talk to you. That is unless you help me."

"You're not in a good negotiating position."

"Time is crucial, detective. Two people have been kidnapped. The people who took them are a part of why I was at that house. Do this one favor for me and I'll tell you everything. You need to retrieve something for me. If you don't, two people will die."

"Depends on what it is." Palmer hammered the business end of his Bic on the blank yellow legal pad.

"I need you to turn off the camera."

"Does this have anything to do with your brother calling me?"

"Probably. What did he tell you?"

"He left a message. I never called him back. Said something about Lily Zanns, aka Delilah Hussein, being alive, and she has kidnapped your son and girlfriend."

"I'll tell you the whole story when you turn off the camera and tell the guys behind the glass to go get a cup of coffee."

Palmer screwed his lips into a tight pucker as he considered Jason's request. Finally, he turned to the mirror and made a slicing motion across his throat. The light on the camera went dark. Palmer exited the room, returned two minutes later, and sat back down.

"They'll be back in five minutes. Make it quick."

"I'm in trouble and I need your help."

"You are in a shitload of trouble. I don't know if anyone can help you, least of all me."

"Delilah Hussein *is* alive," Jason said.

Palmer shook his head. "Nice try, Mr. Rodgers. She's dead!"

"I can prove it!"

Palmer sighed, shaking his head. "I saw the photos and the bodies on the yacht. You're gonna need a better strategy to get you out of this."

"Hussein contacted me. She confirmed that she has Michael, my son, and Chrissie, my . . . fiancée. I have photographic proof. My son and my girlfriend are gone. If I don't do exactly as she tells me, she is going to kill them. She wants to avenge the death of her daughter, the capture of her son, and her failure to kill two presidents. It's why I was at the house with the man I shot. Hussein is calling the shots. She told me to be there."

"Where is this photographic evidence?"

"It's on a cell phone and a computer flash drive in my brother's Hummer. It's on 65th Street, parked outside the house."

"That Hummer is probably in police custody as evidence," Palmer declared.

Palmer lifted his cell phone and called a number. "There's a Hummer parked on 65th Street. It's involved in the murder there. Make sure we impound it. . ."

Palmer listened for twenty seconds.

"What do you mean it's not there?"

Palmer sighed and hung up. "It seems your brother was able to retrieve the Hummer before they catalogued it. They didn't realize it was part of the investigation."

"So, Peter has the cell phone and the laptop."

"I'll call him and he can bring it to me," Palmer replied. "If I'm convinced, maybe . . . I'll help you."

Jason nodded. "You'll be convinced. Here's what I need."

$$R_X$$

"You want me to do what!?" Palmer demanded. Jason had just finished explaining about the keys, the miniature coffins, the video file, and the audio recording. Palmer removed the toothpick lodged in the corner of his mouth, inspected it, and then replaced it on the other side. The aging detective shook his head.

"If I don't get those keys and report back to her, she'll kill them."

"Where are the keys?"

"They were on the floor in the living room at the address when I was arrested. Where would they be now?"

"The crime scene unit probably scooped them up. If so, they're in the evidence room."

"Will you get them for me?"

"Do you realize what you're asking me to do?"

"I wouldn't ask if it wasn't a matter of life and death."

"I don't know . . . What the hell am I saying . . . No . . ."

Jason felt his body shrink. Palmer's eyes searched his.

"Even if I get them for you, how are you going to drive? You're in custody. And there is no way in hell . . . you're not going anywhere. Don't even think about asking me to release you."

"I'll figure something out. I need those keys. I'll get my brother to make the trip."

Palmer closed his eyes and rubbed his temples. "Those keys are evidence."

"Detective Palmer . . . John, if you were sitting where I am you'd be asking the same thing."

Palmer opened his eyes and studied his prisoner. "I want to see the video on the flash drive, see the images and hear the recording on the cell phone. If I am impressed by what I hear, we'll see."

℞

Ten minutes later, Peter Rodgers's cell phone pealed the Marine Corps Hymn.

Driving up Warwick Boulevard, he had just passed the intersection with J. Clyde Morris Boulevard. Tim, his employee , had dropped him off and waited while Rodgers provided the OnStar representative with the necessary password to unlock his vehicle doors and remotely start his car. His car keys had been in Jason's possession, and right now, he guessed, were somewhere in Newport News Police Headquarters. He had an alternate set at home. There was no time to get them.

Fortunately, the Hummer had been ignored.

Jason had parked the Hummer a hundred yards short of the house where he was arrested. A gaggle of police vehicles were parked outside the residence. A yellow band of plastic crime-scene tape had been strung around the perimeter of the yard. A crime-scene technical truck, its rear doors swung wide, exposed a plethora of evidence-gathering equipment and supplies. Two cruisers, their lights flashing, were parked on the street.

Peter assumed that the Hummer had not been identified as the vehicle driven by Jason, or they simply hadn't gotten to it. He had wasted no time dispatching Tim after the Hummer's engine came to life. Thirty minutes ago, he had jerked it into gear and driven slowly past the house and the police presence. The front door of the house was wide open, every window ablaze. Cops and technicians bandied about as flashes from the photographer's camera strobed through the edifice.

The former marine did not recognize the number. He hesitated then pressed the icon to take the call.

"Peter Rodgers."

"This is Detective John Palmer of the Newport News Police Department."

"You have Jason in custody?"

"That's correct."

"What do you want from me?"

"Your brother says that you have evidence that . . ." Palmer hesitated, lowering his voice. " . . . that Delilah Hussein is alive. A phone and a file with a message and video file showing captives. Is this true?"

"That's right."

"Can you send them to me?"

"Are you going to release my brother?"

"That's not possible. He's a suspect in another murder."

The word *murder* sent a sharp pain through Peter's gut. "Then why do you need it?"

"It may help your brother . . . and help us find his girlfriend and his son . . . your nephew. Bring the phone and flash drive to police headquarters."

Peter glanced down at the cell phone emblazoned with the number two in grease paint and the flash drive. The laptop lay on the passenger-side floorboard. He didn't want to end up in custody beside Jason. It would not help Michael and Chrissie's cause.

"Negative. Give me your phone number and I'll send them to you."

Chapter 31

The Watcher strode to the glass doors of the Newport News Police Headquarters on Jefferson Avenue for the second time in the last hour. The time was twenty-two minutes after midnight. At the moment, he appeared to be a man without a care in the world, his gait unhurried and casual. He checked his watch, calculating the time. His appearance was much different than during his first trip here an hour ago. He had donned a pair of thick-rimmed glasses, a blonde wig, a white t-shirt, jeans, and a brown leather bomber jacket. Now, he was back in his dark suit and fedora. If his timing was correct, he had less than a minute.

Hussein's plan had gone to hell. The Watcher was improvising.

Before Jason had killed the tattooed beast, his former military training and spy tradecraft was taxed by this convoluted, perilous mission. Now he was in uncharted territory. Every neuron in his body fired, hypersensitive to every detail.

He yanked open the door and strode into the two-story foyer lined with the portraits of officers who had paid the ultimate price. His eyes registered everything but carried the indifferent look of a bored man trying to pay a parking ticket. He stopped and appeared to study the paintings. The foyer was semi-dark at this late hour. By the nearly empty parking lot, he guessed the building was sparsely populated

After glancing at his watch, The Watcher approached the reception desk. A sleepy-eyed, but pleasant black woman smiled up at him.

"Hi, I'm Doctor Alberti. I need some help . . ."

Three . . . two . . . one . . .

A muffled bang sounded over his left shoulder. The Watcher feigned a jolted surprise.

"What the hell was that?" he said, ducking.

"I don't know," the black woman replied, alarmed.

Smoke roiled from under the restroom door, spilling into the foyer.

"It's a fire," The Watcher shouted.

The woman circled the desk and approached the men's room door. She disappeared from the man's view as she pushed it open. The Watcher pressed the button on the remote control in his jacket pocket beside the badge. A second explosion fired.

The black woman shrieked, staggering backward from the cloud of smoke. The orange hue of fire glowed inside the bathroom. A man and a woman appeared from a side door, saw their fallen comrade, and rushed to her aid. The Watcher joined them.

"I heard you say you were a doctor. Are you?"

"Yes," he said.

"Can you help?"

"Definitely."

The Watcher knelt. "Can you hear me, ma'am?"

The woman did not respond. He checked her pulse and turned to her co-workers.

"We need to get her away from here. A conference room, maybe," the man in the dark suit said.

"Sure, this way," the man replied. "Just off the hallway."

They lifted her. The Watcher and the other man carried the receptionist toward the swinging double doors leading inside the building. The woman swiped a key card, held open the heavy doors, and pointed to a conference room. They sat her in a comfortable chair.

"Get her a wet cloth and some water," the Watcher commanded. "You," he continued, pointing at the man, "call an ambulance and the fire department. Then get a fire extinguisher and call 911! I'm going to my car to get my medical bag. I'll be right back."

The woman rushed off. The man dialed the conference room phone.

The Watcher headed for the nearest stairwell.

℞

As John Palmer walked to the evidence locker, he rubbed his sweaty palms together. Not since he was a rookie patrolman twenty years ago had he recalled feeling this nervous. He had chomped on the ever-present toothpick in his mouth for the past two hours, shredding it. He spit the remnants into a small waste can moments before he slid his leather wallet containing his shield and identification card through the opening in the thick, grated metal toward the clerk.

"Hey, Steve. I need to see the personal effects of the vic, William Luther. They were brought in hours ago."

"Sure John. Slide your card into the slot."

Palmer slid his key card through the pad, logging the time and his badge number into the system.

"It's in aisle seven, top shelf. Here's the case number." The clerk handed him a slip of paper.

Palmer thanked him and headed into the stacks of boxes neatly catalogued on rows and rows of metal shelving. A phone rang. He found the aisle and stepped in. He scanned the top shelf and found the box. Palmer pulled it down and placed it on a small wheeled table a few feet away.

He lifted the lid and hesitated. Palmer walked back to the main corridor and snuck a peak back at the clerk's desk. The clerk was on the phone and engaged in conversation.

What the hell am I doing?

He had been asking himself that question for the last hour, ever since Jason Rodgers asked him to get the keys.

What he was about to do was a felony. Tampering with evidence in a crime would end his career. He would lose his pension.

All for a man he barely knew. *It could be a hoax.*

Peter Rodgers had texted the video file uploaded from the flash drive, along with the voice recording from the cell phone in question. Palmer had watched and listened to them. They lent more than just a ring of truth to Jason's tall tale.

Palmer had met Delilah Hussein one afternoon in her mansion on Riverside Drive for thirty minutes while an officer tried and failed to chase down Christine Pettigrew along the shoreline of the James River. Hussein's rich French accent was unforgettable. The voice in the recording he'd listened to an hour ago sounded very much like hers. As the words slipped into his ear, a lead weight materialized in his gut.

This shit is happening again!

If it was a hoax, Jason, and now Peter, would face a slew of additional charges over and above manslaughter or murder. If it was real, Palmer didn't want the deaths of two hostages on his hands. The detective had seen enough during the assassination attempts to know that Delilah Hussein was more than the Newport News Police could handle. They didn't have time, according to Rodgers, to analyze the recordings for authenticity.

Rodgers had saved two presidents and nearly paid for it with his life. Palmer recalled the sight of Rodgers in the hospital, wounded, beaten, and weak. The man had run into the fray rather than run from it. He hadn't shied away from the fight. Eventually, all his charges were dropped in York County and Newport News.

Palmer decided to go with his gut.

It's real!

Palmer and his wife had lost their only child to cancer nearly a decade earlier. The aftermath was more than she could handle. They were still married, but only in appearance. Their daughter's death had ripped the will to live out of Pat. And he'd almost allowed it to do the same to him.

No one should ever have to bury their child.

As soon as he had seen the image of the boy chained to the wall in the grimy cell, Palmer knew he would not refuse Jason Rodger's request. He just needed to wrap his mind around it. He still didn't know how the keys would help. There was no way Rodgers was being released. But the desperation in the pharmacist's eye and the memory of all Rodgers had been through plucked a nerve in Palmer. So he'd left Rodgers with his rookie partner, Kent Romo, and headed for the evidence room.

Just get it over with!

Palmer removed the yellow copy of a two-ply inventory list from the box. He read over the list and moved the few items around in the box.

"Did you find it okay, Detective?"

Palmer whipped his head in the direction of the words. The clerk was standing at the aisle entrance.

"Are you okay?" he asked. "You look pale."

"No, Steve. I'm fine. You scared the shit out of me . . . I'm just making some notes. The box was right where you said it would be."

The clerk studied Palmer for a beat, then turned to leave. "Okay, let me know if you need anything." Palmer watched Steve disappear, a look of confusion etched on his face.

Palmer removed every item in the box and laid them on the small table: a wallet, some coins in a plastic bag, a jack knife, a cell phone, two guns, and a money clip holding a ten, a five and two ones in it.

Palmer looked in the box again and then at the items on the small table. *What the hell!*

He didn't need to worry about committing a crime.

There were no keys here.

Two seconds later, fire alarms sounded, sending deafening, intermittent blasts through the basement.

℞

"I need a SITREP, now!" Broadhurst demanded, wheezing the words.

"Rodgers has been arrested," someone answered.

"What? When?" Clay Broadhurst rolled himself in the wheelchair to the left of the agent at the workstation.

"The FBI team following him and The Watcher said he visited a house and was involved in an altercation. Shots were fired. A body was removed from the residence. Rodgers was taken into custody. He's being interrogated at Newport News Police Headquarters."

"Shit."

"What do you want to do?"

"Get me the Newport News Chief of Police on the line.

℞

Klaxons blared and red beacons flashed throughout the corridors. John Palmer alternated between a run and a hurried walk along the gleaming first-floor corridor of headquarters. Glancing out the large window of the hallway, he saw fire trucks clogging the circular drive and parking lot. He spied two firefighters walking toward the foyer.

He stopped a uniformed officer as she approached.

"What the hell's going on?"

"Fire alarm. Smoke and fire in the foyer restrooms," she replied. "It looks like they have it contained. It was a homemade smoke bomb and two-minute flamer."

"Anyone hurt?"

"No sir."

Palmer had taken the stairwell in the rear of the building, so he had not seen the commotion. The elevators had been disabled intentionally. The whine of additional sirens in the distance grew louder.

Palmer raced past the elevator and burst out of the stairwell. Fifteen seconds later, he appeared in the homicide squad room. He checked the interrogation room and found it empty. He darted to the holding cell and found it empty.

"Where's my prisoner?" He demanded of a junior detective.

The young man shrugged and said he'd been ordered to evacuate.

"Where's my prisoner?" he repeated.

"I don't know."

"Where's Kent Romo? I left him in charge."

Another negative response.

"He better hope I don't find him."

CHAPTER 32

"Who the hell are you?" Jason demanded, sitting at the wheel of the man's black Cadillac CTS-V.

The man wearing the fedora and the black suit sat in the passenger seat with his weapon, below the level of the dashboard, leveled at Jason's abdomen. The car was parked at the Skymart gas station on Jefferson Avenue on the northwest corner of the intersection with Dresden Drive, south of Hampton Roads Center Parkway.

Jason was familiar with the area. He had played in weekend softball tournaments years ago at a ballfield on Dresden Drive. Across Jefferson Avenue, the W.M. Jordan building nestled at the corner behind ornate shrubs. At the far end of the same building, the central precinct of the Newport News Police Department resided. Several patrol cars sat parked.

This guy had big ones, Jason thought.

He had appeared in the interrogation room as the fire alarms sounded, flashed his badge, and unlocked Jason's handcuffs. In the commotion, he led Jason out of the building

"And what the hell do you want?"

"You failed to complete your mission back at the house," the man stated calmly. "I'm trying to help you."

"Look, I appreciate the get-out-of-jail-free card, Mac," Jason said, "but I'm not sure it helped. The whole Newport News police force is looking for me. And you picked a spot right across the street from the hornet's nest." Jason pointed to the police cars parked across Jefferson Ave.

"Hide in plain sight," the man replied. "You're right. They will be looking for you. So there's no time to waste."

Jason paused, then asked, "You helped me last night after Clyde Hutton's crash."

The man nodded. "Yes."

"You're not a cop, are you?"

The man shook his head. "I'm a little higher on the food chain. I suggest you get back on your quest."

The first opportunity to really study the man presented itself. His aquiline nose split the thin visage in half. The skin was pockmarked with some kind of dermatologic condition. A long scar snaked from under one ear across his throat to the other side.

"And what quest would that be?" He turned away from the man and looked out the windshield, observing traffic zipping by but not really seeing it. The buzzing of a gnat along the inside of the windshield caught Jason's eye.

"Don't play coy, Mr. Rodgers. I'm the one that planted the small coffins with the cell phones in them for you to find."

Forgetting the gun aimed at him, Jason reached out and grabbed the man by his expensive shirt and suit. "Where are they?"

"I don't know"

"Don't screw with me! My family! Where are they? What the hell is your part in this," Jason seethed.

"I don't know where your son and girlfriend are. I told you I am here to help you. I am given orders by a contact I do not know. I keep tabs on you and plant clues for you to find. I keep you out of trouble, which, I might add, it seems, you are quite adept at getting into. For that I am paid quite well."

"Who are you?"

"Just call me The Watcher."

"Why are you helping me?"

"It is in my—and my handlers—best interests to see you complete your mission. The longer you stay alive and continue on your quest, the more information we obtain . . ."

"Who's 'we'?"

"Sorry . . . can't say."

"So I'm just a pawn . . ."

The gnat crawled along the dashboard as the man said this. "You are no more important to me than this bug."

The Watcher slapped the vinyl, crushing the insect. He turned his palm over, revealing a streak of gray dust and mangled insect wings. Opening the glove compartment, he removed a paper napkin and wiped his hands.

"I track your progress. If harm were to befall you, my job would be over." He leaned back, resting the gun on his lap, but making sure the barrel was pointed at Jason. "That's all you need to know."

"So, I guess I don't have to worry about you using that thing," Jason declared.

"I believe you have a deadline, Mr. Rodgers. Did your message not tell you that you were to retrieve the keys and communicate back to whoever is on the other end by one this morning? Would the consequences for you not be dire?" The man glanced at his Rolex. "You have a little more than thirty minutes. I suggest you use them wisely so that you can be on your way."

"Then let me go so I can find the keys. I'll call her and tell her I need more time!"

"She won't give it to you."

"I don't have much choice. As you said, I have only thirty minutes left. So let me go."

"Not yet," the man said.

"You're not making any sense. You're telling me to continue my journey, and you're holding me up. You're going to let me miss my deadline?"

The man checked his Rolex once more. "Another minute more."

The man's eyes shifted to something behind Jason. The man's gaze followed a moving object. Jason turned and saw Peter's large boxlike silver Hummer skidding to a halt in the parking lot.

Peter climbed out, searching.

Jason shot The Watcher a quizzical glance.

The man shrugged. "You can thank me later." He waved the gun and Jason shoved open the car door.

"Pete!"

"Jason!"

The brothers embraced.

"I should beat the shit out of you, little brother. What the hell were you thinking, ditching me?"

"I'm sorry. I told you I didn't want you involved."

"Well, guess what? I'm involved . . ."

"We don't have much time. Do you have the cell phone?"

"Right here," Peter replied, patting his trouser pocket.

Peter opened the passenger door to the Hummer for Jason. Before Jason climbed in, The Watcher, now standing beside the luxury car, called to him.

"I don't have time for sentiment," Jason sneered.

"You'll need these," the man shouted.

He lobbed something at Jason. It rattled in his hand as he caught it. He opened his palm and looked down at the keychain that once belonged to the deceased William Luther, Tattoo Man.

℞

On the video monitor, John Palmer watched a tall, lean man in a well-tailored suit enter the interrogation room. The cop paused the recording and studied the still image. He had already played the video four times. Each time he did, the same two words slipped from his mouth in an incredulous whisper: "Holy shit!" The cop had seen all forms of bravado and daring, both criminal and heroic, in his years as a member of the Newport News PD. This one deserved first prize in both categories.

He rammed a new toothpick between his teeth.

"Who the hell are you?" Palmer asked, speaking to the monitor.

No matter where he stopped the tape, he could not make out a significant portion of the man's face because of the tilt of the fedora and the angle of his head. The man was a real pro.

He hovered the cursor over the play button and pressed once more. The man in the hat entered the room once again and emerged exactly one minute and twenty-five seconds later with Jason Rodgers in tow, uncuffed. Just as he had the previous three times he'd watched.

The pair marched without a trace of urgency or panic toward a rear entrance as officers and plainclothes cops raced by. He couldn't be sure because he never saw it, but based on the man's proximity to Rodgers and the cock of his right arm, it seemed as if he had a gun in the pharmacist's back.

This feels too familiar, he thought. *And it stinks to high heaven!*

The detective rubbed his weary eyes. The clock on his desk read 12:39 a.m. He needed sleep. But he knew that was many hours away. He re-read his notes.

The identity of the dead man in the house on 65th Street was one William Luther, a career criminal involved in a slew of robberies and assaults over ten years. He'd been busted eight times and done time at Greenville for maiming. But Palmer could not be sure why. The judgment had been sealed. The only reason he knew what he did was because he had a friend in the Department of Corrections.

Luther had been involved in an assault on one Jason Rodgers two years ago in the Regional Jail in Williamsburg. Three months later, Luther had been incarcerated at Greenville. Palmer had deduced that the attack on Rodgers had been the reason.

Luther had been allowed entrance into Rodger's cell by a guard named Clyde Hutton. Luther, the tattoo-laden criminal, who had tried to stab the pharmacist with an improvised shank, seriously wounded his victim. But not before Rodgers shattered Luther's jaw.

After he served his time in prison, Luther stayed off law enforcement's radar. He was not sighted until he showed up dead today.

Hutton, the guard, had been fired and bounced from menial job to menial job over the last twenty-five months. Ironically, Hutton also died early yesterday morning in a car wreck after a high-speed chase in northern Newport News. The other car involved was a bright red Mustang registered to . . . Jason Rodgers. Rodgers was injured, treated, and released at the scene.

Palmer had only been able to shake his head and sigh when his underling Kent Romo presented him with this information. Things were spiraling out of control again.

What the hell is it with this pharmacist?

Accused of and framed for the murder of his ex-girlfriend, Sheila Boquist, two years ago, and while being hunted by police, Rodgers was instrumental in thwarting an assassination attempt at the shipyard. The pharmacist had earned a twisted respect from the seasoned detective.

Palmer's gut reaction told him that Rodgers was simply exacting revenge on the pair of men who had tried to kill him. The cop couldn't blame him. If it were him, he might just do the same thing: dispense a little street justice.

Victims, however, couldn't be allowed to take the law into their own hands, no matter how much it was deserved. Rodgers was no doubt a victim.

But was he also a perp?

Two more people were dead—people Rodgers had a motive to kill. He had been present at both scenes. The pharmacist had the means, motive, and opportunity to kill both these men.

Palmer let the tape roll. The man in the fedora pushed Rodgers through the stairwell door and both disappeared from view.

Who was this accomplice? And how had Rodgers recruited him?

The guy's description sent a ripple of familiar angst through the seasoned cop. Expensive dark suit. Sharp features. The calm demeanor in the face of fire alarms and running bodies. He was a well-trained operative. *A spook!* Of that, Palmer had no doubt.

He was going to find out who he worked for. Staying under the radar on this was crucial. He did not want his superiors in the loop . . . not yet. He decided to call the only person who could help.

But first, he wanted his prisoner back. Palmer dialed the dispatcher.

"I want a BOLO placed for Jason Rodgers." Palmer gave the pharmacist's description. He also gave the name and tag numbers of Rodgers's known associates. There was only one. Peter Rodgers, the brother. The pharmacist would seek out the help of the ex-marine. Palmer continued.

"Then I want the video files for the outside cameras. See if we can't get a look at this mystery man."

As soon as Palmer ended the call, the phone rang.

"Palmer."

"John, this is Chief Rangel."

"Yes, sir," Palmer replied, his heart rate jumping. Palmer had been called to the chief's office before. The request usually came through his captain. Palmer had never received a call directly from the chief of police's office, let alone the man himself. Palmer's fatigue evaporated.

"I just received a call from the FBI in Washington. They said we have a man named Rodgers in custody?"

"We brought him in him about two hours ago."

"Washington says he is a person of interest in a case they're pursuing. The attorney general's office is requesting that we release him to their custody. Why was he arrested?"

"He's a suspect in the homicide on 65th Street, sir."

"I see. What do you know about Rodgers?"

Too much, he thought.

"He claims his son and girlfriend have been kidnapped and he was told to go to the house . . . and kill the man."

"Why is Washington asking to have him released? Do you know?"

Yes, I think so! Palmer said to himself.

"No sir," he lied.

"Your name was mentioned by an agent named Broadhurst with the Secret Service. He asked to speak with you. What's this all about, John?"

"I don't know, sir."

The police chief recited a phone number. "He specifically asked for you. You will call him immediately from my office. I *will* be on this call. Now get your ass up here."

℞

"Let's have it," Jason said.

Peter handed over cell phone number two as they drove north on Jefferson Avenue toward the intersection with J. Clyde Morris Boulevard.

Peter checked the rearview every ten seconds, looking for the black Cadillac . . . or police cars.

"Is he there?" Jason asked.

"Nope. All's clear. Who is that guy?"

"I dunno. But he's involved somehow. Said he was the one planting the coffins we've been finding."

"What?!"

"He's also the one who pretended to be the cop who showed up after Clyde Hutton died. He sprung me from jail. He got me the keys!"

"Does he know where Michael and Chrissie are?"

"No. I don't think so."

"Why didn't you get it from him?"

"He had a gun on me, Pete."

Jason pulled up the only phone number in the contact list of the cell phone. Without hesitating, he pressed the green circle at the bottom of the screen.

It rang five times.

"*Bonjour Monsieur* Jason," the thick, husky voice of Delilah Hussein greeted him. "You have accomplished both of your objectives, oui?"

"I have the keys and man in the house is dead."

"Très bien. Je suis impressionné." *Well done. I'm impressed.*

"Now what?"

"The keys are to a box truck, parked near the Norfolk terminals. One key starts the vehicle, the other opens the glove box. The cargo area is locked. The keys to it are at the destination. Do not attempt to open it.

"Look for a man in a Red Sox jacket. The truck will have the word *Vengeance* stenciled on the side. It is parked at the BP station outside the gate to Virginia Marine Terminal. Find it and begin driving. Take the Chesapeake Bay Bridge-Tunnel north. The truck is equipped with an E-ZPass. You will not have to pay the toll. Stay on Route 13 until you reach Mappsville. Take Turkey Run around the bend and find the dilapidated house. The one with the holes in the roof beside a house trailer. Inside you will find the coordinates to your next destination.

"Do not stop for any reason. We are watching you every step of the way. If you deviate from your route, your precious woman will die first in a very uncomfortable fashion."

She had described the directions to find the truck with amazing accuracy. *She lived here for years,* he thought.

"I want proof they are still alive!"

A long silence filled the line. "You will get proof in thirty minutes. For now, you better get moving. You need to get the truck and get to Mappsville before 8 p.m. your time. If you fail, she dies."

"I want to speak to Michael and Chrissie. Now!"

His demand went unanswered. The line went dead.

"Shit," he seethed.

"Well?"

Jason frowned. "Take 64 East. We need to get to the terminals in Norfolk."

Ten minutes later, Peter took a right on J. Clyde Morris Boulevard, heading toward Yorktown. "We'll double back toward Norfolk, then hit Interstate 64." There was no traffic on the road this early in the morning.

He saw a sight in the distance he did not like. "That's not good," he sighed.

Jason looked toward the direction Peter had nodded. A Newport News police cruiser was heading in the opposite direction across the median on J. Clyde Morris. Jason held his breath as it sped past.

"Stay cool," Peter instructed

Five seconds later, the cop switched on his light bar and the siren wailed. He hung a U-turn at an intersection and headed back in their direction.

"Is that for us?" Jason asked.

"We're going to find out?"

Peter continued to drive. A minute later, the cop was thirty yards behind and a lane to the right.

"I think he's going to pass us," Jason said. "Pull to the side."

Peter had the Hummer in the left lane, going the speed limit. He began to cross to the right lane so he could get out the way. The cop veered into their lane ten yards behind them and gave the siren a single blast.

Peter slowed then stopped. Ten seconds elapsed. The cop exited the vehicle, standing behind his open door. The air inside the cab thickened. The cop lifted his service weapon, leveling it at the rear window.

"Get out of the car slowly!"

The sound of additional sirens filled the air. "His backup is coming," Peter said.

"How did they hell did they find us?" Jason said.

"Palmer's no dummy. I'm sure he knew you and I would end up together sooner or later."

"Go ahead and get out, Pete," Jason commanded. "You've already done enough. You don't have to do this for me."

Peter glanced at his brother. "Filling prescriptions isn't exciting enough for you? You had to go and piss off a terrorist. But no! You couldn't piss off just any terrorist. You had to piss off a female terrorist with a permanent case of PMS."

Peter studied the rearview then turned his eyes to the side-view mirror. His right arm was draped casually atop the steering wheel as if he were waiting for a light to turn. The sirens grew louder.

The cop hollered again. "Get out of the car!"

"Get out. I'll go it alone from here," Jason repeated. "I'm running out of time, Pete! I'm going to get them back."

Peter yanked the gearshift into drive and smiled at Jason. "You think Delilah Hussein is trouble? When Lisa finds out what you got me into, you'll prefer dealing with the terrorist."

Peter gunned the engine, spinning the rear wheels.

℞

He'd been working at the cloth in his mouth for some time, pushing his tongue up and out against the cloth and the gag wrapped around his head. He didn't know what time it was and he was exhausted. But a little fatigue was not going to stop him.

The going was slow. At first, the gag did not budge. He jutted his tongue into the cloth over and over, stopping every few minutes to rest. After what seemed like a thousand attempts, Michael felt the gag slip lower. The balled cloth in his mouth blossomed over the gag.

Sweet, musty air seeped into his throat and lungs.

As he continued to work at the cloth, he recalled what he had learned. He was somewhere much warmer than Virginia. His captors were not American. English was not their native language. He guessed he was in another country somewhere south of Virginia. And he was near an ocean.

Most important, he was not alone.

There was another person in the cell with him. It was a woman. Based on the grunts the other person had made as Michael was being escorted out, he guessed she was gagged as well. His mother! Michael was certain of it. It made perfect sense.

Instantly, he was afraid for her. The other guard, the one named Charlie, had spat curses at her. Something had happened while he was outside. Not being able to see or talk to her made the not knowing worse. His imagination ran wild.

Was she okay? Had they hurt her?

He pushed harder and faster with his tongue. The balled cloth inched out millimeter by millimeter. Michael flexed his jaw up and down and sideways, working the gag farther down his face.

Another burst of five tongue thrusts pushed the cloth out of his mouth. He tilted his head back. The gag fell down around his neck.

℞

Detective John Palmer dialed the telephone number on the keypad of the Polycon SoundStation tabletop speakerphone resting in the center of the conference room table adjacent to the chief's office. Chief Anthony Rangel sat at the table along with a city attorney and his deputy chief. The stern, unforgiving scowls on their faces stifled any extraneous conversation.

Palmer spoke with a receptionist and asked for Broadhurst. The room fell silent as the three police officers and the lawyer stared at each other.

"You've got a lot of explaining to do after we are done here," Rangel declared.

Deciding it was time to level with his boss for the first time in two years about his involvement at the shipyard episode, Palmer had outlined how and why the Feds were asking to have Jason Rodgers, a murder suspect, released from their custody.

"Detective Palmer?" Broadhurst replied after Palmer identified himself.

"Agent Broadhurst," Palmer replied, "I'm on the line with my chief." Palmer introduced the two other men on their end. Broadhurst introduced the deputy director of the FBI, Brad Lane, and a deputy attorney general. Broadhurst inquired as to how much the chief knew about the past and current history.

"We are just beginning to understand Detective Palmer's involvement in this scenario," Rangel explained. "Why were we not apprised of past events?"

Broadhurst cleared his throat. This erupted into a spasm of coughing.

"I apologize. Chief, Detective Palmer was asked, in fact, he was threatened with criminal charges if he revealed anything he knew about the events of two years ago. I am warning you and the other men at the table as well. This is a secure line. Silence is paramount. Our teams cleaned up the mess in the towers and kept your officers in the dark. National security.

"I understand," Broadhurst continued, "you have Jason Rodgers in custody. We need him released. He's involved in an operation involving national security at the highest level."

"Rodgers," Palmer began, "is being manipulated by Delilah Hussein . . ."

"How do you know this?" Broadhurst interrupted.

"He told me himself."

"I will not confirm or deny those allegations. I can't reveal any details about the current operation. We need Jason Rodgers released. We are sending a team of U.S. marshals to retrieve him. The attorney general's office is preparing the paperwork now."

"Agent, Jason Rodgers killed a man today," Rangel said, raising his voice. "The media will be all over this. He needs to be held accountable."

"Maybe so, but it will not be today."

"And if I refuse to release him?"

"Chief," another voice on the line broke in, "this is Deputy Attorney General Chad Spiller. My boss, the AG, just got off the phone with the president. He has signed an order releasing Rodgers to our custody. I you fail to comply, you will by charged under the National Security Act with interference in an on-going operation. Do I make myself clear?"

Palmer, the city attorney, and the deputy chief turned their eyes toward Rangel. Rangel pursed his lips and rubbed his chin. "Understood. But I expect him to be returned to us when this is over. Do I make myself clear?"

"Chief," the FBI deputy director chimed in, "Brad Lane. We will look into the situation when the dust settles."

"Okay. But there is one more important detail we need to tell you."

""What is that?" Broadhurst asked.

Rangel looked to Palmer with a wry smile. "Okay Secret Agent Palmer, tell them."

"Gentlemen, I regret to inform you that Jason Rodgers has escaped."

$$R_X$$

The Hummer's 3.7 liter, inline, five-cylinder engine strained its limits as the Rodgers brothers hurtled east on Interstate 64. At 2:20 a.m., traffic was nonexistent. The Hampton Coliseum became a quick memory as they sped past the I-664 interchange. The Hummer's top heavy nature caused it to list as Peter negotiated the gentle curves.

Fifteen minutes earlier, the cop who had pulled them over on J. Clyde Morris Boulevard had jumped back in his cruiser and given chase. He'd closed the distance, as Peter had to slow for a red light near the Jiffy Lube. Peter gunned the engine and popped the left-side tires onto the curbed median to avoid a pair of stopped cars.

The cop had to wait for the cars to part before he could get through. Peter ran two more lights before taking the ramp for the interstate, heading east. They hadn't seen the cop since.

"See anything?" Peter asked, studying the headlight beams cutting through the early morning darkness.

"All clear," Jason replied, looking back.

His lips had not stopped moving when a gray and black blur appeared, lights ablaze, from the ramp at LaSalle Avenue.

"A statie just showed up. He's a mile back . . . and coming fast."

Peter pressed the petal harder, despite it being on the floorboard.

"This five-cylinder engine ain't gonna outrun him," he complained, jerking the wheel to pass a stray Volkswagen.

"Where are we?" Jason asked.

"Passing Pembroke Ave. We're about a mile and a half from the tunnel."

"He's gaining . . ."

Peter eased his foot off the accelerator. The engine's pitch slowed. The vehicle slowed.

"What the hell are you doing?"

"The only thing I can do."

℞

Hussein's two soldats, Pierre and Charlie, sat on either side of the heavy wooden door in the warm early morning Caribbean air. The taller man, Pierre, puffed a thick cigar. The breeze carried away each plume of smoke. Much to Pierre's chagrin, Charlie had changed the guard assignments. They were now on the midnight watch and had pulled sixteen consecutive hours.

"Why are we stuck on the night shift?" Pierre asked. "We are the most senior soldats. Let the young ones lose sleep."

Pierre simply smiled. "What's the difference? Besides, because we are working at night, we avoid the daytime duties."

"I still don't like it." Pierre knew what Charlie was up to.

"C'est ta tourne se charge du garçon, Pierre," Charlie, the larger man said. *It's your turn to handle the boy.*

Pierre, sitting on a thick round stump of wood and leaning against the wall of the building, removed the thick cigar from his mouth. He lifted the Panama hat and peeked at his partner.

"Charlie, tu es trop tôt, mon ami. Nous avons un autre trentes minutes," Pierre replied. *You're too early, my friend. We have another thirty minutes.* "I took care of the boy last time."

"Arrêtes se plaindre," Charlie retorted. *Stop complaining.* "Make sure you take the kid out of *ze* cellar and keep him out. Cette garce down there is going to learn what a real man is. I owe her that much." As he uttered these words, he stroked his still throbbing testicles

"Pas une bonne idée, Charlie." *Not a good idea.* "Madame will not be pleased."

Before Pierre could react, Charlie was upon him, moving with a lithe, smooth motion belying his girth and size. Charlie grasped Pierre's shirt, balling it in his fist. Pierre looked into a pair of wide, wild green eyes. His throat seemed to slam shut. He tried to swallow. The moisture in his mouth evaporated, and it felt like he was trying force sandpaper down his esophagus. Suddenly, he was transported back to the one time before that he'd seen Charlie unleash his anger.

The incident had occurred in western Africa as they trained for this mission. The Boss Lady was in the Middle East. Their bunking quarters were open, barrack-style facilities, with no privacy. Charlie was a man who harbored no embarrassment about pleasing himself at night in the darkened barracks. His fellow soldiers often heard the stifled groans of pleasure coming from Charlie's bunk as he masturbated. He bunked in a secluded area of the space, away from the others. Nonetheless, Charlie pleased himself at night and did so loud enough for the others to hear.

One day, Charlie discovered someone had removed one of his porn magazines from under his mattress. Charlie confronted the suspect. The *soldat* lied, hoping to quell Charlie's anger and avoid the consequences. Everyone knew how much Charlie treasured his skin mags.

Charlie rifled through his compatriot's belongings and found the dog-eared monthly. The Frenchman became apoplectic, dragging the culprit outside. First, he flogged him with his fists. After the second blow, the man went down. Charlie lifted him up, holding him upright with one hand as he pounded him about the head and face with the other like a rag doll. He did not stop until the eyes had closed behind swollen, red tissue. Blood coated every inch of his face. When Charlie realized he was unconscious, he let the body fall to the ground.

Charlie roused him by grabbing a handful of skin under his chin and twisting it until the man coughed and gagged on his own crimson-tinged saliva. The near-comatose man blinked his eyes, unaware of where he was or what was going at that moment. Charlie removed a switchblade. He cut away his trousers and underwear and proceeded to cut off the man's penis.

As the blood-soaked man screamed in agony, Charlie stuffed the severed appendage into his mouth. The witnesses had covered for Charlie, fearful they might be his next victim. The man was buried alive in a shallow grave.

These images replayed themselves in Pierre's mind now as Charlie picked up the Russian-made MP-443 Grach pistol. He lifted the brim of Pierre's hat with the barrel and peered into the guard's eyes. "She will never know. She will not be back to check on them or us for another eight hours. That is, unless you plan on telling her."

Pierre's eyes widened at the sight of the gun inches from his face. "Mes lèvres sont scellées," he declared, making a motion of closing his lips with an invisible key. "Mais, why do you get the woman?" he continued, feigning injustice.

"I'm the senior man. And it was my idea. You can have a go next time." Charlie removed a hundred euro note from his shirt pocket. "Voici, un petit quelque chose pour vous récompenser!" *A little something for your trouble.*

He then placed the barrel of the weapon against Pierre's temple. "And here's my insurance. *Ve* are going back down *zere* . When we do, keep the boy out until you see me return from the cellar. That's when you will know I am done."

℞

"Hello," came the whisper.

Chrissie's chin rested on her chest. She tried to ignore her aching muscles and her legs were cramping. Her arms felt like molten tubes of lead, sending searing blasts of pain to her shoulders.

"Hello?"

Had she fallen asleep? Was she dreaming or hallucinating?

There it was again, barely audible, a throaty whisper cracking on the second syllable.

"Mom? Is that you?"

Chrissie lifted her head. She struggled against the chains, rattling them behind her. She recognized Michael's weak, teenage voice.

"Mfcwaeg!" she grunted, trying to speak through the gags.

"It's Michael," he whispered again. "If you're gagged the way I was, use your tongue to push against the cloth over your mouth. It will come loose, just keep pushing."

Chrissie grunted an agreement.

Michael was here! Jason's Michael was here!

Her hopes soared. A bolus of adrenaline coursed through her, numbing the pain. She worked her tongue against the cloth. She realized how frightened he must be. Chrissie desperately wanted to reach out to him, to speak to him. Then she thought about the implications.

Did that mean Jason was here as well?

There was panic in the young man's voice. The words were querulous and filled with trepidation.

She worked her tongue up and down, back and forth. As she did this, she began to think about what she would say to him.

How would he react?

How would he take learning that she was not his mother?

How would he handle the fact that it was the woman he didn't want becoming his stepmother?

$$R_x$$

The Hummer maintained a parallel course alongside a large eighteen-wheeled semi. The rig was one of two other vehicles nearby on the interstate. In the distance, they could see another car, a sedan, a mile ahead. The driver glanced over at Jason in the passenger seat of the Hummer, and gave a half-salute.

Jason watched the driver's eyes shift to the large side-view mirror. The truck slowed when he spotted the trooper's light and heard the siren. Peter decelerated along with him, keeping the cop blocked. The driver eased the truck onto the emergency lane.

The cop swerved into the lane filling the space once occupied by the semi. Peter gunned the engine. The Hummer lurched forward with more power than Jason anticipated. His head bounced off the head rest. Peter wrenched the wheel hard right, cutting off the trooper. The cop hit the brake. He swerved to the right, into the shoulder, missing the now stopped truck by inches.

In a few seconds, Peter put a hundred yards between the cop and the Hummer. They jockeyed back and forth this way for a mile and a half. As they passed under the North Mallory Street Bridge, Peter slowed, pulling alongside a slower Nissan Ultra, once again, boxing the cruiser in.

"Traffic's getting thicker," Jason observed.

"At this hour?"

Jason played lookout, peering through the rear windshield. Peter's eyes seesawed between the road and the rearview mirror.

"That's not good," Peter declared.

Jason turned to look. "Dammit!"

Both lanes of Interstate 64 were backed up three hundred yards from the entrance before dipping into the tube of the Hampton Roads Bridge-Tunnel. After a second look, Jason realized the problem.

"They're doing road work. The right lane is closed."

With the former Chamberlin Hotel across the water to left, Jason pointed. The cop was pulling alongside. The trooper's front bumper was even with the rear door of the Hummer.

"Get in the left emergency lane!" Jason shouted. "There's a work truck on the right, blocking the way!"

Both sides of the bridge possessed a breakdown lane. The right breakdown lane was the width of a normal travel lane. The left, however, the one Peter was turning the Hummer into, was half as wide as its right-handed counterpart. Peter braked hard and slipped into the narrow left emergency lane, zipping by the mirrors and doors of the unsuspecting, slowed traffic rolling toward the tunnel. The cop closed the distance again, siren wailing. He fell in behind the Hummer, squeezing beside the single line of traffic.

Peter pressed the accelerator, speeding up again.

"What are you going to do?" Jason asked, a tremor in his voice.

"Take a huge chance," Peter shot back.

Chapter 33

Michael listened, filled with anticipation. His mother grunted and groaned in response to his urging. It was taking her forever to undo her gag.

As he waited, Michael wasn't satisfied with being able to speak and breathe. He needed to see.

He'd maneuvered himself backward, attempting to lean against the wall to which he was chained. The chain was too short and he could not continue keeping his butt in the air. The chain pulled up on the handcuffs. His weight hung from the wall. Enjoying the limberness and flexibility of youth and ignoring the pain in his wrists and forearms, he arched his back like a gymnast and was able to touch his head to the rough brick of the wall.

Turning his head sideways, he rubbed the blindfold against the brick. The cloth moved, oscillating against his skin. As he did this, he continued to urge his mother to free herself from her gag.

"Don't stop, Mom!"

He could hear his mother breathing and grunting somewhere in front of him.

The skin on his temple began to abrade and tear. A warm trickle of blood snaked down outside his left eye. He continued, dragging his face in longer, more effective strokes. All his weight was pressed down now on the shackles. His arms felt like they would burn up. Michael ignored it, pushing himself.

Finally, a sliver of dim, silver light penetrated the top of his field of vision. A few more millimeters and he would be able to see.

℞

"We have eyes on Rodgers, Agent," the agent at the screen said.

"Put it on the big screen."

The image on the massive wall screens loaded a moment later, flashing the car chase on Interstate 64.

"Explain what's going on."

"They're on I-64, headed east. They are on the western bridge section of the Hampton Roads Bridge-Tunnel, being pursued by a state trooper."

The image on the screen wavered and moved in and out. In the left emergency breakdown lane, a large square Hummer was being followed by a Virginia State Trooper with his blue lights angrily flashing.

"What the hell is wrong with the picture?"

"It's a private drone. Our agent is in a car following about a half mile behind. The high winds coming from the water are buffeting the machine."

"A private drone? Where are the Bureau's UAVs or Cessnas?"

It was not a well-known fact that government agencies were using surveillance drones and other aircraft, mostly Cessna's, to observe tactical situations inside the continental United States. The FBI had a small fleet of unmanned vehicles hangered at various locations, as well as a larger fleet of piloted Cessnas.

"These events developed too fast to retask our current UAVs or surveillance planes. They are either in for service or on assignment. We looked into borrowing one from the Border Patrol. But there are none in the area. This whole thing will be over before it could arrive. The agent on the ground took it upon himself to purchase a camera drone in a local hobby shop earlier today. We'll switch to our drones when one arrives. We've patched the image into his phone and are uploading it here."

"Is this a government operation or what?" Broadhurst thought for a moment. "I'm glad someone is thinking on their feet."

"Whatever you say, sir."

"Do we know where they are going?" The acid in his stomach had become a bubbling cauldron. Broadhurst removed a plastic bottle of Tums from his suit coat, shook two tablets from it, and began crunching. He swallowed and repeated the procedure with two more.

"I think they're about to be caught, sir. Nowhere to go," another agent instructed.

℞

Fifty feet from the entrance to the tunnel, the state trooper's Dodge Charger hugged the Hummer's rear bumper. A Chrysler minivan in the fast lane, to the right and ahead of the Hummer, its driver confused by the sound of the siren, started to creep into the left-side emergency breakdown lane, cutting off Peter and Jason.

Peter laid on the horn. Instead of hitting the brake, he slammed the pedal to the floor. The bass-toned engine whined higher two seconds before the Hummer's front bumper crumpled the front quarter panel. Peter stayed hard on the gas and, using the Hummer's momentum, pushed the van out of the way and into the rear of the car in front of it. The Hummer squeezed between the Ford and the guard rail. Scraping metal tore down both sides of the vehicle.

Another driver began to pull in front of Peter, this one a tiny, low-to-the-ground Smart car. Peter gunned it again and the Hummer walked over the engine compartment of the subcompact like a monster truck.

"Almost there," Peter hollered, once they were over the mangled car.

The state trooper, now stuck behind the crumpled insect of a car, was blocked.

Peter reached the entrance to the island as traffic inched into the eastbound tube. There was no way to break into the line of cars. He turned off onto the island.

"Now what?" Jason said.

"Start praying."

Peter drove to the opposite side of the island. He checked for traffic and turned right, heading eastbound in the westbound tunnel.

CHAPTER 34

"Shit," the FBI agent in the rental Chevy Malibu exclaimed to his counterpart behind the wheel.

"What's wrong?"

"We're losing battery power. I didn't have much time to charge the battery pack after I bought the damned thing."

"How long?"

"Three minutes."

$$R_X$$

"It's me, Mom. It's Michael."

"Michael?"

"Yes." Michael paused. Something was wrong. His mother's voice was a weak whisper. Higher than normal. "Are you okay?"

"I'm sore. But, I'll live." The voice paused.

The timbre of the words registered with his brain.

"You're not my mother."

"No, Michael. I'm not. It's Chrissie. Your father's . . . friend."

"What are *you* doing here?"

"I have no idea. Are you hurt?"

"No," Michael sighed. "I mean I have a cut over my eye. But I'm fine."

"How did that happen?"

"I did it. I rubbed my head against the wall. I can see over the blindfold with one eye."

"You can see?"

"Yes."

"But you didn't recognize that I wasn't your mother."

"It's dark in here. Only some moonlight through a window."

"What do you see?"

$$R_X$$

"Where's my picture?"

"The drone went down short of the Bridge-Tunnel, sir. The agents are stuck in traffic now."

"Can they see the Hummer?"

"No, sir. The brothers went up the left-hand emergency lane, followed by the staties. Lost sight of them five minutes ago. They eluded the police. They traveled the wrong way through one of the tunnels."

"Keep searching. We have his and the brother's cell phone numbers. Get the NSA tech in here now! Track the numbers. Find them. Now!"

$$R_X$$

"What do you see, Michael?" Chrissie repeated.

There was nothing but silence and Michael's heavy, frustrated breathing.

"Michael," Chrissie began, "I know you wanted me to be your mother. It's a good thing she's not here. You wouldn't want her here, would you? I'm scared. Are you scared?"

Chrissie could hear the boy suck in a long, deep breath. "No, I'm not scared," he said. His words wavered.

"That's good," Chrissie replied. "Do you see anything that will help us?"

"It's pretty dark," Michael began. "That's why I didn't recognize you. We're in a basement. It smells."

"I smell it, too. It's musty and moldy. What else do you see?"

"There are lots of tools. I see a pitchfork, rakes, and a couple of barrels. The kind they use to make wine. There are racks and racks of wine bottles, too."

"When I was outside, the air was warm and I could hear the ocean."

"You were outside?"

"Yeah, I had to pee . . . and do the other thing."

"They took me to a smelly bathroom in here," Chrissie explained.

"Why are you here?" Michael demanded.

"I don't know. I think the people that took us want to get to your father."

"Why?"

A curtain of silence descended between them. Strong wind gusts buffeted the building. Dust and debris floated about. Chrissie felt it on her face and in her nostrils.

"I don't know," she replied.

Her response was the truth. She had no idea why they'd been taken. There was no reason. Everyone from the past was either dead or in custody.

"You need to remove your blindfold," Michael demanded, trying to take control. "Lean back and rub your head against the wall."

Chrissie chuckled. "Michael, I'm not as young as you and my body won't do that." She sensed Michael's power play. He was acting with a machismo she could tell he didn't feel.

"You need to try."

Chrissie leaned back. But her weight caused the chains to become taut and her wrists began to burn. She tried several times. "I can't do it, Michael."

"My mom would be able to do it."

"I'm sure she would," Chrissie scoffed. She tried once more to lean back but was not able to reach the wall. "I guess I'll have to just stay in the dark. You'll have to be our eyes. Is there anything in here we can use to escape?"

℞

The dying Hummer limped, steaming into the BP gas station on Hampton Boulevard outside the main gate at the Virginia International Terminals. Peter had coaxed the Hummer off of I-64, eventually taking

Terminal Boulevard paralleling the railroad tracks to the intersection with Hampton Boulevard

"She said to look for a man in a Red Sox jacket," Jason instructed. "His truck is parked in the lot away from the pumps."

Peter pressed the gas. The Hummer moaned. The engine groaned and sputtered as steam and smoke roiled from under the wrinkled hood.

"This thing's dying," Peter said.

"Just a little farther," Jason urged.

They swiveled their heads, searching. The Hummer stopped near the air station away from the pumps.

"There!" Jason pointed to the left.

Standing near a small building just off the gas station property, an elderly man leaned on a cane, staring the Hummer down. He was swallowed up by the bright-red pitcher's jacket with the words Red Sox scrawled across the front. His face, puckered with leathery skin, appeared shrink wrapped over his facial bones.

Jason hopped out, circling around the front. Peter rammed the Hummer into park and followed as Jason marched toward the old man. The shriveled human removed a nickel-plated revolver from the pocket of his jacket.

Jason showed his hands.

"We don't want any trouble," Jason said.

"There ain't gonna be any trouble as long as I'm holding this," he replied. He stood beside a small shack in the shadow of a wide oak tree.

"We need to find a truck," Jason continued. "I have these." Jason held up the keychain.

"I know what you need to find."

"Where is it?" Peter demanded. "We don't have much time."

"Not so fast, marine boy. Empty your pockets and give me your phones."

Jason and Peter pulled out their wallets, pocket money, the Hummer's keys, and their cell phones. They held them up.

"You . . . drug man," the old man pointed at Jason. "Both cell phones. Yours and hers."

Jason removed both cell phones, his and the one Delilah Hussein had left for them, the cash, his gun, and the ammo. Peter held out his weapon and the keys to the Hummer.

Red Sox Man pointed to a leather bag sitting on the asphalt. "Put 'em in there . . . Good. Now follow me."

The old man backed up and circled, giving the brothers a wide berth.

"There she is," he said.

A mid-sized Freightliner with a twenty foot cargo hold sat thirty yards away. Over the cab attached to the square cargo hold, a sleek blue refrigeration unit hummed. From this unit a long yellow cable snaked over the cab and down the front of the vehicle to an outlet on a small building. Keeping his gun trained on the brothers, Red Sox man removed the cord from the receptacle.

"Look for the crumbling house on Turkey Run Road." He motioned with his arm toward the vehicle. "Have a nice trip."

"The cops are after us," Peter said.

"Don't worry. When they find your truck, I'll be long gone. You'll have a good thirty-minute head start."

Peter and Jason exchanged glances and jogged to the truck. Along the side panel near the rear wheels, in two-inch letters, was the word Vengeance.

Red Sox Man hollered after them. "Two more things . . . No stopping . . . And don't try to open the back! The keys are at the destination."

℞

"They are now on the Eastern Shore," Oliver explained, ninety minutes later. "They have just left the bridge-tunnel and have turned north toward their rendezvous. It should be an hour or so before they get there."

"Any signs of the authorities? police? FBI?" Hussein asked.

"None. The Watcher stayed behind and is monitoring all local, state, and federal agencies for any kind of response. He just texted me over the secure line. There is no activity."

Hussein checked her Rolex.

Oliver knew she was calculating the time remaining. "When does the delivery have to be made?"

"They are starting the production run in twenty-four hours. The cargo needs to be there. Rodgers and his brother should arrive at their final destination in less than five hours. That leaves plenty of time. Phase two of Operation Hygeia will begin then."

"Shouldn't we have someone tailing them? Making sure they don't try something?"

"No," Hussein barked. "We have his son and fiancée. He will not try anything as long as he thinks they are in danger. And we are listening to and watching what's going on inside the truck, remember? That's enough. How are the woman and the boy?"

It was Oliver's turn to check his watch. "I just checked on them. They are fine."

"How many times have you visited?"

"Three times since they arrived. I will check again in a few hours."

"Any problems?"

"None."

"Where is the drone?"

"Just left on its latest sortie. It will return and we will download the messages within two hours," Oliver replied.

"Any issues with our earlier breach in protocol?" Hussein asked.

Oliver frowned. "None that we can detect. Luckily, the live transmissions did not occur for very long. I think we are okay. Our Russian friends have been monitoring their perimeter detection sites around the Atlantic. There have been no reports of any unusual movements by federal authorities like FBI or naval ship or troop movements. Homeland Security is on alert, but nothing is being mobilized."

The breach in communication protocol earlier had risked exposing their operation. Hussein's lapse in judgment was caused by her desperate need to know what was going on with the pharmacist. They had transmitted text messages to The Watcher live with the drone at altitude over the ocean. In her frustrated desperation, Hussein used Jason Rodgers's name, a key word no doubt being monitored by the American intelligence community.

"Continue to monitor the truck. I am expecting a communication from our asset inside Dawson Pharmaceuticals. He will want an update on the shipment."

℞

"When did we receive this?" The deputy director of the NSA asked.

"About two hours ago," came the reply.

"Jesus," the DD said, exasperated. "What the hell took so long?"

"We have not been able to locate the source of the transmission to a specific point. Only to a general range of islands in the eastern Caribbean."

"This name 'Rodgers' refers to the pharmacist?"

"Yes, sir. We believe so. The same message was sent four different times in a thirty minute span, relayed through a communications apparatus somewhere over the Atlantic. Each transmission was separated by ten or so miles."

"Call the National Reconnaissance Office. Get me satellite recon photos over this area. I want every inch of that area photographed. And get me Clay Broadhurst in the SIOC!"

$$R_x$$

"Do you have any idea where this is taking us?" Peter asked.

"Not the foggiest," Jason replied.

Jason, in the driver's seat, had the Freightliner M2 box truck headed north on Route 13. They had just passed over the twenty-mile long Chesapeake Bay Bridge and Tunnel complex and Fisherman's Island and gone "feet dry" at the southern end of the Eastern Shore ten minutes ago.

"We're five minutes from Townsend," Peter said.

"We've got to make contact with someone who can help us," Jason said.

Route 13 bisected the Delmarva Peninsula, normally an easy, unstressed drive along well-maintained pavement. But not this early morning, only minutes from sunrise. The last time Jason had driven here was ten years ago, with Jenny, when Michael was three years old. They had spent the weekend in Cape Charles, a quaint little bayside town with good shopping and uncluttered beaches.

Not much had changed in a decade. The divided, four-lane highway carried traffic north toward Delaware, Maryland, and Washington. Long stretches of the flat roadway allowed for a smooth, comfortable ride.

Traffic lights slowed the journey when small business districts in cities like Birds Nest, Nassawadox, Painter, and Melfa popped up. If you wanted to get away from city living, the Eastern Shore was the place to do it. Jason felt like he'd traveled back in time to what life in fifties

America could have been. But the tranquil environs of gentle farmland, thick-forested stretches of highway dotted with farmer's markets, and down-home country folk were not to be enjoyed this morning.

His unintended reverie was interrupted by a ringing noise.

"What the hell is that?" Peter asked.

Two more rings.

Peter tried to open the glove compartment. It was locked.

"It's on the key chain," Jason declared.

Peter leaned over and wrestled the remaining key from the key chain as it hung from the ignition. He opened the glove box and found another cell phone as the phone rang for the eighth time. This one was marked with a three in white grease paint. "She doesn't know I'm here." He handed it to Jason.

"Hello?"

"I see you have picked up the truck and you are headed north. Most excellent!"

It was her.

"We are about an hour from the address on the paper," Jason replied.

"We have a tracking device on the vehicle and are monitoring your location. No stopping or deviations. Stay on Route 13 until you reach Mappsville. You have plenty of fuel. If you stop or change course, your woman will pay. Understood?"

"Yes," Jason seethed.

"Also, the material you are delivering must be kept below freezing. If you allow the product to thaw, you will never see your family again. Make sure the engine is not turned off for any reason! Acknowledge that you have heard me!"

"I heard you!"

"You brought along a guest, Jason. You were not instructed to bring your brother."

"How did you . . ."

"Our man at the gas station reported in. He said there were two men that approached him. That was not wise."

"My brother will do everything needed. He wants my family back as much as I do . . . How did you know it's Peter?"

Hussein ignored the question. "You should not have disobeyed." Hussein paused, turned, and spoke to someone beside her. "Bring the Pettigrew woman here!"

"What are you doing?"

"I told you. No deviations. Your girlfriend will be held accountable."

"If you hurt her . . . or my son . . ." Jason hesitated.

"What?" Hussein demanded.

"I will drive this truck to the nearest police station. And I will not rest until I find you and kill you. Think I'm kidding? Try me!"

Jason's body shook as he spoke the words. They sounded weak and tremulous. He was taking a gamble. Hussein still needed him. But he was betting with Michael and Chrissie's lives.

A long silence followed. Finally, Hussein spoke. "I will overlook the transgression this time. The next time I will personally put a bullet in her head and video it for you to watch!"

Jason exhaled audibly and managed to say "Thank you!" He sighed. "I have a question."

"I'm sure you have many. In time, they will all be answered."

"Why have me go to all the trouble of getting the keys from William Luther? Why not just have me get the keys from the old man at the terminal?"

"Why, Monsieur Rodgers, that would be no fun, would it? And, by the way, do not try to call anyone. That would be unwise. We are monitoring the phone as well."

Before Jason could reply, the line went dead.

"What did she say?" Peter asked.

"They're tracking the truck. Have a GPS on board. She also knows you are with me. She *knew* it was you! The old man in the Red Sox jacket told her. Said we weren't to make any calls."

Jason's last statement caused Peter's forehead to tighten with concern. "Really?'

℞

"What's wrong?" Jason asked, five minutes later.

Peter held a finger to his lips. He mouthed two words: *No talking!*

"What is it?" Jason whispered.

Stop talking! Peter mouthed again. *I think they're listening.*

Jason: *How do you know?*

Peter: *Something you said.*

What?

She told you do not try to contact anyone. Almost like she was listening.

I got it, Jason replied. *You think they have a microphone planted?*

They may have a camera in here as well, Peter replied, nodding. *I'll look.*

Peter scanned the interior of the cab. He flipped down both visors. He opened the glove box. He did not see anything untoward. Next, he perused the dashboard and the steering wheel. Nothing.

Then Peter noticed a small dial on the rear wall of the cab. It was a temperature gauge. The needle registered a temperature of minus two degrees Celsius.

"Whatever is in the back of this thing is kept below freezing. If we let it thaw out maybe we spoil all their fun," Peter mused.

"I'm sure they are monitoring that as well. If we do that, we risk Michael and Chrissie!"

They came to a red light. Peter's eye narrowed. He angled his head and pointed to the rearview mirror.

What is it? Jason mouthed.

The pharmacist adjusted the mirror. His hand touched something on the underside of the housing. He motioned toward it. Peter leaned forward and checked the backside of the mirror. *There it is,* his brother mouthed.

Jason motioned that he wanted to write something. Peter found a pen and the registration in glove box. He handed them to Jason.

The light turned green. Jason pressed the accelerator. Peter grabbed the wheel and kept the truck straight as Jason scribbled.

Mike?

Peter checked the mirror again and ran his hand along the wires. A small microphone was attached to a wide-angle surveillance lens on the underside of the mirror.

Peter smirked and nodded.

Jason spoke aloud. "This damn mirror is dirty. Hand me something to clean it with."

Peter rummaged around in the glove box and came up with a small piece of cloth from an eyeglass case. "Here, use this," he replied out loud.

Jason drove and wiped the mirror. As he did so, he grabbed the small camera and microphone system and turned it 180 degrees so it faced the roadway.

"Just leave that up there," Jason said, "in case I need it again." Peter gave Jason a thumbs up.

℞

"We can't see them anymore," the technician explained to Oliver as Hussein's aide-de-camp entered the bedroom-cum-tech center.

The technician's heart beat in his chest with the speed of a hummingbird's wings. A palpitation fluttered beneath his ribs, taking away his breath. The technician knew what happened when someone messed up around here.

He had screwed up and breached protocol. The two sodas he had drunk in the last hour had caught up with him. He'd left the terminal to relieve himself and missed what had happened. He summoned Oliver when he returned to his work station and found the camera had been turned around. The brothers were talking about cleaning the mirror. It was a convenient excuse.

"What happened?"

"He messed with the mirror and dislodged the camera. It's pointing at the roadway. We still have audio, though."

"Did they find the camera?"

"I don't think so." The technician replied.

Oliver watched the asphalt and dashed white lines of Route 13 on the Eastern Shore rush past the lens.

"Merde!" he hissed. "Is the GPS beacon still active?"

"Oui."

"I'm going to call the phone in the truck. Keep monitoring."

℞

Jason drove as he mouthed another set of instructions to Peter while keeping one eye on the road.

Find out where the wires lead.

Peter traced the wire leading from the mirror. It snaked up a channel on the back of the mirror support toward the top of the windshield. From there, the wire disappeared under the lining on the interior ceiling. Peter pressed on the cloth, feeling the wire beneath, tracing them until his fingers palpated a hard, square object under the fabric.

Where the rear window met the roof lining, he pulled at the cloth until he freed a small section. Inserting a finger between the cloth and roof, the former marine yanked the cloth down, exposing the underside of the metal roof, the wire, and a small black box.

The black box possessed a steady indicator light illuminated with a green dot. The wire terminated at the small black rectangle, held in place by Velcro. A battery supply of some sort. Peter pulled at the square and removed it from the cab's roof. It separated easily, exposing a hole in the metal through which a small black stubby antenna attached to the square had protruded.

Peter showed it to Jason.

Pull it apart! Jason said.

Peter yanked the wires from the box and antenna as the cell phone began to ring.

Don't answer it! Jason mouthed.

℞

"We've just lost audio, *Monsieur* Oliver."

Oliver blurted several French expletives. "Qu'est-ce que c'est?" *What's going on?*

"Je ne sais pas." *I don't know.* "I can't see inside the truck. Should we notify Madame?"

"Is there anything we can do about it?"

"*Non.* We still have the GPS signal."

"I'll make the call." Oliver lifted his cell phone and pressed Hussein's private number.

"Madame, nous avons une problème." *We have a problem.*

℞

With the ability to speak freely restored, Jason pushed a plan.

"I need to get word to someone about what's going on," he explained. "We can't just keep blindly following her instructions."

"How are you going to do that? We have Hussein's phone, which I'm sure is being monitored. So you can't use that. And who are you going to call? Palmer? He's going to put you in jail . . . again."

"Even if he wanted to help us, which I don't think he does. This is over his head. I need to call Broadhurst in Washington."

"We don't have our phones," Peter said. "To make a call we'd have to stop. You heard her, no stopping!"

"I heard. We have to stay on course and on time, or she'll become suspicious."

"Watch it!"

Jason had been driving in the right lane and was so focused on his brother's words, the truck had drifted, straddling the dashed center line. A blue Chrysler sedan had pulled even with the truck and started blaring its horn as Peter shouted his warning.

"Sorry," Jason whispered after correcting. He blew out a long breath. "Do we have a tail? Any sign of the black Caddy?"

"I don't think so. I've been checking. I haven't seen one."

"We could find and disable the GPS," Jason said.

"That would take forever and we'd have to stop. It's probably under the hood or in the electronics. It would give us away. Can't risk it."

"Then what do you propose?"

"That light up ahead just turned red," Jason said. "I need you to drive. Let's switch positions."

Jason braked at the light, third in line in the left lane at the intersection with Stone Road leading to Cape Charles. Peter and Jason performed the old-fashioned Chinese fire drill before the light turned green.

Peter ground the gears before finding first and slowly accelerated. "What do you have in mind?"

"I'm going to make that phone call."

"How?"

CHAPTER 35

Nine miles and fifteen minutes later, as they passed through Machipongo, Jason rolled down the passenger-side window and leaned out of the cab. The truck accelerated in jerks as Peter awkwardly shifted gears. He waved at an approaching vehicle. A Jeep Grand Cherokee was gaining on them in the right lane, being driven by a burly, bearded man wearing a worn John Deere baseball cap.

Jason motioned for him to roll down his window.

"Can I use your cell phone?" he shouted.

The man scrunched his brow, thought for a second, and flipped Jason the bird before speeding off. He tried this tactic three more times with equally insufficient results.

A few miles later, on the fourth attempt, Jason flagged down the female driver of a white Chevy Malibu. The Malibu pulled even with the truck. She had short spiked black hair. Dark mascara ringed her eyes.

She shook her head no when Jason asked his question, and fell back.

"Damn it," he blurted, rolling up the window.

"We could risk pulling over," Peter said. "She's got us taking whatever's in the back of this rig somewhere. So she needs us. If she hurts them, then she's risking her own plan."

"Would you risk it if it was one of the girls?"

Peter shrugged. "No."

"I've got to know where they are. I've got to make her think we're following along. But we've got to know more. Broadhurst will know. He'll help."

The short, loud blasts of a horn interrupted the former marine. They both looked out Jason's window. The Malibu crept back into view. The spiked-hair woman was mashing the horn in short bursts as her eyes alternated between the road and the truck.

Jason rolled down the window.

"For two hundred dollars, you've got a deal," she hollered.

"Deal!" Jason shouted back. "I'll get into your car at the next light."

Peter picked up Delilah Hussein's cell phone. "I won't be answering this," he said.

Jason, realizing he would not be around to talk to Hussein said, "That's a good idea. If she calls, listen to the message and respond with a text like it's from me."

"Will do." Peter smiled wryly. "By the way, have you forgotten that the old geezer took our phones *and* our money?"

"No, I haven't forgotten."

"Then how are you going to pay her?"

"I'm working on it. Whatever you do just keep driving, I'll catch up with you."

℞

"The brother's cell phones have been tracked to Norfolk, Agent Broadhurst."

"Show me."

The wall screen filled with an overhead satellite view of the Norfolk, Virginia area. Two blinking triangular red icons flashed on a section of the grid. "We've overlaid the phone's signals onto the map."

"Where is this?" Broadhurst asked.

"It's an overhead view of the Virginia International Terminals south of the Norfolk Naval Base."

The blinking icons flashed in the general area of the terminals. "Are those the signals?" Broadhurst asked.

"Yes sir."

"Zoom in."

The screen zoomed in, focusing on the icons. The icons and the detail became more distinguishable. "What street is that?"

"That's Terminal Boulevard with the offshoot to the marine terminal gate. The signal is coming from a gas station."

"Where is my FBI person?" he shouted.

Broadhurst spun, a little too fast. He lost his balance and braced himself on a nearby table. The rapid intake of air into his damaged lungs formed a tickle in his throat. He coughed, trying to clear it.

"Right here, sir." A thirty-something, crewcut appeared.

The cough persisted. Consumed with the urge to clear his congested lungs, he was racked with an uncontrolled spasm. Broadhurst removed a handkerchief from his pocket and covered his mouth. The spasm lasted thirty seconds.

He choked out a question to the FBI agent through the handkerchief. "Where are our FBI agents in the area?"

"Two were in traffic on the Hampton Roads Bridge-Tunnel. They were operating the purchased drone when it lost power. They are returning to the field office in Norfolk where there are three more agents."

Broadhurst lowered the blood-tinged cloth. He noticed the FBI agent's eyes following it as he rammed it into his pocket.

"Have them contact Norfolk PD. I want agents and cops scouring that area. I want those phones found ten minutes ago. And get me a video file from the gas station!"

℞

"Michael, are you there?"

"That's kind of a dumb question. You think I'm going anywhere?"

The early morning sun rose through the small window near the top of the east wall.

Chrissie shook her head. "That's was pretty sarcastic, young man. I know your father didn't raise you to speak to adults that way."

"Well, it was a dumb question."

They sat in silence for a short time. Then Chrissie asked a question she should have asked an hour ago.

"Michael, have you seen your father? Is he here too?"

"I haven't seen him."

"I guess that's good," she sighed.

She decided to confront Michael. "Why do you not like me?" Chrissie asked, turning her blindfolded eyes toward the sound of Michael's voice.

"I don't know."

"So you admit you don't like me?"

Silence.

"Are you mad because of something I did?"

"No."

"Something I didn't do?"

"No."

"Please tell me why then."

"I don't want to talk about it."

Chrissie heard Michael sigh from across the dusty cell. Sensing an opportunity, she urged him.

"Michael, I'm not your enemy. I'm not trying to get between you and your father. He loves you very much. He talks about you all the time."

Michael grunted a guttural sound.

"Tell me, what have I done to you?"

Michael exhaled again. "My father never wanted children. He said he *wasted* all those years. He was talking to you. I heard it."

Chrissie felt like she'd been kicked in the stomach. "Michael, what are you talking about? When did you hear this?"

"When my father was in the hospital. You and he were talking behind the curtain. I walked in. You didn't see me. But I heard him say he loved you all this time and that he wasted all those years."

Now it was Chrissie's turn to exhale. She remembered their conversation in Tidewater Regional Medical Center and the squeak from the hallway. Chrissie had whipped the curtain back. But no one was there.

"Oh, Michael, that was you?"

"Yup. I heard it, don't tell me I didn't."

"No, he said it," Chrissie replied. "Have you never discussed this with your father?"

"No."

"Why?"

Silence.

"Never mind," she said. "I think I know why."

"Why does he love you more than me and my mom?"

Chrissie instinctively tried to move her hands. The hurt in his voice touched something maternal in her. She wanted to wrap her arms around him and embrace him. But the only thing she managed to do was rattle chains.

"Michael, I want you to listen to me . . . very carefully. I'll try to make you understand."

"This ought to be good," he mocked.

$$R_{X}$$

Less than an hour after Clay Broadhurst had requested it, the grainy black-and-white video footage filled the wall screen in the SIOC. Broadhurst, seated in his wheelchair, and Brad Lane and Director of Operations John Beck stood behind the Secret Service agent shoulder to shoulder and stared up at the images. The technicians and agents situated before their computer monitors and screens had collectively stopped what they were doing and were also gazing up at the surreal scene. The time stamp on the screen indicated that the surveillance had been recorded at 3:45 a.m. More than two hours ago.

On the monitor, a battered Hummer, steam seeping from under the damaged hood, pulled to a stop in the far corner of the BP gas station. The vehicle was mostly hidden from view. But Jason Rodgers, the pharmacist, and his ex-marine brother, Peter, alighted from the truck and walked to a person in the shadows. He had positioned himself in such a way that his upper body and face were hidden from the camera. The images also revealed that he was leaning on a cane.

As the two men approached, the partially hidden man removed a gun from his jacket pocket. Jason and Peter Rodgers, in unison, raised their hands in a sign of surrender.

"He's wearing a jacket with wording on the front. Can you read it?" Brad Lane asked.

"Freeze it, right there," Broadhurst croaked as he held a handkerchief to his mouth.

"Can't read it sir. Too many shadows."

An unseen technician halted the recording, reversing it a few seconds to maximize the shot of the obscured individual. The gunman's hand moved the gun, waving it slightly as he spoke to the pair. After fifteen seconds, the Rodgers brothers both removed items from their pockets and placed them in a bag on the pavement. Once that was completed, the stranger backed up out of sight as the brothers followed.

Three minutes after that, a portion of a white panel truck was visible driving off. Only the wheels and a sliver of the cargo hold were visible.

"Stop it there," Broadhurst commanded again.

After a few adjustments, the image froze on a few feet of the cargo hold, the wheels, and chassis of the white truck.

"What's that writing in the truck . . . right there? Zoom in . . . we might get a clue as to the origin of the vehicle."

The image zoomed in, becoming more pixelated and grainy.

"Can anyone read that?" Beck, the CIA man, demanded.

"Yes, sir, I can," an anonymous voice called out.

"Well, don't keep us in suspense."

"It reads: Vengeance."

"Vengeance?" Broadhurst muttered. "That was the name of her yacht!"

Broadhurst lowered the handkerchief from his face as his mouth hung open. Beck's forehead crinkled in confusion, and Brad Lane uttered one word, "Shit!"

℞

Jason raced around the front of the Chevy Malibu and climbed in a moment before the light turned green.

"Just keep pace with the truck," Jason explained. "And I'll get out at another light."

"Just curious, but why can't you make a call on your own cell phone?" The woman snapped, her voice filled with contemptuous curiosity.

Jason blinked in frustration. "I lost it. And it's a very important call."

"And what about your friend's?"

"He lost his, too."

"Let me guess," the young Goth woman said, "your mother had to write your name on all your clothes when you were little, right?"

"Look . . . what's your name?"

"Sheryl. Sheryl Penney. That's Sheryl with an *S*."

"Okay Sheryl with an S, I really need to make a phone call. Can I use yours or can you take me to a gas station or a motel or something? I don't have time to argue with you."

"Sorry," she replied, wiping her forehead with a paper towel. "I get cranky. I'm overdue for my medication."

"Can I use the phone?"

She pulled her phone from her purse at her feet on the driver's side.

"My password is 2-4-8-2-4. Do you know what that spells?"

"No . . ."

"B-I-T-C-H!"

"How appropriate," Jason deadpanned.

She licked her lips and swallowed hard, pulling the phone back.

"What's wrong with you?"

"Nothing . . . I'm fine. Now as that guy in *Jerry Maguire* said, "First, show me the money'!"

CHAPTER 36

The Watcher read the text message from Hussein for the fourth time.

Job well done! Get on a flight as planned, send final payment instructions, and disappear.

He smiled.

It was critical that he get inside her compound, wherever that was.

He had enticed Hussein to allow him to become part of her team with $100 million. The first $50 million installment was paid upfront with the promise of an equal payment when Rodgers was en route to the destination and confirmation of the death of the spy codenamed Hammon. Rodgers, with his brother, Peter, was on his way up the Eastern Shore at this very moment.

Hussein had confirmed that Hammon was dead by sending a photo of the body. The presence of the ex-marine brother of the pharmacist could complicate the mission. The Watcher had considered demanding that the former marine step out of the Hummer in the parking lot of the gas station, leaving Jason to fend for himself. But an instinct told him that Jason Rodgers would need his brother's help. So he'd done nothing. Now, it was time for his next move.

The hard part, he thought. *As if all this hadn't been hard enough!*

He typed his reply, knowing it might take hours to get a response. His request was timed for this exact moment. Hussein would be knee-deep in last minute activities. She would be pre-occupied. And she was inherently greedy. The Watcher had earned Hussein's trust. He prayed she would allow him onto he compound.

Need to meet you! Final payment instructions must be delivered personally.

℞

Jason sighed. "I don't have any money with me."

"I knew it," she said. "I knew it. She spat, "Get out of my . . ."

Sheryl Penney blinked rapidly as if trying to keep her eyes open. Her eyes had glassed over. She looked at Jason. Large droplets of sweat erupted on her forehead.

"Are you okay?" Jason asked.

She had halted midsentence and turned back to the road. Her head lolled back and forth. The Malibu drifted toward a grassy embankment along the side of the road. Jason grabbed the wheel and corrected her course.

"I don't feel so good," she said. "I need to find a bathroom. I knew you were a no good weasel. No . . . money!"

"Okay . . . take your foot off the gas and steer into the breakdown," he commanded.

"Screw you, asshole!"

"Living up to your password, I see. Just take it easy and slow down."

The Chevy stopped at an angle off the road. He hopped out and circled to the driver's side, dragging Penney from the car and pushing her into the passenger seat. Once behind the wheel, he pulled back into traffic. A mile up the road, Jason saw the taillights of the Freightliner glow as Peter depressed the brakes.

The sedan picked up speed as Jason punched the accelerator. He pulled alongside the Freightliner and yelled to Peter.

"Something's wrong with her. I need to get her help. Keep going. I'll catch up."

Peter nodded and drove on. Another mile had slipped under the wheels of the Malibu before Jason pulled into a Valero gas station in Nassawadox. He assisted the Penney woman as she babbled and bitched the whole way into the convenience store.

Inside, halfway to the restroom, she said, "I need my purse. Gotta have my purse."

"I saw a sign for a hospital. Riverside Shore Memorial. I should take you there."

"No," Penney demanded like an insolent child. Get my purse!"

Jason let her lean on a counter by the soda fountain as he returned to the car and retrieved the purse. When he returned, he placed her arm around his neck and walked her to the ladies room.

At the restroom door, Penney said, "I can take it from here. I'm feeling a little better."

Jason scanned her face. Some color had returned.

"Are you sure? What medication are you on?" he asked, searching her eyes.

"None of your goddamned business," she smiled. "Sorry. I get cranky sometimes. Can you put some gas in the car? I'm running low. I'll pay when I come out."

She closed the door in his face.

Back at the pump, Jason stuffed the nozzle into the tank, watching the numbers roll by. The Malibu had been running on fumes. Jason looked around, contemplating his next move. The Penney woman had her phone with her in the bathroom and he had no money to pay for the gas.

$$\text{R}_{\text{X}}$$

"Michael, please give me a chance," Chrissie pleaded.

She had reasoned with him for a long time. But he'd simply said he didn't want to hear it. She'd sat silent for about ten minutes. Finally, she decided to give it another go. He was, after all, a captive audience.

She spoke softly. "Michael, your father and I knew each other many years ago. A long time before you were born . . . a long time before he and your mother were married. We dated for about a year . . . and we were in love.

"He worked for my father, Thomas. Everything was going well. Then something happened . . ."

Chrissie hesitated. Her voice cracked. She didn't want to burden Michael with the minutiae of why Jason had left or the threat of the lawsuit and the tearful break-up on the bench overlooking the James River.

"We couldn't be together anymore. Your father decided to end our relationship after a year. I never saw him again, not until about two years ago. He was divorced from your mother. He came to my father's funeral. That's how we reconnected."

She heard Michael shuffling and his chains rattling. "Why did he break up with you?"

At least he's asking questions.

"Your father had to make a difficult choice. If he stayed on working in my father's pharmacy, The Colonial . . ."

"Your father owned The Colonial?"

"He did. When he died, it became mine."

"So my dad works for you now?"

Technically, that was true. "We run it together. Your father is a good pharmacist. Many years ago, your father broke up with me because there was a mistake made. People blamed your father. They said if he didn't leave, The Colonial would be sued. It would have put my father out of business. It would have ruined our family.

"So your dad decided to leave The Colonial so my father and me could have a good life. He sacrificed a lot. That's the kind of man he is. He cares about other people more than himself. I'm sure wherever he is right now, he's worried sick and is doing whatever he can to find us."

$$\textbf{R}_{\textbf{X}}$$

Sheryl Penney sat on the filthy toilet, bracing her head in her hands, summoning strength. She glanced at the door and saw that she'd forgotten to lock it. But she was too unsteady to stand up again. As a Type I diabetic, she'd always been hypersensitive to changes in her blood sugar. Normally, she was very good about taking her insulin. But the wedge of apple pie loaded with two scoops of vanilla ice cream was wreaking havoc with her sugar levels.

She had not injected herself with five units of Humalog after eating. The phone call from her stupid-ass sister had gone on for thirty minutes, depleting her battery and distracting her from the insulin shot. Her sister, Heather, was in a panic because she'd missed her period and didn't want to be pregnant . . . again. Penney had done nothing but respond with "ums" and "uh-huhs," while Heather got it out of her system.

The symptoms had started with the mounting thirst. Her mouth, dry and parched, felt like a desert. Her bladder was full. She always had to pee when her blood sugar rose. She'd barely made it to the bathroom, sat down, and relieved herself. That's when the spinning set it.

She retrieved the travel case containing her testing supplies from her purse. Her damned, cheap-ass insurance company had been dragging its feet for a year about paying for an insulin pump. They never hesitated to take her premiums though.

Penney held out her hand and watched it oscillate. She fumbled with her One Touch glucometer and managed to shake out a test strip. Her tremor was so violent, though, that she spilled the rest onto the grimy floor. With difficulty, she slid the strip into the slot of the machine without pushing it all the way in.

Next, she removed the lancets—the small needles used to puncture the skin of her fingers—so she could massage a drop of blood. Again, a small army of capped lancets fell to the floor. She palmed one and jammed it into the lancing device. Placing it against the side of her index finger, she pressed the activation lever. The familiar click was followed by the annoying stinging sensation.

After squeezing a crimson droplet from her finger, Penney pushed the test strip all the way into the machine, activating it. The readout counted down five seconds. She placed the droplet at the edge of the strip and the blood wicked into the strip as the machine quaked in her hand.

Three seconds later, the machine registered its reading: 458.

Oh God! She thought. *You idiot!*

Penney removed another leather case from her purse and creaked it open. She removed an insulin-loaded Humalog Kwikpen, twisted on one of the pen needles, and dialed in eight units of insulin.

She rose up and lifted the shirt over her belly. At that point, the dizziness swelled. Penney felt herself sway as if pushed by a strong wind. She began to fall. The last thing she saw was the ever-increasing size of the filthy squares of the tile floor coming up to meet her.

℞

"Is the GPS still working?"

"Yes."

"They have not answered the phone. Is it dead?"

"No, Madame."

"Where are they now?"

Hussein leaned in over Oliver's right shoulder.

"They are here," Oliver replied, pointing to the small icon on the map. *She seems to have calmed down*, he thought.

"What happened to the sound?"

"The pharmacist manipulated the mirror and accidentally hit the lens. Then the power failed. Battery, peut-être?"

"No," Hussein replied. "They found the camera and microphone?"

Hussein had blasted Oliver when he informed her about the failure of the camera and microphone, casting ominous threats toward everyone within earshot. He waited for another outburst now regarding the sound. But none came, only a question.

"We're not sure."

"Have they stopped or has the truck made any unusual moves?"

"Non, Madame! They're on schedule."

"Bien! Perhaps it was just a glitch."

"They are about to approach the drop point. They should find the old house in about fifteen minutes."

℞

"Hey mon. Your woman needs some help," said the clerk, waving his arms as he charged from the building. He was a tall, lanky black man with dreadlocks hanging down the front and back of his polo shirt.

"She done collapsed. The door was unlocked and someone found her on the floor."

Jason had finished filling the tank and raced inside. He pushed through a gaggle of curious onlookers. A woman knelt over the Penney woman with two fingers pressed against her neck. The woman looked up as Jason neared.

"She's alive, but unconscious."

Jason saw the testing meter and supplies scattered across the dirty floor. "She's a diabetic." Turning to the onlookers, he issued a command. "Call 911!"

The trio of onlookers, two men and a second woman, stood transfixed.

Jason pointed at the eldest. "You! Call now!"

He circled the female pulse-checker and picked up the glucose meter with the bloodied test strip still in the slot. He turned it on and the last blood sugar reading displayed on the screen.

"I'm a pharmacist. She needs insulin," he said grabbing the insulin pen.

She was probably on a sliding scale based on her blood sugar levels. He needed to give her a sufficient amount that her sugar levels dropped. But he didn't want to give her so much that it bottomed out and she became hypoglycemic.

The pen had already been dialed in for eight units of a fast-acting insulin called Humalog. There was no box or label containing dosing instructions from her pharmacy. Diabetics were often quite adept at injecting themselves with the correct amount of insulin without referring to the prescription label each time.

That's it, he told himself. *She gets eight units.*

He lifted her blouse, exposing her abdomen. He swabbed her skin with an alcohol pad from her purse. Gently pinching the skin together, he pushed the short, ultra-thin needle in and pressed the plunger.

Jason checked the pulse in her wrist and checked her breathing by placing his ear close to her mouth.

"Ambulance is on the way," a voice called out.

Jason rummaged around in Penney's purse. He found the car keys and the cell phone. "We have another family emergency to tend to. What hospital will she be taken to?"

"Riverside Shore Memorial Hospital," someone said. "Just down the road here!"

"I must leave. Tell my sister," he said, pointing to the woman, "that I'll be back as soon as I can. When the paramedics arrive, tell them I gave her eight units of insulin." He pointed at the most competent-looking person in the small group. It was the woman who'd called 911. "You, do you know how test a patient's blood sugar?"

"No."

"I'm going to give you a crash course."

After explaining the procedure, Jason placed the cell phone in his pocket and ran out the door. Thirty seconds later, he was in Penney's Malibu and speeding off without paying for the gas.

℞

"It still doesn't explain why he thinks he wasted his years?"

"He doesn't think he wasted his years with you or your mother."

"Then why did he say it?"

"Because he was in pain in the hospital. We had just gone through a lot. He was frustrated and just glad to be alive."

"What happened? Why was he in the hospital?"

Jason had told Chrissie the story he and Jenny had given Michael about Jason's hospitalization. It was the only thing she knew to say.

"He was in a car accident."

"I'm not stupid! Don't lie to me. He was not in an accident."

"Well, what do you think happened, Michael?" Chrissie asked with a defiant tone.

℞

Charlie snapped shut the cell phone and smiled at Pierre.

"Was that Oliver?"

"Yup," Charlie triumphed.

"And he's not coming by?" Pierre asked, already knowing the answer.

"Nope. We have another four hours before he checks in on us again."

Charlie stood and hitched up his pants, licking his lips as he did.

"It's time, Pierre." Charlie slapped his compatriot on the back of the head. "Remember, keep the boy outside until you see me return."

$$R_x$$

Following the written instructions, Peter hung a left onto a desolate road called Turkey Run Road.

It's a holler, he thought.

Peter had commanded a young marine in the Middle East named Earvin Johnson. His fellow marines, including Peter, called him Magic, after the famous Los Angeles Laker basketball star. Unfortunately, this Magic had never held a basketball in his hands and couldn't hit the ocean if he was standing on the beach.

Magic was a good-natured, country hick from the Deep South, somewhere in Alabama. He'd used the word holler in a conversation that Peter overheard. Magic told his buddies that a holler is a long, curving country road cut through the forest with scant few houses. Hollers were great places to take a date and shoot squirrels, Magic had told them.

"A real night on the town. You really know how to show a gal a good time," his fellow marines kidded him.

As Peter drove the first one hundred yards along the lonely road, he couldn't help but remember Magic. Unfortunately, Magic was blown into five large chunks of flesh and blood three days later when he stepped on an IED.

I hope we have a better outcome, Magic, Peter thought.

The light intensified as the sun rose over the tree line. However, the large deciduous trees with limbs of freshly sprouted leaves draped over the roadway blocking the luminescence, creating a shadowy, speckled tunnel. A gradual left-hand turn curved another hundred yards away. He flipped on the truck's headlights.

A white-tailed doe stood on the crest of the unmarked humped roadway. The cracked pavement sloped away. The young deer stared into the beam of the truck, transfixed despite the early morning hour. Its eyes glowed an aquamarine glimmer in the shadows. Peter depressed the accelerator with a slow, gentle push. The engine revved. The truck inched along. He mashed the horn. The whitetail jerked and bounded into the forest to Peter's right.

He rotated the wheel, taking the gentle turn with care, not wanting to miss anything. The instructions said that the house he was looking for was abandoned and sported two holes in the aged roof. The headlights illuminated two houses forty yards apart on the right side of the road, set back behind a row of broken hedges. The first was a large white edifice with a single dormer protruding from a well-worn but intact roof coated with pine needles.

Peter guessed there was second dormer on the opposite side of the roof. He couldn't see it, though, through the overgrowth of branches and vines.

The second building was smaller, in better condition, with dark mold stains dotting the siding. It was a nothing more than a small box with a door and a roof.

He slipped past these houses along a linear length of dark asphalt. A quarter mile deeper into the forest, the road meandered right. More trees, more shadows. As he brought the truck out of the turn, a flash, again from the right, glinted fifteen feet into the trees. A metallic strobe caught his eye.

Peter braked and peered beyond the tree line. He let his foot off the brake and let it roll forward. The vague, grayish, rectangular outline came into view. Square black holes dotted the rectangle. As he inched farther, Peter began to recognize the familiar shape of a single-wide mobile home with children's toys scattered long the gravel driveway.

Peter cast his eyes left. If this was the place, the old, abandoned house should be visible. The forest beside the trailer seemed thicker here. The shadows several shades darker.

He had been praying since Jason left the truck that Hussein would not call. If the phone did ring, he was not going to answer it. He did not want to have to explain where Jason was. If she texted, he would stop and reply, pretending he was his brother. But, so far, the phone had remained silent.

Jason's plan to find a phone and to get to Michael and Chrissie was fraught with holes.

Peter stopped the truck with a squeal of brakes and put it in park, but left the engine running. He exited and crossed through the wash of headlights, crossing the overgrown ditch beside the road. He climbed up the opposite bank and walked through a blanket of dead leaves, branches, and brambles. He'd gone ten feet into the forest when he spotted the cracked, bending outline of the dead house.

℞

"I don't know," Michael replied again. "I don't know what happened. Stop playing with me. Just tell me what happened."

Michael had told her three times that he didn't know what had happened to his father. Chrissie had asked the question in different ways. She wanted to take his focus off of the words his father had spoken in the hospital and put it on why Jason had been hospitalized. The more he said "I don't know," the longer she paused between responses.

It was time to give him the news.

℞

Anger still stung Michael, infecting his thoughts and emotions. His breaths were slow and hard as she spoke to him.

"Michael, your father had some very dangerous people trying to kill him and some others. Your father got involved and stopped them. He was injured in the process. So was I. We both almost died."

"Really?" Michael could not contain his surprise at her statement.

"Really."

He screwed up his lips into a tight circle. "Who were these people trying to kill?"

"It's not my place to tell you that. Your father should. I'll let him do it when we see him again. Okay?"

"Yeah . . . okay. Who were the dangerous people?"

"It's complicated, Michael, Suffice it to say that your father was a hero. But we couldn't tell anyone because it's still a secret."

"Dad is a hero?"

"Yup."

They were silent for the next thirty seconds. In that time, Michael's memory was jogged. Her words came back to him as he listened to her conversation with his father that night in the hospital room.

Thank you for saving my life. If you hadn't been right behind that guy, I would be dead, she had said.

His father *had* saved her life. His father was a hero! He saved this woman's life.

Bad things happen when good people do nothing!

Michael felt his pent-up frustration and anger drain from his body.

Chrissie interrupted Michael's thoughts and decided to ask the boy for a request. "Michael, can you do me . . . no, can you do yourself and your father a favor?"

"I guess so."

"I want you to stop being mad at your father about what you heard in the hospital. Can you do that? At least until you hear the whole story . . . from him. Can you do that?"

Chrissie heard Michael sigh heavily. "Yeah, I can do that."

"Great . . ."

They were interrupted by the sound of the heavy wooden door thunking open. They fell silent. Chrissie's heart rattled in her rib cage. She could only imagine the amount of fear assaulting the boy, because hers was monumental.

Slow, heavy footfalls descended the stone steps and moved across the dusty floor, scraping to a halt between them.

Chapter 37

Sunday, April 12

Delilah Hussein plopped herself down in a heap on the Adirondack chair beside the pool under the covered pergola, out of sight of satellites, drones, and any possible surveillance aircraft. She sucked in several long, cleansing breaths as she studied the blood-stained chair opposite her, the discarded flap of ear, the bloodied knife, and the areas where the acid had peeled away the paint on the chair.

Checking her watch, she saw it was almost seven-thirty in the morning. The sun, slicing in horizontally, had lifted over the watery horizon and warmed her face. It felt good, lifting her spirits. She had calmed down since learning about the failure of the technology on the truck speeding toward the rendezvous point. Her concern initially swelled when she learned that Peter Rodgers, the brother of the pharmacist, had tagged along with Jason. In hindsight, she should have instructed Jason to stop the vehicle and tell the former marine to get the hell out. She could have confirmed their compliance through the video feed. But the thought had not occurred to her until after she disconnected the call. By the time she realized her mistake, the drone had returned to its landing pad and was being serviced. In the interim, they lost all video and sound in the cab of the Freightliner. She did not want to risk another phone call at that point. They had already been careless. Thinking that their plan was going to shit, she popped a pill. It had not touched her rising anxiety.

As time passed, her angst plateaued and then waned slightly. There were two reasons for her shrinking concern. First, the truck carrying the two brothers had continued along its route with no deviations. Second, they had arrived at the dilapidated old house on Turkey Run Road in Mappsville, Virginia. The fact that the brothers were there now, meant they were one step closer to the final destination. The fragile but deadly cargo was another step closer to finding its way to the plant in New Jersey. Once there, the cargo would be offloaded and installed in the secret room. Then the waiting would begin.

Oliver had suggested that they simply send a text message to the cell phone with the address or coordinates. But Hussein had reverted back to her fear and disdain of electronics and technology and insisted that the final destination be communicated through a dead drop.

Thanks be to Allah! she told herself. The failure of the camera and the microphone in the truck demonstrated that her techno-fear was justified.

She popped a second anti-anxiety pill into her mouth, following it with two sips of Espresso. She would need the caffeine to counter-act the sedative effects of the anxiolytic. Though she was feeling better about the mission, she didn't need another flare-up of anxiety crippling her ability to think clearly.

As she swallowed the tiny white pill, her cell phone chimed. She checked it. The latest round of data had been uploaded from Reprisal One. There was only one message. It was from The Watcher:

Need to meet you! Final payment instructions must be delivered personally.

Hussein considered the request. She was leery of visitors to her compound, lest they lead the Americans to her. Hammon's visit had taken place on a neighboring island for that very reason.

The Watcher was requesting a meet to deliver the instructions for payment of the final $50 million installment. Hussein steepled her hands before her face. Today was a crucial day in their operation. It would be extremely busy and would spell success or failure. She hesitated to allow The Watcher on the compound. But she could also not afford to lose three or four hours running off to another island to take possession of account numbers and passwords.

I could send Oliver, she mused. *No,* she finally decided. *I need him here as well.* Oliver was the only person she trusted to make sure everything was in place.

Receiving the final payment instructions had to be done by her . . . and her alone. She did not trust anyone to have access to such a large amount of money.

The Watcher's deeds and actions over the preceding twelve months had been exemplary. He'd delivered on every promise—monitoring Jason Rodgers's every move, listening in on his phone conversations, intercepting email, and eavesdropping on him and his girlfriend. The Watcher knew every move the pharmacist was going to make before he made it. He'd corralled William Luther and Clyde Hutton, putting them in place for Rodgers, and delivered the cell phones and the small coffins. He'd rescued Jason Rodgers from the car wreck and the jail in Newport News, allowing her sordid plan of vengeance on the man to continue to play out. Without him, this mission would not have been possible.

Except for the one security slip-up in which he'd used Rodgers name in a text, The Watcher had acquitted himself like a true professional.

Hussein sighed and typed in her reply:

Come to my compound! Get a flight to St. Bart's immediately. I will have a car meet you at Gustaf Airport. Use the password with the driver . . . Amo . . .

Hussein gave him the location and coordinates. Then she laid her head back on the Adirondack chair, closed her eyes, and let the warm breeze wash over her.

Try to relax, she told herself. *The time is drawing near!*

℞

Since leaving the gas station, Jason had driven for twenty minutes. It was almost seven-thirty in the morning. The spring sun had blossomed over the tree line. Jason couldn't remember the last time he'd slept. He felt no fatigue at the moment. He was running on adrenaline and fear.

A surge of healthcare worker's guilt filled him. His job was to assist a person with any kind of health crisis whenever and wherever and to never leave a patient in distress. He couldn't remember anything in the Pharmacist's Oath, the Nightingale Pledge, or the Hippocratic Oath that said a pharmacist, nurse, or doctor was required to stay with a patient when their son's and girlfriend's lives hung in the balance.

He had done everything he could for the diabetic Sheryl Penney, bringing down her blood sugar with a dose of insulin and instructing one of the bystanders to measure it again in ten minutes. Hopefully, an ambulance had already taken her to the hospital.

The Freightliner was long gone. He wondered where Peter was and hoped that Hussein hadn't somehow figured out that he had left the truck. *Relax!* He told himself. *You can't do anything about it now!*

He pulled into the parking lot of The Great Machipongo Clam Shack, found a parking spot away from other cars and lifted Penney's smartphone off of the seat beside him.

He turned it on and entered the password, pressing in the numbers corresponding to the word: B-I-T-C-H. A rotating circle appeared on the phone, followed by a warning: *Low Battery . . . 10%*

He cursed as he pulled up the Safari browser for a website and typed words into the url address bar.

Will the battery last?

His goal: get in contact with Clay Broadhurst, the Secret Service agent in Washington. But he didn't have a number. He had one option because he only had one cell number burned into his memory: John Palmer, the Newport News homicide detective. The same man who, right now, was looking for Jason and Peter so he could put them in a cell. And the man who was probably still fuming over Jason's request to retrieve the keys. He needed Palmer's help and Jason had to find a way to convince the cop to help.

The automated voice on the other end answered. *"Thank you for calling the Newport News Police Department . . ."*

$$\mathbf{R}_{X}$$

Peter approached the door, hanging from the top hinge in its frame. The wood was blanched and weather-beaten. The house was more than just old. It was a rotted, collapsing shell of wood and shingle, looking like the remnants of a bomb blast.

A piercing screech startled him from the right.

Instinctively, he dropped to a knee.

The door to the mobile home had opened. A short, squat, silhouetted woman stood backlit in the doorway. In her hands, she held what looked like a shotgun.

"Who's out there?" the female voice called.

Peter did not respond. He realized it would be futile to remain silent with the idling truck humming behind him. Her disheveled appearance clued him in that she must have been awakened by the truck.

Peter swallowed and called out. "It's me, ma'am. My name's Peter."

"What the hell you want over there?"

Peter heard the distinctive click of a hammer being cocked.

"I got a gun!"

"I don't mean no harm, ma'am. Just checking out this old house. I have a thing for old houses . . . like to take pictures of them," Peter lied.

"This early in the morning?"

"This is when the light is best."

"Where you from?"

"Across the bridge-tunnel."

"That damned bridge-tunnel. Does nothing but allow you crazies over here."

"I promise I'll leave. I just came from inside and I dropped something in there. I'd like to get it. Then I'll leave. I promise."

The woman stood silent, partially concealed in the door. The outline of her jaw revealed the probability of a hard scowl on her face. Her patience was short.

Finally, she said, "Make it quick. Then git your ass outta here."

℞

He is going to show your father's girlfriend what a real man looks like!

The words were spoken without emotion. But they hit Michael like a punch in the gut, sucking the air from his lungs. He trudged forward. A sinking feeling flooded him.

The guard named Pierre had retrieved Michael from his dungeon, leaving Miss Christine behind. Michael trudged up the steps as Pierre pushed him. As they passed the low window to the cellar, the naked light bulb hanging from the rough timbers of the wine cellar ceiling illuminated the scene clearly through the rectangular opening. The wild-eyed guard named Charlie stood over Miss Christine, unbuckling his belt.

The guards had seemed in a hurry to get Michael out of the cellar and failed to notice that the blindfold had slipped a little lower on his face and that Michael could see. Or had they chosen to ignore the fact? Michael had asked why the woman wasn't coming with them. That prompted Pierre's ominous reply.

Michael had been angry with Miss Christine for not being his mother, for being his father's girlfriend. He wanted the person held with him to be his mother. Disappointed that it was Miss Christine, he felt almost cheated. But ultimately, he realized, this was the last place he wanted his mother to be.

He had been angry with his father, too.

Miss Christine's words about his father being a hero had stunned him. Not that he didn't think his father was heroic. *He'd almost been killed and he'd saved some people!* His father was like that. He always did the right thing.

Through the window, Michael saw the guard standing over Miss Christine. Her blindfold had been removed, and there was a look of horror on her face, her eyes looking up at the guard, filled with a sense of the coming unspeakable deeds. Michael felt fear, too. Fear for Miss Christine. The small feelings of jealousy that had consumed him for so long evaporated.

His father had taught Michael a valuable lesson a few years back. A lesson that crystallized now following the uncomfortable ebb of the guard's words.

At school, Michael had watched a smaller boy being beaten by an older classmate. Michael had come home and told his father about the exciting fight, explaining how the older boy's punches drew blood and closed the younger boy's eye.

His father listened without reaction as Michael recounted the story. When he was done, his father asked if the younger boy was alright. Michael said he didn't know.

"And you just stood there and watched?"

Michael's reply was a weak "yes." The question, and the way his father had asked it, communicated volumes about his father's feelings about Michael's lack of action. Instantly, guilt consumed him.

His father's lecture was a simple two sentences: *"Sometimes you have to think about other people before yourself, son. Bad things happen when good people do nothing!"*

Days later, his father had presented Michael with the Saint George's Medal that he now wore around his neck. Michael could feel the medal swinging back and forth across his chest as he walked.

Michael recalled his father's story about Saint George. As the patron saint of England and courage, George stood up to a tyrannical king. He didn't remember all the details. But he'd done what was right, despite the difficulty it caused him.

Whatever feelings he had about Miss Christine—and he understood now how selfish his feelings were—she was about to experience a life-changing assault. Michael's anger and frustration, which had melted away moments ago, now reappeared in a different form, morphed into hatred and motivation . . . motivation to act.

He could not do nothing!

"Oh really. I never liked her anyway. She deserves whatever she gets," Michael lied. "What's your name?"

"Pierre."

"Pierre. That's French for Peter. That's my uncle's name."

"Vraiment?" *Really?*

Michael took two more steps. "Hey, Pierre, I have to pee."

A long, frustrated sigh emanated from the guard along with a breath of smoke over and around the cigar dangling from his lips. *"Sacré bleu.* You Americans have such weak bladders."

"I'm only thirteen."

Pierre walked him over to a tree and began undoing his belt. Michael twisted his hips, stopping him.

"Please, I'm not going to run away. I'd like to be able to take a piss with some . . ."

Michael paused looking for the right word.

"Dignité?" Pierre added.

"Yeah, that's it . . . dignity. For a thug, you seem like a nice guy, Pierre. Not like your buddy." Michael motioned toward his pants with his chin. "Do you mind?" Michael lifted his cuffed hands behind him.

Pierre frowned and looked back toward the building and the cellar.

"Come on, I won't tell. He'll never find out."

Pierre hesitated, then slipped a key into the handcuffs, and Michael's hands slipped free.

"Vite! Vite!" Pierre commanded, pointing at the tree. *Quickly!* He placed the barrel of the gun against the boy's head.

"If you try anything, I will shoot you. My unit in Libya wiped out an entire village because the tribal leader offended Miss Delilah . . . women, children, and old men. Despite being a pain in the ass, I like you . . . for now. But I get paid whether you live or die . . . comprends?" *Understand?*

"No problem."

Pierre was behind him and had been the entire time. Running away was not an option for two reasons. Michael's ankles were shackled, making running away impossible. That and the fact that he could not outrun a bullet.

As he undid his pants, Michael's eyes scanned the terrain near him. Another shriek from the cellar sliced through the ocean breeze. Five feet away, Michael saw something he could use.

℞

"Palmer," the detective barked into the phone, his early morning voice nasal and phlegmy.

The one word spoken by the man through Sheryl Penney's cell phone was filled with stress and fatigue. *Be convincing and do it before the battery dies!*

Jason removed the phone from his ear and glanced at the power percentage on the phone: two percent.

"Hello? This is Palmer!" the cop repeated.

"Palmer," Jason began, his voice filled with authority, "listen to me. It's a matter of life and death. I don't have much time."

"Who the hell is this?"

"Jason Rodgers!"

"Screw you, Rodgers! I don't believe you have the stones to call me after what happened last night. That was a nice touch, asking me to get some keys so you could have your partner bust you out. Who was he by the way?"

"I don't know. I've never seen him before . . ."

"No more favors, son. You've used up all your collateral."

"Shut the fuck up and listen, you pompous ass!"

Jason hesitated, waiting for the cop to respond. His words must have shocked him to the point of speechlessness. After a few seconds, Palmer continued.

"Give me one reason why I should help you?"

"Because it may stop a terrorist attack!"

Palmer's short, stifled sigh filled Jason's ears. He didn't wait for the detective to speak.

"Call Clay Broadhurst. Tell him to trace this cell number. Write this down. I don't have much time . . . my battery may die any moment"

Jason repeated it twice. Without waiting for Palmer to respond, he continued speaking.

"I'm on the Eastern Shore headed north. There is a delivery being made somewhere north of here. Get Broadhurst! Get the Feds to find me. Hussein is up to something. Did you get all that?"

There was no response. Jason repeated the question. "Palmer did you get that?"

Jason pulled the phone away from his ear. The screen on the phone was dark. The battery had died. He had no idea how much Palmer had heard including the tag numbers of the Chevy Malibu.

℞

Peter grabbed the handle of the door and pried it open. It dropped from the rusted hinge and clattered to the rotten wood of the step below, falling to the side.

"I'll just be a second," he called to the woman, hoping she wouldn't fire.

Inside, he turned the phone around and shone the light around the dark space. Debris, broken boards, dirt, and spider webs blocked his way. Everything screamed despair and dereliction.

Everything, that is, except the crisp, pristine, sealed manila envelope nailed to an angled, rotting board. Peter tore the envelope from the nail and stuffed it in the back of his shirt.

He retreated out the door. "Found it!" he called out.

Using the flashlight from the phone, he tiptoed back through the forest debris to the truck. He pushed it into first and drove straight ahead, deeper along the holler.

A mile down the road, he turned the Freightliner around, executing a six point turn on the narrow road. He zipped past the ruins of the house and the mobile home with the grizzled fat woman holding her shotgun. Peter hoped a bullet didn't shatter the window and lodge in his skull. When Peter reconnected with Route 13, he breathed again, the pulse in his head thumping his temples.

He turned north, gunning the engine.

Where the hell are you Jason?

℞

"Agent Broadhurst," Maria Gonzalez, the Secret Service agent's day shift assistant, said. "We just received a phone call from a Newport News homicide detective. His name is John Palmer."

"What did he want?"

"We don't know he's still on the line. Said he'd only talk to you."

"What line?"

Gonzalez held up three fingers. Broadhurst rolled his wheelchair to the nearest landline and punched a button, picking up the handset.

"Broadhurst."

"It's John Palmer in Newport News."

"Tell me you found Jason Rodgers."

"No, but he just called me."

"Where is he?"

"Somewhere on the Eastern Shore. Don't know exactly. He was not very forthcoming. He asked me to call you."

"We already know that. Why is he there?"

"You'll have to ask him. He wants you to call him. Can I text you the number? He gave it to me before the call dropped. He said the battery was dying."

"Go." Broadhurst gave Palmer the cell number.

"What do you want me to do?" Palmer asked.

"Stay by the phone. Call me if he calls you again."

"One more thing. Take down this Virginia tag number." Palmer recited the license plate number. "He's driving a Chevy Malibu."

"Thank you, Detective." Broadhurst ended the call and hollered to an agent across the command center. "You. Here is a cell phone number. I want it tracked and traced. I want to know where it is. I'm dialing the number now. Also, I want these tag numbers run through the NCIC."

Broadhurst dialed the contact Palmer had texted him and lifted the phone to his ear and listened. It rolled to voicemail without ringing. Broadhurst heard the greeting, the squeaky voice of a very agitated female, Sheryl Penney.

"Sonofabitch! Bring up a map of the Delmarva Peninsula."

Seconds later, the screen on the wall switched to an overhead view of the Eastern Shore of Virginia. Broadhurst moved to it. Broadhurst used a laser pointer to highlight the map. "I want two teams to head south from DC. And two more teams from the FBI Office in Norfolk to cross the Chesapeake Bay Bridge-Tunnel, heading north, now!" Broadhurst screamed with what little energy he had left. He coughed, recovered, and continued. "Get me a chopper airborne and scanning the area. Where is the nearest Virginia State Police Office?"

An analyst directly in front of Broadhurst pounded a keyboard. Muted clicks sounded in rapid-fire succession. "Sir, there's an office in Accomack County in Melfa about halfway up the Eastern Shore."

"Get the watch commander on the line."

℞

Charlie stood over Chrissie for several minutes, taking his time and massaging himself into readiness. She looked up at him through a curtain of blood-soaked eyelashes.

At first, Chrissie refused to turn her head toward him.

"Watch me," he had commanded earlier as he stroked. "Or I will cut you then take you as you bleed to death. Watch me, whore!"

He had unchained her hands and legs from the wall. Her wrists were still chained together. But her legs were completely free now. He stood between her legs, spread-eagled on the dirty floor. Charlie kicked her about the legs and buttocks, pummeling her. Then he launched several kicks about her head. Chrissie curled into a ball. Despite the pain he was causing her, she sensed his growing frustration. Not satisfied to just hurt her, he wanted more. The monster wanted to violate and humiliate her, mouthing invectives in French. Her reddened face swelled and bled. She sensed an urgency in him, an uncontrollable desire feeding him. He was making her pay for the blow to his manhood.

"I'm sorry," Chrissie pleaded. "Please don't hurt me anymore. I'll do what you want me to do." Tears leaked from her eyes, mixing with the grime on her face. She tasted the saltiness on her lips. "Please don't do this!"

That's when the beating had ceased and Charlie had dropped his pants and began stroking himself once again.

Now, Charlie stopped massaging himself. His trousers were still open, hanging from his hips. His manhood, hard and angled toward the ceiling.

"Puta!" he seethed. *Whore!* "D'Accord!" *Okay!* "I will stop beating you. But we are not done! Take off your clothes!"

Chrissie pleaded with her eyes. An animal rage resided in the Frenchman's eyes. She had never before seen such a quality in another human being. His chest heaved in a slow, methodical manner.

As she cowered before this beast, she knew she was a dead woman. He would ravage her and then kill her. Even if she managed to survive rape, whoever was holding them was going to kill her and Michael to torment Jason.

Everything she did now was buying time in a life that would be cut short. She had to buy as much as possible . . . for her and for Michael. She prayed he was safe and not being tormented . . . or not already dead.

Chrissie reached deep into her soul and summoned courage she had never before grasped.

"Take them off now or I will rip them off!"

Chrissie forced a tense smile. She placed her cuffed hands on the hem of her shirt and began to lift it.

℞

"I'm transferring my screen to your terminal," the technician said.

Broadhurst was already seated in his wheelchair at the three-screened terminal. "What am I looking at?" he wheezed.

"It's a blow-up of the Delmarva Peninsula, specifically, Route 13, in Parksley, north of Accomack. He's about five and half miles south of Mappsville."

Broadhurst watched a blinking red dot on his screen moving slowly north along the yellow line marking State Road 13. An identical image displayed on the massive wall screen simultaneously.

"How did you find him?"

"The Malibu is equipped with Lo-Jack."

Broadhurst smiled, shouting his reply as best he could in his weakened state. "The state police are closer than any of our units. Get their asses on him. And find out where we can land a helicopter.

Thinking a moment, the Secret Service agent turned to another agent several workstations to his left. "You," he demanded, pointing. "Have the agents from the Norfolk Field Office mobilized to the Eastern Shore yet?"

"No, sir. They are getting ready to leave now."

"Good. Tell them they are, instead, to go to Jason Rodger's home and search the place."

"Do we have an address?"

"You're the goddamned FBI. I'm sure you can find it."

"What about a warrant?"

"This is national security. He's not home. He's on the Eastern Shore. Screw the warrant!"

CHAPTER 38

"Alright already," Pierre said. "Finish up."

Michael had finished peeing ten seconds ago. But he pretended he was not done. He waited another few moments and demonstrated the task was completed by shaking up and down.

"Pierre," Michael said, "with all that's going on, my stomach is upset. I have . . . you know . . . diarrhea. Very nasty."

Grunts and shrieks filled the air, Miss Christine was putting up a good fight. But she still needed his help.

"Mon Dieu," Pierre replied, "go behind that tree. But stay where I can see you."

Michael shuffled over to the large palm tree, his leg irons rattling, closer to the object. He pulled down the blindfold so he could see better. Pierre was oblivious.

He crouched, slid his pants to his ankles and pretended to evacuate his bowels.

"Your friend seems to be having a good time in there," Michael observed.

Pierre grunted, lighting a cigarette. "I get her next time."

Michael reached down with his right hand, his pitching hand, and grabbed a rock the size of his fist. He sucked in two quick breaths. He would have one chance. If he missed, he would die. A bullet would rip through him. If he did nothing, Miss Christine might die.

Bad things happen when good people do nothing!

Michael rose up pretending to be done. Squeezing the rock under his arm, he snapped his jeans closed. He let the rock slide down into the fingers of his right hand. It was oblong with sharp edges.

That's good, he thought. *If I hit him, it will do more damage.*

"Stay there, Pierre," Michael called out. "It's pretty disgusting back here. I'm coming out."

There was just enough play in the ankle chains to allow him to shift his feet. Any good ballplayer—and Michael considered himself one—pointed his shoulder at his target and stepped into his throw for maximum velocity and accuracy. The ankle chains would not allow him to step. This heave would be all arm, like he was turning a double play at second base with the runner at his feet.

He peeked out from behind the tree and spied Pierre, dropping the stub of his cigar to the ground and crushing it under his foot.

Now!

The chains at his feet rattled. Michael pushed out from behind the tree, his shoes scuffing the sandy ground. Hearing the commotion, Pierre started to raise his lowered head. Michael stared at his target, the small space between the Frenchman's bushy eyebrows.

Aim small, miss small!

He rotated his upper body as he had done thousands of times on the pitcher's mound. Pointing his left shoulder, he cocked his right arm behind him. Pulling down and back with his left arm to create torque and rotation, Michael slung his right arm up and out in a three-quarter arm slot, just like his pitching coach had instructed. He released the rock as his arm reached full extension.

Michael felt a pain and heard a pop in his elbow as the rock left his hand.

The words "Please God!" slipped from his lips.

PART FOUR

CHAPTER 39

Fifteen hundred miles to the northwest, the large black Chevy Tahoe skidded to a stop in the driveway of Jason Rodger's York County home. A mother pushing a three-wheeled stroller across the street stopped and looked on in wide-eyed amazement as a team of five agents all wearing blue windbreakers emblazoned with the large gold letters, FBI, on their backs rushed to the front door. One carried a large black ram.

In five seconds, the door crashed open and the men disappeared inside, fanning out through the residence, two upstairs, two downstairs, while the leader strode into the kitchen.

The first thing that caught his eye was the black smartphone, lying face down on the kitchen counter. A large white numeral one had been painted on its back. Under the phone, he spied a torn slip of paper with numbers scribbled on it.

$$\text{R}_{\text{X}}$$

The rock pierced the stiff ocean breeze, traversing the twenty feet toward the guard. Michael's stomach flipped as he watched it tumble end over end in its trajectory.

Pierre's eyes were still directed toward the ground and coming up when the projectile left Michael's hand. It somersaulted and dropped. He watched the stone begin to tail off course.

It was going to sail by Pierre's left ear. He was still focused on crushing out the cigar stub when the sound of Michael's whooshing clothing alerted him. His eyes searched for the source of the sound. At the same time, Pierre removed his foot from the squashed cigar. In doing so, his weight shifted from one foot to the other, causing his head to move into the path of the hurtling rock.

It struck him above the right eye with a sharp crack. Pierre's head snapped back and to the side. Small droplets of crimson became airborne around his head, arcing into the breeze.

Pierre staggered and reached for his face with both hands. His gun tumbled into the sand. Pierre twisted and fell face first to the ground.

Michael stood transfixed for several seconds, amazed and paralyzed while Pierre groaned and squirmed on the ground.

Move!

Hobbling over to the fallen weapon, he picked it up and shuffled toward the wounded man. Blood seeped through the fingers covering his face onto the grass and sand. His legs squirmed about as he writhed in pain.

His father and his uncle Peter had shown him how to handle a weapon. He found the safety and clicked it off. Staying out of reach of the fallen guard, he raised the handgun, holding the grip with both hands.

Fueled by adrenaline, his fear was gone, replaced by the frustration and helplessness of captivity. He leveled the gun at Pierre's torso. He had been firing guns at his uncle's gun shop with his father and uncle since he was nine years old. The targets were always paper. He had never fired in anger.

Manhood was upon him now. He closed one eye and pulled the trigger.

℞

Nothing happened.

There was no flash from the barrel. No recoil, forcing the gun back higher. The trigger clicked against the trigger guard. Michael pulled it again with the same result.

He pulled back the slide, exposing the empty chamber. He turned the gun upside down and looked at the bottom of the grip. It was hollow and dark. It held no magazine. Michael whispered expletives.

He eyed Pierre again. The Frenchman had stopped moving. His face rested in both blood-covered hands. One leg was bent out to the side. Michael studied his chest. It rose and fell. The man was alive but unconscious.

Another cry spilled forth from the wine cellar.

Michael felt time ticking away.

He skirted Pierre, staying out of reach, and shuffled toward the building. Kneeling by the small rectangular window, Michael peered in. In the dim light, what he saw horrified him.

℞

Chrissie's shirt and bra were off. Her jeans and panties hung from one leg. One eye was swollen and almost closed. Blood, dirt, and sweat smeared her face.

With her hands free from the wall, Chrissie planned on fighting Charlie. Months ago, after much prompting, Jason had shared a few details of his encounter with the male pharmacist in the towers the day of the christening at the shipyard. He had shown her the two-fingered attack to the eye that had ended the fight with Delilah Hussein's assassin son.

As she'd disrobed for Charlie, Jason's description of his attack came to her. She had planned to try the same maneuver. But the guard had foiled that plan. Once her clothes were off, Charlie had chained her wrists to the wall once more using a long length of chain, slapping her a few more times for good measure, leaving her legs unchained and free for obvious reasons.

He yanked her hard. The long length of chain allowed her body to become completely horizontal; her back on the cold, dusty floor. Her exposed breasts swayed as she struggled and squirmed. Nothing but a few short inches stretched between her loins and an exposed Charlie. He knelt between her legs with his own pants around his ankles.

The guard leaned forward, attempting to kiss her.

Chrissie turned her head, avoiding his putrid breath.

"Bitch," he spat. "Kiss me!"

His fist came down hard again on Chrissie's cheek.

He grabbed a handful of hair and yanked her face toward him, lowering himself once more, and put his lips on hers.

This was not going to happen without a fight!

Chrissie opened her mouth. As his filthy lips connected with hers, she grabbed his lower lip with her teeth and clamped down with all the strength in her jaw. Blood seeped into her mouth a moment before he screamed like a dying animal. Chrissie did not let go. She twisted her head, pulling him by the mouth side to side. His right fist slammed down on her face repeatedly, trying to make her let go. Chrissie pulled her face farther to the right, ripping the flesh.

She opened her good eye. Through the blood and sweat and Charlie's stringy, wet hair, Chrissie detected movement to her right. She saw Michael coming at them.

He held a long, rusty pitchfork in his hands, poised to strike.

℞

Jason swerved the Malibu into the left lane, zipping past a slower car, an older model sedan being driven by a hunched old lady who had to look through the steering wheel to see the road.

He guessed he was about thirty minutes from the first rendezvous point. But he couldn't be sure. Penney's phone was dead and he had no map. Time was of the essence. He would drive until he found the Freightliner.

As he scanned the roadway, Jason's eye caught a flash from the rearview mirror. He studied the shaking image on the glass in the morning glow of light. His heart sank.

Three dark police cars, single file, their lights bars angrily spewing spasms of multicolored lights, rapidly closed the distance. Virginia State Troopers!

Shit! I can't be arrested again! Need to get to Broadhurst!

Jason pressed the accelerator. The Ford's engine hesitated then whined to a higher gear. Jason was forced back into the seat. The lead car shrank in the mirror.

The traffic around Jason began to pull off the road, leaving him isolated. The line of police cars split, creating two lines, one in each lane. Two by two, they gave chase and moved in.

The four cylinders of the Malibu were no match for the cruisers' high-torque engines. The phalanx of police cars were upon Jason quickly. He was now in the right hand lane and the two cars to his left had pulled even. The lead car sped up and took up position in front of him while the second car stayed even with the Ford. The two cars behind him stayed stacked close to his bumper. He was boxed in.

Jason glanced at the car beside him, its light bar pulsing reflections off automotive metal and glass. The trooper behind the wheel met his gaze and motioned for him to pull over.

Jason sighed, checked the rearview mirror then slowed. The tires crunched the gravel along the side of the roadway. Each state car stayed in their positions relative to the Ford, leaving Jason without an escape.

Not wanting to be accidentally shot, Jason kept his hands on the wheel and in plain sight. Two troopers approached from the driver's side, their guns drawn. Jason sensed movement and heard soft footfalls to his right. Two more troopers stood on the passenger side near the rear window, guns also drawn.

One cop yelled through the Ford's glass.

"Step out of the vehicle. Keep your hands where I can see them!"

Jason swallowed hard and moved his hand to the door handle. He pulled on it and pushed open the door. It felt like a ship's anchor.

He stepped out and raised his hands over his head.

"Turn around and put your hands behind your head!"

Jason complied. In fifteen seconds, his hands were in hand cuffs again. With a state trooper on each side, he was led to a cruiser and placed in the rear seat of the lead car.

The four cars sped off single file, heading north, with Jason in the second car, with two State Troopers up front and one beside him.

Jason explained what had happened earlier with the woman named Sheryl Penney. "Can you please make sure someone gets her to a hospital?"

The trooper in the passenger seat looked back at Jason with a confused smile.

"Please," Jason asked.

The trooper called in and requested they check on the woman.

"How did you find me so fast?" he asked when he'd finished his transmission.

The cop in the passenger seat turned. "Got a call from Washington. Some government agencies are good at what they do. Now sit back and shut up!"

℞

Three steps away now, Michael advanced. More slowly than Chrissie would have liked. She could see how petrified he was. The pressure in her skull increased. Her head felt like it would explode.

Two . . . one . . .

At the last moment, Chrissie released her grip on Charlie's devastated lower lip. Blood coated both their faces.

Michael lunged, thrusting the rusty farm implement at Charlie. The guard saw Michael at the last moment. He rolled away, trying to avoid the thrust.

The corroded tines penetrated the guard's flank above the hip. Charlie howled, spitting a curtain of blood into the air. He grabbed at the tines.

The boy did not hesitate. He pulled the pitch fork out, plunging once more with much greater force. This time it delved deep above the belly button.

Charlie opened his mouth and what was left of his lower lip dropped, a severed flap of flesh. He screamed. Both hands grasped at the tines again, trying to remove it. It did not budge.

He tried to kick at Michael, missing the first time. The second one connected with his arm, knocking him to the floor. Charlie gripped the pitch fork again, removing it as he screamed. Michael scampered away, pushing himself across the floor on his backside. Slowly . . . awkwardly, Charlie struggled to his feet, naked from the waist down, with blood seeping from multiple wounds. The lower half of his face was nothing but blood, exposed teeth, and torn flesh. The guard wavered from side to side but managed to inch toward Michael. A walking dead man.

Charlie lowered himself to the dirty floor. Michael breathed easier.

He's going to die, Michael thought.

Charlie picked up the blood-stained pitchfork and struggled back to an erect position. Hunched over, he walked, dragging one leg, toward him. Michael peered into the eyes glaring at him over a curtain of mutilated, crimson flesh. Michael's heart skipped in his chest, followed by the sensation that it might stop.

Michael's weapon was about to be turned on him.

℞

"We have Rodgers in custody. Where do you want him?"

"Bring him here to FBI headquarters. I want to know as soon as he arrives."

Broadhurst sank into the chair at his workstation, his head spinning. He lowered it into his hands.

"Agent, are you okay?" Gonzalez asked.

"No, give me a minute."

℞

Michael scooted farther backward, sliding on his butt. He stopped against the brick wall under the window. Charlie was fifteen feet away, limping and dripping, in his direction.

"You should have run," Charlie declared in a wet, barely comprehensible lisp. "Now . . . you are . . . going to die . . ."

In his peripheral vision, Michael saw Miss Christine struggling. Her face and bare torso covered in blood. Her eyes wide with fear for him.

Michael brushed up against another tool. A metal rake. He grabbed it, leveling it at the crazed human. Charlie swung the pitchfork in a quick, sideways arc. Its bloodied tines connected with Michael's rake, knocking it from his hands, clattering to the floor.

The thirteen-year-old bent to a crouch, staying on the balls of his feet. His heart felt like it would fly from his chest. His breaths came hard and fast, but he still could not suck in enough air.

Charlie lunged, stabbing the pitchfork at him. Michael jumped to his left. The tines sparked against the bricks. Michael grabbed the distal end of the wooden shaft. Charlie tried to pull it back out of his grasp twice but Michael did not release his grip. The guard swung the tines into Michael. The boy never released his grip, remaining stiff-armed, not allowing it to connect with his body.

Charlie tugged a third time, yanking harder. Michael let go. Charlie reeled backward, stumbling onto his buttocks, nearly on top of Miss Christine. The pitchfork landed on the dusty floor. Michael careened hard against the wall.

Still on her back and with arms chained to the wall, Christine wrapped her free legs around the weakened guard, pinning his arms to his sides.

Charlie struggled, trying to slide away. She tightened her squeeze.

Slowly, Charlie wriggled one arm up between his torso and Miss Christine's leg. He pushed against her leg, freeing himself. In an instant, he was on her. His hands went to her neck and began crushing her windpipe.

Chapter 40

"Get our asset in New Jersey on the line," Hussein commanded.

Two minutes later, Oliver handed her the secure satellite phone.

"What is the password?" the male voice on the other end demanded.

"Hygeia," Hussein replied.

"This is Quinton Boyd. Proceed."

"Allo. Comment allez-vous?" Hussein asked. "Is everything ready?"

"Everything is as well as can be expected."

"That statement does not fill me with confidence. Can we depend on you and your man?"

"We will not fail. When can we expect the shipment?"

"It is en route as we speak."

"How long?

"Three hours. Is the room ready?"

"Yes, temperature is at the prescribed 28 degrees Fahrenheit. What about payment?"

"The money will be wired when you secure the package and provide us with video evidence that is in place. I want to see the drums with their identification numbers visible being placed into the hold."

"It will be done."

$$R_X$$

Christine struggled to get air into her lungs. The guard's large bloodied hands had clamped off her throat. With her arms chained above her, she was defenseless. She flailed her legs, trying to bend her right leg up to put it between her and Charlie's chest.

She couldn't execute the maneuver. Each attempt became weaker.

She stared up into the distorted, torn face. The muscles in her neck burned under his grip. Christine opened her mouth in one last effort to allow air in.

Nothing!

The black curtain began to close.

Before it completely descended, a shadow crossed before her dwindling field of vision. A quick, thin, darting outline. Something warm splashed her face, a jet of warm stickiness. The taste in her mouth was a familiar one. Blood.

The shadow retreated to the right and in once more. The pressure on her throat and neck eased. Cool, dank, delicious air flooded into her lungs. She gasped a long, deep breath. As blood rushed back into her head, a large volume of Charlie's blood hit her face and mouth.

Opening her eyes fully, she spied snippets of the violent scene through a blood-coated curtain. Charlie's dead weight slumped on her naked chest. The skin of her wrists, supporting the man now, began to tear. The pain, though excruciating, felt good. She was alive!

"Help me," she squeaked.

Michael shuffled into view, his trousers and arms covered in crimson splatter. His eyes wide with terror, the shaft of the pitchfork whose tines were buried into Charlie's neck, were clutched in his hands. Michael's gaze, far away and unfocused, remained riveted on the dead man.

"Michael, please help me. Get him off of me."

Several seconds later, he reacted.

He grimaced, pulling the pitchfork from the man's neck. Christine used her legs to push and partially squirm from under the body.

"Pull him off."

Michael circled the body and grabbed a fistful of shirt, pulling with all his might. He elevated the corpse a few inches, allowing Christine to scooch free. Michael grabbed the ankle and slid him another foot.

Michael looked into her eyes, tears welling. Fear consumed him, his mind now absorbing the extent of blood and gore. He furrowed a brow and turned away.

Chrissie could not see him. But she heard him, retching, emptying the contents of his stomach near the body.

$$R_X$$

The helicopter landed on the tarmac in the middle of the H on the helipad. The hangers and buildings and their layout were familiar to Jason. He'd been here before.

"This is Andrews Air Force Base!"

"It's called Joint Base Andrews now," the agent beside him said, "but it's the same place." He pointed to a two vehicle convoy of Chevy SUVs approaching. "Here's your next ride."

Before he could fire any more questions, Jason was whisked by another team of FBI agents to the second vehicle. Pinned to the back seat by the g-force created by the accelerating SUV, Jason closed his eyes and prayed that Hussein had not discovered that Peter was alone in the truck and that Michael and Chrissie were still alive.

$$R_X$$

Standing on wobbly legs, Chrissie looked down at the carnage. She was covered in crimson. The body of the dead guard was bathed in blood. The face a mutilated piece of meat.

Using a small hand tool he found along the wall of the cellar, Michael worked hard for ten minutes, gouging out the soft mortar fastening the iron rings to the wall, freeing her. Her wrists, still wrapped by the handcuffs, were sore and lacerated. Chains, handcuffs, and iron rings dangled from each wrist.

The boy retrieved a dirty cloth from atop one of the wine racks. Michael carefully wiped Miss Christine's face with the cloth, removing the blood, grime and sweat. Miss Christine winced as he gently caressed the cloth around her swollen eye and lips.

Michael removed his shirt. Kneeling beside her now, he worked his sweaty shirt over her head and into the arms. His feet, still chained together by a single strand of chain did not allow him freedom to move freely. His eyes were swollen and red. Tear tracks snaked lines through the dirt and sweat on his face. He saw the folded clothes their captor had placed on one of the wine racks. He fetched them and changed quickly behind one of the wine racks.

He returned to her, kneeling beside her as she sat on the floor. Now that her nakedness was covered, Michael looked at her without awkwardness. She smiled at him. Michael collapsed into her arms. With no words to describe what they'd just experienced, they sat in each other's arms, making no sound.

Finally, with his head still buried in her neck, she whispered.

"Thank you, Michael. Thank you. You saved my life."

Michael squeezed her tighter. Christine could feel his shoulders bobbing. As each second passed, she felt the tension release from his body. His sobs increased in number and strength.

When he'd finished crying, she spoke, "Let's get out of here. Where is the other guard?"

"He's unconscious outside. I hit him with a rock."

Christine placed a hand on his cheek and smiled again.

"We need to get the keys to these chains," she said.

Michael eyes widened. He glanced at the body warily and shook his head.

"Don't worry," she calmed. "You've done enough."

Christine moved to the body and patted Charlie's pockets, avoiding a look at the corpse's face or naked butt. She found the lump in his trousers and pulled the keychain from the blood-soaked pants. She found the key and freed herself from the chains and handcuffs. Then she unshackled Michael's leg irons.

"Let's go. I don't want to be here anymore."

CHAPTER 41

Rain angled down from the slate gray sky like bullets, pelting the outside of the four-story grandstand overlooking the track in North Baltimore. Inside the glass, four casual but well-attired men sat at a square table twenty yards from the finish line. Three large, green-and-yellow John Deere tractors hummed by in wing formation dragging large iron plates across the dirt of the oval track, smoothing the pockmarked mud created by the horses' morning workouts.

Three of the executives of Dawson Pharmaceuticals poured over their racing forms and tip sheets, pondering their next wagers. With no races at Pimlico today, they were betting on races simulcast from tracks around the world. Amid the paper and cellphones on the table, four-rocks glasses containing various levels of bourbon sat surrounded by a plate of half-eaten Oysters Rockefeller.

The fourth man, sitting distracted near the vaulted glass, watched the tractors make their way around the oval. His name: Juan Santos, chief executive officer of Dawson Pharmaceuticals. The distant look in his eyes belied a lack of concern for the upcoming races.

"I'm going for the longshots for the rest of the day. I should be wiping my arse with these tip sheets for all the good they do me," Sir Quinton Boyd complained. Boyd, the vice president of Injectable Production sat beside his boss, Santos, and faced the other pair at the table. "I'm down five thousand quid already. I need to recoup my losses."

"Stop griping, Quint. You're royalty for God's sake. That's a drop in the royal piss pot. Just ask the queen for an advance against your allowance," Andrew DeNiro chided him. DeNiro, Dawson's VP of marketing and strategy, straightened his polka-dot bow tie against the starched white button-down shirt. The leather patches on his tweed sports coat gave him the appearance of a tenured professor. His bald pate reflected three circles of light from the fixtures hanging above. "And that sounds like a wonderful strategy. Throw good money after bad! Just like a researcher."

Boyd sat more erect, defiant and proud. His cool blue eyes hardened. His British accent notched an octave haughtier. "I'm not royalty. I was knighted for my clinical research. And I only met Her Majesty on the day I was knighted." His head of snow-white, perfectly-coifed hair glistened against his tan face.

"I like Cloverbrook, Tecumseh, and The Bard in the sixth race at Aqueduct," Anson Wellington announced. Wellington's short, stout frame, round face, and the flabby skin waggling under his chin made him look like a bullfrog. As the chief financial officer, Wellington retained the facts and figures of Dawson's books with computer-like clarity.

"How much are you betting, Duke?" DeNiro asked.

"A grand on each," he replied. "And I've told you a thousand times, don't call me Duke."

"Why?" Boyd added. "The Duke of Wellington is revered in the United Kingdom. He conquered that heathen Bonaparte."

Santos winked at his money man. "I'm taking Sly Fox to win, place, or show."

"How much?" Boyd and DeNiro asked.

"The usual," Santos replied.

"Come on, boss," DeNiro said. "You're killing me."

"You guys know it's the same bet every race. A Lincoln on each one to win, place, or show."

"Only a fifteen-dollar bet, JS?" Wellington chided. "I know how much we pay you."

"I knew I made the right decision when I hired you. You always show a real proclivity for numbers."

Wellington shook his head.

Santos slapped the table. "It's time to talk turkey, gents!" Santos glanced at his watch, then the scoreboard in the infield. Santos turned to Boyd. "We have twenty minutes until post time. Let's figure this plan out. Is it doable?"

$$\text{R}_{\!\text{x}}$$

They ascended the stairs and looked through the small portal cut in the planks of the old door, watching and waiting. Now, Michael slowly pulled open the heavy door. The warm breeze pulsing through the door felt like a slice of heaven. But the elation was cut short.

"Circle the building immediately!"

The volume of the spoken words and the alacrity with which they were delivered told them the speaker was close. Very close!

Christine snuck a peek around the door frame. A gaggle of guards carrying weapons and wearing matching uniforms of khaki shirts and dark blue jeans had fanned out behind the tall, dark-skinned leader who stood over Pierre who was trying to get to his feet.

Morning was in full bloom. Sunlight glowed everywhere. The tall, muscular leader stopped short and continued barking orders in French. A nauseating ache leadened Chrissie's gut. *Oliver!*

She turned to Michael. "Too late. They're here. We have to get back inside."

They moved back down the stairs, through the cell past the dead body and the pooling blood. The room that had been their prison was an anteroom for the rest of the building. She led Michael by the hand to the entryway to the next room.

Thin shards of light cut into the long, narrow space from the ceiling-high windows. Mostly empty except for empty wine barrels and wooden crates, Christine spied a large wooden door similar to the one at the top of the stairs.

"There! Hurry!"

Racing to it, they both saw the large, rusted padlock hanging from a steel hasp.

A low-pitch, muffled, and irritated voice could be heard at the top of the stairs in the anteroom. Oliver barked loud, single-word exclamations. Then a profanity-laced tirade in French.

In the anteroom, his words halted. He'd seen the body.

Their only avenue of escaped was blocked. They had no time to sift through the keys.

"This way," Chrissie whispered.

She led him to a cluster of barrels stacked haphazardly in the corner near the locked door. Putting her hands on Michael's shoulders, she pushed him behind the stack.

"Get down and stay down," she whispered. "Find the key that unlocks that door."

"What are you going to do?"

"I'm going to buy you some time." Christine put an index finger to her lips.

$$R_X$$

Boyd nodded, dabbing a line of sweat on his forehead.

"What's wrong, Quinton. Are you getting sick?"

"Maybe," he lied. "Not feeling well."

"Well why didn't you stay home?" Santos demanded.

"Probably should have. But I'll be okay."

Boyd was not ill. He was nervous. Nervous about the ongoing clandestine operation at the New Jersey plant. An operation about which only he knew all the details. Angelo Sheppard was a pawn who had been strong-armed into helping build and secure the Vault. The three other men who were going to dispose of the driver of the truck were mercenaries being paid well for a one-time job.

No one knew the full extent of the operation. No one except Boyd. He had been in on the plan from the beginning, recruited and paid by Delilah Hussein's organization to make sure the deadly contents currently en route were used according to her plan.

Boyd was the most unlikely jihadist on the planet. He did not look or act the part. An older Caucasian male with a lineage going back centuries, he was sympathetic to the cause of the Arab people and the discrimination and suffering they had endured for centuries.

Boyd cleared his throat. "We can produce a million doses for that one day. Not a problem. My only concern is that we won't have enough remaining. If we sell a million doses on that one day, it could create a shortage for the rest of the season and we won't have enough to make it through November."

"How many doses will we need to manufacture for the entire season, then?" Santos asked.

"Counting the million for that one day," Boyd replied, blowing out a long breath, "twice as many as last year. About six million. If we run the plant three shifts until August 1, we can make it."

"And the cost, Anson?"

Wellington shifted in his seat. The chair creaked. "We anticipate a seven-percent increase in ingredient costs over last year. It will require an investment of one hundred and eighty mill. But will we be able to obtain enough in the appropriate ingredient volumes to meet production needs?"

"I've checked with our suppliers. They have the eggs and other ingredients in the pipeline already. I've placed a hold on it. They can ship as long as we provide a financial commitment within two weeks."

"How much of a commitment?"

"Half."

Santos whistled. "Ninety million?"

"We can do it," Wellington stated. "We have $60 million in cash reserves. We can tap into our lines of credit for the remainder. But this had better work, Juan. If it doesn't, we will be headed down a treacherous slope when it comes to the balance sheet."

"I know the risks, Anson," Santos replied. He looked at DeNiro. "Andy, can we get the product stocked in the pharmacies."

"Most definitely, sir. Getting them into the drugstores will be easy. I have reached out to the CEOs of all the major chains. We're offering them a thirty percent discount if they pre-book by June 30. They'll bite on that offer."

"What about our partnership for the one-day push?"

"I spoke with John Gibson, the CEO at Drug-Rite. They want to be the leader in administrations the day of the promotion. We have slotted them for one million doses. They can leverage down payment, a deposit of five million for the shipment before we begin their production run."

"Good. What about advertising?"

"Our marketing department is developing a television and radio campaign now. We expect to have a plan on your desk by the end of next week. A print media campaign will hit the major magazines as well."

"Cost?"

DeNiro was ready "Three million, tops."

Santos nodded his approval. "Excellent. So what's the bottom line on this program?"

"If we sell seventy percent of the doses," Wellington chimed in, "we will see a net of $20 million. Breakeven is fifty-five percent of doses."

"This is a bold plan, Juan," Boyd observed. "It will be a major coup. If it works, Dawson will become the first name in this market segment. The Mercks, the Glaxos, and Pfizers will be wringing their hands."

"You're right, Quint. It is a bold plan. Andy, I want you to wait as long as possible before we launch the ad campaign. Then flood the market. I don't want our competitors to have a chance to respond with their own versions of this event. And no discussions with anyone outside the executive team about the increase in production." Santos drummed the menu lying on the table with his fingers.

"What's wrong?" DeNiro asked.

"If it fails, the board will want my head on a platter. Can we sell it to them?"

Boyd responded, "I've already reached out to several members. They can be convinced. If we get Jones, Mitchem, and Newman on board, the rest will fall into place."

"Okay," Santos replied, "the board meets in two weeks. I want a presentation ready by Wednesday so we can go over it."

℞

For several long minutes, Christine stood in the doorless entryway connecting the filthy back room with the wine-cellar-cum-prison cell, summoning courage. Oliver's attention was focused on the body and blood. He stood in profile under the harsh light of the naked bulb. Then he turned away from her.

Christine shuffled into view.

Oliver whipped around and faced her, his eyes wide with surprise at her appearance and battered face. Their intensity morphed into angry orbs. He stepped to within three feet of her.

Christine wanted to cower, but steeled herself.

"Where is the boy?"

Christine managed a shrug and an even weaker reply. "He's gone."

Oliver turned as if to look at the carnage. He uncoiled at the waist, slinging his long right arm in a tight, powerful arc. The back of his closed fist cracked on her cheek.

Christine's head snapped to the side. A streak of white stars flashed in her vision. She stumbled and fell into the wall beside the entryway. A fresh dose of warm blood filled her mouth. She spit it onto the floor.

"Where is the boy?"

"I told you. He's gone," she replied without looking up.

"Bullshit!" Oliver walked to the body and kicked it. "How did you manage to kill Charles with your hands in chains? He was stabbed. Someone else did that."

"I'm a very talented woman."

Oliver moved toward her again, towering over her. She prepared for another blow.

He kicked her in the gut, expelling the air from her lungs. She gasped a silent scream. Finally managing to take a breath, a sharp, stabbing pain flowered in her rib cage.

Chrissie heard footsteps approach. Pierre stood near the base of the stair, his head wrapped in a dirty cloth angled over the damaged eye. Christine smiled as the horror of his dead comrade spread across his face.

Oliver gave him an order in French. Pierre hesitated.

"Maintenant!" *Now!*

Pierre sidled past Oliver and Christine, giving his commander a wide berth and entered the dark back room in which Michael was hiding. She heard him moving about. Barrels were tossed here and there as he searched. Christine lay on her back now. She could see a small portion of the back room and what Pierre was doing. It would only be a matter of minutes before Michael was discovered.

Soon they would both once more be chained on the walls. Under heavier guard, no doubt. Their escape attempt had failed. But they had inflicted serious damage. One was dead. The other seriously injured. More importantly, she knew with certainty that Oliver and Delilah Hussein were behind their abductions.

How had she survived? Or was Oliver running the show now?

Christine moved her head to the side, looking after Pierre. Her eyes searched the stack of barrels, trying to make eye contact with Michael. She could not see him.

Pierre shuffled back into view. She expected to see Michael being dragged by the hair. Pierre's eyes, filled with frustration and terror, portended a dark encounter with Oliver.

Christine smiled. He was alone.

℞

Oliver listened as Pierre delivered the message in soft, hesitant French, trying to minimize the impact of the news.

Imbécile!" Oliver spat. "Stay here!" He stepped over Christine and moved into the back room.

Oliver scanned the filthy back room of the wine cellar himself, swinging the large mag-light back and forth. *Idiots*, he thought. He had personally vouched for Charlie. Now he was dead. After this was over, there would be hell to pay. Heads would roll. Literally! He hoped his wasn't one of them.

Discarded wine barrels lay scattered about. Black mold dotted the walls, creating map-like continents along the painted white cinder blocks. He trekked around the perimeter checking behind every barrel. He kicked over every cask, spilling vinegary remnants along the dusty floor.

Five barrels stood near one corner of the room in a triangular formation. Oliver opened two of them, flashing the light inside. The third drum was heavy, sloshing with liquid. He tried to lift the lid off, but it was fastened tight.

Oliver placed his heavy boot against the top, knocking it on its side. The barrel oscillated back and forth along its convex exterior. A dark liquid oozed from small cracks between the slats, several gulps splashed onto his boots and pant legs.

Oliver knelt to examine it and was accosted by the unbearable stench of excrement and urine.

Merde!

This is where prisoners, past and present, had been allowed to relieve themselves.

Three minutes later, Oliver concluded his search. The boy, in fact, was gone.

$$R_X$$

Pierre and Oliver dragged Christine back to the wall. Oliver berated his injured *sentinelle* with each step. They chained her in a sitting position with her back to the wall, Charlie's carcass only inches from her feet.

Oliver issued a final directive.

"She is not to be released or unchained for any reason. She can piss and shit herself where she sits. Charles nearly compromised this mission because he wanted some pussy. The boy was smarter than you. You better hope we find him."

Pierre cowered. "What about the body?"

"Leave it where it is." He turned to a third *soldat* standing nearby. "Get two more *sentinelles* to stand guard. Alert everyone. Find the boy!" He pointed to Pierre. "You. . . come with me."

$$R_X$$

Christine suppressed another smile as she leaned against the wall with her arms splayed against the bricks like Christ on the cross. Tears welled in her eyes.

Amazing! Somehow he'd found a way to escape.

CHAPTER 42

At the same time, in western Virginia inside the Red Onion State Penitentiary, breakfast was two hours late. It normally arrived by 7:30 a.m. It was now twenty minutes after nine.

Five trays wheeled on a stainless-steel cart, each covered with a clear plastic cover and labeled one through five with a handwritten numeral on a white label affixed to the cover, were pushed through the security checkpoint by the female corrections officer.

"I'll be back in an hour," she said

Griffin leered at the same woman who'd escorted him to Deputy Warden Travis's office twenty-four hours ago.

"Fuck off, asshole," she whispered, smiling back.

He ogled her as she disappeared beyond the security checkpoint.

"Don't go there, man," one of the other guards guffawed. "She's a man-eater."

"We'll see," Griffin retorted. He paused, then said, "Why don't you serve up breakfast."

"No problem, man," one of his new co-workers replied. The unit manager showed Griffin how to open the wicket in the steel door of empty cell number one. "Start with two and work your way around. The wickets are covered shelves. Open the cover, like this, insert the tray, then close and lock the lid so the inmate can retrieve it."

"Thanks man, I got it from here."

The six-celled unit held only five inmates. Cell number one, cur-rently vacant, was awaiting the next violent high-value target. Griffin delivered breakfast to inmate two, a six-foot-seven black man with a torso that looked like the trunk of a redwood. Griffin closed up the opening and moved back to the cart, wheeling it to cell three. He removed Cyclops' tray, placed it on the top of the cart, and pretended to inspect it by running his hand over it.

Griffin placed his hand in his pocket and removed something. Griffin rapped three times on the steel door. He then unlocked the wicket, opened the cover, placed the tray on the shelf, and reclosed the cover.

"You're new. Where's Baker?"

"That's none of your business. And I'm not new. I'm thirty-nine years old. Now shut up and eat!"

Before Cyclops turned to take the tray to his bunk, Griffin tapped on the glass of the door then placed his palm flat on the glass.

He watched Cyclops' eyes go wide at the sight of the marking on his hand.

$$\mathrm{R}_{\mathrm{X}}$$

Curled up and cramped in the dark, wet space, Michael had waited for what seemed like hours. Any move he made sloshed the liquid, making noise. He had remained motionless the whole time. But now his muscles were cramping, and he was becoming restless.

The stale air suffocated him. The pungent liquid soaking his feet and legs stank with the acrid sting of vinegar and the sickening odor of urine and feces. The old wine barrel had been used as a toilet. Michael had puffed his cheeks, trying to keep from vomiting in his first minutes inside by using slow, short breaths.

Michael had heard the first man enter. He'd tossed barrels about. When he got to Michael's barrel, he tried to move it. Discouraged by its weight, he moved on. Then the second man approached and knocked the barrel on its side. It took every ounce of Michael's strength to keep a seal on the lid and keep from rolling through the top. He pulled down tight against the rim. He closed his mouth and eyes and held his breath as the semi-solid mixture waved back and forth over him, covering him in filth.

Now he feared if he released the lid and showed himself, one of the goons would be standing there waiting for him. It was impossible to tell if he was alone. All he could hear now was the sound of his own breathing, the soft rustle of his flesh and clothing and the gentle lapping of the fetid liquid.

After Miss Christine had disappeared into the front room, Michael had left his position behind the barrels and moved to the door. His curiosity more powerful than fear, he had listened as the large man questioned Miss Christine.

Peeking through a gap in the wood, he'd watched in horror as he hit and kicked her. Christine did not give him the answer he wanted, namely where Michael was hiding. He cringed with each blow, fearing that she would rat him out. When she didn't, he was oddly relieved.

She had protected him!

He had thought about jumping from the shadows and coming to her defense. But he was more valuable to both of them free. If they were both captured, they would not escape again.

He needed to find a better hiding spot. While the large man shouted at Pierre, Michael searched, desperately looking. As he looked around, he placed his hand on the top of one of the barrels. The lid moved. He pulled it open and his nose was met by the vulgar mixture.

Seeing no other choice, he climbed in.

The circular top had a rope handle in it. Once inside, he inverted it and pulled it over the opening. Holding his breath, he pulled down on the rope with all his might, creating the impression the barrel was sealed.

His arms were weak and tired from the constant tension of pulling on the rope. He shook them out one at a time, trying not suck in too much disgusting air. Unable to stand it any longer, Michael decided it was time to go.

Releasing the tension on the rope handle, Michael gently lowered the lid to keep it from crashing onto the floor. The boy peered through the round opening, studying the dark surroundings, looking for any movement and listening for any sound. Satisfied there was no one in the immediate area, he belly-crawled over the lid and onto the dirty floor. Crouching behind one of the still-upright barrels, he peered toward the soft, yellow cast of rectangular light created by the doorway to the anteroom.

Thankful for the relative freshness of the cellar air, Michael allowed himself several long, deep breaths. Still, he saw no movement and heard no sound.

Staying low and shaking out his arms, he duck walked toward the entrance of the anteroom. He stopped at the rough frame and peeked around the doorway.

CHAPTER 43

Like his cell, the exercise space was miniscule. They COs referred to them as yards. But, they were more like cages, the kind one would see at a zoo housing a medium-sized an animal. The pair of COs escorted Cyclops to the open cage. He knelt, facing into the cage. The leg irons were removed. The cage was closed. Cyclops, keeping his back to the COs, placed his hands through the fold-down wicket in the chain-link gate, allowing the burly CO to remove his wrist shackles. Once unchained, the prisoner rubbed his wrists and shuffled into the small outdoor rectangular prism. His own private cage.

Relegated to a minute portion of the facility, Cyclops had never seen the entire prison complex. From what was visible, the facility was huge. An angled and angry conglomeration of white brick, concertina wire, and tall chain-link, spreading out over hundreds of acres. His guess was predicated on the fact that a vast swath had been cleared in the mountainous terrain. Ironically, though the facility was enormous, the spaces he inhabited were tiny, cramped, and isolated. The walls inched in on him every day in the secret, detached pod of the prison.

This maximum security prison, deep in the countryside far from populated areas, kept its inmates locked down twenty-three hours a day except for the solitary hour in which they were allowed to make small laps inside these inhumane chain-link boxes.

The truck that had delivered him many months ago had swerved and jostled along a sinuous roadway, climbing a steep incline. Cyclops had formed a theory as to their general location by studying the climate, the surrounding landscape, and his position relative to the sun. He was still in the United States. After being taken into custody two years ago, he had been rushed into emergency surgery to repair his obliterated eye, and his other wounds had been attended to.

A few days after that, they stopped giving him pain medications and the intensive interrogations began—the water boarding, the electric shock, and painful insertion of all sorts of probes into his anal cavity and penis. He'd broken, of course. Everyone does. The only question was how long you lasted. It had taken them over forty hours.

Cyclops adjusted his eye patch, buried the painful thoughts, and turned back to his observations about his surroundings. He'd been driven by secure bus to a second safe house and ultimately to the Red Onion. The COs had told him the name of the site, but not the location. A precaution, he guessed, that would keep him from communicating his location to anyone wanting to break him out. Not that he'd ever been allowed to speak with anyone not connected with the prison

The security measures here had been designed for society's most violent criminals. Serial murderers and rapists, men with no consciences. Their every movement was regulated and watched. If he had been allowed to mingle with the general population, the prisoner knew he would not last a week. But there was no general population here—everyone was in solitary confinement.

His attempted crime, though murderous and brutal, was not warped. His was a political statement, an act of war against a nation whose imperial proclivities needed to be thwarted.

And yet he was not one of these brutal, antisocial degenerates. He was a thinker, elegant and refined, well trained in the art of killing with a body that was strong, athletic, and well-cared for. His swarthy skin was not riddled with piercings, facial hair, or tattoos, except for the small squiggly line on his forearm. It was the same marking that his sister, his mother, and Oliver all possessed. And now, the guard who'd served him breakfast had shown him the same marking on the palm of his hand.

The seemingly insignificant act had caused Cyclops heart to soar. His dream of getting out of this Underground, once remote, now seemed real. Outside the prison, forces were at work to free him. He'd looked at the special gift he'd found with his breakfast and read the simple instructions.

Cyclops had recorded a simple recording to be delivered to the object of his scrutiny. A short message with enormous consequences.

Stepping into his private cage, he flexed his tight muscles and squinted against the bright sunlight with his one good eye. He worked his neck, tilting his head back and forth, cracking the bones of his upper vertebrae before he began his walking laps around the cage. His yard was one of six that lay side by side. Six chain-link cages. His target was two cages away.

The object of his scrutiny had once been a protégé, a fellow conspirator who had collapsed under the pressure of the moment. A weak American with no stomach for the dirty work of a bloody coup d'état.

Cyclops, once known to the Americans as pharmacist Sam Fairing, but whose real name was Sharif al-Faisal, had not spoken to the weasel Steven Cooper since they'd been captured. The two men communicated across the expanse of concrete, chain-link, and concertina wire through looks and slight facial movements. Cooper (Faisal was sure that was not his real name) always held a pleading, sunken gaze, begging for forgiveness. Faisal always smiled a reassuring grin along with a nod, as if to say, "Everything is alright."

He placed his hand in his jumpsuit pocket and fingered the tiny envelope that had been folded many times into a ball of paper.

Cyclops moved to the corner of the cage, near his neighboring inmate's. The communication was quick and whispered. They had developed a connection over the last two years because each was brought to his exercise cage at the same time every day. It could not be called friendship. You didn't make friends here.

The COs were always watching, monitoring every move. Though they were separated by wire and fence, they were not allowed to engage in conversation or to stand near the fencing or each other. But there was no other way to accomplish his task.

The two men made some oval laps inside the cramped space of their cages. Cyclops moved clockwise, while his neighbor moved counterclockwise. Their laps were timed so that they arrived at their common chain-link wall simultaneously with their backs to the corrections officer standing watch. As they converged on their first lap, Cyclops whispered a statement.

"*I have a gift for you my friend.*"

The two prisoners circled again.

"*What is it?*" his neighbor replied.

On the next lap, Cyclops began to explain. "*I need you to deliver something to someone!*"

And so it went. With each lap, Cyclops laid out instructions for his neighbor to deliver something to Steven Cooper two cages down.

The inmate in the neighboring exercise cage moved to within four feet of the fence near Cyclops, as had been pre-arranged. Cyclops did not know he'd done it, but his new CO Griffin had somehow reconnoitered the situation and arranged a special present for the neighboring inmate's assistance. The neighbor had eyed Cooper, bringing him in on the plan. As each man lapped their cages, word was eventually relayed to Cooper that a small present was coming his way.

"*It will be done. Give me three minutes,*" the neighbor explained to Cyclops on one of the last laps.

Without he or Cyclops ever having set eyes upon each other, the neighbor moved off toward the entrance to his private cage. He began shouting and spreading his arms, drawing all eyes and attention to him.

"Rejoice in the Lord . . ."

Everyone looked, including the two corrections officer in the area, casting their eyes toward him and not on the eye-patched Cyclops. Cyclops slipped the small wad through the fence. It fell to the concrete and came to rest in the corner of his neighbor's cage as he continued to rant. Cyclops quickly turned away, continuing his exercise laps and smiling at the apparently crazed inmate.

℞

Delilah Hussein circled her prey, showing no emotion.

Pierre had been allowed to sit alone with his thoughts for a few hours in a dark windowless room in the residence guarded by several sentries. Oliver had told him that Madam Hussein was asleep and she would deal with him when she woke. Now, she had been pacing around him for five minutes on the lawn outside the residence

She's very controlled, Pierre thought. *No anger in her voice. Maybe I have a chance.*

He knelt before the matriarch of The Simoon, avoiding eye contact, waiting as she made each circle. Oliver was behind him, but close. The warm breeze evaporated the sweat as soon as it formed on his body. The bloodied bandage angled over his face covered his eye and temple. The wound throbbed and radiated pain in every direction.

With each question she tossed in his direction, her words cut. "And this was all Charlie's idea?"

"Oui, Madame. I took the boy out to make urine. While I was gone, Charlie decided to . . . have his way with the woman."

"And he told you nothing of this?"

Pierre lifted his head and managed a quick glimpse as she passed in front of him. He lowered his eyes, seeing only the flow of her silk sari and the dark skin on her sandaled feet.

"Non. Il était un cochon," he declared. *He was a pig.*

"Je vois," came the soft reply. *I see.*

Her soft footfalls circled again, stopping directly behind him. Pierre did not move a muscle.

Hussein spoke once more. "You understand that in order for our plan to work. Monsieur Rodgers must know that his son and girlfriend are in our custody and are safe. He must believe that he will get them back in one piece . . . or we have no ability to control him, n'est-ce pas?"

"Certainement, Madame."

"Now I am told the boy is missing . . . escaped. You allowed him . . . a thirteen-year-old . . . to overwhelm you. You were bested by a pubescent teenager."

"Oui," Pierre replied in a throaty whisper, barely audible above the breeze.

"I suppose," Hussein continued, "I should consider his escape from you a stroke of good luck, because the young man was able to stop Charlie from raping the woman. Had he not escaped, he probably would have completed the task."

She completed another lap. Pierre studied her feet and the hem of her sari.

"Look at me," she commanded.

Pierre lifted his head as far as he could and looked into the dark gray eyes.

"Was it not fortunate that the boy was able to stop Charlie?"

"Oui."

"Your job was to look after our guests, n'est-ce pas?"

Pierre did not have the courage to speak. He nodded, moving his head only an inch.

"Où est le garçon?" *Where is the boy?*

He felt a soft, warm dribble of urine slip down his pants. The breath in his chest caught.

"Je ne sais pas." *I do not know.*

"Tant pis." *What a shame.*

Pierre lowered his head, avoiding her penetrating stare. "Look at me, *Monsieur*."

Pierre complied. When their eyes met again, the gaping bore of a handgun was directed at the furrowed space between his eyes. Her hand twitched as she pulled the trigger.

A brilliant flash erupted from the dark circle of metal. An incredible agony coursed through his skull.

Then he saw nothing.

℞

The sight stirred Michael's gut.

He had been peering around the doorway for ten minutes, waiting and watching. Afraid that someone was there, lying in wait for him. The thirteen-year-old stood frozen in the doorless entryway.

Acid welled in his throat. He suppressed the urge to vomit. Miss Christine was chained in a sitting position to the wall; this time her back was against it and her arms were splayed like Jesus on the cross. She was gagged and blindfolded once more. Her head rested on her chest. From the slow, soft heaving of her chest, Michael guessed she was asleep.

Charlie's body lay a few feet in front of her, untouched from the moment he'd died. The pool of blood around it was a large round circle, mixing with the dust and dirt. The pitchfork lay a few feet away, covered in *his* crimson hand prints.

Deciding it was safe, Michael moved toward her. He stepped on the balls of his feet, his strides short and tentative. He swiveled his head, checking every angle. His heart thumped in his chest. After ten feet, he stopped and listened. He swiveled his head again and checked behind him.

He resumed his journey across the wine-cellar floor through the racks of wine bottles. The body loomed in front of him, getting larger and more gruesome. The pool of blood around the dead guard had stopped expanding. It was impressive and nauseating in its size. The edges of the puddle became damned up as the dirt impeded its progress. He couldn't avoid looking at the ravaged flesh of the face, bluish in death. The lower lip had been devoured. His naked legs and butt were pale and blue. Lifeless!

Michael gave the corpse a wide birth. So wide, he stumbled into the far wall. The wall he'd been chained to not long ago. He fell to his knees, scuffing the rough concrete.

Miss Christine jumped at the noise. "Who's there?"

Her head whipped back and forth, trying to ascertain the direction of the sound. She drew her legs in close to her body, readying for a kick.

"No, please! Not again!"

"It's me, Michael. Miss Christine, it's me," he whispered.

Miss Christine cocked her head, then smiled. "Michael?"

"Yes," he whispered.

"Can you free me?"

"I think so."

Michael circled the corpse and knelt by her side. He removed the chain of keys from his pocket and began inserting them into the lock restraining her left arm. Two minutes later, both arms were free.

"Where are the guards?" Michael asked.

"Probably outside. Everyone is looking for you! Let's get out of here."

They crept up the steps to the large wooden door. Christine peered through the small barred window cut in the horizontal planks. Two different guards sat there in place of Pierre and Charlie. She ducked back out of sight and motioned for Michael to follow her.

They made their way once more past the body and returned to the back room filled with discarded wine barrels. The rear door was dead bolted and secured with a large rusting padlock.

Michael gave her the key ring. She tried several keys with no success. Then she tried the largest, oldest looking key, inserted it, and turned. The mechanism was corroded and rough, but the lock dropped from the U-shaped hasp.

Christine pushed at the door. It did not budge. She tried several more times, again with no luck. Michael pressed his back against it and exerted all the pressure he could summon using his legs, while Miss Christine drove her shoulder into it.

After several minutes, they dropped to the floor in exhaustion. Sweat poured from their skin.

"What do we do now?"

Miss Christine looked at Michael. She crinkled her face in the dim light and sniffed.

"Can I tell you something, Michael?"

"Yes."

"Promise you won't get mad?"

"I guess."

She smiled. "You stink."

Michael looked down at his wet, stained clothing. He sniffed. "Yeah, I guess I do."

They both chuckled.

"Let's keep trying," she said.

℞

Three hours later in the mountains of western Virginia, Steven Cooper sat back on his uncomfortable cot inside the Red Onion, looking at the tiny gift.

The guard had deposited him back in his cell fifteen minutes earlier. He waited that long before he stood and turned away from the camera mounted in the corner. He removed the wad of paper, setting it on the desk across from his metal cot.

His heart thumped as he studied it.

This was the first communication he'd received from Sam Fairing since they'd been captured in the fourth-floor condo in the north spire of the Windsor Towers on that fateful day. Cooper had tried many times to communicate with small gestures and facial expressions across the exercise yard.

Though communication of any kind was forbidden and punished, Cooper had used facial tics, half-smiles and small shrugs to show Cyclops that he was remorseful for his cowardly actions, including spilling everything he knew about the failed operation.

The technique used to extract information—Cooper was quite familiar with it—was effective. Hypothermia: standing naked in a cell kept at a constant temperature of fifty degrees and regularly doused with cold water to accelerate heat loss. Cooper knew what was coming and did not want any part of it. He'd cracked in only an hour.

But despite telling them everything, he had not been spared. Next came being forced to stand, handcuffed, with his feet shackled to an eye bolt in the floor for endless periods of time. He had to balance his weight on one or two of his foot muscles. It created an intense amount of pain in his legs. Eventually, they failed him.

Cooper couldn't tell for sure. But it appeared that Cyclops had forgiven him for his transgressions using similar gestures and looks. He sported mixed emotions about the contact Cyclops had made. For some strange reason, he wanted the Muslim to forgive him. Cooper chided himself. When a man makes a choice to commit an act and then shows his cowardice in the heat of battle, it leaves an indelible sense of failure.

He recalled a quote he'd read from one of the books in the prison library:

Burn from my brain and from my breast
Sloth, and the cowardice that clings,
And stiffness and the soul's arrest:
And feed my brain with better things.

Cooper wanted to feed his brain with better things.

He picked up the clump of paper and unfolded it.

A small disc slipped from the folds and fell into his open hand. Cooper studied it, then turned his eyes to the hand-scribbled words on the page. The writing was miniscule, barely readable. Because his eyes were going bad, he wore reading glasses. Even they were unable to magnify the text enough for him to read it. So he grabbed a large magnifying glass and began studying the message:

My fellow brother-in-arms:

I am happy to see that we are incarcerated together. Our cause is still alive. You have a second chance to make good. Another mission is upon us. We are to be freed to continue our journey. The small disc you have received is a small transmitter containing a message from a secret friend. Place it in your ear and hear the instructions for our next mission.

Allahu Akbar!

Cooper picked up the small disc, the diameter of a pencil eraser. From the pad of his index finger, he examined it. One side was sticky and coated in some kind of glue. The opposite side looked like a miniature circuit board.

He sniffed it. It smelled sweet and acidic at the same time.

Cooper looked up at the camera keeping constant tabs on him and back at the disc on his forefinger.

Could it be? Was he being given a second chance?

He placed the disc on the skin at the entrance to his ear canal. With a gentle pressure, he pushed it in. Almost immediately, he felt a sting, a tiny electric shock.

A weak, tinny voice spoke to him, emanating from the tiny disc. Cooper had not heard the voice since he'd been brought here. He recognized it despite the poor quality of the recording.

It was Sam Fairing! Sharif al-Faisal! Cyclops!

The timbre of the first words sent a calm through him.

"Hi, Steven!"

That feeling lasted a moment as the next words spilled out. An icy chill sliced up his spine.

"Vengeance is mine!"

Cooper scratched at his ear, trying to remove the disc. But it had slipped deep into the ear canal. The stinging sensation in his ear spread throughout the skin of his head and face. In a matter of seconds, his whole body began to crawl as if covered by thousands of insects.

The words repeated.

"Vengeance is mine!"

The crawling sensation increased. Now, it felt like millions of insects were inching over him, biting him. His throat thickened and narrowed. His breaths came harder, faster. Less air was getting into his lungs. A low whistle penetrated the stinging in his ears. It was the sound of air trying to get into his chest.

His heart rhythm changed to a weird, uncomfortable thumping, strong and irregular.

Cooper's head began to swim. The walls waved. A warm liquid oozed from his nostrils. Cooper moved his hand to his mouth and nose. His fingers came away coated in crimson. Collapsing to the floor, his body twitched. A moment before his eyes closed for the last time, the three words in that tinny, ominous voice repeated themselves.

"Vengeance is mine!"

℞

Cyclops, lay in his bunk two cells removed from Steven Cooper's. It had been three hours since he'd been tasered for his outburst in the exercise yard. He knew it was coming. His neighbor had created a diversion so Cyclops could drop the small gift. Then, in turn, the one-eyed prisoner had created his own commotion allowing his neighbor to pick up the small wad of paper, giving him the chance to pass it along to Cooper, the intended recipient.

It was a small, but necessary price to pay. Exhausted, as if he'd just finished a marathon, his motor skills had finally returned but his muscles still ached.

He spent those hours resting, recovering. But, he also spent them waiting. Waiting for the rushed, panicked movements of the corrections officers. That would tell him it was time to initiate the next phase of his plan.

The death of the weasel would only be a matter of time.

Cyclops also spent that time contemplating his fate.

He remembered how close they had been to striking down the infidels in Newport News. It would have been a swift, crushing blow, creating panic and worldwide terror. Stock markets would have crashed. The world would have recoiled in shock and horror. If the Americans could not protect two of their most important people against The Simoon, how could anyone be safe?

He had been a hair's breadth away from pulling the trigger, sending the fifty-caliber projectile through the white screen, puncturing the cloth, and ripping through weak flesh and bone.

He would have been hailed a hero by the coalition he'd been tapped to lead—a coalition that would have united the Arab governments of the world, one he would have guided out from under the yoke of American colonialism.

But they had failed. He was holed up here, a prisoner no more important than a common criminal. If the failure itself hadn't been enough, the memory that he had been thwarted by a no-name stung Cyclops even deeper.

Jason Rodgers wasn't a law enforcement type. He was a pharmacist with, Cyclops grudgingly admitted, a strong will, a sense of purpose, and training in a martial art and weapons.

He had experienced it in the brief but fateful altercation in the condo of the Windsor Towers. The pharmacist's technique, the way he'd handled himself and the handgun as he entered the condo—Jason Rodgers had been a formidable opponent.

Nonetheless, the pharmacist must pay. He would pay. If he ever got out of here, Sharif-al-Faisal, the Cyclops, would see to it.

I am invincible!

I cannot and will not be defeated!

I have not won all the battles, but the war is mine!

I am Sharif-al-Faisal!

I am Sam Fairing!

He rubbed the patch over his mutilated eye. It was gone, nothing more than scar tissue over a deep hole in his skull. It ached with phantom pain from time to time. He had become the one-eyed monster of Greek mythology.

I am the Cyclops!

I am Brontes! The blacksmith of the Gods, forger of weapons that will strike the mighty lethal blow to the American Titans!

I am the Cyclops! And I will have my revenge!

Though he wasn't there to see it, he knew exactly when Steven Cooper placed the deadly poison disc in his ear. Though the doors and walls of his cell were solid cement and steel, the commotion caused could not be quelled.

Corrections officers rushed past his cell. Five minutes later, a stretcher arrived and was whisked past his small cell. Another few minutes after that and the stretcher reappeared, being wheeled in the opposite direction.

Cyclops caught a glimpse of a medical person performing chest compressions as they rushed by.

A smile crept across his face. It was now time begin the second phase. He would wait several hours. He did not want the medical team being distracted with attending to the dead-or-dying Steven Cooper. He would need the medical team focused only on him when the time came.

Cyclops checked the digital clock on the small shelf in his cell. Soon, he would begin his escape.

Chapter 44

"What am I doing here?" Jason demanded. "Who the hell are you? Where the hell am I?"

Jason sat in the den of an affluent, private residence outside Washington, DC. The dark wood furniture of the massive office was upholstered with brightly patterned fabrics and accented with highly-polished brass lamps. In the center of the desk rested a brass banker's lamp. A green shade shone a perfect cone of light on the leather blotter.

A varied assortment of expensive Hummel figurines, antique handguns, and pens in cushioned cases lined wall bookshelves, dotting spaces between leatherbound tomes. Framed photographs and citations covered the walls above an ornate chair rail. Four decanters holding bronze liquids sat perched on a small corner table surrounded by crystal rocks glasses.

Sitting in a chair directly opposite a large, expensive desk, Jason scanned the room. Five stern-faced men in dark suits, four of them about his age ringed the walls. The fifth, his face lined with fine wrinkles that framed a pair of intense blue eyes, was an older gentleman around sixty. The perfectly trimmed, close-cropped, silver hair hinted at a military pedigree.

Jason's eye caught the small bar, and suddenly he wanted a drink.

The older man noticed Jason's glance. "My apologies, Mr. Rodgers. Can I offer you a something?"

Jason nodded.

He wore a dark navy suit and a crisply starched shirt. The red tie glowed against the white fabric of starched shirt. He poured three fingers of an amber liquid into two glasses, stepped over to Jason, and held one out. Jason accepted it.

As the man circled the desk to the thick, cushioned executive chair behind it, Jason placed the glass to his lips and gulped down the scotch, wincing as it burned its way into his stomach.

"Do you know who I am?"

Jason shook his head. "No."

The fact that he was now sitting in front of someone from the federal government meant his ploy had worked. This fact concerned him and at the same time offered him a glimmer of hope. He was one step closer to finding Michael and Chrissie. He had abandoned Peter, leaving him to deal with the delivery of whatever lethal cargo the truck held. He tried not to think about what Hussein would do if she discovered that Jason was not in the truck.

"I am Giles Doyle, director of the Secret Service of the United States."

"What am I doing here? I have no business with you. I need to be speaking with someone from the FBI."

"For now you get me. I apologize for interrupting your quest."

"My quest? You know about that?

"Of course we know. The government has many agencies at its disposal. You didn't expect that Delilah Hussein would organize an assassination attempt on two presidents and that we would let it go at that, did you? I also know that your son and girlfriend have been taken and that Delilah Hussein has them."

"How long have you known she was alive?"

"We found out two weeks ago."

Jason shuddered. This whole thing, for him, Peter, Michael, and Chrissie, had started forty-eight hours ago. 'Are you shitting me? Why was I not told?"

"That was not my call."

Jason shook his head. He narrowed his eyes. His next words were laced with contempt. "I could have taken steps to safeguard my family!"

Director Doyle absorbed Jason's reaction without a flinch or narrowing of the eyes. In a soothing, calm tone, he said, "Jason . . ."

"That's Mr. Rodgers to you!" Jason glared. He coughed and continued. "So why hasn't she been taken down? It would have saved me a lot of trouble."

Doyle nodded, then frowned. "I understand . . . Mr. Rodgers . . . that decision was made at the highest level. You have to understand there was concern that any communication with you could have been intercepted, or any actions taken by you after that communication could have tipped Hussein and her group that we are on to her, creating the chance the she could elude us. We need the element of surprise."

Jason lifted an eyebrow as if saying: *I don't give a shit.*

"We had no idea she was going to kidnap your son and Miss Pettigrew." Doyle leaned forward. "Well maybe we can help each other out. We were hoping you might fill in some of the gaps."

"You need my help finding her?"

"It would be a service to your country."

"You guys knew she was alive. You knew what happened in Newport News. You knew she could retaliate against me and my family. No one bothered to inform me. And now you want me to help you?"

"Mr. Rodgers," Doyle said, placing his drink on the end table, "her continued existence was and is a matter of national security. We know The Simoon has plans to attack the United States. We believe that attack is underway right now. But we do not know what it is, or where it is going to happen. She is using you to carry out part of her plan. What is in the truck?"

Jason gnashed his teeth. *They knew! They knew two weeks ago!*

Jason lowered his eyes to his lap and studied his hands. His fingers blanched as they dug into the fabric of his trousers. *Betrayed!*

Michael and Chrissie's kidnappings could have been prevented!

Jason uttered the only two words that came to mind. "Fuck you!"

The words appeared to hit Doyle like a speeding truck. He appeared to be swallowing his initial, angered gut reaction.

"You asked a Newport News cop to contact us on your behalf. You reached out to us, remember?"

Jason pushed out a long breath. "Yes."

"So you must think we can help, right?"

"I don't have any other options."

He sighed. "I understand your anger. But you're wrong. We didn't know what was happening. We still don't. Hussein's plan, whatever it is, needs to be stopped.

Jason couldn't get past what seemed obvious. "Perhaps, if you had warned me, and by proxy her, she would have ceased operations and halted the attack."

"Doubtful," Doyle retorted. "I repeat: if we had warned you, it could have alerted her that we knew. We couldn't risk that. According to our expert on Hussein, she's filled with a need for revenge."

"So I'm a pawn. A chess piece to be sacrificed."

"Jason," Doyle persisted, "you contacted us through Detective Palmer. You wanted the government involved because you want your boy and your girlfriend back. You came to us. You're here now. Make the most of it!"

Jason, at a loss for words, shook his head slowly

"Do you want your family back?" Doyle continued, raising his voice.

The betrayal Jason felt, the knowledge that they had known, had temporarily derailed him. Then the realization hit him. He was going to have to work with these men whether he liked their decisions or not. There were no other options.

"We suspected you would be distrustful. So we brought in someone we know you can trust . . . and someone that trusts you."

Confusion mixed with a swirling maelstrom of frustration. A rattling sound interrupted Jason's fugue. Coming from behind him, it reached a crescendo a few feet away. Jason turned for a glimpse. His eyes registered a shriveled form in the wheelchair.

Several long moments elapsed. A flicker of recognition passed through Jason's mind. Doyle said the words before Jason's mind formed the name.

"Mr. Rodgers, I believe you know Special Agent Clay Broadhurst."

℞

"The brothers stopped at the rendezvous point," Oliver explained. "For about twenty minutes. They proceeded and are now heading north on Route 13 again."

"That is good news, Oliver, mon cheri," Hussein replied. "Has Pierre's body been disposed of?"

"Oui, Madame. It has been dropped in the ocean four miles offshore."

Hussein placed a gentle hand on Oliver's shoulder as he sat at the computer terminal showing the blinking icon on the screen. She squeezed until Oliver winced. Hussein placed her lips beside his ear.

"You have let me down, Oliver. Your men royally screwed up. You better hope we find the boy," she threatened. Hussein's breath caressed the side of his face and neck, making him tense his muscles. "How long until they reach Dawson?"

"With no stops, should be three to four hours."

Hussein smiled. "No more screw ups." Oliver nodded as Hussein reached down and placed a pair of boning scissors on the table beside the keyboard. Instantly, Oliver's two missing pinky fingers began to ache.

℞

Moments earlier, Jason Rodgers and Clay Broadhurst had studied each other for several moments. Each nodded to the other, acknowledging a mutual respect borne out of a common fate forged in the Windsor Towers in Newport News.

"Did you know?"

"No. I don't like any of what's happening either, Jason," Broadhurst replied. "I have made my objections known to Director Doyle, quite vehemently."

Broadhurst shot a brief, harsh glance at his boss. Jason turned to see disgust register on Doyle's countenance.

These two don't like each other! Jason thought. For some strange reason, this fact comforted him.

Broadhurst continued. "To be fair to the director, the decision to not warn you came from above him . . . at the highest level!"

"So he said," Jason replied. "The president, the man I helped to save, decided he would not return the favor."

"It's more complicated than that," Doyle interrupted.

Jason studied Broadhurst's weak, emaciated appearance. He'd lost an egregious amount of weight. His clothes hug from his frame. The eyes were dull. The man was a breath away from death.

"Let me help you, Jason. I owe you. Let *me* return the favor."

"Maybe."

"You don't have a lot of options," Broadhurst whispered. He lifted a white handkerchief to his lips and coughed several times into it.

Ten seconds later, Jason nodded.

"Good. Where is your brother now?"

"I don't know."

"Where were you going?"

"Don't know that either."

"Then what the hell was the plan?"

"We were supposed to get more information at a location somewhere north of Exmore on the Eastern Shore. We would get further instructions then. Peter has probably already been there."

"Where on the Eastern Shore?"

"Turkey Run Road in Mappsville. Get me a computer and I'll show you on Google Earth."

Broadhurst removed his cell phone from his jacket and dialed. "Get a response team mobilized. Eastern Shore of Virginia." He ended the call and turned to Jason. "Show me where exactly."

℞

"The Greek Monitor has initiated contact," the deputy director of operations of the CIA said.

"How?" John Beck, the director of operations of the Central Intelligence Agency asked.

Beck was acquainted with the secret CIA black site inside the Red Onion State Penitentiary in the mountains of western Virginia, staffed with corrections officers serving in a dual capacity as CIA operatives. These select agents drew two salaries, one from the Virginia Department of Corrections and a second, covert remuneration from the Central Intelligence Agency. Their directive was to maintain order in accordance with state protocols for the five ultra-secret political prisoners and collect information for the Agency, passing along any data gleaned from the inmates for evaluation by analysts at Langley.

In the wake of the security breach and assassination attempts, Beck had tasked the deputy director with placing an alternate agent onsite at the prison. This agent was an ultra-paranoid safety measure made necessary by the leaks and moles discovered in Washington. Someone whose presence was known only to the deputy director and Beck. Beck didn't know the agent's name. The deputy director did. The Greek Monitor's sole mission was to watch the watchers. The dual agents at the Red Onion had no idea they were being scrutinized. Beck did know the agent was a woman who delivered meals to the ultra-secret detention unit.

"She sent an email with the code "GPI," the deputy director explained.

"GPI?" Beck asked.

"It means 'Greek Protocol Initiated.' It references the fact that Cyclops, al-Faisal's self-anointed nickname, is a mythical Greek figure."

"Okay, give me the details."

"She used a polygraphic substitution cipher in a long email to a phony boyfriend we set up months ago . . ."

"I don't need those details, just what's going on at the Red Onion."

"Okay, first, there's this." The lieutenant dropped a flash drive and a file on the director's desk.

"What's this?"

"Clayton Usher has been missing for the last forty-eight hours . . ."

"Tell me something I don't fuckin' know," Beck spat.

Beck had been briefed in the days and weeks following the assassination attempts in Newport News about the presence of a deep-cover mole inside the Agency. A classified team of select Agency personnel was assembled to find the double agent. They narrowed their search to three possible suspects. The trail ultimately led to one man who stretched head and shoulders above the other two possible spies. His name was Clayton Usher, director of communications at Langley. Codename: Hammon.

Shortly after the assassination attempts in Newport News, Hammon's activity ceased. He had gone underground. But the team had traced his activities, whereabouts, communications, and personal

finances, and by cross-referencing it with known activities of the perpe-
trators of the assassination attempts and information gleaned through
the intensive interrogation of Cooper and Sam Fairing aka Sharif
al-Faisal, they were able to train their sites on Hammon/Usher.

Beck always chuckled at the term intensive interrogation. He pre-
ferred to call it what it was: torture. And it was very effective at extracting information.

Beck and his task force had been watching, listening to, and monitoring Usher for eighteen months, waiting for Usher to make a false
move or contact that would confirm their suspicions. He had received
an email several days ago, then disappeared. The codebreakers were still
trying to determine if the email was a coded message. At present, he
had eluded their surveillance and was "off the grid," causing Beck two
sleepless nights.

The deputy director ignored Beck's sarcasm. "This flash drive and
file belonged to him. These were dropped off at my desk last evening."

"What the hell does this have to do with the Red Onion?"

"This confirms he's the guy we've been looking for."

Beck flipped through the file. "Summarize."

"He left this note." The DD handed Beck a single, handwritten missive. Beck scanned it. "It says that he was meeting with Delilah Hussein
yesterday. The note is dated three days ago. He left instructions to have
the drive and the file delivered to us by courier if he did not return by 3
pm yesterday. It arrived at 4:30 pm. I spent last night and this morning
studying and verifying it. It contain details of the assassination attempts,
spreadsheets, financials in offshore accounts, the whole nine yards."

"And he hasn't returned?"

The DD shook his head.

"Is he dead?"

"Don't know. I have agents combing his home, office, and personal
accounts. We'll have a preliminary report in a few hours."

"What was Usher meeting with Hussein about? Getting out of the
country?"

"We don't know . . . neither did he. She requested the meeting."

"Where did they meet?"

"Usher carried with him a GPS transmitter, giving us a trail of his
movements?

"Where did he go?"

"He went to Bonaire."

"Where the hell is Bonaire?"

"It's an island in the southern part of the Caribbean Sea, just north of Venezuela in South America."

"Okay, then what?"

"The electronic trace disappeared there."

"What do you mean 'disappeared'?"

"Just that. The electronic transmission being sent to his laptop simply stopped."

"Let's get some satellite pictures of the island."

"I've already arranged it. The NRO's KH-12 Kennan satellite, part of the Keyhole program, has a bird on close orbit over the south Atlantic right now. Sign this." The deputy director slid a memo to Beck.

"What's this?"

"Your permission to retask the satellite. I will send it through the proper channels and have the NRO reposition it over Bonaire."

Beck scribbled his name on the document.

"Good work."

The DD smiled. He was used to Beck's belittling comments. He had learned long ago to ignore them. He had just been given the most lavish compliment he'd ever heard Beck utter.

"There's one more thing, John."

Beck peered at him like an impatient father waiting for more bad news from a troublesome child.

The DD continued. "A few hours after the scheduled meeting Usher had with Hussein, we intercepted a communication from our agent in Syria, the double agent in ISIS. He was contacted by someone representing Hussein asking to place a CO at a prison in the U.S."

"No shit! The Red Onion?"

"Didn't say."

"Did you contact the Virginia Department of Corrections?"

"Yesterday. Discreetly. At about four in the afternoon a man named Dalton Griffin met with the deputy warden, Jeremiah Travis. His first shift began this morning."

Beck nodded, acknowledging the obvious. The DD nodded along with his boss.

"How and why did they replace him?"

"According to the Greek Monitor's email, Josh Baker, Cyclops' CO, died along with his family. An apparent murder-suicide. He was replaced by a CO named Dalton Griffin. Dalton is *not* employed by the Agency."

"How did *that* happen?"

"We're still looking into that."

"We have more moles?"

"Could be."

Beck pushed out a long sigh and rubbed his temples. "The director and the president are going to have my balls for breakfast. Go on."

"Within twenty-four hours of taking over Baker's duties for Sharif al-Faisal, aka Cyclops, inmate Steven Cooper was dead. They found an implant inside his ear. We believe it contained a touch poison that was passed to him by the Cyclops. We're reviewing the video from the prison now."

The director had been forwarded ultra-secret daily reports from the Greek Monitor unit inside the Red Onion. She transmitted secure emails two to three times a week from a secure server at her home near the prison to an equally secure server offshore. Through several relays, the email arrived in the deputy director's inbox, was decoded by the DD himself, and hand delivered to Beck for review. Until this moment, her communications had been devoid of any controversial information.

"Do you want me to have Griffin relieved and interrogated?"

"Is there any indication that an attempt to free al-Faisal is in the works?"

"Not at this time."

Beck shook his head. "I don't like it. Tell the Greek Monitor to keep her ear to the tracks. Get me George McNamara. I want an extraction team on standby, ready to go. If we get word of any more unusual activity at the Onion, any sign they are trying to get al-Faisal out, we move! Is that clear?"

"Absolutely. Move to do what? Stop the escape?"

"Delilah Hussein wants her son back. We know that. We haven't pinned down her location yet. The electronic trail is varied and inconsistent. Broadhurst is sure she will make an attempt. We are going to use this to our advantage."

"I'll have the Greek Monitor report every eight hours."

"Excellent," Beck said. "Hopefully, retasking the satellite will give us a better idea where she might be."

"I'll contact the FBI director myself, so you can make your request."

The director nodded. "Make it happen."

$$\text{R}_{\text{X}}$$

They crouched, scanning the terrain. Michael and Chrissie had stayed out of sight in the shadow of trees on the property.

Michael pointed to the area where Pierre had taken him to relieve himself and where he had hit him in the face with the small boulder.

"This way. Quick," Christine said.

They peered around the corner. Seconds later, a phalanx of men appeared. The leader pointed in the direction of the wine cellar. The squad of men fanned out, dispersing. Two ran toward their former cell.

"We need to get away from here," Christine whispered. "Follow me."

She checked the expanse of ground behind the wine cellar and led Michael toward the rear corner of the compound and a tall, green, chain-link fence. She pointed toward a narrow cave of darkness created by a copse of trees. They ran, crossing the exposed distance.

When they reached the shadows, they stopped and dropped to the sandy earth inside the chain-link barrier.

They lay beside each other on their stomachs, chests heaving.

"Who are these people?" Michael asked in a whisper.

Christine recalled the image of Oliver standing over Pierre, his form backlit by the morning sun.

Despite the various traumas she had survived in the last two days and the warm breeze, the sight of Oliver sent an Arctic shiver through her. Her mind quickly registered Michael's hands desperately clutching her arm.

She repressed the image. "You don't want to know," she replied.

$$\text{R}_{\text{X}}$$

A second wheelchaired man rolled himself into the spacious room behind Broadhurst. Unlike Broadhurst, his legs were not covered by a blanket. In fact, Jason immediately noticed that this man had no legs.

"And," Doyle continued, "this is Special Agent Tom Johnson. Agent Johnson served with your brother in the marine corps."

"Hello," Jason replied, remembering hearing the name. "This reunion is a very nice and all. But I need to find my son and Christine."

"We are . . . I am working on that," Broadhurst croaked. His voice sounded like a dying electric toy. The high pitch trailed off as air seeped from his lungs. "Jason, we can help each other."

The director interrupted. "Mr. Rodgers, what Clay is trying to say is that if you help us, we may be able to help you."

Jason had recognized his plight moments before. But something deep inside him caused him to continue to object. As if that might cause them to be more careful when it came to getting Michael and Chrissie back. "So the lives of two people I love very much depend on my helping the Secret Service? These are American citizens that have been kidnapped by a terror organization. And you're using them as pawns."

"The sooner you get used to that fact, the sooner we can move toward getting them back," the director shot back.

Jason frowned and shook his head slowly

"We need to know what Hussein has asked of you. What is she forcing you to do?"

"I told you I don't know"

"Tell us everything that has happened. It may hold a clue as to what she is attempting. I promise we will do everything we can to get your son and your girlfriend back."

Jason's shoulders sagged. He had depleted his stores of resistance. Delilah Hussein had manipulated him. Michael and Chrissie were not coming back unless he worked with these asses.

"Okay . . . okay," he relented. "But I swear if you don't live up to your promise, I will scream everything I know from the mountaintop. I'll tell everything that happened with the attempted assassinations and what is going on now. Are we clear?"

Director Doyle nodded. "You have my word."

CHAPTER 45

Dalton Griffin had checked three of the five cells on the cell block. He worked backward from number six. He worked conscientiously, but he served more than one master: The Virginia Department of Corrections and the organization that was paying to help extract the prisoner known as Cyclops.

The other four correction officers were employees of the state prison system, but they also worked for the Company, the CIA. Only a few people in the state system knew the true nature of their double service—the chief warden, who oversaw the Red Onion; his supervisor, the chief of corrections operations; and the director of the Virginia DOC himself. Griffin knew that the director of VADOC could have anyone placed anywhere in the state prison system.

The rub was that Griffin did not work for the CIA. He was employed by a shadow organization ensconced in the government apparatus with ties to an outfit external to the Feds. He didn't know how he had been placed in a CIA black site posing as a CIA agent. The how and the why of how he'd arrived at the Red Onion did not matter. He had a job to do. A job he was being paid very well to accomplish. One he was about to perform.

The prisoners segregated here were five of the most dangerous persons in the world and had tried in one way or another to terrorize the United States of America. They were political prisoners, none of whom had been tried or convicted in an American court room. Their crimes or suspected crimes had been so dangerous and insidious that they had been whisked away without a trial or access to legal aid. Not even the guards knew what their treasons were.

Except, of course, Dalton Griffin.

In fact, Griffin knew one inmate's story quite well, that of Sharif al-Faisal, aka the Cyclops. Of course, Griffin had come by this information through unofficial channels.

He had checked his accounts hours before leaving for the Red Onion.

His official accounts, checking, savings, and 401k held about a hundred thousand. The corrections officer collected his pay from the Department of Corrections and lived in a modest home on the outskirts of Big Stone Gap in the southeast corner of Virginia. His neighbors knew him as a tough but quiet state employee.

Griffin had been on the payroll of the Simoon for the past eight months. The money they offered was substantial. All they asked was that he be ready when the time came to provide his services. They had deposited $15,000 each month for the last eight in a third account in the National Bank of Abu Dhabi.

Griffin studied the monitor on the desk before him. Each CO had his own private computer terminal through which he could monitor his charge. Cyclops was resting on his back on his cot, with his hands behind his head. His eyes were closed. Griffin couldn't tell if he was asleep or just meditating.

He glanced at his fellow officers. They had spoken little to him in his first twenty four hours on the unit. He was an outsider. If he had been placed as a guard at the Red Onion, Griffin knew that someone up the chain was also working with his Middle Eastern compatriots.

America is infected with traitors, he thought.

He had received the call forty-eight hours ago, been briefed in a two-hour video conference, and instructed as to what his mission was. He had been tasked with delivering the small package inside the breakfast tray. And to be ready when the time came hours later.

The unit had been shaken to its core by the breach. When they'd found Steven Cooper in his cell, his body cold and blue, they tried CPR and took him to the infirmary. But it had been a futile effort.

An urgent, encrypted communication had been fired off using a secure cell phone to the overseer of the program at Langley informing him of the death. Orders were issued to keep close tabs on all the other prisoners.

He watched now as Cyclops stood up and turned his back to the camera. Griffin watched the prisoner lift a hand to his head. The head moved as if he'd placed something in his mouth. The guard looked around the unit.

Suddenly, Cyclops dropped to the floor. Griffin checked his watch. Prayer time wasn't for another hour. Confused, Griffin stood and walked to Cyclops' cell. He peered through the thick glass embedded with chicken-wire window.

"Code Red, cell five!" he shouted into his shoulder mike. He rapped on the window. By the position of the body, he knew they were about to record their second death in the last six hours.

℞

"That's everything," Jason said as he collapsed onto the sofa. Over fifteen minutes, he'd poured out the details of the last two days. The retelling exhausted him almost as much as the actual events.

He had begun with the kidnappings, finding the business cards with the microprinting on them, followed by digging up the mini coffins. He capped it off with the request to get the keys from William Luther and then the struggle in the 65th Street home, followed by Luther's killing, and the escape from the jail with the assistance of The Watcher. Jason recounted the car chase to retrieve the box truck with the refrigerated cargo hold from an old man in the Red Sox jacket at a gas station, the locked rear doors with a key waiting somewhere at whatever destination lay before them, and instructions to drive up the Eastern Shore. He told them about leaving the truck and Peter, and jumping into Sheryl Penney's car to use her unmonitored phone.

"Where is this Watcher?" Doyle asked.

Jason shrugged. "Is he one of ours?"

Doyle paused as if thinking about whether or not to divulge that information. "No," he finally said.

"Who is he?"

"Dunno. What's in the truck?" Doyle asked, changing the subject.

Jason shrugged. "Don't know. The cargo area is locked. We were given specific instructions not to open it."

"We dispatched a team to Turkey Run Road. Nothing was found except an old house and we scared the shit out of a family in a mobile home. The woman there confirmed a truck stopped there. The driver went into the old house and came back out five minutes later."

"So he made it there?"

Doyle nodded. "Can you contact Peter?"

"I would if I could, but our phones were confiscated. The man at the gas station took everything before we got into the truck."

"Will your brother try to contact the authorities?"

"Pete was a topnotch marine . . ."

"I can vouch for that," Agent Johnson chimed in.

"He'll do whatever it takes. But he won't jeopardize Michael or Chrissie."

"Let's hope," Doyle continued, "we hear something soon."

℞

One hundred and fifty miles northeast, inside the Dawson Pharmaceuticals manufacturing plant, Angelo Sheppard rapped three times on the door. The word Security was stenciled on the frosted glass embedded in the thick oak. Without knocking or warning, he pushed it open.

"Hey, Gus."

"Hello, Mr. Sheppard. Pretty quiet tonight. What's up?"

"I'm sorry to ruin your night. But we have a gaggle of kids on the grounds. Northeast corner near the road."

The uniformed guard sat before a computer monitor with eight boxes arrayed across its screen. Each block contained a video image from feeds around the grounds. At the bottom of each block, shortened, condensed words indicated which camera was providing the image. Every few seconds, some of the images flickered, changing to a view from another camera.

Gus pressed several keys. The eight blocks disappeared, changing to one large view of the well-manicured lawn in front of the building.

The guard manipulated a joystick and panned the camera, zooming it in and out at various points.

"I don't see anything sir."

"They were there a minute ago. Can you check it out?"

"I'm not supposed to leave the control room. Kevin is at lunch. He went down the road and took the security vehicle."

Sheppard nodded. He already knew this and had timed his visit to coincide with the other guard's absence. The guards were not supposed to leave the premises. But they had been doing so for about six months. "I understand. But these guys looked like thugs. I'd hate for you to have to explain to one of the VPs why they damaged something or hurt someone on your watch. I'd feel better if you went out there. After all, you're the one with the gun. And I won't tell anyone that Kevin left the grounds."

Gus looked at the screen and back at Sheppard, weighing his options.

"I'll watch the monitors while you're gone," Sheppard persisted.

"Okay. I'll be right back."

As soon as Gus was gone, Sheppard sat down and went to work. He'd sent the rent-a-cop to the farthest corner of the campus, buying himself as much time as possible. Sheppard had practiced what he was about to do for the last three weeks. He punched the keyboard until the eight-image array returned. Then he moved to the network video recorder and squeezed behind it, pushing the small stand on which it stood away from the wall. He lifted the small cloth covering the cables and studied the sight. The small rectangular box, no bigger than the size of a large VCR, held forty-eight ports into which ran an army of coaxial cables. Dawson was currently using forty of the forty-eight available ports.

Thank God they haven't upgraded to IP cameras! Analog cameras made this task much easier, he thought.

Each analog camera around the plant, forty in all, was hardwired via a coaxial cable with its feed running from ports in the wall into the back of this network recorder.

Sheppard found the five ports he needed and unscrewed each coax cable from them. He removed five small devices called repeaters from under his shirt. Each was identical—a small black box with a four-inch coaxial cable protruding from one end and a coax receiving port on the other. Sheppard screwed the first unsecured cable into a repeater then connected the repeater's cable to the network recorder, thus placing the device between the cable from the wall and the network recorder.

He walked back to the screen and checked the image corresponding to that port. The repeater recorded a short ten second video from the image on that camera and continuously looped it back to the monitor.

He left the security room and ran the fifty feet to the hallway the camera monitored and switched off the lights in the hallway. The corridor went dark. Sheppard then returned to the security office, out of breath. He rechecked the image for that camera and saw that the image showed the lights still on in the hallway. He smiled. *It's working. The cameras would not record movements by anyone in these hallways or on the loading dock!*

Sheppard repeated the process with the four remaining ports and cameras, inserting a repeater between the network recorder and the coaxial cable. He checked his watch. He had planned on fifteen minutes, start-to-finish. Everything was done with three minutes to spare and there was still no sign of Gus. Sheppard covered the back of the NVR with the small black cloth, covering the repeaters, and pushed it back into place. He pulled up the camera feed of the front lawn and saw Gus the Guard standing on the grass.

His covert activities could now be conducted in total secrecy. Sheppard would return tomorrow after his covert activities had been conducted and remove the repeaters. If everything went according to plan, by the time anyone discovered what was going on, Sheppard would talk Gus back out of the office and remove the repeaters.

Sheppard hated the sneaking around. If he didn't, he was sure Quinton Boyd would end his career. All of this would be over soon.

℞

The Greek Monitor sat at her computer in the cramped one-bedroom extended-stay hotel just outside Clintwood, six miles east of the Red Onion. The small suite had an open-ended lease. She had a feeling the message she was going to send would mark the end of the CIA's need for her surveillance.

She typed her message into the email that would eventually find its way through various relays to her handler, the deputy director of operations of the CIA. The woman had been typing and crafting the message for the last hour, perfecting it, then using the polygraphic communications cipher to encrypt it.

The two paragraphs outlined how Cyclops had been taken from his cell, unconscious or dead, only hours after Steven Cooper had been confirmed as a casualty. All of this happened during one shift. Dalton Griffin was the variable. The new corrections officer had been on duty for less than eight hours when these crises occurred.

Her final coded words to the deputy director were: *Cyclops is no longer on site. I followed the vehicle and know where they have taken him.*

She typed in the coordinates. Satisfied, she pressed enter and the email disappeared.

$$\text{R}_{\text{X}}$$

An hour later, Sharif-al-Faisal awoke with a sharp intake of air into his lungs. The room spun. The ceiling seemed to rotate above him. He felt as if he was about to spin off the cold, steel slab.

He closed his eyes again, quelling the nausea and the spinning. Slowly, his senses returned. His ears picked up a soft, rhythmic beeping. A female voice penetrated the fog of his mind.

He's coming around. Increase the rate of the reversal agent. Bring it up to fifteen micrograms per hour.

The blurry face of a very attractive woman filled his field of vision. The soft lips rippled as her mouth formed words that did not quite register. Faisal blinked rapidly. The facial image strobed. Her blonde hair was pulled into a tight ponytail and a stethoscope hung laterally around the collar of her white lab coat.

"Where am I?"

"Just relax," the woman said. "It will take several hours for the reversal agent to take full effect and for you to regain all your faculties."

"Where am I?" Faisal repeated.

The doctor disappeared. A diminutive man wearing another starched lab coat replaced the woman. A pair of silver eyes peered at him from under a bald head and over a tightly cropped goatee.

"You are coming around nicely," the man said.

Faisal asked the question a third time. Still no one would answer him.

"Leave us," a third voice commanded.

The receding footfalls were followed by the clicking of a metal door latch. Sounds exploded around him as if through a loud speaker.

The drug!

The man attached to a third voice came into view from the opposite side of the bed. Faisal turned his eyes and gazed up at him. The man's head was turned, looking to the foot of the bed, as if waiting for the doctor's to leave. After a few seconds, he rotated his head and looked at Faisal, not speaking for a full fifteen seconds.

Dressed in a black turtleneck sweater under a tweed sports coat, he studied the patient with his hard black eyes.

"Welcome back."

Al-Faisal tried to sit up. A firm hand pressed him back down.

"Not yet," the man instructed. "Let the reversal agent do its thing."

"What happened?" Al-Faisal asked. The words sounded foreign to him, as if spoken by a drunken man.

"Everything went as planned. You took HH-34. It worked as it was supposed to."

Al-Faisal frowned in confusion.

"You died and we brought you back."

"Where am I?" al-Faisal asked. The words felt like they were coming from outside his body.

"In a safe hospital in rural West Virginia, an hour from the prison. Now relax. In a few hours, we will move you out of here . . . to be reunited with your mother."

℞

Four hundred miles northeast of the safe hospital, Peter Rodgers sat behind the wheel of the Freightliner with the engine running. His hands rested on the steering column, gripping the vinyl. He had not moved a muscle since the man standing ten feet from the cab had ordered him to place his hands on it. It was late Sunday afternoon. The parking lot itself was deserted, save for the idling truck.

"Are you Jason?"

"Yes," Peter lied.

"Where's your brother?"

"I left him at a coffee shop on the way."

"I was told there would be two of you." The man's face was covered with a black bandana much like outlaw cowboys once wore. Peter couldn't discern the make of his weapon. But it was a large caliber that would cause a lot of damage.

"Sorry about your bad luck," Peter intoned calmly. "It's just me."

"Turn off the engine and get out. Now!"

Peter cut the engine, pushed open the heavy door, and stepped down. He stood beside the open cab with his hands raised, palms facing the gunman.

"So what is the going rate for secret deliveries to Dawson Pharmaceuticals in New Jersey?"

"Shut up!" The man removed a cell phone from his jacket pocket and pressed a preprogrammed number.

"Are you an American?"

"I said shut up!"

The man's gun hand wavered. His eyes darted about as if he'd forgotten what to do next.

This guy's a nervous wreck.

Peter pressed his luck and the man's patience. "You know treason carries the death penalty."

"If you say another word, I'll shoot you right here. My orders were to secure you and your brother . . ."

"Well, I'm glad I made him get out of the truck."

Someone answered. The gunman spoke to the person on the other end. "Where the hell are you? He's here. Get the fuck over here!"

Thirty seconds later, a dark sedan pulled to a stop in front of the truck. Four men exited. Two flanked Peter. Before the hood was placed over his face, Peter saw the second pair of men climb into the truck.

He was tossed roughly in the back of the sedan beside a third man, whose presence he could feel. The former marine's hands were bound in front of him. Peter heard the truck engine rev and move off. Seconds later, his head jerked backward as the car accelerated away.

CHAPTER 46

Angelo Sheppard alighted from the Freightliner, leaving the engine running so the refrigeration unit continued to cool the hold. The car with his new compatriots and the driver of the truck had sped off to God-only-knew-where. Sheppard didn't know what was going to happen to the man. It didn't look good. Boyd had never told him guns would be involved. Suddenly, Sheppard felt like a criminal.

Keep your mouth shut and do the job, mate!

Sheppard walked through the door alongside the loading dock. A few seconds later, the large roll-down garage door lifted. The production manager rolled a six-foot, motorized, flatbed dolly onto the dock. He removed the only set of keys to the rear door of the hold, unlocked the double padlocks, and lifted the door open.

A blast of freezing air and a cloud of fog hit him in the face. Sheppard rolled the motorized dolly into the truck, its electric engine emitting a low whine. There was no time to waste. The ten drums had to remain below the optimal temperature of twenty-eight degrees.

Wearing thick work gloves, he lifted the tall, slim drums coated with frost onto the dolly. He estimated that each weighted fifty pounds. He would be lugging five hundred pounds through the hallways of the plant.

This Sunday had been chosen as the perfect time to make the transfer. The plant had been shut down for the weekend for a thorough cleaning and decontamination before the production run next week. Sheppard had ensured that the sanitizers finished yesterday, Saturday, leaving the plant empty. Save for the security guards on site, Sheppard was the only person inside the plant.

Two minutes after starting, he had finished hefting the drums onto the electric dolly. He had practiced the journey from the loading dock to the secret room many times, trimming his time to a consistent five minutes.

With the truck still running, Sheppard pressed the lever on the steering mechanism, much like the brake handle of a motorcycle. The dolly rolled slowly off the truck, bumping onto the concrete loading dock, and through the open garage door.

He checked his watch and started the timer. He motored the machine to his right, disappearing into the shadow of the plant.

$$\mathbf{R}_{\!x}$$

The deputy director of operations of the CIA sat at his desk in his home office. The soft glow of the computer screen illuminated his face with a blue hue. The machine beeped as an email arrived in his private, secure inbox.

It was from the Greek Monitor.

He clicked on it and stared at a jumble of letters organized in varying length from one letter to ten. The DD opened a decoding program and accessed it. He copied and pasted the encrypted message into the software and hit enter.

The disorganized alphabet transformed into two paragraphs of readable text.

"Shit," he said aloud, twenty seconds later.

He printed the page and folded it in two. Jumping from his cushy leather executive chair, he rammed the email into his pocket. A minute later, he was on his way out the door. As he backed out the driveway of his Fairfax home, his cell phone was pressed to his ear. The director of operations line was already ringing.

$$\mathbf{R}_{\!x}$$

The hood, filthy and soaked with some kind of noxious chemical, exuded a medicinal odor. *Something from the pharmaceutical plant,* Peter concluded. *Hope I'm not being poisoned.*

Fifteen minutes later, the sedan skidded to a halt on a gravelly surface. The front doors swung open, followed quickly by the rear doors. Peter was yanked out. With his hands still bound, he fell from the vehicle, landing hard on his shoulder.

A strong hand pulled him up by the shirt and ripped the hood from his head. Peter blinked at the sudden barrage of light. After several moments, his eyes adjusted and he scanned his surroundings, assessing. They were in a clearing, deep in a wooded area. A cloud of dust swirled about the recently stopped vehicle.

It was still light, but the sun was going down. He guessed it was past six in the evening. It was still early spring, but it would be dark soon.

Two of the men, also wearing masks, flanked him as the third masked man, the nervous one who had held him at gunpoint in the parking lot, rammed his gun into his beltline, then removed a cell phone and initiated a call. In short, clipped tones, he gave a short burst of vital information to the person on the other end. Peter could hear the response clearly. A heavily accented male voice responded on the other end. Peter could not make out their meaning. *Could be French!*

The voice asked a series of rapid-fire questions, perhaps inquiring about the delivery and its whereabouts. Then Peter could understand the words coming from the voice of the man on the other end.

"Yes," the masked man repeated several times. "The delivery has been secured. Angelo has taken possession of the truck."

"Have you taken the drivers into custody?" the voice asked.

"No . . . I mean yes. I mean . . . there is only one driver."

"What? Who is it?"

"It is the man named Jason."

"Where is the brother?"

"He said he left him at a coffee shop. What should we do? Do you want us . . ." The masked man locked eyes with Peter before continuing. He then turned his back to him. "Do you want us to kill him?" the man whispered. Peter did not hear the words but he could guess. It was as if they had been shouted in his ear.

A long silence ensued as the man waited for a response.

Peter held no cards. Bound by the hands and guarded by two large men with large guns, he would not get three steps if he tried to run.

Despite these long odds, he was not about to stand idly by as they put a bullet into his brain.

The voice came back on the line, muttering words Peter could not understand. The masked man turned and held the phone up and snapped a photo of Peter's face. Fifteen seconds later, he dispatched it.

A minute later, the phone rang. The male voice on the other end had been replaced by that of a female. The high-pitched and irate timbre spewed epithets Peter did not catch.

The masked man, through the cloth over his face, attempted to respond but was unable to. Thirty seconds elapsed before the pitch and speed of the woman's words decreased.

The masked man stepped to within a foot of Peter. He lashed out, twisting at the waist, with a right cross to Peter's cheek. The former marine dropped to his knees.

The masked man stood over him. "You are not Jason Rodgers. You are his brother. Where is he?"

Peter spit a mouthful of blood into the dirt. The two men on either side of him lifted him to his feet. Peter squinted and spat a bloody gob into the leader's face.

"I want to speak with whoever is on the other end of that phone. Is it Delilah Hussein?"

The leader's eyes went wide. Then his cheeks lifted slightly, telling Peter the man was smiling.

He held the phone to up to Peter's cheek. Peter spoke into it as blood flowed over his bottom lip. "I do not know where Jason is. But wherever he is, I'm sure he's on his way to find you."

$$\text{R}_{\text{X}}$$

Sheppard checked the isolated hallway, making sure that no one was around. The video cameras had been taken care of. He and his cart of frozen drums were invisible.

What had happened to the driver of the truck?

Boyd had told him he would never see the three men who had taken the driver. He did not mention that other men were involved until this morning. Sheppard felt like a man trapped in a watertight compartment with the water level rising.

He pushed the cart into the Vault and closed the door, locking it behind him. Removing his cell phone from his pocket, he videoed each drum, making sure to get a close up of each container's serial number. He flipped the switch on the large metal cylinder. The entire assembly lifted, exposing the fogged, subterranean, grave-sized hole lined with stainless steel.

Carefully, Sheppard moved each of the drums into position in the hold so that each was beneath one of the ten tubes dangling from the larger vat.

Will connect those later, he told himself.

The production manager considered the roads he'd taken and choices he'd made in the last few years that caused him to end up where he was at this very moment. And he wished he'd never agreed to meet Boyd that day.

One March afternoon twenty-five months ago, Quinton Boyd, the vice president of the Injectable Division, had appeared in the cafeteria. The Brit asked Sheppard to meet him after work for a drink, saying it would be worth Sheppard's time. Later that day, Sheppard met the pharmaceutical executive at Bill's Olde Tavern in Hamilton, just outside of Trenton, about twenty minutes from the plant.

For the first five minutes, Boyd tried to make small talk. The effort was all the more lame because of his British accent.

"Mr. Boyd, I don't have much time. I have to get home. My wife needs to go to work. She works night shifts and my son is ill. With traffic, it's going to take me an hour to get home from here," Sheppard urged.

"I know," Boyd countered. "I'm sorry about your boy. I'll get right to it."

Boyd produced a folded USA *Today* newspaper from within his jacket and slid it across the booth. Sheppard began to open it.

"Don't remove the envelope until later," Boyd had said.

"What's this?"

Boyd smiled and took a long pull on his Guinness. "I know that you have many medical bills. This should help. There'll be more later."

"I don't understand."

"You are now part of my team, Angelo."

"What team?"

"Juan Santos and I . . ."

"Santos, the CEO?"

"Yes," Boyd had nodded. "We are initiating a covert program which will revolutionize our industry. It has been approved by a small subcommittee of the board of directors and is so top secret that only a handful of people know about it. Once we prove that it works, Dawson Pharmaceuticals will become the leader in our industry segment."

"Is this legal?"

"Let's just say we have to produce some significant results before we go public. Your job will be to help us build a secret storage facility inside the plant. It will require you to oversee construction of the secret room when the plant is quiet."

"Can we count on you?"

"And if I say no?"

Boyd forced a thin smile over his crooked bowtie. He leveled a hard glare at him. "Then you will lose your job . . . and I will see to it that you don't work in the industry ever again. Your life will be all at sixes and sevens! That's how we Brits say…all fucked up!"

Sheppard had reluctantly agreed. Boyd pushed the newspaper and the envelope closer to Sheppard.

"Keep your mouth shut and you will be able to retire in a couple of years, son. If not, your life will become very uncomfortable."

Angelo Sheppard had kept his mouth shut and collected more than three hundred thousand dollars under the table. Now, the Vault was finished and he had placed the drums. But something was very wrong. The truck had arrived with the delivery and the driver had been taken away at gunpoint by masked men.

What the hell was in these drums?

With his hand shaking, Sheppard again removed his phone and recorded the drums in place in the frozen room. Satisfied, he lowered the larger vessel back into place.

He then pulled up the video files on his phone and sent them via secure text to Quinton Boyd, who would send them up the chain.

"Why is the Secret Service doing this? Isn't that the CIA or FBI's job?" Jason demanded.

"Trust me," the director replied. "Since the sitting president and his father, the former president, were targeted for murder, every agency has been tasked with finding those responsible. All appropriate agencies are working together on this."

"I have Delilah Hussein's voice," Jason began, "on a recorded message and have a video file showing my son and my girlfriend being held captive."

"We know that," the director interrupted.

"How?"

"We have ways. We have someone inside their organization. We know that there is a plan and that it is underway. But the target has been kept very close to the vest. Only a few people know the true target. Our agent isn't one of them. The video file was sent to us via our mole. We have been trying to analyze it to gather clues as to Hussein's location."

"So you don't know where she is?"

"We are getting close. But we may not have enough time before her plan is executed. You can lead us to her. And at the same time, you may be able to help your son and girlfriend."

"Tell me how."

℞

The masked man held the phone back up to his ear and listened. The tone of the voice on the other end told Peter that Hussein had issued an ultimatum to the gunman standing in the wash of the headlights on this deserted stretch of roadway.

As the leader listened to her harsh words, Peter glanced to his left at the tall skinny man flanking him. Then he cast a quick look to his right. This guy was stout and muscular. The stock of a snub-nosed revolver jutted over his belt. Both men wore dark kerchiefs pulled high over the bridges of their noses.

He's thicker, Peter thought.

Peter addressed his guards, "You guys ever seen the Jesse James story?"

They guards regarded him with hollow, menacing glares.

"Piss off," the stout man replied.

"Jesse James is one of my favorite cowboy tales."

The leader spun.

"She wants to know where your brother is," the leader demanded.

"I told you I don't know."

The man spoke into the phone, turning away once more. "He says he doesn't know."

A pause ensued. Three words came through the phone. They registered instantly in the marine's ears.

"Then kill him!"

The man on the phone nodded. Peter watched the back of his head bob down then up. "Will do," he replied.

He began to rotate, reaching for the weapon he'd stuffed into his belt.

As soon as he heard the man's reply, Peter initiated his maneuver. With a lightning quick move, he raised his bound hands and dropped them around the neck of the man standing to his left. With all the force he could generate he yanked down on the back of the man's neck with his duct-taped hands, forcing him to bend at the waist. At the same instant, he raised his knee, ramming it into the criminal's forehead. The bone-on-bone impact sounded like the crack of a bat on a spring afternoon.

In almost the same motion, Peter lifted his bound arms from around the man's neck as he dropped to the gravel. The man to his right reacted, but his timing was a fraction late. Peter spun, lifting his arms, cocking his right elbow and swinging it.

The point of his elbow caught the man square on the cheek, snapping his head to one side. Peter reached down and pulled the revolver from the man's belt before jumping behind the staggering man. The masked man at the front of the car, holding the phone, had leveled his weapon and fired.

The round struck the heavy guard in the lower abdomen. Peter held the man upright. A second shot rang out, ripping through the man's shoulder. He groaned as air escaped his lungs in a rapid whoosh.

Peter pushed the wounded man toward the gun-wielding, phone-holding leader. As the heavy guard fell forward, Peter saw the leader's eyes following his compatriot's downward trajectory. That split second allowed the former marine to rip off one shot.

It exploded into the man's shooting arm. The masked leader spun and dropped to the gravel, dropping the gun. The leader, though down, scrambled for the fallen gun.

Peter aimed and pulled the trigger a second time. The trigger clicked and the revolver spun. *Nothing!*

The leader had taken hold of the gun with his good arm, his left, and was bringing it around. Peter pivoted and ran behind the idling car. Two shots zipped past him.

He dove into a roadside ditch overgrown with tall grass, rolling several times to its valley. Peter collected himself and, staying low, bolted for the tree line.

℞

An hour later, Peter, his hands still bound with duct tape, trudged along the two-lane deserted stretch of roadway framed by trees and shrubs. The traffic was sparse, an occasional truck or car passing by every ten or twelve minutes. The sun had begun its descent to the horizon. Darkness would envelop the area soon.

When a pair of headlights approached, Peter stepped into the tree line. The sight of a strange man with his wrists bound would not invite drivers to stop. Besides, he wasn't sure if the goons were still alive or if they would pursue.

Dawson Pharmaceuticals, as he recalled, was situated along State Road 602, in Camden which cut through swatches of farmland, slanting northeast, paralleling Interstate 295. As he approached the pharmaceutical plant, the farmland turned into suburbs. He shouldn't have to go far to find some kind of civilization. After they had driven from the parking lot, they did not travel for more than fifteen minutes. So he was still relatively close to the plant.

After he had taken refuge in the woods from the remaining gunman beside the desolate roadway, Peter ran through trees and brambles as deep as the thickets would allow putting distance between him and the killers. After he'd humped about two hundred yards, the sedan's engine pitched higher. Tires spewed dirt and stone as it sped away.

Now, Peter bundled himself against the chilly spring night, plodding along and pondering his options. Jason was God-only-knows-where.

But Peter knew Jason would be scratching and clawing a way to find Michael and Christine. Peter decided his only option was to find a phone, lie about his predicament, and contact the only man he knew to call.

After thirty minutes of humping in the growing darkness, the former marine stopped and knelt to tighten the knots on his tennis shoes. He had retied the second knot awkwardly with his bound hands when he spotted a flickering light through the forest to his right.

Peter studied it, moving his head back and forth. The light remained stationary as he moved, peering through the dense foliage. It was a spotlight.

He left the roadside and entered the dense forest a second time, picking his way through a hundred yards of trees. He emerged on the other side in a clearing, where he gazed upon a cluster of three one-story buildings.

Several minutes later, he stood on the porch of the main residence, a farmhouse. He mashed the doorbell several times. When no one responded, he opened the storm door and rapped once on the metal door.

The porch light came on. The curtain in the window twitched. Then the door cracked open.

"Who are you?"

The voice was male and husky. The eyes were hidden by shadow. Peter could make out a bulbous nose in the sliver of light penetrating the opening between the door and the jamb.

Keep it simple!

"Sorry to bother you at this hour, sir. I need help! I need to call someone."

"What century do you live in? No cell phone? You think you're gonna roll an old man. I ain't no ham-and-egger from Chicopee Falls."

Peter didn't understand what the hell that meant. He shook his head. "No sir, I left it back home. Just one call."

"You know what they say in Russia, son?"

"Uh . . . no sir."

"They say, 'Tough shitski!'" The diminutive man cocked the hammer on the sleek, shining shotgun. "Now git the hell outta here!"

Peter showed him his tied wrists.

"It's a matter of life and death."

"What the hell? Is this some kinda joke?"

"No . . . no joke. I was taken by some goons. Managed to escape and walk here."

"Where you from?" The old man eyed him with suspicion.

Peter lifted his arm and scratched his nose. "Virginia. Smithfield. I promise just one call and I'll leave you alone."

Peter felt the unseen eyes studying him for a long time. The door opened a foot more.

"I'm gonna have Old Bertha here on you the whole time. One wrong move . . . you got it?"

"Yessir."

"Make it quick," the voice ordered. "A guy can't be too careful."

"Thank you very much, sir."

Peter pulled open the storm door and stepped in. That was when he got a better look at the over-under, double-barreled shotgun angled toward his face. The two black circles of the muzzle stopped him in his tracks. His eyes whipsawed between the gun and the face of the old man holding it.

The man looked to be about eighty and stood no more than five-nine. The red-skin hung like jowls from his face. He wore a faded wife-beater t-shirt and boxers adorned with red flowers. His rail-thin legs were covered with white curls of hair. Peter sensed a lot of fight in this small dog.

Peter recognized the gun. "Nice shotgun. I believe it's a Caesar Guerini Tempio Field Gun. Runs a pretty penny."

The old man smiled, backing up a step. "Damned right, sonny; thirty inch barrel, 28 gauge, with a Prince of Wales grip. Cost me over seven grand. At this range, you'd look like Swiss cheese. And don't think I won't. I killed a man back in '81. I'll do it again too if I have to."

Peter raised his hands. "I don't mean no trouble. Just need a phone."

The man waved the gun toward the back of the house. "In the kitchen."

Peter inched past the man, who followed with the weapon pointed at the small of his back. He dialed his home landline awkwardly with his wrists taped together. It rang ten times before voicemail picked up. Peter hung up and dialed Lisa's cell phone.

"Where the hell are you?" she asked.

"I'm somewhere in New Jersey," Peter sighed.

"New Jersey? How did . . . Where is . . ." Peter could hear the concern in her voice.

"Lisa. I'm sorry. I'll be home as soon as I can . . . Listen to me . . ."

Peter stopped speaking as her sobs mingled with panicked exclamations. He was not angry with his wife. He felt sorry for her. The girls and he were her whole life. And Peter's escapades with Jason two years ago, no doubt, were revisiting her again because she had been kept in the dark. The mind fills in the gaps.

"Honey, I need you to go to my computer . . ."

Lisa did not respond. Her crying increased in volume. Her responses were barely coherent. "Not at . . . home. At my . . . sister's . . ."

The crying disappeared followed by a few seconds of fumbling on the other end.

"Peter?!"

"Donna?" Peter said. Donna was Lisa's older sister and the woman Lisa always turned to in a crisis.

"Yeah," she retorted. "You listen to me you sick sonofabitch. You've put her through enough. She's barely stopped talking about all the crap that happened two years ago. Now you disappear again without . . . Your wife is worried sick . . ."

"I know . . ."

"Then get your ass back home and take care of your family!"

The line went dead.

"Donna?"

Peter stared at the phone then turned toward his host. The old man had lowered the shot gun and was smiling.

"You're not going to shoot me?" he asked.

The old man screwed up his lips. "I could hear everything your women folk said. If I did shoot you, I think I'd being doing you a favor."

Peter chuckled. "You might be right."

"I'll be right back," he said.

Peter redialed the number but it rolled to voice mail. He tried twice more with the same result.

The old man returned with a bottle of whiskey, two rocks glasses, and a pair of scissors. He cut the duct tape from Peter's arms.

"Whenever things go to shit, I break out the Knob Creek. Good stuff!"

He filled both with three fingers of the amber liquid and handed one to Peter.

"My Gladys has been dead for ten years," he said, raising his glass. "She was a great cook. I haven't had a decent meal since she passed. But she could make my life miserable. Once, I left the seat up after takin' a leak at two in the morning. She went in an hour later, tried to sit down in the dark, and fell in. On her deathbed, one of the last things she told me was to remember to put the seat down."

Peter raised his glass. "Here's to our women."

They slugged back the whiskey.

"I need to make one more call."

"Help yourself," he replied, pouring two more shots.

He lifted the phone to dial and stopped. "What's your name, sir?"

The old man grinned. "Are we going to be friends now?"

"Maybe."

"Name's Perechoduk. Dennis Perechoduk. Friends call me Ducky."

Peter dialed the only other number he remembered. In two minutes, he had John Palmer on the line.

"I swear," Palmer began, "between you and your brother, the Newport News PD is going to have to create a division just for all the shit you two start. Do you two think I'm your personal answering service?"

"You talked to Jason?"

"Yeah. He called me several hours ago."

"Where is he?"

"By now, he's probably in Washington DC, a guest of the FBI. So what's your story?"

"I delivered the package to a pharmaceutical company called Dawson Pharmaceuticals. I have no other information. I don't know what's happening but it ain't good. I need to call someone in Washington."

"Well, call Broadhurst of the Secret Service. He appears to be running an operation up there. You gotta a pen?"

Peter motioned that he needed to write something down to his guest. Ducky retrieved a pen and paper. Peter jotted down the number.

"You do realize you and your brother still have to answer for running from the police, and Jason is a suspect in the death of a man, right?" Palmer added.

"We'll have to deal with that later," Peter explained.

"Where are you?" Palmer asked.

"I'd rather not say. I'm a fugitive, remember? Thanks for the phone number."

"No problem. I'll arrest you and Jason when you get back."

"Of course, you will."

Peter hung up before Palmer could trace the call, afraid that he would in fact send officers to arrest him. He turned to Ducky. "Thanks for the use of the phone. It's not often people help strangers these days," he said. "Mind if I ask why?"

"I noticed the art on your forearm when you scratched your nose on the porch."

Peter lifted his right arm. "This," he replied, showing a tattoo of an eagle, globe, and anchor.

"I was in the corps. Did three tours in 'Nam between '65 and '71 with the second marines."

Peter winked at the old man. "I owe you one, Ducky, and so does my brother. I need to call someone in Washington. Is that okay?"

"Ding dong, you're gone," Ducky smiled, nodding toward the phone. "Sounds serious."

"It is," Peter responded. He pushed out another breath. "It is."

<h1 style="text-align:center">CHAPTER 47</h1>

"Where are you taking me?" Al-Faisal demanded three hours later. In a wheelchair being escorted to the hospital exit by John, a CIA agent and Simoon mole in the Company, Cyclops had a pounding headache. Awake but groggy, the cool clean West Virginia air energized him as they waited by the curb.

"To a safe house in Manassas. You'll wait there until we receive instructions from your mother on how to repatriate you."

John pushed al-Faisal through the open sliding-glass-door exit. A black panel truck idled at the curb. The driver and a man riding shotgun exited the vehicle and assisted John in lifting the chair into the back. Al-Faisal sat in the second, bench-like passenger seat.

"Tell your mother I said hello." John slammed the door shut and tapped it twice. The van moved off.

℞

The man in the woods a hundred yards from the safe house in Beckley, West Virginia, lowered the field glasses and removed the headphones from his ears. He turned off the two-foot-long ultra-sensitive K300 microphone and lifted the satellite phone to his ear.

"They just took him out of the safe house," the CIA agent said into the device. "They're headed west on Route 19."

"Roger that," came the reply. "Keep your eyes on the safe house. We're sending a team to get them. We have eyes on Cyclops from above."

The agent looked into the sky and saw the drone circling overhead, soundless and no more than a speck.

℞

Thirty minutes later, just inside the Virginia–West Virginia line, al-Faisal asked, "How much longer?"

The driver shouted over his shoulder. "We're on Route 55. It's another thirty more miles. Probably an hour on these back roads."

The van sped past a small clearing. A low-slung farm building with several vehicles parked on the grass appeared through the window and just as quickly disappeared from sight.

"Can you hurry it up?"

"Sit back and shut up! We'll get there when we get there."

Al-Faisal muttered. *Damn Americans. Never in a hurry!*

The terrorist stretched his arms and twisted his torso. The effects of the drug that had stopped his heart lingered. His muscles felt like heavy, wet concrete. As he turned, through the rear window of the van, Al-Faisal saw three sedans approaching at high speed two hundred meters back.

"We've got company," he shouted.

The driver glanced in the mirror and saw the caravan. "We'll let them pass," he replied. He turned his eyes back to the roadway and slammed on the brakes.

"What the . . . ?"

The tires screeched along the asphalt as the van fishtailed to the left. Blue smoke erupted from the wheel wells. Three more sedans ahead of them had appeared from driveways hidden in the trees, blocking the way. The rear echelon of SUVs did the same.

Before another word was uttered, fifteen uniformed agents appeared surrounding the van, wearing black tactical gear with FBI emblazoned on their bullet-resistant vests. Automatic weapons and handguns were trained on the driver and passengers.

"Hands on the dashboard! Now!"

The two men complied.

"Move and you die, here and now!"

The driver and passenger-side doors were flung open, along with the rear panel. The two men and al-Faisal were led to separate vehicles. The van was commandeered by two agents. In less than three minutes, the van and six sedans formed a single line of vehicles heading east along Route 55 toward Manassas.

In one of the sedans, al-Faisal sat flanked by two heavily armed, helmeted agents. His hands and legs were now chained and shackled. He looked at one of his captors just as a hood was placed over his head.

"Where are we going?"

"You are now a guest of the United States government. We'll be in Washington in ninety minutes. Enjoy the ride."

℞

Hours later, another caravan, this time a three-vehicle motorcade, zipped through the darkened city streets of the nation's capital. Jason sat beside the director in the backseat of the first car.

"What's going on?" Jason demanded. "How can I can help you?"

The director of the FBI, George McNamara, formed a tight-lipped frown. He was about to speak when his cell phone rang. Jason listened as the man said a few words, then spent the next thirty seconds listening.

"Excellent," he said to the caller. "That's at least a start. Thanks, Special Agent."

"Well?" Jason persisted. "I deserve some answers."

McNamara was undeterred. "That was Clay Broadhurst. He's dying by the way. The bullet he took in that stairwell in the condo towers really screwed him up. He's developed lung cancer. He doesn't have much time left. He's technically been on medical leave ever since the assassination attempts two years ago. But we can't keep him away from the office. He's been over seeing this operation and studied what happened at the shipyard in Newport News, and why."

"Admirable. I have a great deal of respect for Agent Broadhurst. But, what does it have to do with me?"

"We have a general idea where Delilah Hussein is. We have been trying to track her down for the last two weeks."

"So you guys never really believed she was killed in the explosion on the yacht?"

"No, we believed she was dead. We only found out she was alive in the last two weeks. Our analysts reopened the case and found that the bodies of the man and woman on the exploded yacht in the James Rivers were not those of Hussein and her manservant Oliver. They did not have the tattoos. We have been trying to track her whereabouts ever since. These things take time."

The caravan turned right onto Eighth Street.

"So what's your plan, and how does it involve me?"

"You want your son and woman back. She wants her son back. We're going to arrange a trade. And you are going to lead us straight to her."

"A trade?"

℞

Jason exited the black SUV still surrounded by FBI agents, but this time not as a fugitive. Jason, the director of the Secret Service, and ten agents stood aside as a large square truck approached.

They were in an underground parking garage deep beneath Washington.

The square rig looked like an armored car, except it was painted black with FBI in four-foot white letters on the rear. A pair of guards exited the cab. They moved to the rear door and opened it. Another phalanx of guards wearing riot gear and helmets, and sporting automatic rifles, spilled out.

Seconds later, a man in an orange jump suit was escorted from the truck by another pair of guards and two more plainclothes men wearing jeans and short haircuts. The prisoner shuffled down from the truck, chains clanking. A thick strand circled his waist. His handcuffed wrists were secured to these irons. Another set of links draped from the waist to a pair of leg irons restraining his ankles. A black hood covered the man's head.

The detainee was smaller than Jason.

Jason's confusion multiplied when one of the plainclothes agents spoke to the director.

"We don't think this is a very good idea. This guy is dangerous."

The director smiled politely. He spoke with an even tempo dripping with patience. "Tough shit. The decision has been made and it was made at the highest pay grade. It's out of my hands now." The director turned to his men. "Bring him here."

The prisoner was led to the director and Jason. The man stood a few feet away. He was surrounded by guards, their rifles and batons poised.

"Take it off."

A guard grabbed a fistful of cloth and ripped the hood from the man's head.

With his mental and physical state frayed, Jason's ability to control his impulses had eroded. The constant worry about Michael and Chrissie had been gnawing it him.

He needed to find them and be with them. It was the only thing that mattered. Their lives—and his—depended on nothing else.

Yet, the path to finding them had twisted and turned in unexpected directions. No matter how close he was, the distance between him and his loved ones seemed to increase with each passing hour. Frustrated and fragile, he didn't think his body could react to anything else placed in his path. That is, until the hood was ripped from the prisoner's head.

The dark skin. The eye patch. Jason starred into the soulless face. The pharmacist would not remember the next few moments.

His arm shot out, slamming into al-Faisal's head. Jason leapt on him pummeling him with blows about the head. He landed two perfect punches, the sharp cracks cutting through the underground garage. Three FBI agents wrapped Jason up and tore him away.

The director strode over to Jason, who lay on the pavement, looking up at the senior law enforcement official.

"Did you get that out of your system?"

Jason cleared his throat and pushed himself erect.

"Well?" the director persisted.

"Yeah, I guess so," Jason replied.

"Okay, then. Let's get your family back."

THE END

THE CYCLOPS REPRISAL

PART ONE

CHAPTER 1

Monday, April 13

They exited the elevator into a stark-white sterile corridor. The hallway ended at a large white metal door. The FBI director opened it, walked in, and held it open for Jason.

The pharmacist stepped in and looked down upon a semicircular indoor amphitheater. At the lowest level, ten large screens, six feet high and ten feet wide, were mounted on the wall. Four screens showed satellite images of various locations around the world. The remaining six displayed data scrolling over a black background.

Its multi levels were occupied by the stepped stages of the theater crammed with computer stations, terminals, and secure phones. Fifteen men and women were seated at these stations and other locations. Certain smaller computer screens were synced displaying the computer's information on the larger screens.

"Welcome to the SIOC," McNamara declared.

On the highest level of the center, a large conference room overlooked the massive technological display below. The common walls were floor-to-glass, allowing for a panoramic view. From this vantage point, agents in the enclosure could observe the goings-on in the command post.

"Jason," FBI Director George McNamara began, "has agreed to help us. I want everyone to brief him on Operation Dust Storm."

The faces around the table shot the director shocked glances.

"Sir, he's not cleared," one woman objected.

"I just gave him clearance!"

No one made a movement to comply.

"I mean it," he persisted. "Just give him facts. And do not mention what security agencies or databases were accessed. Give him the important details."

Throats were cleared and papers shuffled.

"Tom, you start."

The wheelchair bound Tom Johnson opened a thick file and spoke in a slow, methodical manner, reciting facts.

"Two weeks ago, we learned that the explosion on the yacht after the assassination attempts was staged."

"How did you come to know this?" Jason asked.

"We intercepted a communication between someone in Newport News called The Watcher and an unknown subject that caused us to question the conclusion that Hussein was dead. A special team was dispatched to look into the explosion. It was determined that the bodies on the yacht were not those of Hussein and her associate. That information was not shared with the local police . . . or anyone else for that matter. We knew that Lily Zanns, aka Delilah Hussein, was alive. We brought in the FAA and began to look at all flights, commercial and private, originating from the area in and around Newport News.

"The tail letters on Hussein's plane and its transponder signal were cross-referenced with electronic flight records from the FAA's mainframe. All flights are tracked and saved at their headquarters here in DC. Hussein and her associate flew to a few miles of the coast of North Carolina. The plane's track terminated over the water. At first, we thought they may have crashed into the sea.

"We checked with the Coast Guard and the Navy, looking for a record of a crash and/or recovery operation. There was nothing. But we did find a report of an abandoned aircraft, a float plane, matching the tail numbers of her aircraft."

"Hussein," Jason began, "was off the grid. I understand she had no papers, no social security number. How did she manage to buy a plane?"

"She had no paper trail as Lily Zanns. But she did have one as Delilah Hussein. The plane was owned by an organization based in Syria with ties to The Simoon."

Johnson continued his explanation. "The plane was found empty, floating on the ocean waves. There was no sign of foul play. We assumed that they rendezvoused with others."

At that point another gentleman unknown to Jason took over.

"Back checking, we cross-referenced the shipping lanes and routes for the day after the assassination attempt and were able to determine that two ships were in the area at the time the plane's flight terminated. Both ships' crews were interviewed. It was learned that two people, a dark-skinned man and a woman, were rescued from the sea in a rubber raft in the early morning by a Liberian tanker headed to Cuba.

"Based on the interviews, we determined that the man and woman debarked in Cuba and disappeared."

A third man picked up the story.

"Let me stop you right there," Jason interrupted. "Where is Agent Broadhurst?"

McNamara tapped the table. "Clay is ill. He is resting right now. Continue."

"Since that day two weeks ago, we have continuously monitored all communications looking for any key words associated with Delilah Hussein and her organization, The Simoon, from anywhere in the world. The single communication we intercepted two weeks ago led to this area of the world."

The man picked up a remote and pointed it at a blank monitor on the wall of the conference room. The screen came to life showing a world map. Slowly the image zoomed in on an area highlighted by a sizable rectangle.

The western wall of the box stretched from below Panama on the Pacific side north to the Gulf of Mexico. The top border ran west to east between Cuba and the southern tip of the Florida peninsula. The top right corner of the box floated over the middle of the North

Atlantic. The eastern line dropped south to a point east of French Guiana. The southern side of the immense quadrilateral stretched east to west through the northern countries of South America: French Guiana, Suriname, Guyana, Venezuela, and Colombia.

"That's a sizeable area," Jason commented.

"More than 3.2 million square miles," the man replied.

"I thought the government had all these resources at its disposal to monitor and locate the bad guys. Why can't you pin her location down?"

"Given enough time we will find her. The problem is time," McNamara explained. "An operation is underway. We need to find her. She's using some kind of sophisticated cloaking mechanism to hide the source of her electronic and voice transmissions. Normally calls are routed through satellites and cell towers which makes tracking them relatively easy. Hussein's communications, when they occur, are sending hundreds of signals out in a three-hundred-and-sixty-degree pattern."

"So trace the signals back to where they all converge . . ."

"We've thought of that, young man. The origination point of the calls changes every time a call is made or a secure text is sent. It can vary anywhere inside this rectangle you see on the map."

"How do even know this is Hussein?" Jason demanded.

McNamara smiled as if explaining a simple concept to a child. "We have other assets around the world that have confirmed communications are coming from this area. We have teams analyzing large amounts of electronic data. And that's all I will say about that. Again, continue."

The agent with the remote continued. "We've cross-referenced each communication with known cell towers and transmission points. None of the calls can be traced to a specific cell tower. It's a complicated algorithm which we can solve. We will need time. Time we don't have."

"So she's somewhere in the Caribbean but you don't know where."

"Exactly," said the director.

"How do you expect to contact her if you don't know where she is?"

The director stood up. "Thank you, gentlemen." He turned to Jason. "Follow me."

Chapter 2

"Agent Broadhurst?" the special agent said into his phone.

"Who is this?"

"Peter Rodgers. Jason's brother."

Broadhurst shot up from his recumbent position. He regretted the sudden movement. His head swam. Dizziness washed over him. A tide of nausea swelled. The dying agent sucked in several rapid breaths, expelling them quickly. He pushed back the urge to vomit.

"Are you there?" Peter Rodgers demanded.

"Yeah . . . yeah, I'm here."

"You don't sound too good."

Hoping to catch a few moments of much-needed rest, he had found an empty office inside the SIOC complex, hung his suit coat and tie on a chair, and lain down. He checked his Bulova. It was twenty minutes after midnight. Sunday had turned into Monday. And he'd only managed thirty minutes of shuteye-in the last twenty four hours.

"Where the hell are you?"

Broadhurst swung his legs off the small cot in an empty office of the SIOC hallway.

"I've been trying to call you for the last four hours. I've left you three messages. Where the hell have you been?" Rodgers shot back.

"Things are crazy up here," the Secret Service agent said. "A lot of things going on."

In fact, Broadhurst's phone had been charging when he lay down. The battery died four hours ago. He had plugged it in beside him on the small sofa. The call from Rodgers had been relayed from the SIOC to his cell phone while he was sleeping.

"Again, where are you?"

"I'm in New Jersey. Where's my brother?"

"He's here with us. Have you delivered the truck?"

"Is Jason okay?"

"He's stressed . . . naturally . . . but okay. Have you delivered the truck?"

There was a hesitation on the line. "Yes, to a drug company in Camden. Dawson Pharmaceuticals."

"Give me your address. We'll send a team for you."

℞

The director opened the windowless door. The room, also windowless, was also crowded with computer stations arrayed in a circle. At each station, headset-wearing technicians punched keys and talked on phones while monitoring displays.

"What you see here is confidential. Do you understand?"

Jason nodded. "More so than everything else I've seen? You don't need to keep telling me that!"

The director nodded. "Good point. Take a seat."

Jason sat at a small table in the corner of the room.

McNamara continued. "You were contacted by Hussein and asked to go to various locations after you listened to information on a number of cell phones, correct?"

"Yes," Jason replied, nodding.

"Where are the cell phones now?"

Jason thought a moment. "The second is in a leather bag somewhere in Norfolk. The man who handed over the truck made us give it up. The last cell phone was still in the truck with Peter."

"And the first?"

Jason thought a moment. "I think we left it at my house in York County."

The director opened a drawer and removed something from it. "Is this it?" he asked, dropping a black smartphone on the desk. It landed face down so Jason could see the large number one scrawled in white grease paint along its back.

"That's looks like it," Jason asked.

The director nodded. "We retrieved it from your home."

"You broke into my home?"

"In the interests of national security, yes. We have done nothing with the phone pending confirmation that it was the one you used earlier . . . and we have formulated a plan."

"Okay . . . so now what? Just call her and ask for a trade?"

"Basically, yes. Your instructions were in a text on this phone. You are going to send her a text . . . exactly what we tell you to say, along with a photo. If she wants her son back, she'll be in touch."

"And you think she'll just agree to this?"

"Based on the information Broadhurst has learned about Delilah Hussein from FBI profilers and CIA sources in the last two years, yes. She adores her son . . . and will do anything to get him back again. Plus she wants you."

℞

An hour later, Jason, in another secure area of FBI headquarters, stood in a starkly lit hallway of an underground floor, ten stories beneath the SIOC. The director opened a plain wooden door. Jason, the director and a third man with a Canon single lens reflex camera hanging around his neck, entered.

Seated in the center of the empty room, chained to a wheeled metal chair, was the assassin-pharmacist Sharif al-Faisal. The thick cloth hood had been placed over his head once more. Jason knew it was the pharmacist formerly known as Sam Fairing because the squiggly tattoo was clearly visible on the inside of his right forearm.

Leather straps had been fastened across his chest, legs, and arms. His ankles were shackled together along with his wrists. Four members of an FBI tactical team wearing black body armor and toting MP5 submachine guns were positioned in each corner of the small room no more than a step from the prisoner.

"Stand behind him!" the director ordered. "And please try not to hit him."

Jason moved behind al-Faisal. The technician with the camera who had accompanied them in the elevator handed a fresh newspaper to Jason. Yesterday's edition of the *Washington Post*.

The director stepped forward and ripped the hood from al-Faisal's head. The swarthy-skinned Cyclops blinked rapidly, finally focusing his eyes on the director. The FBI director placed a page in Cyclops' hand, bound at the wrist. Jason saw several lines of large font print on the paper.

"Hold it up," the tech commanded Jason .

Jason held the paper out in front of him, exposing the date and headlines above the fold.

"You," the director ordered, "read the words on the page."

The prisoner lowered his head and closed his eyes. The director screwed his lips into a tight circle at the side of his face. "I said read the words!"

Sharif al-Faisal did not move. He crumpled the document and tossed it to the floor with a flick of his bound wrist.

The director turned to one of the armed agents and tossed his head toward the captive. The agent moved to al-Faisal's chair. Instinctively, Jason stepped back.

The agent grabbed the prisoner by the hair and yanked backward, speaking several words in Arabic. Al-Faisal managed a nod. The agent retreated to the corner.

"Now, read!"

The director motioned for Jason to step back behind the chair and raise the newspaper. McNamara picked up the crumpled paper, smoothed it on his thigh and forced it back into Cyclops' hand.

The technician raised the Canon EOS MS and began the video.

"Begin," the technician directed.

Sharif al-Faisal focused on the paper and began recording:

"I am alive. The escape attempt failed. The Americans know you have an operation underway. If you want to see me again, you must cease that operation immediately."

Sharif al-Faisal hesitated, leveled his eyes at the camera and shouted, "Allahu Ahkbar!"

The armed agents moved in and wheeled Cyclops out of the room.

"Get him out of my sight!" the director managed, as the door closed.

Cyclops could be heard shouting through the walls *"Allahu Akbar!"* to the sound of pounding boots traveling along the tiled floor.

The director motioned for Jason to follow. In a room across the hall, they sat once more at another table. The technician typed a message into the cell phone marked number one in grease paint. He had transferred the video file from the Canon to the smartphone. When he finished, he slid it to Jason so he could read the message:

Ms. Hussein:

As you can see, we have your son in custody. He was captured in his escape attempt. Your attempt to free him was thwarted. The American government has me in custody and I am no longer able to move freely.

You have my son and Christine Pettigrew. We both want our loved ones back. They are offering you an exchange: your son for my son and Christine Pettigrew. But you must halt all operations in your attack currently underway.

Jason Rodgers

Jason handed the device back. The technician looked to the director who nodded once. The agent hit send. The phone whirred as the message transmitted.

Jason turned his eyes to the director. "Now what?"

The director spoke, "Now we wait."

"Even if she agrees, I still have a lot of questions about how I'm going to pull this off."

"We're working on a plan."

"What did your man say to al-Faisal to get him to cooperate?"

"Sharif al-Faisal was reminded that if he failed to help us, he would be revisited by our interrogators."

℞

The tepid Caribbean gusts angled the warm rain toward the soft sands of the island. Extremely fatigued, Hussein allowed herself a moment to remember less stressful days. Reprisal One, the communications drone, had made its return fifteen minutes ago, bringing with it another data dump.

She had awoken from a short nap and needed to clear her mind. Remembering Amo and her commitment to him always helped her refocus.

Those days many years ago were happier ones. Before her Amo had been toppled from power and forced to hide like a rodent in a hole, she'd spent glorious days in opulence by his side at locations all around Iraq. In his palaces, filled with servants, extravagant meals of lamb and rice were followed by voracious lovemaking in beds larger than most of the rooms in the house she had occupied in Newport News, Virginia.

She thought those days would never end.

But they did. She vowed after watching her Amo's botched execution to avenge his death—and the loss of her sumptuous life.

As she sat on the patio of her villa now, letting the rain pepper her face, she renewed her pledge to her fallen lover, the Butcher of Baghdad. She also renewed her pledge to her son, bolstered and invigorated by a mother's double loss—his incarceration and the death of her daughter.

She vowed to continue to peck away at the Great Satan, not only for her lost lover, but for her dead daughter and her missing son, a son she hoped to have by her side once more.

The matriarch had actually spoken to Peter Rodgers, the pharmacist's brother. The former marine should be dead by now. But Jason Rodgers was still alive. Somehow, he had managed to remove himself from the moving truck heading up the Eastern Shore of Virginia without being detected. Hussein had been beside herself earlier. But she had calmed down. Hussein knew that she would face Jason Rodgers again. She did, after all, still have his woman and son.

Hussein did not hear the footfalls, but rather sensed the presence of the person behind her. His stealth told her that it could only be one person: Oliver.

"And what about Charlie's body?"

"He is still lying in the wine cellar for the woman to see and smell. Her punishment for trying to escape."

"I thought you told me that Charlie could be controlled."

"I searched his room in the bunkhouse. I found half-digested pills behind one of the toilets. He must have been spitting them out. He tricked me."

Hussein cast her manservant a withering stare. "I will deal with your incompetence after this mission is complete. Charlie has jeopardized everything. I cannot control Jason Rodgers if we don't possess his loved ones."

"I understand."

"Jason Rodgers has disappeared. Those idiots in New Jersey sent us a photo of . . . the brother. By now, Peter Rodgers is dead. Where is the pharmacist?"

Oliver sighed. Hussein took this to mean that he did not know and was smart enough to remain silent.

"Jason must be delivered to me. He will watch the lives of his son and woman being snuffed out just as he killed my beloved daughter."

Oliver nodded.

"Where is the boy?"

"We are searching every hectare on the mountain. He will not get far. The compound is ringed by fences. If they managed to get outside the fence, there is only thick tropical vegetation. Our men are scouring everywhere. We will find him."

Oliver faced Hussein, who was standing now. She reached down and grabbed a handful of crotch. Oliver rose up on his toes, trying to alleviate the pressure on his testicles.

"You better, my love, or I will cut off another appendage. And this time it will not be a finger."

"Oui, Madame," he croaked.

She released her grip. Oliver lowered himself. Hussein studied him. "What is it now?"

"I know where Jason Rodgers is."

"Most excellent. Tell me."

Oliver held out the secure cell phone.

"I dispatched the drone on its predetermined course to cell tower five in Jamaica. It returned fifteen minutes ago and I decoded it."

Hussein accepted the phone. Oliver stepped out of arm's reach. Hussein read the text message and watched the attached video of Jason Rodgers and her son. She heard her son's voice for the first time in two years. Tears welled in her black eyes. Hussein placed the phone on the table as a maelstrom of emotions assaulted her.

"How has this happened? I thought Sharif made his getaway?"

"I do not know, Madame. The last communication we received from our contact in the CIA said that Sharif made a successful escape from the prison. He lost contact after he departed. He must have been taken after leaving the safe house but before they made it to the airport."

Hussein paced the brick-paved patio. Oliver stood like a mannequin, letting her work through the emotions and come to a conclusion.

Finally, Hussein turned toward him.

"I want my son back."

"Je comprends, Madame," Oliver began. *I understand.* "Without saying it, this message tells us one thing. The Americans have not been able to locate our position. This is an attempt to find us. Otherwise they would have attacked the compound."

"Oui, Oui. C'est vrai." *Yes, it's true.* Hussein crossed her arms across her chest. She lifted a finger and tapped her pursed lips. "Mais, it also tells us one more thing." Hussein walked to Oliver. She raised up on her tiptoes and tried to kiss him on the cheek. Oliver moved backward, remembering earlier threats.

"Fear not, mon cheri."

Oliver lowered his face. Hussein delivered a peck and smiled. "It also means the Americans do not know what we have planned. We are closer to successfully delivering our blow."

"So we are going to refuse to the exchange and continue with our plan?"

Hussein shook her head. "No, we are going to get Sharif back . . . and the Americans will not know where we are. Call al-Raqqah. There are arrangements to be made. I want you to send the following message to Jason and the Americans."